'For better or worse, we're together by our child for our lives—and the only way we're going to get through it is by always being honest with each other. We will argue and disagree, but you must always speak the truth to me.'

Natasha fought to keep her feet grounded and her limbs from turning into fondue. But it was a fight she was losing. Matteo's breath was warm on her face, his thumb was gently moving on her skin and scorching it, and the heat from his body was almost penetrating her clothes.

She'd kissed him without any thought, a desperate compulsion to touch him and comfort him flooding her, and then the fury had struck from nowhere. All her private thoughts about the direction he'd taken his career in converging at the realisation he'd thrown it all away in the pursuit of riches.

And now she wanted to kiss him again.

As if he could sense the need inside her he brought his mouth close to hers, but not quite touching—the promise of a kiss.

'And now I will ask you something. I want complete honesty,' he whispered, the movement of his words making his lips dance against hers like a breath.

His other hand trailed down her back and clasped her bottom to pull her flush against him. His lips moved lightly over hers, still tantalising her with the promise of his kiss.

'Do you want me to let you go?'

Bound to a Billionaire

Claimed by the most powerful of men!

Felipe Lorenzi, Matteo Manaserro
and Daniele Pellegrini.

Three powerful billionaires who want for nothing—
in business *or* in bed. But nothing and
no one can touch their closely guarded hearts.

That is until Francesca, Natasha and Eva are each
bound to a billionaire…and prove to be a challenge
these delicious alpha males can't resist!

Don't miss **Michelle Smart**'s stunning trilogy

Read Felipe and Francesca's story in

Protecting His Defiant Innocent

Already available

Read Matteo and Natasha's story in

Claiming His One-Night Baby

Available now!

And look for

Daniele and Eva's story in

Buying His Bride of Convenience

October 2017

CLAIMING HIS
ONE-NIGHT BABY

BY
MICHELLE SMART

First Published in Great Britain 2017
By Mills & Boon, an imprint of HarperCollins*Publishers*
1 London Bridge Street, London, SE1 9GF

© 2017 Michelle Smart

ISBN: 978-0-263-92536-4

Printed and bound in Spain
by CPI, Barcelona

Michelle Smart's love affair with books started when she was a baby and she would cuddle them in her cot. A voracious reader of all genres, she found her love of romance established when she stumbled across her first Mills & Boon book at the age of twelve. She's been reading and writing them ever since. Michelle lives in Northamptonshire, with her husband and two young Smarties.

Visit the Author Profile page at millsandboon.co.uk for more titles.

For Adam xxx

CHAPTER ONE

JAW CLENCHED, HIS heart pounding an irregular beat in his chest, Matteo Manaserro watched the coffin being lowered into the consecrated ground of Castello Miniato's private cemetery.

Surrounding the open earth stood hundreds of Pieta Pellegrini's loved ones, friends, family, colleagues, even some heads of state, with their security details standing back at a discreet distance, all there to say a final good-bye to a man who had been respected the world over for his philanthropic endeavours.

Vanessa Pellegrini, Pieta's mother, who had buried her husband, Fabio, in the adjoining plot only a year ago, stepped forward, supported by her daughter Francesca. Both women clutched red roses. Francesca turned around to extend a hand to Natasha, Pieta's widow, who was staring blankly at the wooden box like an ashen-faced statue. The breeze that had filled the early-autumn air had dropped, magnifying the statue effect. Not a single strand of her tumbling honey-blonde hair moved.

She lifted her dry eyes and blinked, the motion seeming to clear her thoughts as she grabbed Francesca's hand and joined the sobbing women.

Together, the three Pellegrini women threw their roses onto the coffin.

Matteo forced stale air from his lungs and focused his attention anywhere but on the widow.

This was a day to say goodbye, to mourn and then celebrate a man who deserved to be mourned and celebrated. This was not a day to stare at the widow and think how beautiful she looked even in grief. Or think how badly he wanted to take hold of her shoulders and...

Daniele, Pieta's brother, shifted beside him. It was their turn.

Goodbye, Pieta, my cousin, my friend. Thank you for everything. I will miss you.

Once the immediate family—in which Matteo was included—had thrown their roses on the coffin, it was time for the other mourners to follow suit.

Striving to keep his features neutral, he watched his parents step forward to pay their last respects to their nephew. They didn't look at him, their son, but he knew his father sensed him watching.

Matteo hadn't exchanged a word with them since he'd legally changed his surname five years ago in the weeks that had followed the death of his own brother.

So much death.

So many funerals.

So much grief.

Too much pain.

When the burial was over and the priest led the mourners into the *castello* for the wake, Matteo hung back to visit a grave on the next row.

The marble headstone had a simple etching.

Roberto Pellegrini
Beloved son

No mention of him being a beloved brother.

Generations of Pellegrinis and their descendants were buried here, going back six centuries. At twenty-eight, Roberto was the youngest to have been buried in fifty years.

Matteo crouched down and touched the headstone. 'Hello, Roberto. Sorry I haven't visited you in a while. I've been busy.' He laughed harshly. In the five years since his brother's death he'd visited the grave only a handful of times. Not a day passed when he didn't think of him. Not an hour passed when he didn't feel the loss.

'Listen to me justifying myself. Again. You know I hate to see you here. I love you and I miss you. I just wanted you to know that.'

Blinking back moistness from his eyes, his heart aching, his head pounding, Matteo dragged himself to the *castello* to join the others.

A huge bar had been set up in the state room for the wake. Matteo had booked himself into a hotel in Pisa for the next couple of days but figured one small glass of bourbon wouldn't put him over the limit. His hotel room had a fully stocked minibar for him to drink dry when he got there. He would stay as long as was decent then leave.

He'd taken only a sip of his drink when Francesca appeared at his side.

He embraced her tightly. 'How are you holding up?' He'd been thirteen when his uncle Fabio and his wife, Vanessa, had taken him into their home. Francesca had been a baby. He'd been there when she'd taken her first steps, been in the audience for her first school music recital—she'd murdered the trumpet—and had beamed with the pride of a big brother only a few months ago at her graduation.

She shrugged and rubbed his arm. 'I need you to come with me. There's something we need to discuss.'

Following her up a cold corridor—the ancient *castello* needed a fortune's worth of modernisation—they entered Fabio Pellegrini's old office, which, from the musty smell, hadn't been used since the motor neurone disease that eventually killed him had really taken its hold on him.

A moment later Daniele appeared at the door with Natasha right behind him.

Startled blue eyes found his and quickly looked away as Francesca closed the door and indicated they should all sit round the oval table.

Matteo inhaled deeply and swore to himself.

This was the last thing he needed, to be stuck in close confines with *her*, the woman who had played him like a violin, letting him believe she had genuine feelings for him and could see a future for them, when all along she'd been playing his cousin too.

It seemed she had been with him every minute of that day, always in the periphery of his vision even when he'd blinked her away. Now she sat opposite him, close enough that if he were to reach over the table he would be able to stroke her deceitful face.

She shouldn't be wearing black. She should be wearing scarlet.

He despised that she was still the most beautiful woman he'd ever seen and that the years had only added to it.

He studied the vivid blue eyes that looked everywhere but at him. He studied the classically oval face with its creamy complexion, usually golden but today ashen, searching for flaws. Her nose was slightly too long, her lips too wide, but instead of being imperfections they added character to the face he'd once dreamed of waking up to.

And now?

Now he despised the very air she breathed.

'To summarise, I'll take care of the legal side, Daniele takes care of the construction and Matteo takes care of the medical side. What about you, Natasha? Do you want to handle publicity for it?'

Francesca's words penetrated Natasha's ears but it took a couple of beats longer for her brain to decipher them.

She'd struggled to pay attention throughout the meeting Francesca had called, the outbursts of temper between Daniele and Francesca being the only thing that had kept her even vaguely alert.

'I can do that,' she whispered, swallowing back the hysteria clamouring in her stomach.

Ignore Matteo and keep it together, she told herself in desperation.

God, she didn't know anything about publicity.

She knew Francesca thought she was doing the right thing, inviting her to this meeting of siblings—and the Pellegrinis considered their cousin Matteo to be a sibling—and that Francesca assumed she would want to be involved.

Any decent, loving widow would want to be involved in building a memorial to their beloved husband.

And she *did* want to be involved. For all his terrible failings as a husband, Pieta had been a true, dedicated humanitarian. He'd formed his own foundation a decade ago to build in areas hit by natural disasters; schools, homes, hospitals, whatever was needed. The Caribbean island of Caballeros had been hit by the worst hurricane on record the week before he'd died, wrecking the majority of the island's medical facilities. Pieta had immediately known he would build a hospital there but before his own plans for it had fully formed his own tragedy had struck and he'd been killed in a helicopter crash.

He deserved to have this memorial. The suffering people of Caballeros deserved to benefit from the hospital Francesca would steamroller into building for them.

So Natasha had striven to pay attention, not wanting to let down the loving Pellegrini siblings who'd been a part of her life for as long as she could remember, since her father and Fabio had been old school friends. She'd never had siblings of her own and as soon as it had been announced she'd be marrying into the family the closeness had grown, even during the six long years of their engagement.

If only Matteo weren't there she'd have been better able to concentrate.

There had not been one occasion in his presence in the past seven years where she hadn't felt the weight of his animosity. Polite and amiable enough that no one could see the depths of his loathing, whenever their eyes met it was akin to being stared at by Lucifer, her soul scorched by the burn of the hatred firing from green eyes that had once looked at her with only tenderness.

She could feel it now, digging into her skin like needles.

How could Francesca and Daniele not feel it too? How did it not infuse the whole atmosphere?

A part of her understood why he despised her as he did and, God knew, she'd tried to apologise for it, but it had been seven years. So much had changed in that time. She'd changed. He'd changed too, turning his back on the reconstructive surgery he'd worked so hard to specialise in and instead going the vanity surgery route. With his twenty-eight clinics worldwide and the patent on a skincare range he'd personally developed that actually worked in reducing scars and the signs of aging, he'd gone from being a dedicated professional surgeon to an entrepreneur who fitted surgery in when he had the time. Matteo had amassed a fortune that rivalled the entire Pellegrini estate and Pieta's personally accrued wealth put together.

He'd even changed his surname.

He'd become famous with it. Tall with dark good looks, olive skin, strong jaw and black curly hair that he'd recently had cropped short, it had been inevitable. 'Dr Dishy' the tabloids called him. It seemed she could barely pass a newsagent or log on to the internet without seeing his seductive face blazing out at her, normally with some identikit lingerie model or other draped on his arm.

Today his usual arrogance had deserted him. Even with the laser burn of his loathing infecting her, she could feel his anguish.

Pieta had been more than a cousin and surrogate sibling. He'd been Matteo's closest friend.

Her heart wanted to weep for him.

Her heart wanted to weep for all of them.

Matteo pulled his car up by the kerb and turned off the engine. The grand town house he'd parked opposite from stood in darkness.

Slumping forward over the wheel, he closed his eyes.

What was he even doing here?

He should be in his hotel room, drinking the minibar dry. He'd made that arrangement assuming Natasha would be staying in the *castello* with the rest of the family. He hadn't slept under the same roof as her since she'd accepted Pieta's proposal.

But she hadn't stayed. A couple of hours after their meeting to discuss the memorial for Pieta she had made the rounds to embrace everyone goodbye. Everyone except him. By unspoken agreement—unspoken because he hadn't exchanged more than a handful of words with her in seven years—he'd kept a great enough physical distance between them that no one would notice they failed to say goodbye to each other.

He put his head back and breathed deeply, willing his heart to stop this irregular rhythm.

What the hell was wrong with him? Why was it today of all days that he couldn't shake her from his mind? Why today, when he was mourning his best friend and cousin, had the old memories returned to haunt him?

He could see it so vividly, leaving his room in the *castello* to head outside to join the rest of his family in the marquee for his aunt and uncle's thirtieth wedding anniversary party. Natasha had left the room she'd been sharing with Francesca just a short way up the corridor from his at the same time. His heart had skipped to see her and he'd been ecstatic to see the necklace he'd sent for her eighteenth birthday there around her slender neck. He'd been disappointed not to make it to England for her party but he'd been a resident doctor at a hospital in Florida close to where he'd been to medical school. An emergency had cropped up at the end of his shift, a major car crash with multiple casualties that had resulted in all hands on deck. By the time they'd patched up the last casualty he'd missed his flight.

He'd been taking things slowly with her, waiting for her to turn eighteen before making a physical move. And then, in that cold *castello* corridor, Natasha in an electric-blue dress, the epitome of a chic, elegant woman, he'd realised he didn't have to back off any more.

All the letters and late-night calls they'd been exchanging for months, the dreams and hopes for the future they'd shared, had all been leading to this, this moment, this time. It was time for their future to begin right then and he'd fingered that necklace before taking her face in his hands and kissing her for the very first time.

It had been the sweetest, headiest kiss he'd ever experienced in his then twenty-eight years, interrupted only by Francesca steamrolling from her room and clattering up the corridor to join them. If she'd been three seconds earlier she would have found them together.

Three seconds.

What would she have done, he wondered, if she had caught them in that clinch?

Because only two hours later Pieta had got to his feet and, in front of the three hundred guests, had asked Natasha to marry him. And she'd said yes.

Matteo rubbed his eyes as if the motion could rub the memories away.

He shouldn't be thinking of all this now.

Why had he even come here, to the house she had shared with Pieta?

A light came on upstairs.

Had she just woken? Or had she been in the darkness all this time?

And was Francesca right to be worried about her?

Francesca had cornered him as he'd been making his own escape from the wake and asked him to keep an eye on Natasha while she, Francesca, was in Caballeros. She was worried about her, said she'd become a lost, mute ghost.

Although Natasha and Pieta had only been married for a year, they'd been together for seven years. She might be a gold-digging, heartless bitch but surely in that time she must have developed some feelings for him.

He'd wanted her feelings for Pieta to be genuine, for his cousin's sake. But how could they have been when she'd been seeing them both behind each other's backs?

Other than the few social family occasions he'd been unable to get out of, he'd cut her out of his life completely. He'd blocked her number, deleted every email and text message they'd exchanged and burned all her old-fashioned handwritten letters. The times he'd felt obliged to be in her presence he'd perfected the art of subtly blanking her in a way that didn't draw attention to anyone but *her.*

He should have just said no to Francesca. Lied and said he was returning home to Miami earlier than planned.

Instead he'd nodded curtly and promised to drop round if he had five minutes over the next couple of days.

So why had he driven here when he'd left the *castello* fully intending to drive straight to the hotel?

Natasha pushed Pieta's study door open and swallowed hard before stepping into it. After a moment she switched the light on. After going from room to room in complete darkness, in the house that had been her home for a year, her eyes took a few moments to adjust to the brightness.

She didn't know what she was looking for or what she was doing. She didn't know anything. She was lost. Alone.

She'd stayed at the wake as long as had been decently possible but all the consolation from the other mourners had become too much. Seeing Matteo everywhere she'd looked had been just as hard. Harder. Her mother pulling her to one side to ask if there was a chance she could be pregnant had been the final straw.

She'd had to get out before she'd screamed the *castello* down and her tongue ran away with itself before she could pull it back.

The rest of the Pellegrinis were staying at the *castello* and with sympathetic but concerned eyes had accepted her explanation that she wanted to be on her own.

At her insistence, the household staff had all stayed at the wake.

This was the first time she'd been alone in the house since she'd received the terrible news.

Feeling like an intruder in the room that had been her husband's domain, she cast her gaze over the walls thick with the books he'd read. A stack of files he'd brought home to work on, either from his law firm or the foundation he'd been so proud of, lay on his desk. Next to it sat the thick leather-bound tome on Stanley and Livingstone she'd bought him for his recent birthday. A bookmark poked out a third of the way through it.

Her throat closing tightly, she picked the book up and hugged it to her chest then with a wail that seemed to come from nowhere sank to the floor and sobbed for the man who had lied to her and everyone else for years, but who had done so much good in the world.

Pieta would never finish this book. He would never see the hospital his siblings would build in his memory. He would never take delivery of the new car he'd ordered only the day before he'd died.

He would never have the chance to tell his family the truth about who he'd really been.

'Oh, Pieta,' she whispered between the tears. 'Wherever you are, I hope you're finally at peace with yourself.'

The sound of the doorbell rang out.

She rolled into a ball and covered her ears.

The caller was insistent, pressing the doorbell intermittently until she could ignore it no longer. Wiping the tears away, she dragged herself up from the study floor and went down the stairs, clinging to the bannister for support, mentally preparing what she would say to get rid of her unexpected visitor.

Please don't be my parents. Don't be my parents. Don't be my parents.

Bracing herself, she unlocked the door and opened it a crack to peer through.

Certain she must be hallucinating, she pulled the door wider.

Her heart seemed to stop then kick back to life with a roar.

Matteo stood there, shining like an apparition under the brilliance of the moon.

He'd removed his black tie, his white shirt open at the throat, bleakness in his eyes, his jaw clenched, breathing heavily.

Their eyes met.

Neither of them spoke.

Something erupted in her chest, gripping her so tightly her lungs closed.

Time came to a standstill.

There they stood for the longest time, speaking only with their eyes. She read a hundred things in his; variations of pain, misery, anger and something else, something she hadn't seen since the beat before he'd taken her into his arms for the only kiss they had ever shared seven years ago.

This was the first time she'd seen him alone since that kiss.

She would never forget the look in his eyes from across the marquee when she had said yes to Pieta's proposal only two hours later. That would be with her until the day she died. The regret at all that had been lost would live in her for ever.

Her foot moved of its own accord as she took the step to him and placed her palm on his warm cheek.

He didn't react. Not the flicker of a muscle.

Matteo stared into eyes puffy from crying but that shone at him, almost pleading.

All the words he'd prepared melted away.

He couldn't even remember getting out of his car.

Her trembling hand felt so gentle on his cheek, her warmth penetrating his skin, and all he could do was drink in the face he'd once dreamed of waking up to.

A force too powerful to fight took hold of him, like a fist grabbing his insides and squeezing tightly.

Suddenly he couldn't remember why he hated her. All thoughts had evaporated. All he could see was her, Natasha, the woman he had taken one look at nearly eight years ago and known his life would never be the same again.

CHAPTER TWO

THE WORLD AROUND them blocked itself out and, without a word being said, Matteo crossed the threshold, kicked the door shut behind him and lifted her into his arms.

Their eyes locked together. Her fingers burrowed in the nape of his neck and he carried her up the stairs and into a bedroom. There he laid her on the bed and, his heart hammering in his throat, closed his eyes and brought his lips to hers.

Her taste…

When she parted her lips and his tongue swept into her mouth, the sweet, intoxicating taste he'd never forgotten filled him and from that moment he was lost.

In a frenzy of hands and heady kisses, they stripped each other's clothes off, items thrown without thought, a desperation to be naked and for their bodies to be flush together. Then he speared her hair with his fingers and crushed her mouth to his, teeth and tongues clashing as if they were trying to peel the other's skin and climb inside.

There were no thoughts, no words, only this potent madness that had them both in its grip.

He cupped her small perfect breasts then took them into his mouth, her moan of pleasure soaking right into his bloodstream. He ran his hands over her smooth belly and followed it with his tongue before going lower to inhale her musky heat.

He devoured her, not an inch of her creamy skin with the texture of silk left untouched or without his kiss.

Never had he experienced anything like this, this combustible, primal need to taste her, mark her, to imprint himself into her.

To worship her.

Natasha was adrift in a world she'd never been to before, Matteo her anchor, and she clung to him as if he were all that was left to hold onto, dragging her fingers through his hair, touching every bit of smooth skin she could reach with her needy hands. Every touch seared her, every kiss scorched.

His kiss from seven years ago had flicked something on inside her, a heat that had briefly smouldered before the direction of her life had extinguished it. Now he'd switched it back on and it engulfed her, flames licking every part of her, heat burning deep inside her, an ache so acute she didn't know where the pleasure ended and the pain began. She could cry with the wonder of it all. All those years of living without this…

And it wasn't enough. She needed more. She needed everything.

As if sensing her thoughts, Matteo snaked his tongue back up her stomach and over her breasts, climbing higher to find her mouth and kiss her with such passion that it sucked the air from her lungs.

His hand found her thigh and pushed it out while she moved the other and wrapped her legs around him.

His erection brushed her folds and she gasped for breath at the weight and hardness of it then gasped again when he pushed his way inside her.

There was no pain, there was too much heat and fire

racing through her for that, just a slight discomfort as her body adjusted to this dizzying newness.

And then there was a moment of stillness from Matteo, a pause in the frenzy.

Suddenly terrified he'd sensed or felt something wrong, she grabbed the back of his head and kissed him deeply, hungrily.

And then she forgot to worry, forgot about everything but this moment, this time, and welcomed his lovemaking, the feel of him inside her, the pleasure taking over, taking her higher and higher until the pulsations burst through her and rippled into every part of her being.

As she absorbed these beautiful sensations with wonder, Matteo's movements quickened, his lips found hers and with a long moan into her mouth, he shuddered before collapsing on her.

For a long time they simply lay there, still saying nothing, the only sound their ragged breaths and the beats of their hearts echoing together through their tightly fused bodies.

Then, as the sensations subsided and the heat that had engulfed them cooled, something else took its place.

Horror.

She heard Matteo swallow into her neck, then his weight shifted and he rolled off her, swung his legs over the bed, and swore, first in his native Italian and then in English.

Coldness chilled her skin.

It was just as well she was lying down for if she'd been on her feet she was certain her legs would have given way beneath her.

What had they just *done*?

How had it happened?

She couldn't explain it. She doubted he could either.

Feeling very much that she could be sick, she stared up at the ceiling and tried to get air into her tight lungs. If she could get her vocal cords to unfreeze she might very well swear too.

After a few deep breaths to steady himself, Matteo got to his feet and went in search of his discarded clothing.

He needed to get out of this house. Right now.

He found his shirt under her dress. One of his socks was rolled in a nest with her bra.

Nausea swirled violently inside him.

What had they just done?

Why the hell had he got out of his damned car? Why hadn't he driven off?

He pulled on his black trousers, not bothering to do the button up, then shrugged his shirt on, not caring it was inside out.

His other sock had rolled half under the small dressing table that had only a thin glass of dried flowers on it. That this was clearly a guest room was the only mercy he could take from this.

Stuffing his socks into his jacket pocket, he slid his feet into his brogues and strode to the door. Just as he was about to make his escape a thought hit him like a hammer to the brain.

His hands clenched into fists as recriminations at his complete and utter stupidity raged through him, every curse he knew hollering in his head.

Slowly he turned around to look at her.

She hadn't moved an inch since he'd rolled off her, her hands gripping the bedsheets, her eyes fixed on the ceiling. But then, as if feeling the weight of his gaze upon her, she turned her face towards him and wide, terrified eyes met his.

That one look confirmed everything.

It didn't need to be said.

Natasha knew as surely as he did that the madness that had taken them had been total.

They had failed to use protection.

And he knew as surely as she did that Natasha wasn't on the Pill. Pieta himself had told him they were trying for a baby.

A thousand emotions punching through him, he left without a single word exchanged between them, strode quickly across the street and into his car.

Only when he was alone in it did the roar of rage that had built in his chest come out and he slammed his fists onto the steering wheel, thumping it with all the force he could muster, then gripped his head in his hands and dug his fingers tightly into his skull.

Another twenty minutes passed before he felt even vaguely calm enough to drive away.

He didn't look at the house again.

Two weeks later

It was taking everything Natasha had not to bite her fingernails. It was taking even more not to open one of the bottles of Prosecco that had been in the fridge since Pieta's funeral. She hadn't drunk any alcohol since the wake. If she started drinking she feared she would never stop.

Francesca was due any minute to go through the plans for the hospital they were going to build in Pieta's memory. To no one's surprise it had taken her sister-in-law only one week to buy the site and get the necessary permissions to develop on it. Her sister-in-law was possibly the most determined person Natasha knew and she wished she had an ounce of her drive and a fraction of her tenacity.

For herself, she seemed to have lost whatever drive she'd ever had. She felt so tired, like she could sleep for a lifetime.

Where this lethargy had come from she didn't know, had to assume it was one of those stages of grief she'd been told to expect. Everyone was an expert on grief, it seemed. Everyone was watching her, waiting for her to crumble under the weight of it.

And despite everything, she *was* grieving, but not for the reasons everyone thought. Her grief was not for the future she had lost, but the seven years she and Matteo had both wasted.

Mixed in with it all was that awful sick feeling in her belly whenever she remembered how the night of the funeral had ended.

God, she didn't want to think about that but no matter how hard she tried to block the memories, they was always there with her.

The bell rang out.

She blew a long puff of air from her lungs and tried to compose herself while the housekeeper let Francesca in.

Footsteps sounded through the huge ground floor of the house Natasha had shared with Pieta and then Francesca entered the study with her brother, Daniele. It was the figure who appeared behind her brother-in-law that almost shattered the poise Natasha had forced on herself.

As was the custom with her Italian in-laws, exuberant kisses and tight embraces were exchanged with whispered platitudes and words of comfort. Then it was time to greet Matteo.

Bracing herself, she placed a hand loosely on his shoulder, felt his hand rest lightly on her hip as they leaned in together to go through the motions of something neither could forgo without arousing suspicion. When the stubble on his warm jaw scratched her cheek she was hit by the vivid memory of that same cheek scratching her inner thigh and had to squeeze her eyes tightly shut to block the image, something she *must* forget.

But she could smell his skin and the scent of his cologne. Smell him. Feel the strength of his body, the curls of his dark hair between her fingers...

It had been a terrible mistake, something neither of them had needed to vocalise.

She didn't know it was possible for someone to hate themselves as much as she hated herself. She owed Pieta absolutely nothing, she knew that, but...

She just couldn't believe it had happened. Couldn't believe she had lost all control of herself, couldn't work out how it had happened or why.

It was as if some madness had taken hold of them both.

For one hour she had left behind the girl who had done everything she could to please her parents to the point of abandoning the life she'd so desperately wanted, and had found the hidden woman who had never been allowed to exist.

Protection had been the last thing on either of their minds.

They'd been stupid and so, so reckless.

Francesca hadn't said she would be bringing her brother and cousin with her. It hadn't occurred to Natasha to ask. Daniele and Matteo both ran enormously successful businesses that took them all over the world. She'd assumed their input for the hospital—especially Matteo's—would come at a later date.

But then she looked properly at Francesca and understood why Daniele at least had stuck around in Pisa. Her sister-in-law looked more bereft than she had at Pieta's funeral. More than bereft. Like the light that had always shone brightly inside her had been extinguished. Daniele would never leave his sister in this state.

And Francesca looked closely at Natasha in turn. 'Are you okay? You look pale.'

She gave a rueful shrug. None of them could pretend they were okay. 'I'm just tired.'

'You're holding your back. Does it hurt?'

'A little.'

The housekeeper brought in a tray of coffee and biscotti, which distracted them all from Natasha's health. They sat around the large dining table onto which Francesca placed a stack of files.

Natasha couldn't even remember what the meeting was for. Matteo being under the same roof as her had turned her brain into a colander.

Why had he come? Was it to punish her?

Every time she'd seen him over the past seven years had been a punishment she'd accepted. She'd let him kiss her and then hours later had agreed to marry someone else, in front of him, in front of everyone. Not just someone else, but his cousin and closest friend. She'd let the moment when she should have told him about Pieta slip by in the haze of his kiss.

Would things have been different if she'd told him, either then or in the weeks beforehand when Pieta's intentions had suddenly become clear? Or would the outcome have been the same?

She'd called and left dozens of messages but Matteo had never answered and he'd never responded. He'd cut her off as effectively as he'd wielded his scalpel.

If things had been different, though, would her life have been any happier? She'd long stopped believing that. Matteo wasn't the man she'd thought him to be. He wasn't a man any woman with an ounce of sanity would consider spending her life with unless she was a masochist. It wasn't just a love of wealth he'd developed since the days she'd fancied herself in love with him; he'd developed a hedonistic streak to match it. No man who had a new woman on his arm every week could ever be content to settle down with only one.

Daniele took control of the meeting, explaining where they were with the project and how he and Matteo were planning a trip to Caballeros in the next couple of weeks. It was hoped construction would begin soon after.

'That quick?' Natasha found the energy to ask.

'It's Caballeros, not Europe,' Daniele answered with a shrug. 'Bureaucracy doesn't exist there in the way we know it.'

'Have you had any publicity ideas?' Francesca asked, reminding Natasha of the role she'd agreed to take in the project.

'I'm sorry, but no.' She stared at the polished surface of the table in her shame. All she'd done these past two weeks was drift. 'I'll get thinking and send you some ideas over the next few days.' She rubbed her temples, hoping she wasn't promising something she would fail to see through. The more publicity they had for it the more donations they would receive, the more donations they received the more staff they could employ.

Dull thuds pounded behind her eyes. As Pieta's next of kin this was her responsibility. Everything concerning her husband's foundation now rested on her shoulders and so far she'd abdicated all responsibility for it.

She would abdicate that responsibility for ever if it was in her power.

At some point soon she would have to think things through clearly but right now her head was so full yet so loose that she could hardly decide what she wanted to eat for her breakfast never mind make decisions that carried real importance.

She couldn't carry on like this. She didn't know if it was shock at Pieta's death or what had happened with Matteo that had her like this but she had to get a grip on herself.

There was a whole new future out there waiting for her and sooner or later she needed to figure out what she wanted from it. So far, all she knew with any real certainty was that she would spend it alone. She would never remarry. She would never allow anyone, not a man, not her parents, to have control over her again.

Francesca raised a weary shoulder. 'There's no rush. The end of the week will be fine.'

Eventually the ordeal was over. Chairs were scraped back as her family by marriage rose to leave. Following suit, Natasha rose too but as she stood, a wave of dizziness crashed over her and she grabbed hold of the table for support.

Francesca, who'd been sitting next to her, was the first to spot something amiss and took hold of her wrist. 'Are you okay?'

Natasha nodded, although she felt far from okay. 'I'm just tired. I should probably eat something.'

Francesca studied her a while longer before letting her go. 'You know where I am if you need me.'

Considering that Francesca looked as bad as Natasha felt, the suggestion was laughable, but it had come from her sister-in-law's kind heart so she would never laugh at her even if she had the energy.

Burning under Matteo's equally close scrutiny, she found she could only breathe normally when the front door closed behind them.

Needing to be alone, she sent the housekeeper out to do some errands and sent silent thanks to Pieta for agreeing with her request that their other staff not live in. How sad was it that she had to request such things, like a child asking a favour from a parent?

Everything about her marriage had been sad. Its ending was the least of it. She'd had no autonomy over any of it.

Now the dizziness had passed she realised she was famished. She'd felt a little nauseous when she'd woken and had skipped breakfast, which had saved her the worry of deciding what to eat, and had managed to forget to have any lunch.

Opening the fridge, she tried to think what she fancied to eat. The housekeeper had stocked up for her and there was choice. Too much choice. After much dithering she took a fresh block of cheese out, then found the biscuits to go with it.

Her stomach was growling by the time she unwrapped the cellophane from the cheese but when she took the knife to it, the smell it emitted turned the growl into a gurgle that flipped over violently.

She chucked the entire block of cheese into the bin then clutched her stomach with one hand and her mouth with the other, breathing deeply, willing the nausea away.

It had only just passed when the doorbell rang.

She stood frozen, hesitant over whether she should open it. Her house had been like Piccadilly Circus for the past two weeks and all she wanted was to be on her own.

It rang again.

What if it was her mother-in-law? Vanessa had been a frequent visitor since Natasha and Pieta had married, and had visited or called daily since his death. Whatever Natasha was going through was nothing compared to what Vanessa was living with.

And yet, even though she continued to tell herself it was bound to be her adorable mother-in-law at the door, she found she couldn't draw the least bit of surprise to find Matteo there instead.

'What do you want?' she asked, tightening her hold on the door frame. There was no audience for them to pretend cordiality.

'I want you to take this.' He held up a long, thin rectangular box.

It was a pregnancy test.

CHAPTER THREE

THE PALE FACE that had opened the door to Matteo turned whiter. 'I'm not pregnant.'

'Take the test and prove it. I'm not going anywhere until you do.'

Her gaze darted over his shoulder.

'Expecting someone?' he asked curtly. 'Another lover, perhaps?'

Her lips tightened but she held her ground. 'Vanessa likes to drop in.'

'The grieving mother checking up on the grieving widow? How charming.' It sickened him that his aunt—like the rest of the Pellegrinis—all thought the sun rose and set with Natasha. It had been Francesca's worry and compassion towards the young widow that had set the wheels in motion for the events that had led him here today. 'If you don't want her to find me here and have to explain why I have this with me, I suggest you let me in.'

A long exhalation of breath and then she stepped aside.

For the second time that day he entered Pieta's home with the same curdle of self-loathing as when he'd entered it the first time. Revulsion. At her. At himself. At what they'd done.

Until Pieta had died Matteo had been in this house

only once, when Natasha had been in England, visiting her parents.

'Have you had a period since...?' He couldn't bring himself to finish the question.

Colour stained her white face at the intimacy of what he'd asked. 'No,' she whispered.

'When are you due?'

Her throat moved before she answered. 'A couple of days ago. But I've never been regular. It doesn't mean anything.'

'You're tired. You have a backache. You used the bathroom three times during our two-hour meeting.' He ticked her symptoms off his fingers dispassionately, although his head was pounding again. They'd made love at her most fertile time. 'My flight back to Miami leaves in three hours. Take the test. If it's negative I can leave Pisa and we can both forget anything happened between us.'

Neither of them said what would happen if the test proved positive.

He held the box out to her. She stared at it blankly for a moment before snatching it out of his hand and leaving the reception room they were still standing in. Her footsteps trod up the stairs, a door shut.

Alone, Matteo took himself to the day room and sat on the sofa, cradling his head in his hands while he waited. In the adjoining room was a bar where he and Pieta had had a drink together. The temptation to help himself to a drink now was strong but not strong enough to overcome his revulsion. He'd already helped himself to his best friend and cousin's wife. He wasn't going to add to his list of crimes by helping himself to Pieta's alcohol.

He'd read the instructions himself. The test took three minutes to produce an answer.

He checked his watch. Natasha had been upstairs for ten minutes.

The seconds ticked past like minutes, the minutes like hours. All he had to occupy his mind were the furnishings the man who'd been like a brother to him had chosen. He couldn't see any sign of Natasha's influence in the decoration.

She'd once wanted to be an interior designer. He remembered her telling him that during a phone conversation held when he'd returned home after an eighteen-hour shift.

Matteo had thought he could never hate himself more than he had when he'd been ten and his dereliction of duty had ruined his little brother's life. The loathing he felt for what he'd done with Natasha matched it, an ugly rancid feeling that lived in his guts. The loathing he felt for Natasha matched it too. Damn her, but she'd been Pieta's wife. Hours after burying her husband she'd thrown herself into his arms and he...

Damn him, he'd let her.

He wished he could erase the memories of that night but every moment was imprinted in him. He'd woken that morning with the vivid feeling of entering her for the first time and the certainty that something had been wrong. It was a feeling that nagged at him more, growing stronger as time passed.

He rubbed the nape of his neck and cursed his fallible memory.

Natasha had been no virgin. She'd been married, for heaven's sake, and had been trying for a baby with her husband.

Another five minutes passed before he heard movement.

She appeared in the doorway.

One look at her face told him the answer.

'There's got to be some mistake,' Natasha croaked, clinging onto the door frame for support. 'I need to do another test.'

She'd stared at the positive sign for so long her eyes had gone as blurry as the cold mist swimming in her head.

For two weeks she'd refused to believe it could happen. She'd refused to even contemplate it.

They had been reckless beyond belief but surely, *surely* nature wouldn't punish them further for it? Surely the guilt and self-loathing they both had to live with was punishment enough?

Eyes of cold green steel stared back at her. It was a long time before he spoke.

'That test is the most accurate one on the market. If it's showing as positive then you are pregnant. So that leaves only one issue to be resolved and that's determining who the father is.'

Afraid she was going to faint, she sank onto the floor and cuddled her knees.

'When did you and Pieta last…?' The distaste that laced his voice as he failed to complete his sentence sent a wave of heat through her cold head.

For the first time in her life she didn't know what to say or do. Whenever life had posed her with a dilemma the answer had always been clear. Do what her parents wanted. It was why she'd married Pieta.

But now her parents were the least of her considerations.

'Do I take your silence to mean that you and Pieta were active until his death?'

How could she answer that? She *couldn't*.

'If your last period was a month ago then it stands to reason you and I were together when you were at your most fertile. However, all women's cycles differ to a certain degree so if you and Pieta were intimate until his death there's a good chance he could be the father. Who else is in line?'

Her head spinning at the medical knowledge that meant he had a much better understanding of how her body worked than she did, she didn't understand what he meant. 'What?'

'Don't pretend you don't know what I mean. Who else have you had sex with in the past month?'

She recoiled. 'That's offensive.'

His laughter crackled between them like a bullet. 'Don't get me wrong, you're playing the grieving widow admirably but you were like a dog on heat with me so it stands to reason there have been others.'

A dog on heat?

She covered her ears, digging her nails into her skull.

A dog on heat?

How had he not *known*? And him a doctor?

There had been a moment, when he'd first entered her, that he'd stilled, but it had only been a moment, and then she had kissed him again, as desperate for him to continue what they'd started as she had been terrified he would figure out the truth.

'I'm waiting for an answer.' His curt voice cut through her thoughts. 'How many others?'

She remembered a time so long ago when his rich voice, the Italian accent faint behind the impeccable English, had always softened around her. She guessed that's what happened when you created a business re-puted to be worth billions out of nothing, your basic humanity was thrown in the gutter along with your principles.

'No one.' She raised her head to look him square in the eye. 'There has been no one else.'

He stared back for the longest time before nodding and getting to his feet. 'A scan will pinpoint the date of conception to a degree of accuracy so we can use that to determine who the likely father is.'

His cutting tone sliced through her.

Then the thought of a scan, of seeing the little one growing inside her...

Suddenly it hit her that she was pregnant.

She was going to be a mother.

Placing a hand to her belly, she blurred out Matteo's bitter face and imagined the life growing inside her.

Hello, my little one, she said silently to it, overwhelming joy spreading through every part of her.

She'd wanted a child for so long. After everything that had gone on with Pieta she had thought it would be a long and torturous road to get there if it ever happened and if she'd ever decided to take the road he'd wanted to conceive one. But it had happened as if by magic.

She was going to have a baby.

'How can you be smiling at such a time?' Matteo said acidly. 'Is this amusing to you?'

The smile she hadn't even known she was wearing fell but as it fell her spine straightened.

Whatever the future held for her, even if it was only humiliation, she had her little seed to think about. She couldn't fall into despair. She would be strong. She would be a mother.

'I'm pregnant,' she said, eyeballing him. 'You cannot know how long I have wanted this so, yes, I will smile and rejoice at my child's conception because it is a miracle.'

His jaw clenched, Matteo eyed her back with mirrored loathing. 'You intend to keep it, then?'

Of all the stuff he'd thrown at her, this was by far the cruellest. 'How can you ask such a thing?'

He breached the distance between them and placed a hand round the nape of her neck. Bringing his face close to hers as if examining her, he said with icy quiet, 'Because I know you, Natasha. You're selfish. You think only of yourself and what advances you.'

Stunned into silence at his closeness, at the warmth of his skin on hers, the fingers almost absently stroking her neck, memories of their one time together crashing through her, Natasha had to blink to get her brain back in gear. Breathing heavily, not taking her eyes from his, she raised her arm to find the hand laid so casually on her and dug her nails in as hard as she could as she shoved it away.

Raising herself to her full height, which was almost a foot shorter than his six-feet-plus frame, she said as icily as she could through the tremors in her voice, 'You don't know me at all. If you did you wouldn't have to ask if I wanted to keep it. I will do more than keep it. I will raise it and I will love it.'

Once she had longed for this.

If her eighteen-year-old self had been told that in seven years she would be carrying Matteo's child she would have danced for miles with joy.

But she couldn't tell him that. He wouldn't believe her if she did.

He rubbed the flesh of his hand where she'd stabbed him with her nails.

'I hope for your child's sake that your words aren't as

worthless as they usually are but time will tell on that. I've a friend who runs a clinic near mine in Florence with the newest, most accurate scans. I'll take you there. She'll be able to pinpoint the date of conception to at least determine if I'm in the frame as father. Her discretion will be guaranteed and I think one thing we can be in agreement on is the need for discretion.'

Natasha forced herself to breathe.

Everything was happening so quickly. She couldn't let him railroad her but likewise she had to do what was best for her and her baby and until she'd decided what she was going to do, she needed all the discretion she could get.

Oh, God, the implications were too awful to think about.

How many lives were going to be ruined when the truth came out?

The worst of it was she would never be able to tell the full truth. No one could know.

Like Matteo couldn't know that she already knew of an excellent clinic, this one in Paris, where discretion was also guaranteed.

And he couldn't know that he was the only man in the frame for the father of her baby.

Fighting back another bout of dizziness, she nodded sharply. She had to keep it together. 'When?'

'In a fortnight. The baby's heartbeat should be detectable by then.'

'So soon?' She'd known for twenty minutes that she was pregnant and he was saying her baby's heart was already forming? That was just mind-blowing.

He nodded grimly. 'Pregnancy is taken from the date of your last period so in a fortnight you will be classed as six weeks pregnant. Only the scan will be able to give us a reasonably accurate conception date.'

'And I'll be able to hear the heartbeat?'

'We both will.' His face a tight mask, he headed for the door. 'I'll be in touch.'

Only when she heard the door close did she sink onto the sofa and hang her head between her knees.

Soon she would be hanging it in shame.

All the people who were going to be hurt, Vanessa, Francesca... Ever since she'd married Pieta she would catch them looking at her belly, knew they were searching for the signs of swelling, the signs of life growing inside her. Since he'd died the stares had become more obvious. She knew how badly they wished she was carrying Pieta's child. Francesca was already suspicious.

She sat back and rubbed her temples.

She didn't have a clue how to handle this. Whatever she did, everyone would be hurt. Hopes were going to be raised then not just dashed but crushed. Then there was the Pellegrini estate itself...

This was too much.

Overwhelmed by the jumble of thoughts raging through her head, Natasha burst into tears.

It had to be like this, she told herself, hugging her belly, the urge to protect her little seed already strong, even if only from her tears.

The real unvarnished truth would destroy every single one of them, Matteo included.

Better to take it on the chin and have the world, including her own parents, think her a slut than for that to happen. She could hardly bear to think of the disdain and disappointment in their eyes when they learned she was pregnant and that Pieta wasn't the father.

Marrying Pieta was the only thing she'd done in her

twenty-five years that had pleased them. It had given them the opportunity to brag to the world that the great Pieta Pellegrini was their son-in-law and it was an opportunity they never let pass by.

Natasha dried her eyes and blew out a long breath.

All the tears in the world wouldn't change things. She was going to be a mother and that meant she had to be strong for her child's sake.

And all the tears in the world didn't change the fact that it was better for the world to think her a slut than for everyone to know that Matteo was the only candidate for father of her baby.

The world could never know that she had been a virgin until the night she'd buried her husband.

The clinic Matteo had booked them into was tucked away in a beautiful medieval building in the heart of Florence. To the unwitting passer-by it could be home to any of the numerous museums and galleries the city was famed for.

The interior was a total contrast. No one entering could doubt they were in a state-of-the-art medical facility.

The cool receptionist made a call and moments later Julianna, the clinic's director, stepped out of a door to greet them.

Matteo had met Julianna, a tall, rangy woman in her midforties, a number of times at conferences. They welcomed each other like old friends, exchanging kisses along with their greetings.

Then he introduced her to Natasha and they were taken through to the pristine scanning room where everything was set up for them.

'Are you happy for Dr Manaserro to stay in the room while we do this?' Julianna asked Natasha in English.

Her eyes darted to him with an inflection of surprise before she shrugged her slim shoulders. He doubted she'd ever heard him addressed by that title before.

'You will be a little exposed,' Julianna warned.

Another shrug. 'He can stay if he wants,' she answered tonelessly.

Matteo experienced a pang of guilt that was as unwelcome as it was unexpected.

Today was the first time he'd seen Natasha in two weeks. In the intervening period, other than arranging this scan, he'd done his best to forget her and the pregnancy.

The chances of him being the father were extremely slim, he'd reasoned. Even if the scan confirmed that he could be, he still knew it wasn't likely. They'd only been intimate the once whereas Natasha and Pieta must have...

His guts twisted violently as he thought of all the times they must have been together over the years. Pieta and Natasha had been actively trying for a baby. Pieta had told him that the last time he'd seen him.

And she was happy to be pregnant. She'd called it a miracle. Was that because of her longing for a child or because she was happy that a part of Pieta might be living inside her? Surely she must have felt *some* affection for her husband, whatever her actions the night of his funeral?

Surely she wouldn't have reacted like that if she'd thought there was any chance *he* might be the father?

Dio, he shouldn't be thinking like this. It felt too rancid inside him.

Since she'd accepted Pieta's proposal hours after

their one kiss, he'd pushed Natasha out of his mind, never thinking of her, never thinking of her and Pieta together. Only when he'd been in her presence had his loathing of her come out of the compartment in his head he'd put her in, and on those occasions he'd learned to hide it by ignoring her wherever possible. He'd moved on very quickly and in any case Pieta was too good a friend and too close a cousin for Matteo to let a woman come between them.

Pieta hadn't known Matteo and Natasha had been building a long-distance closeness which, looking back, had been strange as he and Pieta had often swapped stories about women. At the time it had felt too...special to be spoken of, which with hindsight had been comical. He must have been caught in a bout of sentimentality and had made sure never to have such ludicrous thoughts again.

If it was indeed Pieta's child then he too would celebrate to know a part of his best friend lived on, even if the mother the child had to live on through was a deceitful bitch.

It *had* to be Pieta's. The alternative...

It would destroy everything.

So he'd left her alone and fought the urge to call every five minutes and make sure she was eating and sleeping properly.

Looking at her now, he didn't think she'd had a square meal since he'd last seen her.

'Okay, Natasha, you are looking at this as a dating scan, I believe?' Julianna said.

She nodded.

'Have you seen a doctor or a midwife yet?'

She shook her head.

'Are you thinking of having the child here or in England?'

Her eyes darted to him again.

Julianna smiled reassuringly. 'It's okay, there are no right or wrong answers.'

'I haven't thought that far ahead,' she whispered.

'You have plenty of time to decide but you should be monitored. The obstetrician we employ here is the best in Florence or I can recommend a female for you if that would suit you better?'

Matteo, feeling perspiration break out on his back, had to bite his tongue to stop himself from cutting in. Now they were here, the ultrasound screen switched on, he wanted to get this over with.

But that appeared to be the end of the questioning.

'Are you ready to do this?'

'Yes.' It was the most animation he'd heard in Natasha's voice since she'd opened the door to him earlier.

'Lie down and lift your top and lower your skirt to your hips so your stomach is exposed.'

Matteo trained his eyes on the screen.

When Natasha was ready, Julianna tucked tissue around her lowered skirt and took her seat.

Even though he wasn't looking directly at her, he saw Natasha flinch when the cold gel was applied to her stomach.

Julianna then picked up the probe and pressed it over the gel. As she worked, all three of their gazes were fixed on the screen.

'There it is!' she said in delight. 'See, Natasha? There is your baby.'

Natasha craned her neck forward, trying hard to see what was there. 'Where?'

'There.' Julianna put a finger to the screen. 'See?'

Natasha really didn't know what she'd been expecting to see—a fully formed miniature baby this soon into the pregnancy was too wild even for her imagination—but had hoped it would be more than a blob. But then Julianna pressed some keys on the keyboard on her desk and the blob came into sharper focus. It was still a blob but there was something more defined about it that got her already racing heart ready to burst out of her.

'Do you want to hear the heartbeat?'

A moment later the most beautiful sound she'd ever heard echoed through the room.

She didn't dare look at Matteo. If there was anything other than joy on his face it would taint this special moment for ever.

So she continued to look at her little walnut now frozen on the screen and listen to its healthy heart beating while Julianna did whatever she was doing on her computer until her eyes blurred and the beats were no longer distinguishable.

Eventually Julianna pushed her chair back and wiped Natasha's belly clean with another, softer tissue.

'I would say that so far everything is looking good and healthy.'

'So far?'

The older woman smiled. 'I am a medical practitioner. We never talk in absolutes. What I can say with all honesty is that right now your child is developing well and you should be happy with that. As for when it's due...' She gave a date at the end of June.

Natasha closed her eyes. When she had searched the internet and put in the date of conception, every site she had visited had given this same due date within its narrow parameters.

From the way Matteo shifted in his seat, he had done the same maths.

He knew the due date made it impossible for Pieta to be the father. The date of conception was firmly after his death.

He knew the baby was his.

CHAPTER FOUR

NATASHA HAD TO wait until they were back in his car before she had an inkling of what Matteo was thinking.

'This changes everything,' he said after a long period of silence.

'Not really,' she refuted quietly. 'You already knew it could be yours.'

'I know, I was praying that it wasn't,' he spat.

She dug her nails into the palms of her hands. She'd had two weeks to prepare for this moment, researching everything she could about pregnancy whilst hiding any nausea or backache from her steady stream of visitors.

If she hadn't been in such shock at the test coming up positive—who could expect to fall pregnant on their very first time of making love?—she would have been able think much more quickly on her feet and not put Matteo through the turmoil he must have been in over the past fortnight. When he'd asked when she'd last been intimate with Pieta her brain had been too frazzled to think of a straight-up lie. How badly she'd wanted to tell him the truth and spare him all the uncertainty.

The truth would shatter him. The truth would shatter everyone.

It had to be this way. As hard and as painful as it was, it was the lesser of two evils.

If there was a hell she would surely be sent to it for all the lies of omission she'd had to tell and would continue having to tell.

'Do you have any idea of the nightmare you've pulled me into?' he said scathingly, driving them out of the city and into the Tuscan hills.

'The nightmare *I've* pulled you into?' she retorted, raising her voice. 'As far as I recall, you were there too. I accept I behaved badly but you behaved badly too so don't you dare place all the blame on me.'

He changed gear with so much force she thought the gearstick would snap.

His jaw clenched, he drove them on in silence.

As a rule, Natasha loved Tuscany. She loved the glimpses of vineyards and olive groves, the old hidden monasteries that would suddenly spring into view, some old and decrepit, others renovated, beautiful whatever their states. Today the scenery passed her by without notice. Not until they entered a town they hadn't travelled through on their way to Florence did she realise he was taking a different route back.

Her heart sinking, she knew where he was taking her.

Sure enough, soon she caught her first view of Castello Miniato, centrepiece of the Pellegrini estate Pieta had inherited in its entirety when his father had died just weeks after their wedding. The estate he'd married her for.

Matteo pulled the car to a stop outside the fortressed wall surrounding the *castello*.

'What do you see?' he asked her roughly.

'Is this a trick question?'

'No.'

'The *castello*.'

She'd married Pieta in these grounds—thankfully

not in the *castello*'s chapel as that would have made their marriage even more of a mockery—with a heart that had felt dead. She'd seen the expectation on her mother's face and the silent nod of encouragement to put her best foot forward. She'd felt the pressure of her father's fingers digging into her upper arm, had thought of the vast amounts of money Pieta had given her parents during their long engagement and had dragged her feet towards him.

Pieta had been waiting under the floral arch. His expression had been neutral. It could have been anyone walking towards him.

She wished she'd had the courage to turn on her heel and run.

The *castello* she'd adored for so long, the castle that had fired her young imagination with thoughts of knights and maidens, had been the main reason Pieta had married her. They'd spent only a handful of nights there but she had grown to detest it, a manifestation of the trapped desperation she'd found herself in.

'Why are we here?'

'To remind you of what you married into. The inheritance of this estate is on hold until there is no longer any possibility you're carrying Pieta's child. But it's more than that—they're all waiting to see if you're carrying a part of *him* in you. They're all hoping for it, Vanessa, Daniele and Francesca, and now you are pregnant but it is medically impossible for it to be his, so I am going to ask you this one more time and I want you to think very carefully before giving me your answer. How many other men did you sleep with in the days before and after you and I slept together?'

Blood heating with loathing and humiliation, Natasha forced herself to meet his baleful glare. 'None.'

'You are sure about that? There was no one three days either side of when we were together? This is important, Natasha.'

'I know very well how important it is and I am telling you there was no one. You're the father.'

A low sigh escaped from him as he bowed his head over the steering wheel.

The hard reality of their situation crystallised in him. For two weeks Matteo had been able to tell himself it was too remote a chance for him to be the father. Natasha's vehement denial of there being anyone else held the ring of truth in it.

'I'm going to want a DNA test done when the child's born,' he muttered, thinking aloud, 'if only for my own peace of mind.'

She laughed derisively.

The anger he'd been holding onto spilled over. 'Do you have any idea of the destruction this is going to cause? This isn't just your life, it's mine too. Vanessa took me in when I was thirteen years old and treated me as if I were her own son rather than her husband's nephew. Daniele and Francesca treated me like a brother. This is going to cost me my family so you can be damned sure I want concrete certainty about the paternity if I'm going to lose everyone I love because of it.'

'Stop this right now,' she said tightly. 'I know how much you love them—I love them too, but you *are* the father and no amount of burying your head in the sand can change that.'

His lungs had closed so tightly he had to force air into them.

His phone vibrated. Taking advantage of the distraction, he pulled it from his jacket pocket.

It was an email from Julianna. Attached was a picture of the scan and a brief message asking him to forward it to Natasha.

He opened the attachment and, staring at the tiny life so small the resolution of the attachment struggled to distinguish it in any great detail, he felt a little of his anger deflate.

All the arguing and recriminations in the world didn't change the one undisputable fact that Natasha was pregnant and...

And he was the father.

Something flickered inside him, a bloom that expanded into his chest, up his throat, seeping into his brain, filling him with an emotion he'd never felt before because the emotion had never existed in him before.

He was going to be a father.

How could he deny it?

He couldn't.

Dio, he was going to be a father.

It was his child growing in her belly, no one else's.

It was time to accept responsibility for this because the other undisputable fact was that their child was innocent and deserved all the protection it could get from both its parents and also because Natasha was right. Burying his head would cause more pain to Vanessa and his cousins in the long term.

'We won't be able to keep this a secret for long,' he said, thinking aloud. 'The pregnancy is going to be noticeable soon. People—Vanessa and the family—will assume it's Pieta's. Their hopes will be raised.'

'They're going to be so hurt.' He heard the catch in her voice. 'They're going to hate me.'

'They're going to hate us both, but we can protect them from the worst of it.'

'How?'

'Come to Miami with me. I'm flying to Caballeros with Daniele tomorrow. We should only be there for a couple of days. When I get back I'll take you home with me. We can say you need a break from everything. In a month or so we can tell them you're pregnant with my child. It'll be easier for them to accept we turned to each other for comfort and that a relationship grew naturally than to accept the truth of the child's conception.'

'You want us to lie?'

'No, I do not want us to lie. I despise dishonesty but what's the alternative? Do you want to return to your parents in England and—'

'No.' Her rebuttal was emphatic.

'Then coming with me is the only answer. If you stay in Pisa, and Vanessa and the others think there is even a chance you are carrying Pieta's…' To build their hopes up only to cut them away would be too cruel. 'We need to show a united front starting from *now.*'

'So you do accept the baby's yours?'

'Yes. I accept it's mine and I will acknowledge it as mine. Come with me and I will protect you both, and we will have a small chance of making the pain of what's to come a little less in the family who have shown both of us nothing but love and acceptance. They have suffered enough.'

She rested her head against the window and closed her eyes. He hated that even looking as if she hadn't slept in a month she was still the most beautiful woman he'd ever laid eyes on.

Eventually she nodded. 'Okay,' she said in her soft, clear English voice. 'I'll come to Miami with you. But only for a while. We can fake a burgeoning relationship, I can get pregnant, and then we can split up.'

'We stay together until it's born.'

Her eyes flew open to stare at him with incredulity. 'That's seven and a half months away.'

'This is your first pregnancy. You need my support.' He remembered his early hospital rotation in the ER when he'd been a junior resident. He'd dealt with numerous pregnant women admitted with complications, knew first-hand that pregnancy was unpredictable.

'Support? You were talking about a DNA test only a few minutes ago. If that's your idea of support, I'd much rather go it alone.'

'Damn it, Natasha, I'd convinced myself there was no way the child could be mine! I wanted it to be Pieta's, I didn't want it to be mine. I wanted to be able to wash my hands of the situation but I can't. I *do* accept it's my baby you're carrying but this isn't going to be easy. Not for either of us. I am not going to let you go through the pregnancy alone, so get that idea out of your head.'

'What happens when it's born?' she demanded to know. 'How much involvement will you want?'

'I don't know!' He thumped the steering wheel in his anger.

This could not be happening. Natasha was having his child. It was going to destroy everything and everyone. But he would not let it destroy his child.

He was going to be a father. He could feel the magnitude of it building inside him.

It had been many years since he'd even considered fatherhood. He'd wanted a wife and a family once, a long time ago when he'd met a woman who'd stolen the breath from his lungs with one look. Until that point he'd been so focused on his surgical career that relationships had passed him by, his affairs with the opposite sex short and on occasion sweet, but never interfering with his focus.

The Rawlings were old friends of his aunt and uncle

but the first time he'd personally met them had been during the Christmas period when he'd been in the third year of his residency in a Florida hospital. He'd left Italy at eighteen to study medicine there because it was one of the best medical schools in the world, but had still travelled back to Pisa whenever he could.

He'd arrived late on Christmas Eve, the annual party Vanessa and Fabio threw in their sprawling Pisa villa already well under way. He'd taken one look at the sophisticated, beautiful woman chatting in a group by the enormous Christmas tree and had been instantly enamoured. But then he'd learned that she was only seventeen and had backed right off.

Seventeen? He'd thought she must be at least in her midtwenties.

Being under the same roof meant he'd got to know her a little. What he'd learned had made him want to learn more. Shy on the surface, a little probing had revealed a keen intelligence, a dry sense of humour and a maturity well beyond her years.

He'd returned to America days later, unable to stop thinking about her.

When he'd returned to Italy for Easter, the Rawlings had again been in residence. This time the chemistry between them had been tangible. He'd left with her phone number and the memory of her making him promise to call as soon as he arrived back in Florida so she wouldn't worry about him arriving safely.

No one had ever worried about him arriving anywhere safely before and it had touched him deeply.

He made the call. It became the first of many. Soon it became a habit to call as soon as his shifts at the hospital were over. They emailed. They wrote. They texted. They lived in different continents but it was only a physical separation. He told her things about himself he'd never shared with anyone. He opened himself up and laid himself bare as he'd never done before.

He was content for them to build a relationship from afar, knowing it wouldn't be long until she came of age and they could be together properly. It was the same for her too, going as far as Natasha looking into universities stateside so they could be together.

Spending over a decade studying and working to achieve his goal of being a surgeon had taught him that nothing worthwhile came easily or could be rushed. To him, Natasha was worth waiting for. It was more than desire, it was a meeting of hearts and minds he could never have explained to anyone because he couldn't explain it to himself. She'd tapped into something in him that he hadn't known existed, a need to create a family of his own. And she'd seen something in him no one else had either. Something good. She knew about the childhood fire that had left his brother so severely disfigured that Roberto had become a recluse, yet had never judged him for his part in it. She'd defended him from himself.

Matteo had always known he would never operate on Roberto himself, even when he qualified as a reconstructive plastic surgeon. Never mind it being unethical, he'd barely coped in the waiting room whenever Roberto had endured the many surgeries and skin grafts he'd needed over the years. To be effective, surgeons needed detachment. He could never have been detached operating on his brother. So he'd researched new techniques and the best surgeons performing them while at the same time researching proven topical remedies for burn scars, determined to come up with something practical that would help his brother. Natasha had had no medical knowledge but had listened and encouraged him.

Discovering that he'd opened his heart and laid himself bare to a lie and that she'd been playing with him had hit him right in the gut. But he'd got over it. He'd hardened his heart against her and had soon considered himself to have had a lucky escape. Since then he'd been far too busy, first finishing his residency and qualifying as a surgeon and then building his businesses, to waste his time thinking about her. Thoughts of a family had been put on the back burner. Life was short and he intended to enjoy it and to hell with the woman who'd played him for a fool.

He didn't deny it had given him satisfaction to imagine her reading the media tales of his self-made wealth and know she would be kicking herself for choosing the wrong cousin.

The irony that she would be the mother of his child after all would be laughable if the situation itself wasn't so tragic.

Taking another long breath, he controlled his tone to say, 'No, I *do* know. I'm going to want full involvement. This is our child and we will raise it together.'

'Together?' Her blue eyes flashed. 'I'm happy for us to raise it as some kind of team but only because I know it's best for the baby, but don't get any ideas about me living with you after it's born or marriage or anything like that because I won't.'

'You have no worries on that score,' he shot back. 'You are the last woman I'd ever consider marrying.'

'Good,' she spat, 'because it will never happen.'

He sucked in a breath, trying to keep a lid on his temper. 'We will work out maintenance and custody arrangements that suit us both and works for our child, but that's a long way off. Right now the priority is for you and I to pretend to be a couple falling in love.'

Her disbelief turned into a bark of bitter laughter. 'You? In love? As if anyone in their right mind would believe that. You're pictured with a different woman every week.'

'I will do whatever is necessary to protect my family and if that means being celibate while we fake a relationship then that's a sacrifice I'm prepared to make. We have to make this convincing.'

His uncle and aunt had taken him in when he'd been at his lowest, when the tension between himself and his father had become a poisonous living being. Fabio and Vanessa had loved him and cared for him as if he'd been a child of their loins. He wouldn't be able to protect Vanessa from the horror of Natasha's pregnancy but he could at least spare her and his cousins the truth of its conception and spare their hopes from flaring that a part of Pieta still lived on through her.

'I'm prepared to make some sacrifices but what about you?' he asked, turning it back on her. 'Can you make people believe the grieving widow is capable of finding love again so soon after burying her beloved husband?'

Instead of displaying the vehement outrage he was sure would come at him, Natasha covered her forehead with her hand. 'Trust me, I am an expert at faking things.'

Natasha sat in the living room waiting for the doorbell to ring. Her bags were packed, her affairs in order, passport at the ready, everything done to uproot her life for the foreseeable future.

Matteo's solution, as much as it troubled her to think of living under his roof, was the best way forward. Really, it was the only way. Francesca's unexpected visit just fifteen minutes after Matteo had dropped her home after the scan had proved that.

Francesca had come to tell her in person that she was getting married. Even with her own troubles and the guilty ache in her heart evoked just by being with her sister-in-law, Natasha had been taken aback by the news. Francesca had had a life plan in which getting married had been relegated to occur at least a decade from now. She hadn't planned on falling in love, though, and although she'd tried to mute her happiness, her radiance shone as brightly as the enormous rock on her wedding finger.

Her understandable self-absorption had stopped Francesca scrutinising Natasha with her usual zeal and she had left without asking if she'd had any publicity ideas yet for the hospital in Caballeros or even checking her out for signs of physical change, for which Natasha had been thankful.

For the first time in her life she'd developed a decent pair of breasts. If these changes were already showing, what would come next? Francesca was training to be a lawyer; inquisitiveness came as naturally to her as breathing. Next time those prying eyes would notice.

Leaving Pisa was the best way forward. She couldn't go home to England. That was unthinkable. She dreaded her parents' reaction when they learned of the pregnancy and the identity of the father as much as she dreaded her in-laws' reactions.

Her parents had forced this marriage on her. They hadn't cared that she'd had feelings for another man, hopes and dreams for a future with him. They hadn't cared when Pieta had dragged their engagement out over six long years. They'd never asked if their marriage was a happy one. If she'd told them the truth about it, they wouldn't have cared. They wouldn't have cared that she'd been trapped with no way out and no means to leave him. There would have been no help from them.

When she'd called her father to inform him of Pieta's death, his first question once the platitudes had been done with was to ask if she could be pregnant. Her mother had asked the same thing at the funeral.

Not even her mother-in-law had been so insensitive to ask that and it was her son who'd died.

Her parents' hopes for a pregnancy had nothing to do with any longing for a grandchild. For them it was all about the money.

So, yes, Matteo's option was the only sensible one.

Sensible and right. Right for her baby.

For all his hostility and for all the fallout he would endure, he wasn't shirking his responsibility. After what had seemed like hopeful beginnings for them, they'd been on the fringes of each other's lives for almost eight years and had spent one incredible night together. They both bitterly regretted that night. They didn't know each other. They didn't trust each other. They needed to use this time to form some kind of relationship that would allow them to raise their child in the spirit of togetherness and not as enemies.

All of this felt rational. Sensible. She needed to put her best foot forward and do her best, as her mother always liked to say, as if she were the leader of some Girl Guide group taking charge on an exciting expedition rather than a mother doing what was best for her child.

Her parents had never done what was best for her; they had always done what was best for them.

She could not live like that any more.

She'd lived her entire life as a pawn to be used, first by her parents and then by her husband, never good enough as she was, never *being* enough as she was, just a sad sap of a girl with a desperation to please.

When her baby was born she would think and do only what was best for it and she would do it on her terms, no one else's. But until then...

Best foot forward and do her best, and don't think about what it would do to her emotionally living with Matteo under his roof. That should be the least of her worries, but when her pulses surged to hear the door-bell ring, she knew it had the potential to be the greatest of all the dangers.

CHAPTER FIVE

MATTEO'S JET, WITH *Manaserro* emblazoned in bold red lettering on its sides, was ready for boarding as soon as they'd been whisked through security. Take-off occurred within minutes.

After showing Natasha all the facilities, including the bedroom, which he said was for her use during the long flight, Matteo settled himself at his desk and turned his tablet on.

He raised his brows when she took the seat opposite. 'Don't you want to get some rest? You look tired.'

That she could not deny. The pregnancy hormones were making her exhausted but she'd been so wound up over the guilt of their plans and all the other things weighing on her conscience that she couldn't switch her brain off to sleep.

'Maybe later. Tell me how it went in Caballeros.'

He shrugged and put his tablet down. 'I can honestly say I've never been to such a dire country in my life.'

'That bad, was it?'

'Worse. Francesca's fiancé—' He suddenly interrupted himself. 'Did I tell you she spent one week there and fell for her bodyguard? They're getting married.'

Natasha nodded. 'Francesca told me.'

'Her fiancé is not a man to be messed with and the

hospital site itself is secure. He's got men permanently posted there for the duration of the construction process but the Caballeron government is corruption itself.'

That came as no surprise. Caballeros was infamous. Ranked the sixth most dangerous country in the world, drugs and crime were rife. Daniele had insisted Francesca, who'd been hell-bent on getting the hospital site approved as a memorial to Pieta, only travel there with heavy protection.

Thinking of Daniele made Natasha chew her bottom lip, the weight of her conscience pressing down extra hard.

'Did you tell Daniele about us?' she asked in a small voice.

He grimaced again and sighed heavily. 'I set the seed and told him you were going to fly out to Miami for a break. He didn't seem to be bothered by it.' Suddenly he slammed his fist down on the desk, real anger on his face. 'How do you do it?' he demanded.

'Do what?'

'*Lie*. Daniele trusts me. It didn't occur to him that I was feeding him a steaming pile of manure. How does it come so naturally to you?'

'It doesn't,' she said, stung. 'I *hate* lying. It's deceitful.'

'Stop the pretence. Lying comes as naturally to you as breathing—you told me yourself that you're a pro at faking things.'

She clenched her teeth together knowing she deserved that comeback. She *had* told him that. He couldn't know she'd been referring to her marriage and the mountain of lies it had been built on.

'It was your idea for us to play it like this,' she reminded him icily, 'and you can't tell me you haven't told a bagful of lies in your time.'

'Not in my personal life.'

'You lie in your professional life?'

'There isn't a physician alive who hasn't told a white lie.'

'And what do your lies consist of? *Yes, your nose is huge, let me shrink it for you and charge you a vast amount for it*?' she taunted. 'Although from what I've heard you're too busy swanning around the world building your empire to bother with the nitty-gritty of surgery itself.'

His green eyes turned icy cold. 'I don't swan around, whatever that means. I employ the best surgeons from the top medical schools in my clinics and we operate under a strict code of ethics. A doctor's first duty is to do no harm and I am insulted you would imply otherwise. I have never lied to a patient but in my residency days I did on occasion lie to a relative at the patient's request, like with the mother who wanted to spare her child from knowing the prognosis of the cancer eating at her brain until she thought the child was in the right place to handle it. Those lies were told to prevent further suffering.'

She stared at his tight, angry face. For the first time in seven years she saw a glimpse of the man he'd been before, the man who'd been passionate and driven about his work, a man she'd thought no longer existed.

'Why did you turn your back on it?' she asked, unable to hide her bewilderment.

'I didn't. I became an entrepreneur alongside it.'

'You were going to be a reconstructive surgeon. You took the most direct routes to it that you could find...'

'And I *am* a reconstructive surgeon. I perform enough

to keep my skills sharp, but the surgeons in my employ fix people who are unhappy with how they look. That's what I always set out to do.'

'No, you didn't. You wanted to fix people who were maimed and disfigured. You never said anything about opening your own clinics. The skin cream you wanted to develop was to help your brother...'

'My brother died,' he said, drumming his fingers on the desk, the glint of danger in his eyes.

'I know and I'm sorry.' She knew that when Matteo was ten and his brother Roberto eight, Roberto had been seriously injured in a fire that had left him with horrific internal and external scarring. It was a miracle he'd survived to live another twenty years. When she'd heard of his death she'd known Matteo would be devastated.

Poor Matteo. One minute he must have been on top of the world, qualifying as a surgeon after so many years of hard work, then only three months later, when he'd hardly had the time to taste his success, the brother he'd adored and had longed to make better had died.

She had wanted so badly to reach out to him but had known her words of condolence would not be wanted. They wouldn't be wanted now either.

Adopting a softer tone, she said, 'I just remember all the conversations we used to have. I remember the ideals you had back then.'

'Those?' he mocked. 'They were a young doctor trying to impress a beautiful woman with his humanity.'

Heat spread low inside her at the backhanded compliment. 'So you *are* a liar, then.'

His sensual lips pulled into a smile but the eyes didn't change, holding hers with that dangerous yet somehow seductive glint. 'Not lies. I merely chose to alter the path I was taking. That's the beauty of life—it's full of options, something I am sure you're familiar with. After all, you chose to marry Pieta, heir to the Pellegrini estate, rich in his own right, when there would have been other options available to you. And now you're a reasonably rich widow you will have a pool of men to choose from to make husband number two.' The smile became cruel. 'Or have you already got a man in mind, *bella*? A rich surgeon perhaps who can comfortably keep you in the lifestyle you've become accustomed to?'

Even his endearment of *bella* sounded like a mockery.

'I've already said I don't want to marry you,' she snapped. 'I don't want to marry anyone.'

'But, *bella*, I don't trust a word you say so why should I believe that? If you're secretly hoping my invitation to live with me during the pregnancy means I have some latent feelings for you, you're wrong. I admit that once I did have feelings but you killed them when you accepted Pieta's proposal and I realised you'd been toying with both of us. If I ever marry I would need to trust my wife. I would require some form of loyalty and faithfulness and we both know you're incapable of any of that.'

Natasha's stomach shredded under the weight of his malevolence but she refused to cower under it. 'You haven't lived my life; you know nothing about me. And how dare you speak of loyalty as if it's an attribute you own when you bedded your best friend's wife on the day of his funeral.'

The mocking glint disappeared. Matteo rose to his feet, towering over her, his face dark and menacing. 'That is something I will regret for the rest of my life. You're a gold-digger. You chose Pieta over me because he had money and back then I had little—you see, *bella*, I do know you. I know you come from a greedy, grasping family who spent my cousin's money as if it was going out of fashion and his death means the gravy train is over. You only inherit his personal wealth, substantial, I admit, but nothing compared to the income you enjoyed from the Pellegrini estate when he was alive. Was that why I came back in your favour now I'm so much more than an overworked doctor?'

Matteo watched the colour drain from her face as he spoke but felt no guilt. He only spoke the truth. Pieta had mentioned a number of times about helping Natasha's parents out. He'd described them as leeches.

'You came to *me*,' she hissed, rising too and leaning on the desk between them, blue eyes spitting brimstone. 'You're entitled to your opinions of me—I can't change them, I know that—but you're not entitled to your own facts. You turned up at *my* door, not the other way round. We were both there, we both know what happened just…happened. It wasn't planned and I will not have you twist things round so that you can absolve yourself of any blame. Our child's conception is on both of us so you can damn well stop putting it all on me.'

Matteo threw his head back and clenched his jaw before looking at her.

Dio, even in anger she was beautiful. All she wore was a pair of slim fitting jeans and a navy top that fell off the shoulder, and she still filled his loins with an inexplicable craving.

He wished he had the power to eradicate their night together from his memories.

It hadn't even been a whole night. Barely an hour.

The most explosive, fulfilling hour of his life.

It had been an eruption of desire so intense and all-consuming it should have burnt itself out there and then, not remain simmering in his blood.

Natasha had the potential to drive him out of his

mind. She was a Pandora from mythology, beautiful, beguiling, radiating innocence but inside full of deceit. Natasha had the jar in her hand that when opened was going to unleash hell on his earth.

But she was right that it wasn't fair for him to put all the blame on her.

Wasn't that exactly what his father had been doing for twenty-five years, blaming Matteo for the fire rather than accepting his own responsibility for it?

He would never be like his father.

He *had* gone to her. It had been he who'd kept his finger on the buzzer until she'd opened the door. Even now, with a month's distance from the event, he had no insight into his own motives. He still couldn't understand what had compelled him to get out of the car and cross the street to the house.

Whatever the underlying reason, it didn't change the outcome. They were having a baby together.

'You're right,' he said, sitting back down with a sigh. 'The guilt belongs to us both. I shouldn't put it all on you.'

Her stony glare didn't drop an inch.

He rubbed his forehead, trying to ease the pressure building in it. 'Look, the next seven, eight months are not going to be easy for either of us.'

'No, they're not,' she agreed, her voice a fraction calmer.

'Like it or not, our baby ties us together. I've seen first-hand how destructive warring parents can be. I saw it all the time during my residency, parents who could hardly stand to be in the same room as the other even when their child was seriously ill. I don't want our child to suffer because of us. For our baby's sake, I'm willing to try and look past what went on between us before and build some kind of relationship that isn't based on loathing.'

Her eyes flickered. 'Really? You can stop throwing the past back in my face?'

'I can try. I'm never going to trust you but for better or worse we're now always going to be involved in each other's lives. I'm prepared to try. What about you? Are you willing to try too?'

Her gaze didn't leave his but there was a discernible softening in her eyes, a slight crease forming in her brow as if she was thinking.

She stayed like that for a long time.

Then her lips pulled together and her throat moved before she nodded and whispered, 'Yes. I'm willing to try.'

He almost put out his hand to invite her to shake on their truce but stopped himself before his fingers had moved more than a fraction towards her.

It wasn't just his fingers that yearned towards her. It was all of him.

He cleared his throat. 'So now that's settled, would you like me to order you some food?'

She shook her head and looked away. All the fire that had spilled out of her just a short while ago had been dampened. Now she looked lost.

'I'm not hungry. I think I'll take you up on your earlier suggestion and get some rest.'

'Whatever you wish.'

She walked to his bedroom with a gait that was almost a shuffle. When she reached the door she looked at him again. Even with the distance now between them he could see the crease still in her brow and something that looked like pain in her eyes.

'I know you won't believe me but I never meant for

any of it to happen. I never meant to hurt you. I...' She swallowed and bit into her lip.

Something reached out from his chest and clenched around his throat. Suddenly feeling that he could choke, he waved a dismissive hand. 'You didn't hurt me.'

Natasha closed the door behind her and put one clammy palm to her chest, the other to her mouth and blinked back the hot tears that had filled her eyes.

Despite his denial she knew she'd hurt him all those years ago.

She'd hurt them both.

Drained, her head pounding, she pulled the shades down, removed her shoes and lay on Matteo's king-size bed.

Soon these erratic feelings swirling inside her would subside and she'd be able to breathe.

The soft sheets had a delicious freshly laundered scent to them she found comforting.

Matteo had slept in this bed before. Many times.

How many women had slept in it with him?

She squeezed her eyes shut.

She couldn't afford to allow herself to care. Matteo was the father of her child but he could never be anything more. That ship had sailed. Even if it hadn't, and even if she wasn't determined to grab her freedom and live her life free from anybody else's chains, Matteo would not be the one.

If she'd thought marriage to Pieta had been hard she could only imagine the hell Matteo would have put her through.

He thought a few months of celibacy was a *sacrifice*. God alone knew how many times he would have cheated on her if she'd married him. He went through women like most people went through their laundry.

He wasn't the man she'd believed him to be all those years ago. She'd thought him a man of integrity. She'd believed him when he'd said he wanted to be the world's foremost reconstructive surgeon. The life he'd chosen, however, was the antithesis of those early dreams.

No, he most definitely was not the man she'd believed him to be. And now she was fated to be tied to him for the rest of her life.

The first two weeks in Miami passed a lot more easily than Natasha expected. That she was given Matteo's guesthouse at the back of his waterfront home helped. She'd expected to be physically living under the same roof as him but instead had her own place complete with her own private swimming pool. She'd yet to venture any further into his home than the utility and kitchen. They rarely saw each other but when they did they were at great pains to be polite to each other.

So far, their *entente cordiale* was holding up.

Matteo worked long hours. His headquarters and the clinic he personally practised from were only a mile from his home on Biscayne Bay but he made frequent trips across America to his other clinics.

The only real time they had spent together had been a visit to an obstetrician friend of his, who had asked her a myriad of questions and examined her with such a gentle touch that she'd found herself reassured. Whether she had her baby here or in Pisa, she would be in excellent hands.

Pisa...

At some point in the near future they would return there. The plan was for Matteo to return to Caballeros with Daniele when the structure of the hospital was complete. They'd decided that would be the best time to confess the pregnancy.

She was thinking all this as she sat with her legs in the guesthouse pool, soaking up the last of the day's sun, soul music playing gently through the earphones, sipping on fresh orange juice brought to her unasked by a member of his friendly staff. So lost in her own world was she that she didn't hear any sign of another's presence until a shadow crossed over her.

Turning her head, she found Matteo standing over her.

She whipped the earphones out, sloshing juice over her hand in the process.

'Sorry if I frightened you,' he said wryly.

'I wasn't expecting you back yet.'

'I finished sooner than expected.' He'd gone to Los Angeles the day before, preparing to open a new store that would sell his magic creams; the two he already had there were bursting at the seams with clients desperate to hand their money over for the miracle of reducing their crow's feet.

She could still hardly believe that the topical lotion he'd been intent on developing all those years ago to reduce his brother's burn scars had turned into such a phenomenon.

Two years after she'd become engaged to Pieta, Matteo had finally qualified as a surgeon. At some point in those two years he'd found the successful formula because he'd launched the lotion as a skin moisturiser six months after qualifying, only months after Roberto's death. It hadn't just helped reduce burn scars but acne scars and wrinkles too. It had been a word-of-mouth sensation that had gone viral on social media within days. Initially selling online, he'd since cannily resisted the pleas from department stores worldwide to stock it, instead selling it from the medical clinics he'd opened at an alarmingly fast rate and then opening his own dedicated stores.

While she admired the drive and dedication it must have taken to make such a success of himself in such a relatively short time, she'd never forgotten the humble doctor he'd been who'd wanted only to help his brother and be the best surgeon he could be. In all their long talks he'd never once said anything about money being a motivating factor in his life's choices. Of all the choices he'd made since his brother's death—and it was obvious to her that Roberto's death had been the trigger behind the new life Matteo had pursued—this was the one she found the saddest.

From his jacket pocket he produced a paper napkin from a well-known coffee shop chain. Crouching at her side, he took the hand covered with spilt juice and wiped it.

Taken aback at the gesture, Natasha didn't have time to resist.

Her cheeks flaming, both at his unexpected touch and the realisation she was sitting before him in nothing but a one-piece swimsuit, she muttered, 'Thank you.'

'How have you been?' he asked, removing his shoes and rolling his trousers up to sit next to her, dipping his large feet in the warm water.

'Good, thanks.'

'No more dizzy spells?'

'None.'

He nodded. 'Sleeping okay?'

'Yes.' Surprisingly well.

'That's good. You will let me know if you have any concerns or worries?'

'I've already promised that at least ten times.' This had been something else she hadn't anticipated, that

Matteo would take such an active interest in the pregnancy. Although they had seen little of each other, he messaged her frequently to check that she was feeling all right and had his staff check on her regularly. The guesthouse was connected to the main house by an enclosed glass walkway and there were intercoms in every room that connected straight to his head of housekeeping, who lived in the staff house. Natasha had her privacy but in her time here she'd never felt lonely or abandoned. And that was something else that surprised her. In Pisa, she'd hated living with staff. She didn't find it at all intrusive coming from Matteo's staff, who were a lot more relaxed and upbeat than those Pieta had employed.

'I'm just reinforcing the message.'

'Consider it reinforced.'

Their eyes met, a brief moment of humour flickering between them before she turned her face away to stare at their feet in the water. She never doubted his concern was all for the health of their growing baby.

'The foundations for the hospital have been completed,' he said.

'Already? That was quick.'

'Bureaucracy doesn't exist in Caballeros. The San Pedro Governor is behind the project so it's all systems go. Daniele's been out there again. He's paying his staff triple time to work through the night.' Natasha remembered the agreement that had been made that Pieta's foundation would pay for the site and that Daniele would pay the construction costs and for his own staff to build it. It would be costing him a fortune.

'You've spoken to him?'

'A number of times. He expects the shell of the building to be done within a month. He wants me to go back with him then, before they start the finishing process and it's too late to make any changes I think are needed from a medical standpoint.'

Matteo leaned back on his arms and breathed in the air, trying to unknot the tension that had become a permanent thing in him and always tightened whenever they spoke of Daniele or the other members of his family.

'Has anything been said? About us?' she asked quietly.

'He asked how you were doing. Said Vanessa was missing you.'

She bowed her head and hunched her shoulders.

'She keeps messaging me,' she whispered then swallowed. A tear rolled down her cheek. She wiped it away with the back of her hand. 'I don't know how to respond. It's the same with Francesca. She's called me three times. I try and keep things light and non-specific but I feel so guilty. They've been so good to me and it's killing me to know I'm going to break their hearts.'

He dug his fingers into the grass, resisting the compulsion to put an arm around her. Natasha evoked feelings in him he couldn't begin to understand. She always had.

He had no control over his body's responses to her; even now he was having to fight his own head to tune out that she was wearing nothing but a pretty striped swimsuit and that before she'd hunched herself over he'd seen a glimpse of breasts that had swollen since he'd last seen her only three days before.

It was the need to resist temptation that had seen him travelling more than normal these past few weeks and working the hundred-hour weeks he'd not done since his residency days. Being with her was too much, a constant battle that veered between wanting to shout and shake her, and wanting to pull her close and make love to her again.

He'd promised to try and put the past behind them but, damn it, it was hard.

But he had made that promise and he knew that however hard it was for him, she would be suffering more. She was carrying their child.

Keeping a distance between them might be good for his state of mind but she was under a huge amount of stress. It might suit him better to cast her as an unfeeling cow but that was far from the truth. His clinics in Los Angeles had seen him cross paths with many actresses, good and bad. He could spot a phoney a mile off. Natasha's distress about the Pellegrinis' reaction to the pregnancy was genuine. He'd brought her to Miami in part to support her through this pregnancy. It was time he started holding up his side of their bargain.

'When was the last time you left this place?'

Startled blue eyes found his. 'What do you mean?'

'According to my staff you rarely go out.'

She managed a weak smile. 'Have you got them spying on me?'

'Not spying, more keeping an eye on you. You've got too much thinking time on your hands and it's making you worry about something neither of us has any control over. You need to keep busy, *bella*. We can start by going out for dinner. Have you any favourite foods you like?' As he asked the question he remembered a long ago conversation about her love for spicy food. He blinked the memory he hadn't thought of in nearly eight years away.

'I'll eat anything.'

He pulled his feet out of the water and stood up. 'I'll

have a think about a decent restaurant. Come over to the main house when you're ready.'

Then he picked up his shoes and walked barefoot into his home.

CHAPTER SIX

NERVES CHEWED NATASHA'S stomach as she walked up the marble steps and into Matteo's vast house. It was the first time she'd gone further than the room she knew was used as a utility but which looked like an art gallery, and one of the kitchens, which had the same feel to it. If one didn't know its purpose you could assume it was anything. The first time she'd gone in it the chef had casually mentioned it was the smallest of the kitchens. Turned out Matteo had three of them.

A member of staff appeared and with a smile took her through the house. As they walked, she gazed around in astonishment at the uniqueness and beauty of it all. The exterior was a work of sleek art in itself, with masses of glass and white stucco, but the interior… Everything flowed, the many staircases gave the illusion of floating…it was incredible, a work of art come to life. No wonder Daniele, the architectural brain behind it, had won awards for it. At the time of completion, a year ago, it had been valued as the most expensive property in the whole of Miami.

She was taken through to a vast room, the ceiling at least two storeys high and with an abundance of cream sofas and armchairs, easily enough to seat two dozen people with space to spare.

Left to her own devices, Natasha looked out at the spectacular view of the bay, the sky shades of pink under the setting sun. The room seemed to jut out and touch the bay itself.

She turned round and stared up at what appeared to be a floating balcony but which she quickly understood was a walkway that was part of the second floor. What new delights were there to discover up there?

A glass wall that reached all the way up to this strange yet beautiful indoor balcony soon revealed itself to be a cabinet but it was the huge canvas print beside it that really caught her attention and she walked over to examine it in more detail.

The print was a photograph of two beaming young boys, the elder no more than ten, the smaller one only a couple of years younger. They were sitting on a bench, arms wrapped around each other, their cheeks pressed together, identical curly black hair almost fused into one mass.

'Sorry to keep you waiting.' Matteo's rich tones vibrated through the room.

Natasha looked around but couldn't see him.

'Up here.'

Craning her neck, she found him peering down at her from the floating balcony. A wry smile of amusement on his face, he walked the length of the balcony then disappeared from view, reappearing moments later on the other side of the room.

He must have travelled down a staircase hidden from view.

He'd changed into a pair of crisp navy trousers and a light grey open-necked shirt, his tall elegant frame carrying it off with a panache that made her think of Christmas perfume adverts that always featured suave, gorgeous men and lithe beautiful women. It was the swirls of exposed hair coming through the shirt that had her heart pounding so hard. She remembered so vividly running her fingers through that hair...

Swallowing hard as he strode towards her, she turned her attention back to the print and pointed a trembling finger at the older child. 'Is that you?'

He stood beside her and looked at it.

Fresh cologne filled her senses.

'Yes. I was nine when that was taken.'

'And is the other boy your brother?' It was a silly question really as other than the size difference they could have passed for twins.

'Yes.'

There was a long stretch of silence between them.

'I really was very sorry to hear Roberto died,' she said quietly. 'I know how much you loved him.'

They'd briefly mentioned Roberto's death on Matteo's jet over, but the conversation had turned into a spew of bitterness from him that had stopped her saying anything more about it.

If Matteo had been nine in this picture, then the fire that had torn their lives apart must have happened within a year of it being taken.

She blinked back hot tears as she looked at the happy faces of a life gone by.

Many stories had swirled in the aftermath of Roberto's funeral, gossip and whispers between the family members about a spectacular row between Matteo and his father. Natasha knew the two men's relationship had been strained since the fire, knew Matteo thought his father blamed him for the fire, something that had always made her heart wrench and her blood boil.

She'd never learned what the row at the funeral had

been about but it had been serious enough for Matteo to legally change his surname within weeks. It could only have been intended as a snub to his parents—Manaserro was Vanessa Pellegrini's maiden name. He'd chosen the family name of his uncle's wife. As far as she was aware, Matteo and his parents hadn't spoken since.

As Matteo stood looking at the last happy picture ever taken of his brother, he knew Natasha was thinking of the fire. He'd told her about it himself during one of their many marathon phone calls. He'd told her everything, how he'd been only ten years old when his parents had gone out for lunch leaving him in charge of eight-year-old Roberto, how Roberto had stolen a box of matches from the kitchen and taken them to the barn at the back of their house without Matteo even noticing he'd left the house, and how Roberto had lit those matches one by one, seeing how long he could keep each flame going. It had been a hot day after a period of hot weeks without any rain. The barn had been a tinder box and Roberto had been lucky to escape with his life.

Matteo had escaped with nothing more than the nightmares of his brother's screams, which had sounded as if they'd been dredged from the bowels of hell itself, and his own screams when he'd heard his brother's and had raced out of the house to find him. The image of his brother's small body engulfed in flames haunted him. If the gardener hadn't acted so quickly to douse the flames, Roberto would have died right before his eyes.

Natasha was the only person he'd shared this with. He'd never even told Pieta the sheer horror of what Roberto had been through and what he'd seen.

He hadn't held anything back from her, not his father's complete withdrawal of affection towards him, his belief that his parents blamed him for the fire, the increasing arguments and cold hostility that had culminated in him leaving the family home at thirteen to live with his uncle's family, not the visits back home to see his brother that had only been undertaken when his father had been out, not the many surgical procedures Roberto had endured throughout the rest of his life and for which Matteo had always sat in a separate waiting room from his parents.

He'd trusted her. He'd trusted her with everything.

The worst of it was she'd consoled him. He'd thought she believed in him. Her soft voice had given him comfort.

Then she'd taken his trust and ripped it to shreds.

They stood before the picture for a few more moments in silence before Matteo sighed deeply. It had all happened such a long time ago but sometimes, like now, it might have happened only yesterday.

'Come on,' he said. 'Let's go and eat.'

He led her out to the secure docking bay at the side of his mansion where a gleaming yacht awaited them.

'Is this yours?' she asked with an inflection of surprise.

He nodded and waved a hand to greet the captain awaiting them on deck.

'I've never noticed it before.'

'Have you been round this side of the house?' he said drily.

'No,' she admitted.

'There's your answer.'

'Where are we going?'

He pointed to the island floating in the bay some distance before them. 'Key Biscayne. It's quicker and more pleasurable to sail there rather than drive. How are your sea legs?'

'I guess we're about to find out.'

Within minutes they were standing at the front of the yacht, leaning over the railing as they cut through the water, her blonde hair whipping behind her.

'You like it?' he asked.

She nodded, a wide grin forming, the first real flare of joy he'd seen on her beautiful face in such a long time that it pierced his chest to see it now.

He turned his gaze from her to look at the approaching Key Biscayne. 'Why haven't you explored any of Miami since you've been here?'

'I don't know my way around.'

'I told you when we got here that you only had to ask and a member of staff would be happy to drive you or accompany you anywhere you wanted to go. You're not my prisoner, *bella*.'

'I know I'm not.'

'Then why stay in all the time? Miami is one of the most vibrant cities in the world.'

She shrugged and put a hand to her face to shield herself from locks of thick hair falling into it. 'Where would I go?'

'I don't know. The beach? A café? One of the museums? Jungle Island? An art gallery? A nightclub— there's plenty of those.'

She gave a wry smile. 'I can just see pregnant old me dancing the night away in a sweaty nightclub.'

So could he. Vividly. That long honey-blonde hair swaying, that lithe body in the slim-fitting off-the-shoulder blue-and-white-striped dress she was wearing, moving to the music, wrapped around his...

He blinked the image away and took a breath to drive away the burst of heat in his loins.

'You're pregnant, not dead. There's plenty of exclusive clubs here you can go to that aren't the sweaty places you're thinking of.'

'On my own?'

'I'm not speaking literally. I'm just saying you should be making the most of being fit and able to do things while you can. In a few months you'll be waddling like a duck with a watermelon for a belly.'

'You make it sound so delightful. I look forward to waddling like a duck.'

He grinned at her dryness. He didn't think for a minute that Natasha would ever waddle. She had too much elegance.

It struck him then that he would be there to see the changes in her. He would watch her belly ripen and her breasts grow.

He would be there for all of it. Nothing on this earth would make him miss any of it.

He wondered what changes had already happened that weren't yet visible to his eye, what physical shifts Natasha could feel within her.

'Do you really want to spend the pregnancy stuck in my little patch of the earth?' he said in a teasing tone that belied the depth of his thoughts and the emotions shooting through him.

'It's hardly little.'

'You know what I mean.'

She sighed. 'Yes, I do know. There's lots of reasons but the main one is because I'm trying to save money.'

'You're short of cash?'

'If I spend it frivolously I will be. I have no job. I'm pregnant with no employment history so there's no realistic prospect of me getting one in the foreseeable future.'

'I know you won't inherit the *castello* and the rest of

the family estate but you're going to inherit Pieta's personal wealth.'

'I don't want it. It wouldn't be right.'

'Don't be ridiculous. You were his wife. It's yours by right.'

'I could accept that if I'd contributed to it in any way but I didn't. Everything he earned was his and it was all earned without any help from me.'

'You provided a home for him.'

She shook her head, her hair swishing gently around her shoulders. 'The house was his. The staff were his. The furnishings were his and to his taste. Everything was *his*.'

There was an undertone to her words that raised his antennae.

'You were together for seven years,' he said slowly, trying to figure out what that undertone could mean or why something in his gut told him to listen to it.

'But only married for one. We didn't live together until we married. I cannot in all good conscience take that money, especially not now that I'm having your baby. I could never live with myself.'

His incredulity deepened.

She'd married Pieta for his money. And now she was planning to walk away from it?

A dozen more questions formed but they'd arrived at the dock by the quayside restaurant he'd booked them into so had to wait until they were at their table before he could ask them and the next dozen that formed in quick succession.

They were shown to a table overlooking the waterfront, the distant Miami skyline lighting up like a silhouette under the rapidly darkening night sky.

'This place is so *glamorous*,' Natasha said when they

were seated, her eyes too busy darting around the eclectic restaurant to bother looking at the menu she'd been given. 'Have you eaten here before?'

'I brought my Miami staff here for our Christmas party.'

'Lucky staff. The last time I ate out was at a stuffy ambassador's residence.'

'Not glamorous?'

'If you like old-fashioned glamour.'

'You don't?' He thought of her house in Pisa. Pieta had been a collector of antiques, his tastes shining through every item on display. Now he thought about it properly, there had been nothing of the Natasha he had known all those years ago in that house. It was as if her personality had been subsumed by her husband's.

She hesitated before answering. 'Not particularly. I'm more of a modern girl. What do you recommend to eat?'

'The lobster's good.'

She pulled a face. 'Lobster's boring.'

'Really?'

'Too sweet.' She peered at the menu and pulled another face. 'What the heck are Peruvian potatoes?'

'Potatoes from Peru?' he suggested drily.

She met his eye and sniggered. 'Maybe they come wrapped in a llama.'

He grinned. 'You should try them.'

'I will. Seed-crusted halibut, Peruvian potatoes, wild mushrooms, sea beans and red pepper coulis. Perfect.'

Their food ordered, drinks set before them, Matteo settled back and watched Natasha continue her unabashed admiring of the restaurant's decor.

'You know what I don't understand?' he said.

'What?'

'Why you gave up your plans to be an interior designer.'

The amusement that had flared between them faded, to be replaced by wariness. 'It just never happened.'

'Why not? You still did the degree you wanted in it, didn't you?'

He could tell by the look in her eyes she was remembering how seriously she'd been considering moving to America to do her degree at the Art Institute of Tampa. She'd sent him the prospectus. He'd looked at places to live that were commutable for them both.

She gave a slight nod. 'I ended up doing a BA in Interior Architecture and Design.'

'In England?'

Matteo had tried never to discuss Natasha with anyone over the years and he'd limited his trips back to Europe as much as he could, but it had been impossible not to hear chatter about her. By accepting Pieta's proposal she'd been embraced into the bosom of the Pellegrini family. It had been natural for them to pass on information about Pieta's fiancée to him. They'd assumed he would be as interested as they were. Everyone had assumed that once she'd graduated, they would marry. It had taken another three years for that to happen, although Pieta had bought an apartment for her in Pisa, close to his sister's apartment.

Tales of her had rarely come from Pieta himself. If he ever had spoken of her it had usually been in practical terms, never romantic.

She nodded again.

'Why didn't you take it any further once you graduated? Didn't you enjoy it?'

She gave a wistful smile. 'I loved it. I like to think I was good at it.'

'So what stopped you pursuing a career? You were engaged to a well-known man with contacts all over the world. It would have been easy for you to build a client list.'

'I know.'

'So what stopped you?' he repeated. 'Was it just that you preferred being a lady of leisure?'

Something flickered in her eyes before they flitted away from his gaze.

'I'm not picking a fight here, I'm just trying to understand.' He tried to keep his voice reasonable but as he asked the question he could feel the old anger swelling inside.

This was an extension of their earlier conversation and Natasha's insistence that she wouldn't accept her rightful inheritance. She'd spoken with such sincerity that he had to remind himself to tread carefully. It would be too easy to take her words at face value.

He must not allow himself to forget how he'd fallen for her sincerity before.

Had she been telling the truth on his yacht? Or was she trying to paint herself in a favourable light with him? And if so, for what purpose?

He'd spent seven years telling himself he didn't give a fig for her but the truth was her betrayal had lived in his guts like poison; he could feel it now, uncoiling inside him, the memories of his misplaced faith and trust in her biting into him.

He leaned forward and lowered his voice, trying to read what emotion lay behind the blue eyes staring back at him. 'Why did you choose him over me, Natasha? I always thought it was the money. Was it that? Was it the money and the lifestyle?'

Her hands had balled into fists but there was no fight in her returning stare, just starkness.

His chest rising heavily, Matteo took a large drink of his wine and stared hard at the anguish on her face. He should have ordered something stronger. 'I need to know why. I want to put the past behind us but every time I think I have, something reminds me and it all kicks back in. You strung me along for months...'

Her head shook but her lips stayed stubbornly stuck together.

'Talk to me.' Realising his voice had risen, he strove to lower it again. 'Tell me, Natasha. Make me understand.'

'Look...' She relaxed her hands and took a gulp of her grape juice. Before she could say what she'd intended their meals were brought to the table and laid before them with a flourish.

Natasha looked at her artfully displayed dish and struggled to hold on.

In the space of a minute she'd completely lost her appetite.

Matteo seemed in no rush to eat his food either. He didn't touch his cutlery, just sat there, eyes fixed on her, waiting for her to speak and explain herself.

She couldn't blame him. This conversation had been a long time coming.

She took another drink of her juice. How she wished the grapes had been fermented into wine. It would make this easier.

'I know you don't believe this but everything you and I talked about and the plans we made, I meant it all.'

Natasha knew before the words had finished leaving her mouth that it was the wrong opening gambit.

His eyes narrowed dangerously. 'If you meant any

of it then why were you seeing Pieta at the same time? Did you decide to string us both along until you worked out which of us would make the better husband and give you the better lifestyle?'

'Do you want to hear my side or not?'

There was the slightest flare of his nostrils before he inclined his head.

'I didn't string you along for months. The first time Pieta showed any interest in me was at my eighteenth birthday party. I didn't even think he would turn up for it. I assumed a party like that would be beneath him.'

She'd been devastated when Matteo had called to say he'd missed his flight and wouldn't be able to make it. She'd known it wasn't his fault and that his job wasn't one he could drop—his job, back then, had been a case of life or death. So she'd put a brave face on her disappointment and instead turned her calendar over to the following month when they would both be in Pisa for his aunt and uncle's wedding anniversary party, and drew a tiny heart in the corner of that date.

His jaw clenched. 'You strung me along for that long?'

She shook her head. 'I thought he was being polite.'

'Polite?' Disbelief etched itself on his face.

'He was so much older than me...'

'Pieta is—was—the same age as me.'

Her heart twisted to see the pain that flashed over him at the utterance of his best friend's name.

'But I never felt the age gap with you. Pieta was so serious, he came across as older than his years. He took me to the theatre as a birthday present to see a political play. I hate politics. I didn't have the heart to tell him it was the most boring two hours of my life. Maybe if I'd told him the truth he would have seen me differently and things would have turned out differently too but I didn't and things took on a life of their own. He was in England on business and took me out to dinner a couple of times but I swear I didn't think they meant anything...'

'If they didn't mean anything then why didn't you tell me about them?'

'Because it was during the week you went to Washington for that conference. We hardly spoke that week, don't you remember?'

A pulse ticked in his jaw, his lips tightening.

'Pieta took me to these wonderfully grown-up restaurants and spoke about politics and his humanitarian work. I admit, I was overawed by it all. He was this great man making waves across the world for his philanthropy... I was in awe of him and he knew it, but I swear, I never thought of those dates as dates. The first I knew that he was seeing me in a romantic light was when he asked my father's permission to marry me that Friday, two weeks before his parents' anniversary party.'

'He asked your *father*?'

'That was Pieta all over, wasn't it?' She smiled sadly. 'He took his responsibilities very seriously. It wouldn't have occurred to him to ask me for my views first. He saw the awe on my face and interpreted it as infatuation.'

'And your father said yes?'

'Of course he did. He didn't even have to think about it. It was exactly what he wanted. Pieta was rich and connected and had royal blood in his veins. He was the dream son-in-law to brag about down at the golf club.'

'I can understand why your father would have been keen but that doesn't explain why you went along with it. You could have said no.'

'I did say no.' She squeezed her eyes shut as the memory of her parents' fury played vividly before her eyes. 'My parents knew I was serious about you...'

'Really?' he asked sardonically, finishing his wine.

'Yes! I lived with them, remember? They knew how I felt but they didn't care. They told me to keep my mouth shut about you or I would ruin everything. They told me it was my chance to make them proud after a lifetime of disappointment.'

The scorn in his eyes diminished a little. 'They said that?'

'That and a whole lot of other things too. You had ancient royal blood too but they looked at the wealth Pieta was accumulating, looked at the estate he would inherit and knew that if I married him all their money problems would be over. They were *terribly* in debt. Pieta must have made promises to them because within months of our engagement their debts were gone and he'd paid for them to have an extension put on the house.'

'You agreed to marry him for an extension?' Matteo had picked up his fork and was running his thumb backwards and forwards over the prongs.

'No! That came later. I went along with it because I didn't know what else to do. I wasn't stringing you along, don't you see that? I was playing for time until you got to Pisa for the party and I could tell you to your face what was happening because I couldn't think of a way out.'

'You should have told me as soon as he asked your father's permission.'

'I know that now but at the time I thought it would make things worse. How could I tell you over the phone when you were thousands of miles away that your best friend and cousin wanted to marry me? My head was all over the place. I was only eighteen. I wasn't some cosmopolitan woman with years of experience behind her. I was weak and spineless and I'd got myself backed into a corner I didn't know how to get out of. I wanted desperately to please my parents but at the same time I wanted to be with you. I was waiting for you to get there because I convinced myself you would think of a way out of the mess.'

Natasha took a deep breath and stared at her plate.

Matteo stabbed a roasted shallot with his fork but made no effort to eat it. His eyes were as hard as the tone of his voice. 'You did have the chance to tell me. You made no effort to tell me, remember? But you did let me kiss you.'

She closed her eyes, remembering how she'd taken one look at him in the *castello* and her heart had beaten so hard she'd hardly been able to breathe. After months of increasingly intimate correspondence and phone calls and only a quick snapshot of him on her phone to look at, seeing him in the flesh again...

And then he'd kissed her, their very first kiss—*her* very first kiss—and there had been no breath left to steal. And then Francesca had come barging down the corridor, breaking the moment.

What Natasha hadn't known then was that it had been her last chance to tell Matteo the truth.

CHAPTER SEVEN

NATASHA OPENED HER eyes and forced herself to meet Matteo's unblinking gaze. 'I'm sorry. I thought I'd be able to tell you later that night. I thought I had more time but it was too late. I have kicked myself so many times for not anticipating he would propose publicly like that but I swear I didn't know he was going to do it.'

'Why should I believe you?' he said, not an iota of softening in his stare.

She shrugged helplessly. 'I went to your room in the *castello* that night. I still hoped even then that it wasn't too late for us and that you'd be able to come up with some plan, but you'd gone. I called you but you'd blocked my number—you blocked it that very night. How would I know that if I hadn't tried to call you?'

He *had* blocked her number straight away, Matteo remembered. He'd said goodbye to his family, had managed to force his congratulations to Pieta, walked into the *castello*'s courtyard and into the waiting cab and had immediately blocked her every means of contacting him.

Could she be telling the truth?

'A part of me even hoped you would tell Pieta about us,' she whispered into the bleak silence that had developed between them.

'After he'd publicly proposed and you'd publicly accepted? I would never have humiliated him like that.' He laughed bitterly, his mind reeling from everything she'd confessed.

He looked in the blue eyes that held his. He read the pleading in them.

But what was she pleading for? Forgiveness? Or for him to believe her?

Right then he didn't know what the hell to think or believe.

'You were engaged for six years. You left your parents' home and went to university. You had *six years* to end things with him.'

'When I knew there was no way back with you I decided to stop fighting and just accept it. Accepting it meant pleasing my parents. I told you, back then I was weak and spineless.'

'And you're not now?'

'No.' He saw the defiance bloom in her. 'No. I learned to grow a spine. I had to. And I'm glad I did because it will make me a better mother.' She hung her head and rubbed her temples before looking back at him. 'Just, please, believe my feelings for you were genuine.'

His heart as full as he'd ever known it to be, he nodded slowly. 'Did Pieta ever suspect your feelings for him weren't?'

'Why do you assume his feelings were any more genuine than mine?' Natasha asked before she could stop herself.

'Because he always told me he would know the perfect woman to marry when he found her.'

She clamped down on a burst of her own bitter laughter at the notion. As if her husband had ever looked at her as perfect for anything but the façade he wanted the world to see and the estate he'd wanted to inherit. It didn't matter how hard she'd tried, she'd never been good enough for anyone, not her parents and certainly not her husband.

But she would be good enough for her child and she would do everything in her power to ensure her child never felt that he or she wasn't perfect exactly as they were. She wouldn't diminish them and make them think their best could never be good enough. She would celebrate what they could do and love them regardless of what they couldn't. In short, she would adopt parenting skills at the opposite end of the spectrum to her own parents.

She stared levelly at Matteo. 'I tried very hard to be the best fiancée and then wife that I could be. Do you really think he would have married me if he'd had any doubts?'

Before he could answer, their waitress came to their table and looked at their untouched plates with concern. 'Is everything all right with your food?'

Like a switch had been turned on, Matteo bestowed on her his dazzling smile. 'Everything's great, thanks.'

Smiling, she bustled away.

The interruption had been what they needed.

When Natasha looked at him again he sighed deeply, his eyes boring into her but without the animosity of before.

'We should eat before it gets cold,' he said, finally popping the shallot into his mouth, his tone leaving no doubt that, as far as he was concerned, the conversation was over.

He'd got the answers he was seeking. Whether he believed them or not, she had no control over.

What difference did it make now, in any case? Whatever their feelings had been for each other, it was in the past and it had to stay in the past.

Matteo knocked on the guesthouse door. A minute later Natasha opened it, dressed in a pair of red pyjama bottoms and a black vest. Her usually sleek hair had an unkempt look about it.

She greeted him with one of the smiles that always pierced him in so many different ways.

'I wasn't expecting to see you today,' she said, standing aside to let him in.

'I had a conference call with my clinic managers. We were done sooner than I thought we'd be. Have I woken you?' It was approaching midday.

'I was reading.' She held up the book in her hand. It was a pregnancy book the obstetrician had given her.

'I thought you'd already read that.'

She shrugged. 'No harm in reading it again and there isn't much else for me to do.'

'That's why I'm here.'

'Oh?'

'Have you eaten?'

'What is it with you and my eating habits?' she asked, the trace of a smile playing on her lips.

'I like to be sure you're taking care of yourself. Have you?'

'I had breakfast a couple of hours ago.'

'Then get dressed. I'm taking you out to lunch.'

There was a definite brightening in her eyes. 'Give me twenty minutes. I need to shower.'

He bit back the offer he wanted to make of joining her in it, instead taking a seat at the dining table, following her retreating figure with his eyes. The pyjama bottoms emphasised her bottom, showing its rounded peachy shape beautifully.

He closed his eyes and rubbed his temples.

Since their meal at Key Biscayne ten days ago things had changed between them. It had been a subtle shift but one he felt in his marrow.

He'd gone over her words from that night many times. As hard as it was to override seven years of conditioned loathing towards her, the more he thought about it the more he believed her.

What disturbed him was how much he *wanted* to believe her, and not just because she was carrying his child.

He looked at her now, seven years older, and saw all the things that had been missing before. She *had* been mature beyond her years but it was only now that he was with the fully grown-up Natasha that he realised her maturity back then hadn't been that of a rounded woman with life experience under her belt. She'd been a wide-eyed innocent, blooming as she'd embraced womanhood, excited for her future and what it held. She'd also been a people-pleaser. She'd been almost desperate to please, never giving contrary thoughts or opinions. He remembered how delighted he'd been to find someone so like-minded but now he realised she would have agreed with his tastes and likes whatever they had been.

They'd spent more time together these past ten days. She had no qualms about giving her opinion now and although her tastes did concur a great deal with his own, she never hesitated to voice her own thoughts when they disagreed.

He'd taken her out to dinner a handful of times and to the theatre to watch a musical adaptation of a popular film. She'd clapped along all the way through it. When he'd asked her opinion at the end she'd said that she'd loved it but had wanted to gag the leading lady for her annoying voice.

She was far more interesting now. And somehow more desirable for it, which he hadn't thought possible. He would gaze at her creamy skin and remember how it had felt beneath his fingers. He would look at the honey-blonde hair and remember how it had felt brushed against his shoulder. He would look in the blue eyes and remember the look in them when she'd come with him buried deep inside her.

And he would remember that slight resistance of her body when he'd first thrust inside her and how he'd felt a warning shoot through his head that had been drowned out by the passion of her kisses and the ardour of her response.

If he didn't know better, he would have said that resistance had been the natural resistance of a body unused to being made love to. Which wasn't possible.

But it still nagged at him, playing in his mind like a distant but nearing wind, and though they'd both made a concerted effort not to speak of Pieta or the past since that first meal out, it was there too, hanging between them like a basket of dead flowers.

Until he'd brought Natasha to Miami everything had been cut and dried. He knew who she was and what she'd done. He knew who he was and what he'd done.

Now he was discovering that all his certainties were whispers in that nearing wind and the only thing with any substance to it was his desire for her. It was with him all the time, a constant thickening of his blood, a constant charge in his skin.

When she reappeared thirty minutes later wearing a white summer dress with strappy sleeves and a pair of flat roman sandals, her hair damp around her shoulders, her perfume filling the room as vibrantly as she did just by her presence, he felt the air escape his lungs.

Dio, was there nothing this woman wore that didn't make him want to rip it off?

He got to his feet, keeping his loins under control by the skin of his teeth. 'Ready to go?'

'Where to?' she asked.

'Downtown.'

Natasha strapped herself into the small sports car Matteo had chosen to drive from his vast collection while he pressed the button to put the roof down. The engine started at the press of another button, music pumped out and then he was driving them out of his garage, out of his estate and through the wide open streets of the exclusive gated community he lived in. Soon the verdant verges thick with trees thinned, the large, mostly hidden homes became buildings that steadily increased in height, and the open road filled with traffic.

Downtown turned out to be a thriving metropolis full of character and colour and all kinds of scents. Her hair whipped around her face which with the sun shining down on them acted as an industrial hairdryer.

He drove them round the back of a gleaming skyscraper that looked over the harbour and into the underground car park, coming to a stop in a space with his name on it.

'Handy,' she commented. 'Are these your offices?'

He grinned. 'I need to pop in for a few minutes to sign some documents before we eat.'

There was an elevator a short walk from the parking space. Matteo punched a code and the doors pinged open. Inside, he pressed the button with the number thirty on it.

'Why did you use a code?' she asked.

'It's a security measure. If you don't know the access code the elevators won't work for you. This is an exclusive elevator for my staff and patients.'

They arrived at their floor before she'd even registered the elevator moving.

The medicinal smell hit her the moment the doors opened.

'Do you do surgery here?' she asked in surprise.

'Where did you think I would do it?'

'Not on the top of a skyscraper. I thought these were your administrative headquarters.'

'They're on the next two floors up.'

'But you run your clinic in a skyscraper?'

He laughed. 'Trust me, the facilities here are second to none.'

Three receptionists dressed in white clinical uniforms manned the immaculately clean room with the fabulous views of the ocean they stepped into. Matteo had a brief chat with them while Natasha stared around in wonder at the plush furnishings and tasteful artwork.

It was like being in a hospital that had amalgamated with a five-star hotel.

'I can give you a quick tour if you want?'

'As long as you're not going to give me the hard sell for a buttock enhancement or a new nose,' she jested.

The amusement that had played on his lips since the exhilarating drive over faded. It faded from his eyes too, his stare unfathomable. 'You're the last person who needs anything done.'

It was his tone. The starkness to it. It made her veins heat and her chest fill with a longing that made her yearn to reach out and touch him.

That was all she seemed to want to do. Touch him. And smell him.

She could almost believe he meant it. Almost. But she knew too well that something in her did need fixing. Why else had she never pleased her parents in anything she did? Why else would Pieta have chosen her? She'd been wrong for him in every sense possible but still it had been her he'd chosen to be his wife. It had been her he'd trapped into staying with him even after the truth had come out between them.

She didn't want to think about Pieta.

Since her talk with Matteo ten days ago things had been better between them. They'd both made a concerted effort to build bridges without saying so in words. Like so much between them, it wasn't something that needed saying.

What also didn't need to be said was the reigniting of the chemistry that had always been there, swirling between them but now gaining an intensity she was finding harder to resist.

Resist she must. There was too much danger in it. She'd been besotted by Matteo as a teenager but she wasn't a teenager any more. She was an adult with a little life growing inside her that needed her protection. Learning to find her own voice and not be afraid to speak it had been hard, finding her spine and the courage to stand up for herself harder. She couldn't afford to lose that.

She didn't want to be so vulnerable again. She *couldn't* be. Not for herself and especially not for her baby.

So she swallowed the emotions pushing through her chest and up her throat at the way Matteo was staring at her and forced her tone to be airy as she said, 'I thank you for the compliment but I've always fancied a new nose.'

'Your nose is perfect.'

'Hardly. How about new breasts? We could do a deal—buy one boob, get one free?'

His expression changed, a wryness spreading over his features, as if he too was pulling himself back. 'I think being pregnant has already done that for you.'

The strange almost melancholic moment broken, he led her down a wide corridor and briskly said, 'I can't show you everything as we have patients in residence and surgeries being performed, but I can show you enough so you get a good feel for what we do here. After all, it will be our child who will inherit it all one day.'

'I hadn't thought of it like that,' she said, startled.

'Once everything's out in the open with the family I'll get a new will drawn up.'

'Really? So soon?'

'Death has no favourites. It can strike anyone at any time.' She knew from the look he gave her that it wasn't the patients he'd dealt with during his residency years he was thinking of but Pieta. 'With us being unmarried I want the peace of mind to know that if anything happens to me, our child will automatically inherit without any protracted legal drama. You should get one done too. We should both do everything we can to protect our child.'

'Okay,' she agreed, knowing it made sense, unbelievably touched at what he planned.

He'd said since the scan that he accepted paternity but his talk about a DNA test, although said in the heat of the moment and soon disregarded, had put doubts in her mind. Only small doubts, but they'd been there, tapping away at her.

This simple deed put those doubts to rest and she could hardly credit the relief sweeping through her.

If this didn't prove he accepted paternity then nothing did.

He believed her.

'We'll have to think about guardians should anything happen to both of us,' he said.

'You have given this a lot of thought.'

'I'm not prepared to leave our child's future to chance.' He pulled a tablet out of his pocket and pressed away at it, saying, 'These are the private rooms the patients stay in post-op.' He put the tablet back in his pocket and opened a door halfway up. 'This one's empty.'

Natasha looked inside. It was like no hospital room she'd ever seen. This was a plush hotel room except more clinically clean.

'Any thoughts on guardians?' he asked, closing the door and leading them on to the end of the corridor. Matteo entered a code into a silver box by the end door. It swung open and they stepped into another corridor with a very diffcrent feel to the one they'd just been in. The thick carpcts had been replaced with shiny hard flooring, the soft hues of the walls now brilliant white.

'I don't know. If I thought Francesca wasn't going to disown the pair of us, I'd say her.' She only just managed to stop her voice from cracking.

'She might surprise us.'

'Do you really think so?'

'No.'

She sighed. 'Nor do I. We'll have to see how things go and then decide. But definitely not my parents.'

The grimace he gave showed he felt exactly the same way. 'Do they know you're here?'

'No. I haven't spoken to them since the funeral. They know how to contact me if they want anything.'

He stopped walking abruptly. 'They haven't called you?'

'No. I'm sure they'll crawl out of the woodwork when they think Pieta's inheritance has been sorted. In fairness, I haven't called them either.'

His jaw clenched and he breathed heavily. 'Fairness be damned. You don't owe them anything.'

'I owe them my life,' she pointed out, her heart twisting to see the protective anger on his face. She wanted to stroke that face. She wanted to feel those firm lips on hers again. She wanted it so badly it was becoming like a drug.

Sometimes when they talked she would see more glimpses of the man she'd fallen for all those years ago. Her desire for him then had had such purity to it. Her desire had been innocent, a longing to be with him, to be held by him.

'Anyone can create a life,' he said, his voice low, his face edging towards hers. 'We've proved that. It's how you care for the life once you have it that shows the person you are.'

Almost hypnotised by the intensity in his eyes, she felt her face inching closer to his in turn, her lids becoming heavy, moisture filling her mouth as the electricity of anticipation danced over her skin.

There was no purity to her desire now. She'd lost her innocence long before she'd lost her virginity. Now her desire was a living thing inside her that fed on his presence, a battle she fought harder with every day that passed.

She wanted him. She craved him. She couldn't bear to fall into bed with him again and when it was over for him to roll over and swear at the horror of what they'd done. For her own sanity she needed to keep a lid on her feelings for him but it was becoming harder as each hour with him prised it off a little more.

Because what she needed to remember more than anything else was that they had no future together as anything other than parents of their child. She'd had one disastrous marriage and couldn't contemplate another relationship.

Matteo didn't want a relationship with her any more than she wanted one with him. That did nothing to stop the chemistry between them taking on its own life form. That did nothing to stop her lips parting and her eyes closing as the whisper of his breath played over her skin and his scent played in her senses...

A loud bang jerked her back to reality as the large swinging doors they'd almost reached were slammed open.

Natasha stepped back and swallowed hard, managing a wan smile at the two medics who strolled past them, greeting Matteo loudly as they passed.

He ran a hand through his dark cropped hair and stilled for a moment before going through the doors that had only just stopped swinging.

'This is our operating wing,' he said in a gruff voice, resuming the tour. He reached again for his tablet, which she realised through the daze their almost kiss had put her in had all the information he needed about what was happening at that very moment in his clinic delivered to his fingertips. 'We have operating theatres and recovery rooms, everything you'd expect from a normal, functioning hospital.' As he spoke, a nurse in full scrubs walked past talking on a phone and waved at them.

'We leave nothing to chance,' Matteo continued.

'Room seven's empty. You can look from the doorway but I must ask you not to go inside. No one's admitted without scrubs on.'

He opened a door for her.

Natasha peered inside and gaped. This was an honest-to-goodness operating theatre, just like those she'd seen on the television. Except bigger. And shinier.

'I need to sign some papers off in my office and then we'll go and eat. How do you like the idea of eating by the docks?'

She strove to match the casual tone he'd now adopted, to pretend that they hadn't nearly just locked lips. To pretend her mouth didn't still tingle and her limbs didn't feel weak with longing for him. 'As long as a seagull doesn't try and steal my chips.'

'You want chips?'

She was glad to think of something that didn't involve his hands running all over her body. 'Yes. A big bag of chips. And a big American club sandwich.'

'Then that is what you shall have.'

They were back in the reception area, heading up a different corridor. The door at the end had Matteo's name on it.

He unlocked it and she followed him inside.

Like the rest of the clinic, his office was scrupulously clean.

'Do you see clients in here?' she asked, looking around, keen to look anywhere but at him, not when her heart was still pounding beneath her ribs.

'Those that I take on personally, yes.'

'Do you perform many surgeries yourself?'

'Not as many as I used to do. The business has gotten so big it takes all my time. I make sure I do enough to keep my skills sharp.'

He sat behind his desk and pulled a stack of papers from a tray. 'This should only take me ten minutes. Help yourself to coffee—there's decaf if you want it.'

She could sense him avoiding her gaze as much as she was avoiding his.

'I'm good, thanks.'

Needing to keep her gaze away from him, Natasha passed the time by looking round his office, at the shelves crammed with medical texts, the walls lined with his qualification certificates. His certificate from medical school still bore the name Matteo Pellegrini.

She hesitated before asking something she knew had been a majorly important decision in his life. 'Why did you change your surname?'

CHAPTER EIGHT

FROM THE CORNER of her eye Natasha saw the nib of Matteo's pen hover over a sheet before he pressed it down and signed it, then placed it on the fresh pile he was making. 'Because I no longer wished to be acknowledged as my father's son.'

'It got that bad?' Their relationship had never been the same since the childhood fire that had ruined both little boys' lives.

'Don't pretend you don't know, *bella*. I'm sure you were told all the details.'

'Are you talking about the argument you two had at your brother's funeral?'

He jerked a nod and signed another form.

Pieta had asked her to go to Roberto's funeral with him. It had been one of the only times she'd ever denied him anything he'd asked of her. She'd stood her ground doggedly, pointing out she'd never met Roberto and that seeing as it was going to be such a small, intimate funeral, it would be inappropriate for her to be there. Pieta hadn't wanted her there for support—he hadn't seen Roberto in years—he'd wanted her there for appearances' sake. Even back then she'd known that. Appearances be damned, she'd thought; she wouldn't put Matteo through it. He would have hated to see her there. It would have made a bad day even more difficult for him.

Thinking back on it, her refusal had been the moment she'd discovered that she did have a spine. She'd found it for Matteo's sake.

'I know you two had a blazing row and that you changed your surname two weeks later. I never knew what the argument was about but I assumed the two events were linked.'

'You assumed? You never asked Pieta?'

'I never asked about you, not to him or anyone. Any news I heard about you came about in general conversation.'

Slowly he turned his head to look at her, his green eyes narrowed.

She raised her shoulders and pulled her lips in before saying quietly, 'I had this fear that if I brought your name up, they'd be able to see through me.'

'What did you think they'd see?'

'The truth about our past.'

And the truth that my feelings for you ran deeper than anything I tried to feel for Pieta.

'Eventually it stopped mattering, but not speaking about you became a habit.'

He stared at her for a long time, so hard it was like he was trying to dig into her mind. Eventually he sighed and dragged a hand down his face. 'At the funeral my father said it should have been me he was burying, not Roberto.'

Her mouth dropped open, utter shock thumping her.

'Seriously? He said that to you?'

'Sì.'

'That's *outrageous*. My God, Matteo, I'm so sorry. It must have been the grief talking—he couldn't have meant it.' How could a father say such a thing to a child? Her parents had manipulated her and twisted her emotions to suit their own purposes but never had they wished her dead.

Something sharp clawed into her chest, overlong talons scraping through her heart, making it bleed to imagine what it must have been like for Matteo to bury the brother he loved with one breath and then in the next to hear his own father say he wished him dead.

How could someone be so cruel?

'He meant it. He never forgave me for the fire. I always knew in my heart that he blamed me for it and at the funeral he confirmed it.' Matteo could still hear his father's words in his ear and feel the spittle that had flown from his mouth as he'd delivered his hate-filled words.

They'd buried Roberto under blue skies and warm sunshine, the kind of glorious day his brother had loved for the first eight years of his life but had shunned for the last twenty. He'd hated people seeing the horrific burn scars that had covered his body. He'd refused to look in mirrors, would refuse to enter a room if it had reflective surfaces in it. He'd shunned everyone who wasn't immediate family, only leaving the house for medical purposes. He'd lost all his love for life and become a recluse.

Matteo had said goodbye to his brother, his heart bursting that Roberto's last journey should be so blessed with such glorious weather, grabbing hold of any sign of blessing he could to ease the pain racking him.

Then, as he'd turned from the graveside, his father had snatched hold of his arm and spilled his venom all over him.

'That's *rubbish*.' Natasha looked like she was about

to burst into tears, her face white, her eyes glistening. 'How could it be your fault?'

'I was in charge of him when it happened.'

'You were *ten years old*.'

Somehow Natasha's outrage and upset warmed the coldness that had filled his core as it always did when he remembered that dreadful day.

'I know how young I was and it took a long time for me to accept the blame wasn't mine. It didn't—doesn't—stop the guilt,' he told her slowly. 'Deep down I always knew my father blamed me too and that it was the root cause of our estrangement. I spent twenty years hoping for his forgiveness. I always hoped he would see what I was doing with medicine and be proud of me. I always dreamed of the day he would welcome me back into the fold.' The bitter laugh escaped his mouth again. 'I learned at Roberto's funeral that I would never get it.'

'But *why*? I don't understand. How can he blame you? You were a *child*.' Fat tears shone in her eyes.

Those tears were for him…

Inhaling deeply, he said, 'He left a wilful ten-year-old boy in charge of a wilful eight-year-old. My parents left their two children on their own so they could enjoy a nice long lunch with their friends. To forgive me means accepting his own responsibility for the fire. He lies to himself about it every single day. He's lied to himself now for twenty-five years. He would rather lose two sons than accept his own part of the blame, so if he wishes me dead then to hell with him. When he said what he did at the graveside…something in me snapped. Roberto was gone…there was nothing to keep me there any longer. My last link with my parents was gone. I decided that if I'm not his son and he wished me dead then he didn't deserve for me to have his name.'

'But what about your mother?' she asked with a bewildered shake of her head, her words low and ragged. 'Didn't it upset her when you changed your name?'

'My aunt Vanessa was more of a mother to me than mine ever was and she wasn't even blood. My mother was no better than my father. She allowed me to visit Roberto when my father was away on business but she never stood up for me or insisted, as was her right, that I be allowed back to live in the family home. I was her first born and she washed her hands of me just as he did. Like my father she dishonestly put the blame on me rather than accept her own part in it. So I chose my aunt's maiden name. It felt fitting.'

The tears poured down Natasha's face, her shoulders shaking. Then, so quickly he barely registered her move, she was by his side and taking his face in her trembling hands. She pressed her lips tightly to his, not as a kiss of passion but one that had a clinging desperation to it, her tears splashing onto his cheeks.

Before he could respond or react in any way, she broke away and punched his shoulder, fury now mingling with the distress. 'How could you give it all up?'

'What?' Her sudden turnaround of both conversation and mood had him reeling.

'Your dreams.' She wiped her face furiously but the tears kept coming. 'Your plans to do reconstructive surgery. You keep saying you didn't give it up and only changed career paths but you *did*. You gave up everything you'd worked for. I know you could never have helped your brother surgically but you wanted to help others in the same situation. You *did*. You were so driven and dedicated. It was never about the money for you.' She raised her hands and waved them, taking in the luxury furnishings and the spectacular view he enjoyed. 'It was never about *this*.'

He didn't know what cut through his skin the most, her scornful words or the distress behind them. Both stunned him as much as her tears. Somehow he managed to hold onto his rising temper. 'I wanted to be a surgeon—I *am* a surgeon.'

'A surgeon with his own Jetstream, a yacht and the most expensive property in Miami. You followed the money. Was it to prove a point to your father when being the most brilliant doctor in a generation wasn't enough? You would have been brilliant. I know you would. You had everything there and you threw it away for money.'

'I didn't throw anything away,' he snarled, getting to his feet and kicking his chair back. 'I paid my dues. You know how hard I worked to get through medical school and my residency. I spent over a decade working so hard that there were days I never saw sunlight. I never shirked in my duty, not even when I couldn't feel my feet from standing for so long or when I had to drink gallons of coffee just to keep my eyes open. Yes, I followed the money but so what? Only a fool wouldn't. I developed the lotion for Roberto but it was too bloody late for him. His scarred lungs gave up on him. *Everything* I did was for him but he died, so what was the point? What was the point in working every waking hour when I had nothing to show for it apart from certificates to hang on my wall?

'I saw an opportunity with the lotion to create a skin-care range that worked, and I took it. I make no apologies for that. The money I made from it allowed me to open my own clinics, which made me even more money. I've worked my backside off for years so why shouldn't I be allowed to enjoy it? I'm richer than I ever dreamed possible and, yes, it gives me *immense* satisfaction to think of my father knowing of my wealth and not being able to claim any credit for it because I threw away the name he gave me.'

Stark silence fell between them.

Somehow during his vehement rebuttal they'd finished barely a foot apart, close enough for Matteo to see the exact shade of red slowly creeping up Natasha's neck and over her cheeks.

Her tears had dried up and now she simply stared at him with wide eyes that held his for the longest time before a flash of pain raced through them.

Her throat moved before she whispered, 'I'm sorry. I should never have said any of that. I don't know what got into me.'

'Never apologise for speaking the truth. It might hurt but lies are always, *always* worse.' He looked at the light smattering of freckles over the bridge of her nose and brought his face lower to hers, remembering the feel of her lips on his before the torrent had spewed from her.

He'd never known such passion before. He'd had a steady string of women in his life over the years, pleasant interludes in a busy life, a pretty face to be photographed with when he opened a new clinic and used the media for publicity…

Natasha was right that part of what had driven him had been to prove a point to his father. That *had* been conscious, striving to achieve the riches his father had never been able to find, but it was only at that moment he understood there had been another driving force propelling him forward too.

Her.

Every photo posed for knowing it would be all over the media had been taken with *her* image in his head.

She had been with him of every minute of every day, living in his subconscious, the woman who'd thrown away a future that could have been special for them to be with his richer cousin. And only now, years later, did he realise he no longer believed any of it.

He believed her. He believed right down in his soul that she'd spoken the truth when she'd explained how it had been for her. It had never been about the money for her.

'Seven years ago you kept the truth from me,' he said, running a thumb over her cheekbone, unable to tear his gaze from those beautiful blue eyes. 'If you'd found your voice before it was too late who knows how our lives would have turned out? Maybe we would have married each other. Maybe we would have naturally drifted apart. Neither of us can know.'

Leaning to rest the tip of his nose against hers, he continued, 'We're having a child together, *bella*. I might not have liked what you just said but you've found your voice and have learned how to use it, and you can't know how good that is. I spent too many years distrusting and hating you—I don't ever want to return to feeling like that. For better or worse we're going to be tied together by our child for the rest of our lives and the only way we're going to get through it is by always being honest with each other. We will argue and disagree but you must always speak the truth to me.'

Natasha fought to keep her feet grounded and her limbs from turning into fondue but it was a fight she was losing, Matteo's breath warm on her face, his thumb gently moving on her skin but scorching it, the heat from his body almost penetrating her clothes, heat crawling through her, pooling in her most intimate place.

His scent was right there too, filling every part of

her, and she wanted to bury her nose into his neck and inhale him.

She'd kissed him without any thought, a desperate compulsion to touch him and comfort him flooding her, and then the fury had struck from nowhere, all her private thoughts about the direction he'd taken his career in converging to realise he'd thrown it all away in the pursuit of riches.

And now she wanted to kiss him again.

As if he could sense the need inside her, he brought his mouth close to hers but not quite touching, the promise of a kiss.

'And now I will ask you something and I want complete honesty,' he whispered, the movement of his words making his lips dance against hers like a breath.

The fluttering of panic sifted into the compulsive desire. She hated lies too. She never wanted to tell another, especially not to him. But she had to keep her wits about her because there were things she just could not tell because no matter what he said about lies always being worse, sometimes it was the truth that could destroy a life.

But, God, how could she think properly when her head was turning into candyfloss at his mere touch?

His other hand trailed down her back and clasped her bottom to pull her flush to him. Her abdomen clenched to feel his erection pressing hard against her lower stomach. His lips moved lightly over hers, still tantalising her with the promise of his kiss. 'Do you want me to let you go?'

Her hands that she'd clenched into fists at her sides to stop from touching him back unfurled themselves and inched to his hips.

The hand stroking her cheek moved round her head

and speared her hair. 'Tell me.' His lips found her exposed neck and nipped gently at it. 'Do you want me to stop?'

'Matteo…' Finally, she found her voice.

'Yes, *bella*?'

'Don't stop.'

Her words were all the encouragement he needed. His mouth swept across her cheek to find her parted lips and then he was kissing her with such hunger she melted into him.

The fuse relit in an instant. Need burned bright within her, all the desire she'd been suppressing by the skin of her fingers bursting out of her. She wrapped her arms tightly around his waist, her hands reaching up to clasp onto his back as she kissed him back, her tongue darting into his mouth, dancing against his.

And he held her just as tightly. One hand buried in her hair, the other gripping her to him, devouring her as if her kisses were the air he needed to breathe.

When he broke it and let go of her she almost cried a protest but then he took her face in his hands and rubbed both thumbs across her cheekbones as he stared intently into her eyes. 'I'm not making love to you here.'

Love…?

Although she knew his words weren't meant in the terms of what love itself meant, something in her heart broke free regardless, taking all the air from her lungs.

Only when she'd found her breath did she whisper, 'Then take me home.'

The drive back to Matteo's home passed in a blur. What had been a relatively short journey into downtown seemed to halve, Matteo driving his powerful car to the limit, weaving in and out of the traffic, his jaw clenched, his focus very much on the road before them. Only his right hand, holding hers tightly on her lap as he navigated the roads, showed any awareness of her beside him.

When he pulled into the garage what felt like only minutes later, Natasha shook her head, amazed to find she could remember nothing about the drive. All she'd been able to focus on was their kiss, replaying it in her head, her lips still tingling, her body still experiencing the hard pressure of his body pressed against her as if he'd imprinted himself on her.

As soon as he stopped the car, Matteo leaned over and kissed her again, a deep, heady kiss that sent her head spinning all over again.

'*Dio, bella*, you're driving me out of my mind,' he muttered into her mouth before pulling away to get out of the car.

On legs that felt as if they were new born, Natasha stepped out too. He was by her side in an instant, taking her hand and leading her up the steps of the garage and into the empty house.

She'd never been upstairs and where before she'd wondered a lot about what she would find there, she now found she didn't care, not even when she followed him up the hidden staircase. All she could see at that moment was Matteo. She refused to think about anything else.

But then they stepped into his bedroom and she gasped at the beauty and simplicity of it. It was so *clean* but without being clinical, huge without being oppressive and bathed in light that softened the high walls and gave it such a romantic feel that she felt her belly melt all over again.

She looked at Matteo to find his gaze very much on her, his jaw clenched as it had been during the drive back.

Stepping to him, she reached up to palm his cheek and stare at the face she'd adored for so many years it seemed she'd gone to sleep with it in her mind every night for ever.

He breathed deeply before reaching out to gently brush a fallen lock of her hair away from her eyes.

It was at that moment she realised she'd never got over losing him.

The pain she'd felt when hearing of his father's rejection and wish for Matteo to have been the son that had died had cut as deep as if it had been personally directed at her. Whatever choices Matteo had made with his life since they'd dreamed of building a future together all those years ago, it didn't change that fundamentally he was the best man she'd ever known.

He was the father of her child and she couldn't have chosen a better man for it if she'd been given a list with a thousand names on it.

Was this love? she wondered, dazed at the notion. Or was it just hormones from the pregnancy and a strong case of lust? Whatever it was, the need inside her for him was too strong to even want to fight it any more, not when the green eyes staring back at her were molten with his own unmistakable desire.

And then he hooked an arm around her waist and pulled her flush against him and his hot mouth was back on hers and they were kissing as if they could feed from the other.

Their lovemaking the night they'd conceived their child had been born of a passion fuelled by pain and anger, an old longing that had been kept locked away, out of sight and mind, only to erupt with vengeance at the first opportunity.

This time, as Matteo lifted her into his strong arms to carry her to the bed, the flames had lit to burn as brightly as they had then but this time there was a sense of wonder and a complete sense of rightness.

In a melee of arms and legs, he laid her down, just as he had before but with a tenderness beneath the passion.

When he kissed her, it was with a slow, tempered hunger that was only broken when his hands found the hem of her dress and he pulled it up to take it off her, then smoothed her dislodged hair before kissing her again.

Raking her hands into his short curly hair, Natasha sighed as his lips trailed down her neck, shivered as they brushed over her collarbone.

He bent his head lower, reaching her sensitive breasts that were already much heavier than the last time they'd made love. Kissing each one over her lacy bra, he rested his chin between them and looked at her. 'You're beautiful, you know that, *bella*?'

She swallowed, not wanting to think of all the beautiful women she'd seen him photographed with over the years.

'I mean it.' There was an intensity in his eyes that matched the intensity in his voice. 'No one can hold a candle to you.'

Matteo saw the doubt flicker in her eyes and wondered what Natasha saw when she looked in the mirror. He remembered her jests earlier in his clinic, words said, he knew, to detract from the spell that had woven around them, but there had been something underlying it.

Did she really not see how beautiful she was? Did she really not know that just listening to her voice was enough for his loins to tighten?

Raising himself up, he climbed off the bed and stripped his shirt off and divested himself of the rest of his clothes, her eyes following his every movement.

Only when he was naked did he get back on the bed and trail his fingers from her neck all the way to the line of her knickers, delighting in the way she quivered at his touch.

There was such innocence in her responses that he found hard to get his head around. On the one hand her responses were ardent, her need and hunger for him as visible and as open as a man could wish for, but now, gazing at the almost naked form of the woman he'd dreamed about for years in the hazy daylight, he could believe he was the first man to have ever seen her like this.

Placing a hand behind her back, he lifted her so he could undo the pretty bra hiding her breasts from him. As the lacy material loosened to free her, she tilted her head back and sighed.

The first time they'd made love had been in the dark. Now he could see her perfectly and she was even more perfect than he had imagined. Had her nipples always been that dark or was that the pregnancy working its magic in her?

Dipping his head, he took one into his mouth, eliciting another sigh from her.

As he'd done the first time, he kissed every inch of her, but this time he took it slowly. He wanted to savour it, savour her, to learn everything about her that he could, to find the zones that provoked the loudest gasps and the sharpest digs of her nails into his skin. When he hooked a finger to the side of her knickers, she wriggled beneath him, helping him pull them down her thighs and legs before he threw them with the rest of their discarded clothes onto the floor.

The heat he found in her most feminine part blew his mind and when he brushed over the soft hair and rubbed a thumb over the centre of her pleasure, her eyes widened and a moan flew from her mouth. Keeping a steady pressure with his thumb, he slowly slid a finger into the damp heat. She moaned again and arched her back, her hair falling like a waterfall onto the pillow.

Dio, he had never known anything like this. He could make love to her for ever.

He kissed the softly rounded belly then kissed lower to replace his thumb with his tongue, inhaling the musky sweetness he would gladly bottle and keep on him always.

Her little sighs of pleasure deepened and she whispered his name. Before he could finish what he'd started she wriggled beneath him and sat up, pouncing on him so she straddled him, her arms locked around his neck and her hands cradling his scalp as she fused her lips to his with a hunger that sucked the air from him.

Then she touched and kissed him everywhere, just as he had done to her, his shoulders, his arms, his stomach, his thighs, his aching erection, her mouth leaving a trail of heat on his skin that fired his blood to a level he'd never imagined. And in the fever with which she so beautifully caressed him was a reverence, almost as if she were exploring him with wonder in her heart side by side with the passion that drove them both.

He felt his flesh could burst open to admit her into *his* heart.

Gripping her waist, he manoeuvred them both so she straddled his lap and her legs were wrapped around his waist.

Their lips locked together, he placed a hand flat on her back and laid her back gently, the tip of his burning arousal finding the place it so badly needed to be. Then he entered her, slowly, tenderly until he was burrowed deep inside her tight heat.

The sensations that enveloped him threatened to make him come in an instant and he had to grit his teeth to keep himself in check. Only when he was certain he had himself under control did he start moving.

But, *Dio*, every long thrust built the sensation up to unimaginable levels, every moan and pant from her lips, every scratch of her nails, all combined to make him lose himself in the rapture that was Natasha.

Only when the moans breathing into his mouth deepened and the hand holding onto his buttock gripped tightly and he felt her thicken around him did he finally let himself go with a groan that came from the very centre of his being, plunging so deeply into her that he no longer knew where he ended and she began.

When the explosive pulsations inside him had dulled to a gentle buzz he shifted his weight a little so as not to crush her.

Immediately her arms tightened around him and she raised her face to bury it in his neck.

'If you regret what we just did tell me now so I can prepare myself before I have to look at you again,' she whispered into his skin.

His chest contorting to remember how he'd reacted in the immediate aftermath of their first time together, he held her securely in his arms and rolled onto his back, taking her with him. 'No regrets,' he whispered back, stroking her hair.

How could he regret that? Something that special could never be looked on with regret.

Her small hand groped for his and squeezed and she nuzzled into his chest with a sigh. 'I don't regret it either.'

'Good.' He brought her hand to his lips to kiss it. 'No regrets.'

'No regrets,' she echoed.

CHAPTER NINE

THEY STAYED IN bed until the sun began its descent. They'd made love again and, just as she drifted off, he asked if she was hungry. The mention of hunger was enough to make Natasha's stomach growl and remind her that they'd skipped the lunch he'd promised her.

He laughed and got out of bed. What looked like an ordinary wall had turned out to be a walk-in wardrobe. He disappeared into it, reappearing with a pair of tan shorts on, leaned over to kiss her firmly and said he was going to call a chef from the staff quarters to make them something.

Happy to have a few minutes alone to relive every beautiful moment in her head, Natasha burrowed her face into his pillow seeking his scent.

Making love to Matteo the first time had been an explosion that had detonated itself. This time it had been...

It had been incredible. He'd been so passionate and yet so tender. There had been a connection between them she could never have put into words but it filled her heart with such hope.

But hopes of what? A future together? Him and her and baby makes three?

She grabbed his pillow and pulled it over her head.

One incredible afternoon in bed together did not

make a future. It just made complications and there were enough complications in her life for her to be getting on with.

That didn't stop her waiting impatiently for his return.

When twenty minutes passed without him coming back to the room, concern began to nibble at her. Fishing in the pile of discarded clothes for her dress, she slipped it over her head, intent on searching for him. But no sooner had she stepped out of the room than apprehension suddenly suffused her.

What if he'd left the bedroom and become filled with recriminations again? What if she'd been lying in his bed waiting for his return while he'd been overcome with angry remorse and was trying to think of a way to kick her out and back to the guesthouse?

What if she'd been lying on his bed feeling that she'd slipped into a blissful dream and he'd come to the conclusion that he'd slipped into a nightmare?

She found him in the vast living space she'd been so enamoured with in her first visit there. He was sitting at the table, his long legs stretched out before him, talking on his phone.

He gave an apologetic smile and held out a hand to her.

Her relief was almost dizzying.

It was also terrifying.

She let her fingers drift to touch his and took the seat beside him, her heart thumping madly, her palms suddenly clammy.

Making love like they had had changed everything.

His eyes fixed on her, he continued his conversation, his Italian too rapid-fire for her to keep up. She'd never mastered the language, another regret in her life. It had such a beautiful cadence to it and in the days when she and Matteo had been planning a future together, she'd imagined him teaching her his language.

It had never occurred to her to ask Pieta.

When the call was over, Matteo put his phone on the table. 'That was Daniele. He wants to go back to Caballeros with me at the end of next week.'

She closed her eyes. All the euphoria of their lovemaking, which even her panic about Matteo finding regrets hadn't been able to fully quash, left her. 'Next week? And we'll go to Pisa after?'

'Yes. Next Friday. I'll charter a plane for you and meet you there. It makes more sense than me flying back to Miami to collect you.'

Natasha felt the panic welling up in her and fought hard to stifle it. 'At least that gives us almost two weeks to prepare. Do you think he has any suspicions about us yet?'

Saying the word 'us' felt different from all the other times she'd said it. This time it felt real.

'Daniele takes things at face value so I doubt it.'

She mustered a smile. 'I never got to know him that well. Not like I did Francesca and Vanessa.'

'You're speaking of them in the past tense.'

She met his eyes. 'When they learn about us and the baby my relationship with them will be in the past.'

'Yes. And so will mine.' His admission was like a long, drawn out sigh but then he leaned forward in his chair and stroked her face, staring intently into her eyes. 'There's going to be a lot of pain but we will handle it together. You and me. I won't let them hurt you.'

'It's not me I'm worried about.'

'I know it isn't.' He brought his face close to hers. 'We'll get through this, okay?'

His lips brushed hers, a gentle, soothing caress that

loosened a little of the anguish looping inside her at what they faced and the destruction they were going to cause.

Matteo's words of comfort helped a little but did nothing to ease the guilt that cramped her at what he was going through or the guilt at what she was keeping from him.

A loud cough from the other side of the room broke the moment.

The youngest of Matteo's chefs walked in carrying a tray with two plates covered in silver lids on it.

'Thanks, Leon,' Matteo said. 'Sorry to impose on your night off.'

'No worries. I'll hang around in case you need anything else.'

'If I need anything I'll get it for myself. Take a couple of hundred from petty cash and take your girlfriend out.'

Leon's face lit up. 'You're sure?'

'Sure I'm sure. Pay for any cab on the staff account.'

Leon saluted and scarpered before Matteo could change his mind.

'That was generous of you,' Natasha said, finding she could smile again.

'He was prepared to give up his night off. He's the generous one. Now let's see what we have.' He leaned over the table and lifted the lid off her plate and then the lid off his own to reveal plates heaped with thick-cut English-style chips and thick club sandwiches that managed to be artfully presented.

'You remembered,' she said in delight.

'I'm like an elephant.' He winked. 'In more ways than one. And eating here rather than by the docks guarantees your chips won't be stolen by seagulls.'

She couldn't help but laugh.

'That's better,' he said approvingly before his features

became serious. 'I know it's going to be hard but there's no point in worrying about what's going to happen when we tell them. It's beyond our control. We'll deal with it when the time comes.'

Knowing he was right, she picked up her sandwich and bit into it. 'It's lovely,' she said when she'd swallowed the second bite down. And it *was* lovely. How could it not be? He employed world-class chefs who could make an ordinary sandwich taste as if it had been touched by magic. Everything he owned was the best.

A few minutes later Matteo had wolfed his plate clean and sat back lazily to watch her eat.

As if her eyes were magnets drawn to him, she was helpless to stop from staring back at him.

When she couldn't manage another bite she pushed her plate to one side and took a sip of the juice he'd poured for her.

'You've had enough?' he asked.

She nodded.

'Can I get you any dessert?'

'Can you cook?'

'No.' He grinned. 'I can get one of the local restaurants to deliver.'

She laughed. 'Honestly, I'm full.'

Just as he was about to lean in for another kiss, his phone vibrated across the shiny surface of the table.

Matteo debated ignoring it but knew he couldn't.

That's what came of having a business that spanned the globe, he thought ruefully, swiping to read the message that had come in. Your time was rarely your own.

Today had been an exception, one he felt he should make a regular thing. He rarely worked evenings but his days were always full.

'It's from Francesca,' he said, reading the message.

'She wants to know how I'm getting on with equipment and staffing levels for the hospital.' He rolled his eyes. 'I would have thought her new fiancé would have distracted her from ordering everyone around.'

Her answering grin showed she knew there was no malice behind his observation of his bossy cousin.

'How are you getting on with it?' As she asked, Natasha topped both their glasses up with more juice.

'I've ordered most of the equipment but I'm coming up short on the staff.' Matteo had promised to send his own medical staff to work there for a month to get the hospital up and running, giving them time to recruit permanent medical staff and train local Caballerons to do the auxiliary work.

'What are you going to do about it?'

'I don't know. I'm offering incentives but...'

'Nobody wants to work in such a dangerous country even if Aguadilla and the Dominican Republic are close enough to fly to,' she finished. She scrunched her nose and looked at him. 'Did you really expect it to be any different?'

'What do you mean?'

'You employ doctors and nurses who've turned their backs on healing patients. They're hardly humanitarian sorts.'

'My staff *are* healers,' he refuted. 'They're dedicated professionals.'

'They're professionals,' she conceded. 'But if they ever had ideals they've traded them for money. Your clinics are specifically tailored for the filthy rich. Your surgeons are some of the top earning professionals in the world.'

He hated that she was right. He hated that she must put him in the same bracket. He hated that she was right to.

Like him, the surgeons he employed had paid their dues in the long years of their residencies. Like him, they and the other clinicians he employed had gone into medicine for noble reasons.

She tilted her head and narrowed her eyes as if she was thinking. 'What kind of incentives are you offering? More money, like Daniele's done with his construction staff?'

'Yes. I offered to double their salaries.'

'Forget the money. You want to go for their egos.'

'What do you mean?'

Although she'd only minutes ago declared herself full, she helped herself to a cold chip from her half-empty plate. 'Tell them there will be lots of media at the opening of the hospital like there is when you open a new clinic, and that there's a good chance they'll be interviewed about it and that the world will laud them for their self-sacrifice and humanity. I bet they'll rip your arm off to go there if they think they could make the cover of a magazine off the back of it.'

He shook his head and bit back a laugh. 'I can't believe I didn't think of that.'

'So you think that *could* work to incentivise them?' She looked rather stunned, as if she hadn't thought her idea would pass muster.

'It's a great idea. I've got lots of contacts in the media; we should get in touch with them and get some interest going.'

'I can do that. I did promise Francesca I would take care of the publicity for it and until now I've barely thought about it.'

'I'll get a list together for you. I warn you, it's a long list so you might find it easier to work from my study.'

Her eyes widened. 'Really? You wouldn't mind me working in there?'

'Why should I? Most of my contacts are involved with the fashion and film industry side of the media so it's unlikely to interest them, but they should be able to give you other contacts to speak to about it.'

'Why are your contacts from the fashion and film world?'

'Because the people who come to my clinics and use my skincare range are generally people seeking to emulate what they see on the catwalk and the big screen, whether it's by buying a fifty-thousand-dollar handbag or making improvements to their skin.' He saw the flicker of distaste wrinkle her nose and added, 'That's not all we do, although I can appreciate why you would think it is. When I opened my first clinic I deliberately targeted that market, but the work we do, it's not all breast lifts and tummy tucks and people who want a new nose for cosmetic reasons. We also deal with cancer survivors; women who've had mastectomies and come to us because they know we'll reconstruct their breasts to look so natural that no one would know they weren't real, people who've lost half their noses because of a malignant mole...all sorts of people. It's not all vanity.

'But I do employ the best and I pay them accordingly and charge my clients accordingly for it. We've grown quickly and gained a reputation as the best for a reason—because we *are* the best at what we do. Yes, my staff have enormous egos but they earned them. They worked as hard as I did to become as skilled as they are now, and now they're reaping the rewards for all the dedication and commitment they gave for all those years.'

Her eyes never left his face while he explained the

facts of the situation, delivered because of a compulsion for her to understand.

When he was done a wry smile played on her lips. 'I'm sorry if I came across as judgemental.'

'Don't be,' he urged. He took her hand and kissed it. 'I meant what I said. Always be honest with me. Always tell me the truth. I don't know what's happening between us. I don't know if there ever will be an "us" in the real sense of the word but I know we owe it to ourselves and our child to explore it and see if it leads anywhere, but that can't happen unless we trust each other. I want to trust you, *bella*.'

'I trust *you*,' she admitted in a whisper, those vivid blue eyes huge. He thought he detected fear in them.

What did she have to be fearful about...?

'But what if it doesn't work?' she continued in that same low voice. 'What if the past—'

'Then we deal with it,' he said, cutting her off. 'The past is done. It's the future—our future, our baby's future—that matters. We can make a whole list of what-ifs but neither of us knows what the future holds.' He took a long breath, unable to believe he was having these thoughts and having this conversation with the woman he had so recently despised with every fibre of his being.

But he didn't hate her any more, and as he was the one demanding complete openness and honesty, he had to be honest with himself and admit that his feelings for her had consumed him since the day he'd first set eyes on her. One way or another, she had always been with him.

'Let's just take it a day at a time.'

'One day at a time?'

'One day at a time.'

Her answer was to shift onto his lap, wrap her arms around him and kiss him.

* * *

The most delicious swirling sensation was happening on Natasha's belly. It took a few moments to realise she wasn't in the middle of a dream.

Slowly she opened her eyes to find Matteo propped on an elbow looking at her and trailing his fingers over her naked stomach.

His lips curved into the sensual smile that made her heart skip before he leaned down to brush a kiss on her mouth.

'What time is it?' she asked sleepily. The sun was up but the light filtering into the bedroom was still hazy.

'Seven.'

'Shouldn't you be gone?' He had a full day of surgery booked in at his clinic and then he was flying to Los Angeles to conduct interviews for a new general manager for one of his stores in the morning. He'd promised to be back in time to take her out to dinner tomorrow night.

In the week since they'd become lovers it would be the first time she'd slept without him.

In four days he would fly to Caballeros.

In five days they would be facing the music.

'I should, yes.' He brushed another kiss to her lips. 'Something much more important caught my attention.'

'Oh?'

He circled one of her breasts with his forefinger. 'I was looking at the changes the pregnancy's made to your body.'

'And?' She was barely three months but the changes were there.

'And they're beautiful.'

'Will you still think that when I'm waddling like a duck and covered in stretch marks?' she asked, trying to make her voice jokey, not wanting to admit her fear that the coming changes would be enough to turn him off her.

He rolled on top of her, his erection pressed right at the apex of her thighs, and gazed deep into her eyes. 'Whatever changes the pregnancy makes will only make you more beautiful. Do you know why?'

She shook her head.

'Because every stretch mark and all the other things that come with it will be visible proof of the life you've nurtured. And I'll tell you something else...' He slid inside her and with a groan said into her ear, 'You'll still be the most beautiful woman in my eyes.'

CHAPTER TEN

NATASHA'S PHONE RANG and she dived into her bag, which she'd laid by her feet, glad of the distraction.

In twenty minutes Matteo would be leaving to fly to Caballeros. She read the message and bit her lip.

'Who's that from?' he asked, leaning over and helping himself to a slice of toast from the spread that had been laid out for their breakfast.

'My mother. She wants to know if I've heard from Pieta's lawyers.' She fired a quick message back.

'Is she after money?'

'Probably. They're going to have a fit when I tell them I'm not taking any of it.'

'Are you still set on that?'

'More than ever. I spoke to the lawyer in charge and told him I want it to go to the foundation.'

'When was that?'

'Yesterday when you were at work.' He'd gone to New York for a day-long business meeting. Instead of staying in his Manhattan apartment he'd flown the six-hour round trip to be home in time for bed. 'Sorry, it was an impulsive thing. I never got the chance to mention it to you.'

He shrugged. 'I'm not your keeper, *bella*. So you want all the inheritance to go to the foundation?'

'Every penny. When I think how much work it's been this week for us to drum up press interest and change your staff's minds about working there for a month it brings home how important a healthy bank balance is for the foundation.'

The day after they'd become lovers, Matteo had come home from work with a printout of all his media contacts. Natasha had snatched at it, delighted to have something she could get stuck into for the long periods of time she was alone.

As he'd promised, Matteo set her up in his office so she could work. He even gave her the password for his computer. At first she'd sat in the office feeling like an intruder, her mind fleeing back to the day she'd returned from her brief honeymoon, already knowing she'd made the biggest mistake of her life. Her new husband had turned to her and said his study was his private space and off limits to her. She'd known throughout their long engagement that Pieta craved his privacy but to be excluded from a room of the house she was now supposed to call a home had been yet another kick in the teeth. She hadn't suspected then that the worst kick was still to come.

Matteo never made her feel like a nuisance. He never made her feel that she was intruding in his space. Living with him felt natural.

With increasing confidence, she'd made the calls. As Matteo had suspected, a memorial hospital being built in one of the most dangerous countries in the world was not something that interested his glamorous contacts in the media. However, they'd been generous enough to point her in the direction of editors at the more high-brow end of the media and they *had* been receptive to the idea of covering the story, expressing enough of an interest that Matteo had been able to send a memo to his clinical staff worldwide telling them of the media presence that would be in Caballeros. As a result, over two dozen surgeons and nurses had signed up to spend a month there when the hospital opened. It wasn't as large a number as they'd hoped for, but it would be enough.

It felt good to know that whatever happened between them and the Pellegrinis, they would have played their part in the memorial for Pieta.

'You knew that already surely?'

'The only involvement I had with the foundation was attending the fundraisers and press events with Pieta.' She'd offered to become more involved. If she couldn't work then she'd wanted to be able to do something useful but Pieta had always resisted. His reluctance for her to work had extended to his foundation and she'd had to wait until they'd married to discover why he'd been so loath for her to have any involvement in the running of it other than as an adornment on his arm when he required.

She dropped her phone back in her bag and looked at Matteo. For the first time in her life she lived with someone who made no demands on her or tried to bend her to his will. For the first time in her life she lived with someone who treated her as an equal and a person in her own right. For the first time she lived with someone who wanted to please *her*.

That didn't stop her heart thumping as she braced herself to say, 'I wanted to ask you a favour.'

'Sure.'

'You don't even know what it is yet,' she chided.

'I don't need to know.' He stood behind her chair and put his arms around her waist. She leaned back into him, thinking how right this felt. How right they felt.

'Your guesthouse, can I do it up?'

He stilled. Clearly it was the last thing he'd expected her to ask.

'Please? It's a brilliant space but it's crying out for the interior to be pulled up to the same high standard as in here.'

'And you want to do that?'

'Yes. If you'll let me.'

'How much do you want me to pay you?'

'Nothing. But if you like the end result, you can recommend me to your friends.'

He moved away to take the seat next to her and poured himself a black coffee. 'You want to work?'

'Yes. I want to do what I always said I would do and build my own interior design business.'

'What's brought this on?'

'You sound surprised.'

He looked bemused. 'As far as I'm aware, you've never worked. I thought you liked being free.'

'Well, I don't.' She knew where that idea had come from. Pieta. It's what he'd always said to justify keeping her shackled to him financially. And she, stupidly desperate to please, had let him. 'I always wanted to earn my own money but it was never an option for me. Our baby's due in six months. That gives me time to make a decent go of things. If it turns out that I'm not any good at it then so be it, at least I will have tried.'

'Why was working never an option for you?'

'Pieta wanted me to be available whenever he needed me. A career wasn't compatible with that.'

The bemusement fell from his face, his eyes fixed on hers with that look that always made her feel he was trying to read her mind. Which he probably was.

Eventually, his lips pursed together, he nodded. 'You

are sure about this? You're ready to start building a career for yourself now?'

'Yes.'

'Then you have my support. Go ahead. Do the guesthouse up as you want.'

'That's it? No questions about what I want to do or if it fits in with your own vision for it?'

He shrugged. 'I got Daniele to design a guesthouse so I could have my privacy if I had guests stay. Other than that, I've no interest in it. I'll make you a signatory on one of my accounts so you can spend whatever you need on it and hire whatever tradespeople you need. Pay yourself a wage too. I've been thinking about setting you up with an allowance anyway...'

'I told you, I don't want to be paid for it and I certainly don't want an allowance from you.'

'Pieta gave you an allowance.'

'And it made me feel like a child being given pocket money in exchange for good behaviour.'

The longer she and Matteo were together, the closer they were becoming. There were times she simply ached to confide the truth to him. Matteo demanded honesty above everything else and knowing she was keeping something so fundamental about Pieta from him had settled like a permanent weight in her stomach. She had to keep reminding herself why it had to be like this when the doubts crowding in her head became too much. All she had to do was remember the devastation she'd felt when she'd learned the truth to stiffen her spine against confiding in him. However bad it had been for her, the truth would feel a thousand times worse for Matteo. He'd loved Pieta. They'd been as close as siblings.

But all this didn't mean she couldn't be honest about

the rest of her marriage. Matteo deserved that much from her.

'Before we married I lived in an apartment bought in his name that was never mine. I'm sick of feeling that I'm living on handouts. I'm living under your roof and eating your food—I haven't contributed a penny to anything since I've been here. Doing up the guesthouse for you is one small way that I can contribute and it also gives me the chance to cut my teeth on a project and see if the potential I was told I had at university is really there in me.'

Matteo swallowed back a boulder that had lodged in his throat.

Pieta hadn't wanted her to work. He'd given her an allowance that had made her feel like a child...

Pieta had been his cousin and his best friend but Matteo hadn't been blind to his faults. He'd been arrogant and aloof with an air of superiority born from being the eldest son of an old and noble family and knowing from the moment he could speak that one day it would all be his. But for all that, Matteo had always assumed Pieta would treat the woman he fell in love with like a princess.

He'd always been convinced Natasha's feelings for his cousin had been less than genuine, that it had been the money she'd been attracted to and not the man. It had made him furious to think of her playing with Pieta's emotions to her own advantage but had always assured himself that Pieta was a grown man. If Natasha didn't make his cousin happy he wouldn't be with her.

Now Matteo could see he'd got it all the wrong way round.

The question he should have been asking himself was

whether Pieta had ever made *her* happy. Had he ever made Natasha feel like a princess?

It stabbed at his chest to suspect that the answer was no.

Matteo got out of the car and gazed at the shell of the hospital, astounded at the difference since his last visit there.

Daniele stood beside him and grinned. 'What do you think?'

He shook his head. When he'd last been here the site had been cleared and ground workers had been digging the foundations. Now there stood a sprawling building, unmistakably a hospital, complete with roof and windows. 'Has Francesca seen it?'

'Not in the flesh. I've been sending her updates and pictures of every stage.'

As Daniele spoke a tall, handsome man built like a brick wall strode towards them. Felipe Lorenzi, the security specialist originally hired to keep Francesca safe in this mostly lawless country and now designated the task of keeping Daniele's construction workers and soon Matteo's medical staff safe. He was also the man who'd captured Francesca's heart and would shortly be marrying into the family.

With a pang, Matteo wondered if he would be invited to the wedding. Or would he be cast out of their lives as his parents had cast him out of theirs.

He looked at his watch. Natasha would be boarding her flight to Pisa. In a few hours he would get back on his jet and meet her there. Daniele was taking his own jet back to Pisa too and had already offered a bet over whose pilot could get them there first. His cousin was oblivious to the destruction that was going to be rained down on them all the next day.

But now was not the time to be thinking of that. He had the shell of a hospital to inspect and related issues to discuss. He'd stolen Pieta's wife. He would not ruin his memorial too.

Francesca Pellegrini yawned widely and shoved the box she'd been packing to one side. In two days she would be moving from Pisa to Rome, into the beautiful house her fiancé had bought for them to live in.

He didn't waste time, she thought with a smile. When Felipe wanted something to happen, he was prepared to move mountains to achieve it.

Deciding to take a break before packing anything else, she made herself a coffee and unlocked her phone. One of her guilty pleasures was reading online gossip sites. Unbeknownst to Daniele and Matteo, it was how she'd been able to keep track of their love lives over the years. She preferred for them to think she was all-knowing.

The top stories were about the latest Hollywood divorce, which, being a huge film buff, interested her greatly. Before she could tap on it for more salacious details, a story lower down the page caught her eye.

Her finger hovered over the link for a moment before she took a deep breath and clicked it.

There wasn't much in the way of text, the story mostly comprising photos. The subjects were at a beachside café eating ice cream. The man's face was directly in the frame and unmistakably Matteo. He was leaning forward to wipe ice cream from the mouth of the woman he was with, whose face was mostly hidden from the camera's lens. The second picture showed him leaning in to kiss the part he'd just wiped.

Her blood chilling, she enlarged the first picture, trying to see the woman more clearly, even though her thumping heart already knew who she was. She would recognise that honey-blonde hair anywhere.

The teardrop diamond earring twinkling under the bright Miami sun was the clincher. Natasha had worn those very same earrings at Pieta's funeral.

After staring at the pictures for so long her eyes began to sting and blur, Francesca snapped into action.

'Daniele?' she said when he answered his phone. 'I'm sending you a link. Prepare yourself. You're not going to like what you see.'

Only when Matteo was certain they'd inspected everything that could be inspected and discussed everything that could be discussed did he say they should call it a day.

As they were walking out of the hospital into the blazing Caballeron sun, Daniele paused to answer his phone.

'What?' he said, then took the phone from his ear and stared at it with a bemused expression. He looked at Felipe. 'Your fiancée is a complete drama queen.'

'Francesca?' Felipe asked, concern knotting his forehead.

'Do you have another fiancée?' Daniele jested. 'Oh, here's the mysterious link she thinks I need to prepare myself to look at.'

Watching Daniele open the link, a powerful sense of foreboding settled in Matteo's gut.

When he saw his cousin's eyes crease and dart to his face and then dart back to the screen in his hand, that foreboding deepened.

He just had time to register the darkest, ugliest expression he'd ever seen on Daniele's face before he was slammed into the wall.

Matteo had never been in a fight before but he kept himself fit and had reflexes that could put a boxer to shame. Pure survival instinct had him wrenching himself out of Daniele's stranglehold but the moment he was free, a flying fist connected with his cheek. He punched back, heard and felt the sound of crunching bone, pulled his elbow back to throw another but something as hard as granite attached itself like a vice to his wrist, rendering it immobile.

It was Felipe's hand.

Anyone else and Matteo would have been able to throw them off but Felipe was ex–Special Forces and knew how to use his body as both a weapon and a shield.

'What the hell are you two playing at?' he blazed before saying over his shoulder, 'If you take another step, Daniele, I will knock you out myself.'

But Daniele was already dusting himself down, staring at Matteo with pure loathing, seemingly oblivious to the blood pouring from his nose.

Breathing heavily, trying to get air into his winded lungs, Matteo stared back at the man who'd treated him like a brother, and heard himself say, 'She's having my baby.'

Daniele took a step back, his face contorted, then raised his hand. 'Don't say another word. Don't ever speak to me again. You are no cousin of mine. You're dead to me.'

In silence, Matteo and Felipe, who'd released his hold on him, watched Daniele stagger away and into the car that was supposed to take them all back to airport.

After too long a time had passed, Felipe said quietly, 'I'll get one of my men to collect us.'

'Thank you,' he muttered. 'You should go back to Pisa too. Francesca will need you.'

A meaty hand slapped him on the back in what he guessed was supposed to be a gesture of comfort before Felipe walked away to make the call.

Matteo knew he deserved no comfort and with another twist in his gut he remembered that at that moment Natasha was on a flight to Pisa, ignorant that the explosions they'd expected to deal with tomorrow had already detonated.

The jet Matteo had chartered for Natasha lacked the personal touch of his private jet but was still beautifully apportioned and the cabin crew were all brilliant people who couldn't do enough for her.

So soothing did she find the flight that after a good lunch shortly after take-off, she found her eyes getting heavy and went to sleep. After a four-hour nap she woke to find a dozen missed calls from Matteo but no message.

Cold dread coiled in her belly.

She called him back but reached his own voicemail and had to wait for an hour in nerve-shredding silence before her phone rang again.

'What's wrong?' she asked as soon as the phone was to her ear.

'They know about us.'

The line was terrible, the crackle of interference making it hard to hear. She put a finger to her other ear to try and drown out the background noise of her own flight. *'What?'*

'They know. The paparazzi took a shot of us when we went for lunch at Miami Beach.'

She whistled lowly and rocked forward, coldness filling her head.

They couldn't know. Not like this. Oh, this was awful. 'Natasha?'

'I'm still here.' A loud burst of interference crackled over the line. 'Matteo?'

'Listen to me,' he said, his voice raised, his tone clipped. 'Wait for me at the airport. Don't go anywhere. I'll be landing soon after you. Just wait.'

And then the line went dead.

Scrambling through her phone, a quick search found the pictures Matteo must have been talking about. The headline would have made her laugh if she didn't think she was going to be sick. 'Dr Dishy Serves Icy Treat to New Love.'

Her name wasn't mentioned, which was one small mercy, and her face was mostly hidden. But anyone who knew her well would recognise her. Her family. Pieta's family. They would all know it was her smiling mouth Matteo was wiping the ice cream from and her lips he was kissing.

She'd known that telling Pieta's family would be difficult, especially the part about the pregnancy. She'd known it would be even more difficult for them to hear it. The last thing she'd wanted them to think was that she and Matteo had embarked on a carefree affair with no consideration for the man they'd just buried. These pictures... It could only be worse if they'd been pictured dancing on Pieta's grave.

If there had ever been any hope of forgiveness these pictures had ended it.

Natasha had bitten her nails as a child, a habit finally broken by her mother smearing strong mustard over them. If she had still been biting them then by the time her plane landed she was certain there would be nothing left of them.

They landed in the early morning, the sun only just waking in the frigid cloudless sky.

Coming from the balmy heat of Miami, the dramatic change in temperature was a shock to her system and she was glad of Matteo's reminder to take something warm to change into for her arrival.

Once she'd cleared security she found a seat with a good view of all arrivals and waited.

An hour later he appeared.

Covering her mouth in horror, she got to her feet.

Impeccably dressed as always, in a dark grey suit covered with a lamb's wool overcoat, it didn't detract from his red cheekbone and puffy eye.

She went straight into his arms and held him tightly before tilting her head to look at him more closely. 'What happened?'

'Daniele.'

She closed her eyes and buried her head in his chest, felt his own arms wrap around her and hold her just as tight. 'I'm so sorry,' she whispered.

'So am I.' He rested his mouth on the top of her head, his warm breath swirling through her hair. 'Did you see the pictures?'

'Yes. I had no idea they were being taken.'

'Neither did I.'

'Your poor face.'

Unwrapping his arms from her, he took her face in his hands. 'It looks worse than it is. I think I've broken his nose.'

She turned her cheek to kiss his palm. 'Is he okay?'

'He will be.'

'What do we do now?'

'Now we go back to your house and get some sleep.' That had always been the plan. Natasha needed to pack the last of her stuff and deal with lawyers and all the other things needed to make a clean break.

'Shall we still go and see them later?'

His face tightened. 'Francesca messaged me. They don't want to see us.'

Her message had been emphatic, Matteo recalled, his lungs tightening.

He'd known from the second Natasha had appeared white-faced at the door with the pregnancy test in his hand that he was going to lose his family but he hadn't known how deeply the wound would cut...

He blinked, surprised at his own thoughts.

How had he known that when he'd managed to convince himself for two weeks that the chances of him being the father were negligible?

But you did know. You knew in your heart that you were the father.

Kissing her mouth, he rubbed his nose to hers. 'We're both exhausted. Things will seem better once we've slept.'

Just having Natasha back in his arms already soothed a little of the pain.

CHAPTER ELEVEN

THE HOUSE HAD A COLD, unlived-in feeling that Matteo felt as soon as he closed the front door behind them.

Past the reception room, they went into the day room. The antique bureau in the corner was piled high with post.

'Are you okay?' he asked, rubbing Natasha's back. There had been visible apprehension on her face when they'd pulled up outside the house and now she seemed to have withdrawn into herself.

She looked at him and nodded, her smile rueful. 'It feels strange being back here.'

'Not what you expected?'

She rubbed her arms. 'It feels like I never lived here.' Then she blinked and seemingly snapped herself out of the melancholy. 'I'm going to make a hot chocolate before we go to bed. Do you want one?'

'Hot chocolate sounds good to me.'

She disappeared into the kitchen, leaving him to look around the gleamingly magnificent room. He recalled her saying once that everything here was Pieta's, remembered his own impression of the house that it had all seemed to match Pieta's personality.

There was nothing here of Natasha. His own house in Miami...it was like she'd imprinted herself into the walls. She fitted.

She didn't fit here. She didn't belong here.

This house was like a museum for antiquities.

He brushed his fingers over the surface of the bureau and as he wondered what century it was from, the postmark of the top envelope in the pile of post caught his eye.

Taking hold of it, he looked more closely, trying to comprehend why there should be a letter addressed to Mr and Mrs Pellegrini from Paris's leading fertility clinic. It was postmarked two days before Pieta's death, and from all the marks and stamps on it had been forwarded in recent weeks from Pieta's apartment in Paris.

'I hope you didn't want sugar added to yours,' she said, coming back into the room.

He spun round to find her carrying two steaming mugs, which she carefully placed on coasters on the antique coffee table.

'What's this?' he said.

'What's what?' She took the envelope from him, her hands stilling when she too noticed the postmark and the name of the clinic it had been sent from.

'Aren't you going to open it?'

She looked up at him, the colour draining from her face. There was definite apprehension in her eyes.

'Open the letter,' he commanded.

Still she didn't move, the apprehension now replaced with a hint of fear.

Snatching it from her hand, Matteo ripped the envelope open. Inside were two sheets of paper. He gave one sharp shake to unfurl them, and began to read.

He had to read them three times and even then it still didn't make sense.

'You were going to have fertility treatment?'

Her throat moved and her lips parted but no sound came out.

He held the first sheet up for her to see. 'This is a letter confirming an appointment in the New Year for you to begin fertility treatment and this...' he held the second sheet up '...is the confirmed price list. The letter also confirms that Pieta's sperm test results came back as normal.'

And still she didn't say anything, her eyes huge with an expression he recognised.

It had been the look she'd given him all that time ago when he'd asked the last time she and Pieta had been intimate together. It was the look she gave when she was trying to think of an answer when the truth should simply fall from her tongue.

He rubbed his hand over his head, trying to dull the thuds pounding in it. 'Why were you going the IVF route to conceive a child? This letter confirms Pieta's fertility and we both know you're fertile. You were only married for a year. Pieta himself told me you two only started trying after your wedding—that's too short a time to start thinking you might have fertility issues...'

He checked himself and blew a puff of air out. None of this made sense. None of it.

'Natasha, I need you to be honest with me. Why would a young married couple without any fertility issues like you and Pieta put yourselves through the quagmire that is IVF?'

Her features had clenched so tightly she looked as if she could snap.

'I can't tell you,' she whispered, her head shaking with increasing violence.

If she had simply turned around and said they had both been too impatient to try any longer without intervention he could have possibly accepted that. But she hadn't and her answer made his stomach lurch to his feet.

'If I mean anything to you, if our *child* means anything to you, then you *must*. I deserve to know the truth.'

The colour that had faded from her came back with a vengeance, staining her cheeks, but there was also a sudden calmness about her as if she'd decided to stop fighting the demons and confront them instead.

'If I tell you, you can't tell anyone.'

'What?'

'This is important. You have to promise me.'

A big warning light was flashing, telling him to drop it, telling him it wasn't too late to just stop this conversation and go to bed, that whatever had happened in her marriage to his cousin was none of his business.

But he couldn't listen to it. The nagging feeling about their marriage had become as loud as the siren playing and now, with the door to it prised open, all he needed was to push and the truth would be revealed.

'If that's what it takes to get the truth from you then, yes, I give you my word.'

She raised her chin and looked him square in the eyes. Then she cleared her throat and said, 'Pieta was gay.'

Matteo's first instinct was to laugh. It ripped out of him, echoing off the walls, and then soaked into the silence.

As if Pieta had been gay. It wasn't possible. He'd known him all his life, for thirty-five years. They'd been best friends, cousins, brothers... If Pieta had been gay then the moon really was made of cheese.

Natasha hadn't moved. There wasn't the hint of a smile on her face.

His laughter died as abruptly as it had begun.

'You're lying.'

'No,' she said softly, compassion in her eyes and in her voice. 'I'm not. I'm sorry but *he* lied. To all of you. He was gay.'

'I don't believe you,' he said flatly. 'I don't know why you would tell such lies but it's—'

'I'm not lying,' she cut in. 'We couldn't conceive naturally. He couldn't do it with me.'

It was the way her voice caught when she said, *he couldn't do it with me* and the bleakness in her eyes that made him wonder...

No. She couldn't be telling the truth. He would have known.

Feeling his legs could collapse beneath him, he sank onto the nearest armchair and rubbed again at his head. 'If—and I'm not saying I believe you—but *if* Pieta was gay, why didn't he tell anyone? Why the charade of pretending to be something he's not?'

While Matteo could feel the fabric of his life crumbling around him, Natasha seemed to grow stronger, compassion almost glowing out of her skin.

'Because he knew from before he could talk that he had to marry. It was drilled into him his entire life. It was in the terms of the trust for the Pellegrini estate. You know what it says and it's been the same for hundreds of years—the eldest son inherits but only if he's married. He could never admit who he was. He didn't admit it to himself until he was in his early twenties. He'd been groomed since birth to be the heir and it was a responsibility he took very seriously.'

'And you knew this?'

She shook her head and slumped onto the armchair close to his. 'Not until we got married. He wanted to wait until our wedding before we became physical with each other. I thought he was old-fashioned...'

'Wait, you had no intimacy until you were *married*? You were engaged for six years.'

'We kissed but nothing more.'

'And that didn't set alarm bells ringing?'

'It should have done but, to be honest, it was a relief.' She grimaced. 'He was a gorgeous man but I never felt proper attraction to him, not like I always felt for you. I always hoped that when it came to it, something would switch on inside me. Maybe it would have. I don't know. I was a virgin. I didn't know what I should be feeling…well, I had an idea, of course I did, but… In the end it didn't matter. He couldn't do it.' She inhaled and looked at the ceiling. 'It was painful and embarrassing for both of us but more so for him. I was the first failure in his life.'

Not once in the past seven years had Matteo allowed himself to imagine them in bed together. Now he felt he could easily vomit.

His cousin, his best friend, had lied to him for ever.

And she had lied too.

Dio, after everything they had been through, she'd been lying to him when she knew how important honesty was to him, when she knew how hard it had been for him to trust her again.

'Why didn't you tell me?' he asked roughly.

Her eyes found his, her expression unwavering. 'I was protecting you.'

Anger bubbled like lava so strongly in his veins that he couldn't even speak.

She'd been protecting him? That was the excuse she was going to use to negate her lies?

She took a cushion and pressed it protectively to her belly, as if trying to muffle their voices from their developing child's ears. 'I had to keep the truth about him to myself. I knew it would devastate you. You, his mother, his siblings…you all loved him. Francesca idolised him. How do you think they would feel if they knew the truth?'

'What, that he was nothing but a liar?'

'Exactly that, yes. He kept the most fundamental part of himself a secret. If they learned that now…can you imagine it? If they learned he had never trusted them enough to tell them the truth about himself? When I learned the truth it almost destroyed me. I gave everything up for him. You. A career. Even my own thoughts. Everything I'd believed about him, all my hopes for the future…all destroyed. How could I put them through that? How could I put *you* through that?'

Matteo concentrated on breathing, refusing to look at her deceitful face a moment longer.

How did that old saying go? Fool me once, shame on you; fool me twice, shame on me.

Well, Natasha had fooled him twice. The first time he could forgive himself for.

This time he should have known better.

'Answer me this,' he said, keeping his voice under control by a hair's breadth. 'If Pieta *destroyed* you, why didn't you leave him?'

'Where would I have gone? Back to my parents who'd manipulated me into the mess? I had nowhere to go, no money, no job. He'd seen to that. He'd even sold my apartment so I couldn't go back there. I'd been in Pieta's power and at his beck and call for so long that I couldn't see a way out.'

Natasha closed her eyes. The pain and anger vibrating from Matteo tore at her heart. To learn the man he'd regarded as a brother had been a manipulative bastard and a liar could not be an easy thing to accept. This was everything she'd been trying to protect him from.

'Why the hell did you agree to have a baby with him? Why agree to embark on something as physically painful as IVF for a man you hate?'

'He offered me a child in exchange for my freedom...'

'*What*? And you agreed to that?'

She could almost taste the disgust in his voice.

'No! Please, Matteo, I know you're upset...'

'Right now I am feeling many things but *upset* is not one of them.'

'I understand, I really do—I've been there. Why do you think I chose to keep it a secret? I didn't want to destroy your memories of him, especially when he's not here to justify or defend himself, but please, let me finish.'

'Go ahead. Finish your justification of how you would even *think* of bringing a baby into a relationship like that.'

'It took him months to make me even consider it. He made me many promises; that he would divorce me when the law allowed, that I would have primary custody, that he would buy a house for me and our baby to live in and put it in my name, all sorts of promises.'

'And you believed that after all the lies he'd already told you?' he sneered.

'Things changed between us. The truth being out in the open meant there was nothing left to hide. I knew I would never have another relationship—after what he'd done to me, how could I trust another man?—and I still wanted a baby, very much, so in the end I decided there could be no harm in going to the fertility clinic to discuss what it entailed. That was a week before he died.'

'So you *had* decided to go ahead with it.'

'No.' A wave of sadness flooded through her veins. 'When we got back to Pisa, he was so smug about it all. He took it to be a foregone conclusion that I'd agreed. I realised then that nothing had changed. He still thought he could manipulate me. I could never have trusted his promises.'

'How did he take it when you told him?'

'I never got the chance. The hurricane in Caballeros struck and he went into full-blown humanitarian mode, which for Pieta meant working around the clock with his foundation.' She looked at him, wishing he would meet her eyes. 'And I'm glad of it. I'm glad he died thinking we would have a baby together. I'm glad he died happy.'

With a sigh that could have been a groan, Matteo put his head back and closed his eyes, breathing heavily.

Sliding off the armchair, she knelt by him and put her hands on his thighs. His only reaction was to clench his jaw.

It hurt more than she could decipher to see the pain on his face.

Gently, wanting to take as much of the sting away as she could, she said, 'I know none of this is easy but he kept only one part of himself from you, nothing else. He was still a brilliant lawyer and humanitarian. He was still the man you played late-night poker with over a bottle of bourbon. He was still the man who supported you and was there for you when things became so intolerable in your home that you moved in with his family. Please, don't forget that. None of that was a lie.'

'Do *not* defend him to me.'

'I'm not.' She covered his hand that had clenched in a fist. 'He was a manipulative bastard but that doesn't take away the good things about him. It's not black and white. He was still human. In the end I came to feel sorry for him.'

His burst of laughter was guttural and bitter. 'He dangled you on a string for seven years and trapped you into a farce of a marriage and you felt sorry for him?'

'He trapped me, yes, but he was trapped too. He couldn't be with the man he loved. He'd trapped himself so tightly he could never be free to live his life as nature intended for him to live it.'

He moved his fist from under her hand and pressed his fingers into his forehead. 'I was your first, wasn't I?'

With a sigh she bowed her head. 'Yes.'

'A part of me knew that. I sensed it. I knew... I knew but I couldn't believe because I didn't see how it could be possible.' His fingers moved up to knead into his scalp, his knuckles white under the pressure. 'You let me believe he could be the father of our child.'

His eyes snapped open and met hers. There was a cold steeliness in them that sent shivers racing up her spine.

'I'm sorry,' she whispered.

'"I'm sorry,"' he mimicked. Then, before she could blink, his face twisted and he leapt to his feet. In quick strides he was at the fireplace where a row of antique English pottery sat on display. Swiping his arm across it, he sent them all smashing to the floor.

'*Sorry* does not make things all right,' he snarled. 'You have had weeks, *months,* to tell me the truth.'

Ripping an old oil painting off the wall, he slammed it on the bureau so hard it split, then swiped it over the large pile of post, sending envelopes fluttering in all directions.

'I never lied to you...'

'You were covering his deceit!'

'No, that wasn't it at all,' she implored, getting to her

feet and holding onto the armchair to keep her shaking legs upright. She'd known he would react badly but it was still incredibly painful to witness his anguish. 'I wanted to tell you the truth, I really did, but I couldn't destroy your memories of him.'

'It's my memories of *you* that have been destroyed!' The lava in his veins erupting all over again, Matteo snatched a still full mug of hot chocolate and hurled it at the far wall. 'Everything we've shared has been a lie.'

'It hasn't,' she beseeched.

'You were a virgin! I have lived with the guilt of us making love on the night of his funeral, the guilt of you having my baby, the guilt of what our baby would do to my family... You have let me live with this guilt when you should have told me the truth after you'd done the pregnancy test...'

'I had a choice to make and I made the one I thought was right. I did what I thought was best...'

'You did what you thought was best for *you*, just as you've always done.'

'How can you *say* that? If I'd ever done what I thought was best for me I would have defied my parents and turned Pieta down. I would have married you.'

'Don't flatter yourself,' he scorned tightly. 'I would have seen through you before it ever got that far. You're a liar. You were a liar then and you're a liar now, but you're too clever to lie outright—you lie by omission because you're too spineless to tell the truth.'

She flinched as if he'd slapped her.

Matteo looked away, hating that his first instinct was to haul her into his arms and apologise.

How could he have been such a fool as to trust her again?

He took in the devastation he'd just wrought, the

shattered pottery and crockery littering the floor, along with the dozens and dozens of unopened letters, the cream wall now splattered with hot chocolate, and felt as winded as he had when Daniele had slammed him into the hospital wall.

He staggered back and propped himself against the bureau.

'You're right,' she said, speaking softly but standing tall, breaking the silence shrouding them. 'I've always been spineless. I've always thought there was something wrong with me. I've never been able to please my parents—I always failed them in some way. I couldn't even make a cup of tea correctly, it was always too strong or too milky. I loved to ride horses when I was young. I won a gymkhana when I was eleven and do you know what they said? Not congratulations like any other parent would have, but that my posture had been off. It was all those little things that wrecked my confidence.

'Pieta was this brilliant man and I was in utter awe of him, and once I'd committed to marrying him I deferred to his wishes, just as I'd always deferred to my parents.' I let him dictate everything because I wanted to please him like I always wanted to please them. He *did* keep me dangling on a string but I have to face the fact that I let him. Then I discovered he was gay...' She sucked in a breath, looking as if she could be sick. 'What did that say about me? A gay man who didn't feel even a twinge of desire for me chose to marry me.'

'He chose you because you were a virgin and would have no one to compare him to,' Matteo said flatly.

'Yes. I see that now. I believe that now because of you.' She swallowed and made a move towards him, then checked herself midstep. 'You are the only person in the whole world who has ever made me feel that I'm good enough exactly as I am. I never thought I could trust another man after what Pieta did to me but there you were, where you'd always been, in my heart. You encourage me. You listen to me. You respect my opinions. You make me feel I could be anything I want to be. You let me be *me*.'

A tiny choking sound came from her throat, a tear spilling out of her eye, but she didn't seem to notice. 'I wish now that I'd told you the truth about Pieta and our marriage when the test came up as positive but I truly did think I was doing the right thing. I wasn't lying by omission. I was protecting you because you loved Pieta and I loved you. I've always loved you. I just wish it hadn't taken me so long to see it. I wish I could go back in time and phone you or email or send a carrier pigeon asking for your help when Pieta first proposed. I wish I'd had the courage then that I have now to fix the mess for myself without thinking I needed your help. I regret so many things but that one is my biggest.'

Matteo's listened to her justification with a chest that steadily compacted on itself and solidified. Almost as if they had a will of their own, his feet moved towards her and his hand reached out to touch her cheek. He brushed the tear away and brought his face close to hers, looking deep into her eyes so she would see as well as hear his every word.

'I understand why you chose Pieta over me,' he said quietly. 'I can see that I should have known from the way you kissed me in the *castello* that night that your feelings for me were true. I should have fought for you. I shouldn't have blocked you and cut all communication between us. I accept the blame I bear for that. It's been hard getting over my distrust and loathing of you these past few months but I did get past it and I learned to trust you again.'

A flare of hope flashed in her returning stare but quickly dampened to trepidation, as if she could read his mind and knew what he was about to say.

He brushed his thumb over her mouth, knowing it would be the last time he ever touched her lips. 'And that was my greatest mistake. I should never have trusted you. I have been living with guilt since our first night together and you could have stopped it. You have let me believe so many lies when you know I cannot bear lies.

'The only thing I have ever asked of you is honesty. You know how much I hated myself for the lies we were going to tell about our child's conception...you were going to make *me* a liar when, if you'd only told me the truth, we could have found a better, more truthful way. When I think of everything we've shared and to think you were keeping this from me...it makes me sick to my stomach. You had so many opportunities to confide in me but you chose not to. You made me trust you again. You chose to let me live with the guilt and for me to keep believing the lies until I dragged the truth out of you.'

'I wanted to tell you but I couldn't,' she whispered.

'What you wanted doesn't mean anything. It's what you did that counts. Your actions. You say you love me but I have to tell you, *bella*, you could say the sky was blue and I'd have to go outside to check for myself. I will never believe another word that falls from your pretty lips. My instincts to cut all communication with you back when you accepted Pieta's proposal have been proven right. I was a fool to trust you again.'

More hot tears fell down her cheek and spilled onto his thumb.

'It had been playing in my mind to ask you to marry

me in the future but now I would rather marry the Medusa than spend another minute with you. The Medusa turned men into stone but you've turned my heart into it.'

'You don't mean that.' Her words were barely audible.

'Oh, but I do. The only contact I will ever want with you will be about our baby.' Dropping his hand from her face, unable to look at her another moment longer, he turned around and headed to the door.

He'd stepped outside—when had it become full daylight?—when she caught up with him and grabbed hold of his arm, forcing him round to face her.

'Don't tell me you're just going to walk away?' The tears that only moments ago had streamed like a waterfall down her face had been wiped away, although fresh tears still glistened.

They didn't spill, though.

'Were you not listening to me? Did I not explain myself clearly enough?'

'You explained yourself perfectly well but that doesn't mean you can just walk away. I've screwed up, I know I have, but we can get through this. What we have is too special to—'

'No, *bella*, what we *had* was special, but like your marriage it was a lie.'

'No, it wasn't and you can't pretend it was. I held back the truth about Pieta but I didn't lie to you. Everything we shared, you and me, that was real and you know it was. I love you and I know you have feelings for me too.' Another tear escaped but she didn't crumple. She kept her grip on his arm, her wet eyes boring at him. 'Please, Matteo, don't leave like this. Don't leave us.'

He had to force himself to remain unmoved. Natasha was the greatest liar he'd ever met. How could he believe anything she said or did again? 'Us?'

'We're having a baby…'

'You think I would leave our child?' he almost spat. 'Let me make this very clear, it's *you* I'm walking away from, not our baby. You should know better than anyone that I would never abandon my own child. I would never do what my parents did to me.'

'Then *stay*. Fight. I know you hate me right now but with a little time we *can* get through this. We're so good together. Our baby deserves to have both of us…'

'I agree.' Covering the hand holding his arm so tightly, he prised her fingers off, but before letting them go he brought his face down close to hers. 'And our baby *will* have both of us. But not together. I will never trust you again, and without that trust you and I have *nothing*.'

And then he let go of her fingers and walked down the steps to the path and to his waiting car.

'You let me go without a fight before, are you really going to do the same again?' she said, not shouting but with a timbre in her voice that made him pause.

He inhaled a breath and clicked his key fob.

'You say I'm spineless but you're the spineless one if you can walk away from something so special.'

He opened the door.

'Go, then.' Her voice had turned to steel with none of the softness his heart always melted for. 'But if you drive away now that's it for us. If you drive away now you can only come back for our child because I won't wait for you. If you're too spineless to stay and fight for us I will not put my life on hold for you. If you drive away then you and I are over for good.'

He got into the car and started the engine.

Numb to his core, he drove away. Before he turned out of her street, he looked in his rear-view mirror. The street was empty.

CHAPTER TWELVE

NATASHA SNATCHED UP her vibrating phone. When she saw it was her father, she didn't hesitate to decline the call. About to throw it back on the table, she stopped herself and took a deep breath.

She couldn't avoid her parents for ever. Between them they'd left over a dozen messages. If she didn't respond soon, they'd get a plane over to Pisa and turn up on her doorstep.

She spent a few minutes trying to get her brain to focus on what she needed to say and then composed a short message confirming that, yes, it was true she was pregnant and, yes, it was true the father of her child was Matteo Manaserro and not her late husband. No, she wouldn't be marrying Matteo. She signed off by confirming she would not be taking any monies from Pieta's estate.

Once the message was sent she breathed a sigh of relief.

Whatever she did next would be wrong in their eyes.

She'd spent twenty-five years trying to please them. Finally, she'd accepted she never would. And finally she found she no longer cared to try.

She wondered fleetingly if they would have the audacity to tap Matteo up for money. If they did she could well imagine the reception they would receive for their efforts.

Her phone vibrated again. This time it was one of the journalists she'd contacted about publicity for Pieta's memorial hospital in Caballeros. She declined the call, knowing she should just turn her phone off. The only people she wanted to hear from were the only ones who hadn't been in contact.

She wished they would, even if only to scream and shout at her. The silence was unbearable. Neither Vanessa nor Francesca would answer her calls. She'd gone to Vanessa's villa but had been turned away by the housekeeper.

Natasha's affair with Matteo was headline news in Italy. The great Pieta Pellegrini's widow falling straight into the arms of his equally rich and famous cousin was too juicy a story to ignore. Luck had finally been on her side—they'd only discovered her identity the day after she'd moved into a new house. Three weeks later she and her new home remained off the media's radar.

Two days after Matteo had driven out of her life, she'd walked the streets of Pisa looking for a job and a cheap place to live. She hadn't wanted to stay in Pieta's house a day longer than necessary. It was the focus she'd needed to carry on. She had a child to think about and refused to cry and wallow in self-pity. What kind of example would that set? No, the only way she could help her situation was by taking control of it and setting out as she meant to go on.

She'd found herself a job in a coffee shop within an hour. She hadn't had as much luck with a cheap home but that problem had resolved itself when she'd returned to the house to find a note pushed through the front door and a set of keys.

It had been from Matteo.

In the space of two days he'd bought a house for her

to live in. The note had made clear it was for their baby's benefit and not her own. When the baby was born he would put the deeds to it in its name. He'd also arranged regular maintenance payments effective immediately.

As much as her pride wanted to throw both the house and the maintenance back in his face, she'd resisted. Her baby deserved a decent place to live. Her new job would keep her going until the baby was born. She wouldn't spend a penny of the maintenance money on herself but her baby had a rich father and it wasn't fair to deprive it out of pride. She wouldn't take anything from him for her own benefit.

She'd hardened herself to him completely. If she was so disposable that he could walk away without a second thought, for a second time, then he didn't deserve her tears. That he visited her every night in her dreams was something she had no control over and something she refused to dwell on. It was safer that way. She needed to keep healthy, emotionally and physically, for her baby's sake. Their baby was their only reason for communication now, a few terse messages exchanged about appointments and scans and their baby's health. She knew she wouldn't see him again until the next scan in the new year. She stubbornly told herself that suited her fine.

But she couldn't harden herself to Vanessa and Francesca. Matteo had kept his promise and kept the truth about Pieta to himself so at least they'd been spared that truth.

Their reaction was nothing she hadn't prepared herself for but it still hurt. A small part of her had hoped they would forgive her. A large part of her still prayed they would.

She hoped they'd come to forgive Matteo too, then chided herself for thinking about him again.

And now, looking out onto the street from the dining room of the house paid for by his money and seeing Christmas lights twinkling from the houses across the road, knowing she was going to spend her first ever Christmas alone, she had to keep reminding herself why losing everyone she loved was for the best.

Matteo rummaged through the minibar of his hotel suite but couldn't find the brand of bourbon he preferred to drink.

About to put a call through to room service, he was interrupted by a knock on his door.

Wondering who the hell could be calling at this time of night, he walked the long length of the living area of his suite to the door. If the alcohol he'd consumed that night had done the job as well as he'd hoped, he'd be asleep by now.

He'd drunk steadily all night in the restaurant he'd taken his clinic staff in Florence to, their turn for him to grace their presence at their annual Christmas party. He'd seriously considered cancelling but knew it would result in a huge blow to morale. Tomorrow, Christmas Eve, he would fly to his apartment in New York and pretend to enjoy the festivities alone.

He couldn't even contemplate spending Christmas in Miami.

He was sick of travelling. He was sick of every place he visited reminding him in some way of Natasha, even countries that didn't have the slightest shred of a link with her. He was sick of the paparazzi following his every move.

From utilising the press shamelessly for publicity to promote his business, he now wanted to obliterate every journalist and paparazzo from the face of the earth.

He wished he'd been so lucky in obliterating Florence from the face of his schedule. Knowing Natasha was barely fifty miles away made it much harder to obliterate her from his mind. This was the city she'd had the scan in and he'd learned he really was going to be a father.

But he *had* already known it in his gut, his conscience insisted on reminding him. He'd known it from the second she'd appeared white-faced at the door with the positive pregnancy test in her hand, and had refused to acknowledge it for fear of what the truth would reveal.

He put his eye to the spy hole and stepped back in shock. Maybe the alcohol had worked better than he'd thought.

He took another look. No, there was his cousin Francesca and her fiancé, Felipe.

Apart from one phone call in which she had called him every name under the sun, Francesca had cut him out of her life, just as Vanessa and Daniele had done. Was this the moment his hot-headed cousin had talked her fiancé into beating him up?

Taking a deep breath first, he pulled the door open a couple of inches.

There were no kicks to batter the door in and neither was there any of the expected acrimony on her face. After a moment of awkward silence, she gave a tentative smile. 'Can we come in?'

He pulled the door open to admit them, bracing himself for a punch in the ribs. But as they stepped into his suite he saw the puffy redness of her eyes.

'What's happened?' he asked, concern immediately filling him.

Felipe shut the door behind them as Francesca said, 'Haven't you seen the news today?'

'I've been avoiding the media.' No papers, no magazines and no internet. He didn't need to read the world's opinion of him. None of it could be worse than his own opinion, which had been getting steadily worse, although he couldn't understand why.

Blinking back tears, she handed him a newspaper that had been tucked under her arm.

He took it from her. Before he opened it he knew what it was going to say.

His instincts were right.

Pieta's secret was a secret no more.

'I'll get us all a drink,' Felipe murmured, while Francesca flopped onto the nearest armchair and wiped away a tear.

'Is it true?' she asked him, her eyes pleading with him to deny it, to say that Alberto, Pieta's right hand man for his foundation, the man now purporting to have been his secret lover for over ten years, was a liar.

He dimly recalled Natasha saying Pieta hadn't been free to be with the man he loved. At the time his head had been reeling too much with the magnitude of everything else she'd said to take that in too.

Taking the seat opposite Francesca, wishing he wasn't about to confirm something that was going to break her heart, he nodded.

'How…?'

'Natasha told me.' Just saying her name hurt.

Francesca's face went white as Felipe appeared at her side. She snatched the glass of liquid from his hand and downed it without looking at it or asking what it was.

She pulled the face of a woman with a burning throat then blew out a long puff of air. 'Oh, my God. She knew. Poor Natasha.' She began to cry in earnest. 'Why didn't he tell us? How could he keep such a thing secret? Did he think we wouldn't love him any more? Or didn't he love us enough to tell us? Didn't he trust us?' Then she leaned into Felipe, who'd handed Matteo a measure of Scotch too before squashing himself onto the single arm-chair with her, and sobbed into his chest.

Felipe's steady gaze met his. *No lies*, his look said.

There would be no lies from his lips.

It suddenly struck him that his promise to Natasha meant he was now guilty of lies by omission too.

He would have kept that secret without making the promise.

If Alberto hadn't sold his story, he would have taken Pieta's secret to the grave, not for his sake but for Fran-cesca and Vanessa's. Just as Natasha would have done.

Some hours later, when Francesca and Felipe had left, Matteo sat slumped in his hotel room's armchair and stared at the thick carpet.

He'd never been as mentally drained or as emotion-ally shattered in his life.

But it wasn't the talk of all the secrets and lies his head was full of, it was Natasha.

She'd been with him every minute since he'd left her but saying her name out loud seemed to have opened a sluice in his brain and now he found she was all he could think of. He couldn't rid himself of the urge to call her.

He'd had this urge before, when Roberto had died, a need to hear the soft calming voice that had always had the power to make him feel better. He'd gone into medicine to heal people but in Natasha he'd found the one person who could heal *him*.

He dragged a hand over his face and fought for breath.

He'd thought everything was so clear but it wasn't. He'd been swimming in the fog and now the fog was clearing and his entire life was flashing before him like a reel playing in his head. The happy early childhood ripped apart by the fire, the withdrawal of his parents' affection, the guilt over his brother that had only eased when he'd found the one special person in his life who fully believed in him and who he'd refused to fight for...

Why had that been?

On and on it ran; qualifying as a surgeon, his brother's shame at his scars and refusal to leave the house, his brother's death, his father's venomous words and hatred, changing his name to spite him, creating his empire, every hollow success, Pieta's death, his child's conception, everything forging together into a circle bound by the soft glow of the woman he'd let back into his heart, the woman who'd sucked up all the guilt and fixed all his broken parts without him even realising...

He thought of Pieta and Alberto having to hide and deny their love.

Even if Pieta had found the courage needed to be open and grab the happiness that could have been theirs, death had taken it away from them.

It hit him like a punch in the gut. What he'd done. What his pride and terrified heart had done.

He too had had a chance of happiness.

Natasha had bared her heart and her soul to him and instead of embracing it he'd stamped on it.

She hadn't turned his heart into stone, she'd opened it and moved in.

And he'd thrown it blindly in her face without a backward glance.

Natasha switched the light on in the dark kitchen and filled the kettle. Her early shift at the coffee shop started in an hour and she needed to wake up.

Only a few weeks into her job and already she loved

it. Right then, it was perfect for her. When the baby was born she intended to pursue interior design but for the time being this was just what she needed. It gave her the chance to be with people. She liked seeing shoppers pile into the shop laden with gifts for their loved ones. She liked the smiles, the little conversations conducted in her hesitant Italian, which over the last couple of weeks had suddenly improved by leaps and bounds. She liked the anonymity—if anyone recognised her from the press reports they would dismiss it as an uncanny likeness. She liked the constant smell of fresh coffee. She liked everything about it. She especially liked the reassurance that she wasn't alone in the world. That there *was* a world out there beyond her parents and the Pellegrinis. And Matteo...

Blinking his image away, she reached for a mug, then noticed her phone left on the counter overnight was flashing.

In amazement, she saw she had thirty-three missed calls, forty-nine text messages and over one hundred new emails.

What the heck was going on?

She scanned the missed calls first but there was no number she recognised. It was the same with the text messages until she came to one sent by Alberto.

What she read sent her reeling.

I'm sorry it had to be this way. I couldn't let them trash your reputation any longer. Forgive me for the pain I've caused you.

Gathering her hair together at the nape of her neck, Natasha struggled to control her breathing. She'd avoided all media since her name had been exposed but a quick scan of the internet told her what the apology was for.

She found she couldn't be surprised at what she read. Pieta had once drunkenly confessed to one great love in his life but had refused to name him.

It made sense of the pity she'd often detected in Alberto's eyes when he'd spoken to her through the years. It made sense of his weeping, 'I'm sorry,' when he'd clung to her as she'd said goodbye to him at the wake.

Oh, Alberto, what have you done?

Guilt at his and Pieta's treatment of her had led him to out himself and their relationship. Now the whole world knew.

Now Vanessa and Francesca must know too.

Her eyes fuzzy, her heart sad, she put the phone on the table. She didn't want to read any more. She didn't want to feel that if only she could bounce off the satellites that sent all these calls and messages she would find Matteo and he would make everything better.

Matteo had made his choice and he'd chosen to live without her.

And then the tears she'd blocked for over three weeks burst open again and she laid her head on the table and wept, crying for the love she'd lost, for the love her husband had never allowed to be free and open, and for all the hearts that were breaking.

It was the rap on the front door that cut through her tears.

She hadn't had a single visitor since she'd moved in.

CHAPTER THIRTEEN

APPREHENSION SLOWING HER DOWN, Natasha walked to the door, pulled the chains off then unlocked it and opened the door a crack.

And there he stood. Matteo. On her doorstep, a thin layer of snow falling onto his dark hair and long overcoat.

She pushed the door open wider.

For a long time, nothing was said.

All she could hear was the sound of her frantically beating heart. All her eyes could see was him, as beautifully handsome as he'd been when she'd last seen him. His eyes were bloodshot, though, she noticed. And he needed a shave.

She only just stopped her hand reaching out to touch his face.

Heat rising on her cheeks, the memory of how she'd once given in to the same impulse when he'd turned up at her door the night of their child's conception and then the fresher memory of how he'd cold-heartedly driven away all playing like a concerto in her head, she spun around and headed back to the kitchen.

'What do you want?' she asked, trying to keep her voice civil. However much she wanted to punch him in the face, she had to remember it was his child growing in her belly.

'To make sure you're okay. Have you seen the news?'

'Yes.' She sat herself at the table and looked at him, not inviting him to sit, making sure to keep her features stony and not betray the swirl of emotions rushing through her to see him again.

'Can I sit down?'

'If you want.'

He took the chair on the far side of the kitchen table to her and rubbed at his temples.

'Late night, was it?' she asked in as uninterested tone as she could muster.

'I haven't been to bed yet.'

'Been out partying?'

He sighed. 'No, I haven't been partying. Would you mind if I made myself a coffee?'

'Not at all.'

He pushed his chair back. 'Where is it?'

'I don't have any. I have decaffeinated tea or herbal tea. Knock yourself out.'

'You're not going to make this easy for me, are you?'

'Make what easy? Just tell me what you came here for then you can go on your merry way. There's a coffee shop round the corner you can get your caffeine fix from.'

Matteo had known this visit to Natasha's was going to be hard. After the way they'd parted he hadn't expected her to make things easy for him and he couldn't blame her for it.

She'd laid her heart bare for him and he'd walked away from her.

'I haven't been to bed because I've been up all night, talking to Francesca.'

'Francesca? You've seen her?'

He nodded.

The stoniness on her beautiful face softened a fraction. 'How is she? She knows?'

'She knows.' He closed his eyes. 'She's devastated, just as you said she'd be.'

'And Vanessa?'

'I haven't seen her yet but Francesca and Felipe came to me after they'd been with her.' He swallowed the bile that had lodged in his throat. 'She's in a bad way. They went back to her villa after they left me.'

'And Daniele?'

'I don't know about him. He could be with them too for all I know. I don't imagine he's in a better state than they are.'

She covered her face with her hands and pushed them up to brush through her hair. 'They must be going through hell.'

What could he say to that? Everything Natasha had predicted had come true. She'd known the truth would rip them apart and it had.

The man they'd loved and idolised all his life had not only lied about his sexuality but Alberto's exposé had revealed the truth about his marriage too. They knew their son and brother had married Natasha on a lie so he could inherit the estate he'd so badly wanted.

All their illusions had crumpled in the dust.

To his surprise, Matteo had found himself defending Pieta to Francesca. 'Remember how he was with you,' he'd told her gently. 'Remember the brother who was always there to give you advice and who encouraged you to fulfil your dreams when your parents were set on a different life for you. It isn't black and white. He was still a human and he still loved you.'

They had been so similar to the words Natasha had

used to try and comfort him with that he'd almost choked saying them.

Natasha had kept silent about the lie to protect those she loved when, in truth, she'd been the one hurt the most by it. Pieta had lied to his family but it was Natasha he had lied to and used and diminished for seven years without an ounce of conscience. Matteo could have forgiven him for not confiding the truth about his sexuality—with distance he even understood why Pieta had felt the need to hide it—but he could never forgive him for what he'd done to Natasha. He'd stolen her life.

And he, Matteo, had condemned her for it.

Moving from his seat, he knelt before her, only now taking in the soft white robe she was wearing. She looked different from the last time he'd seen her. Fuller. She looked like a woman on the cusp of blooming with pregnancy.

Whether she would let him be there to witness the dazzling changes soon to come was something he couldn't guess. This was no longer the Natasha who had lived her life wishing only to please the people she loved. That Natasha was still there but with a tougher shell. She'd grown a steely resolve that he couldn't help but admire even though he knew it would make convincing her to take him back that much harder.

But he had to try. He'd let her go twice without fighting for her and if he didn't try now he would spend the rest of his life hating himself and filled with bitter regret.

He took the stiff hand that was on the table and wrapped his fingers around it.

She stilled, her jaw clenching, then inhaled deeply. She didn't look at him.

'When Francesca asked me if it was true about Pieta, I wanted so badly to lie to her and spare her the pain. I should never have condemned you for wanting to spare me and the others that pain, not for a second. I have been living with the truth for barely a month and it's been like a noose around my neck. You've been living with it for so long I can hardly believe it didn't crack out of you sooner. I condemned you for what I considered were your lies of omission when all along you were doing what you always do and protecting the people you love. You have the kindest, purest heart I have ever known and when you told me you loved me I should have got down on my knees as I am right now and thanked God himself for giving you to me.'

Her face changed slightly. The eyes that met his glistened, her breaths deepening, but her mouth stayed tightly pinched closed.

'Do you know what date it is? It's Christmas Eve. Exactly eight years ago I saw you for the first time and something happened in me…it was like you sang to me. I fell in love with you before I'd even heard your voice…'

Now her throat moved and she tried to pull her hand away but he clasped it gently with his other hand too, forming an envelope around it.

'You've always believed in me,' he continued, knowing this was his one and only chance to make things right and that his entire future depended on his next words. 'You've always seen something good in me that no one else could see but I never allowed myself to believe it. It wasn't just my parents who couldn't forgive me for Roberto—I couldn't forgive myself. I knew in my head that the blame wasn't with me but my heart never accepted it, and in my heart I felt I didn't deserve happiness. It was easy to accept you chose Pieta over me when my own parents couldn't stand to be in a room with me, rather than trust in my heart and fight for you because, *bella*, the issue wasn't my trust in you but my trust in myself—can you understand that?

'If I had trusted my heart I would have fought for you but my demons wouldn't let me. There was a part of me that felt I didn't deserve the happiness I knew we would have together. I think I was waiting for you to prove yourself a liar this time round so I could justify to myself how right I was in cutting you off all those years ago because I was too blind to see and accept the truth, not about Pieta but about you and me.'

Her throat moved again and she inched her head forward a little. 'I don't want to hear any more,' she whispered. 'It's too late.'

His heart constricted. 'Maybe it is too late for us. I have to hope that it's not, but if it is then I will respect your decision but, please, let me finish what I came here to say. Let me have that and then I will leave.'

Her eyes closed and she inhaled deeply through her nose.

Sliding his hand around her neck, he pressed his forehead to hers and breathed in the scent of her warm skin. 'I knew something was wrong the night we first made love. I knew in my heart that I was your first but I refused to believe what every nerve and sense in my body was telling me. I was scared of what the truth would reveal, so you see, *bella*, I'm the one who's really guilty of lies by omission because I was too scared to confront what my heart had already told me was the truth.'

She was rigid in his arms.

His chest filling, he pressed his lips to her forehead. 'I'm sorry for hurting you. I'm sorry for every cruel word and deed. I'm sorry for abandoning you. I'm sorry for never fighting for you. I'm sorry for doubting you and for allowing my foolish pride and insecurities to blind me. I wish to God that I'd had the courage to believe in you as much as you believed and trusted in me and I wish I'd had the sense to admit my love for you before I threw it all away.' He found her lips and kissed them with the same clinging desperation she had kissed him with all that time ago in his office. He'd known then, in his heart, that she loved him but had been too blind and untrusting in himself to see it.

And now he had to accept that it was too late.

He breathed her scent in one last time. 'I love you, Natasha. Always know that. If you can never be mine again, know I will always be yours. I will wait for you, for ever if that's what it takes. My heart will always belong to you and the precious life you carry inside you.'

When he pulled away he found her eyes closed and her pale face taut.

He released his hold on her hands and gently stroked her cheek. 'Goodbye, *bella*.'

Natasha knew by the coldness that suddenly enveloped her that Matteo was walking away.

There was a lightness in her limbs and her head, a balloon filled with something undefinable expanding in her chest.

His words reverberated in her ears as his footsteps became more distant.

So many words. So much meaning behind them. So much love and tenderness and pain.

She opened her eyes.

Everything looked different. What had only minutes ago seemed dark was now filled with dazzling light, the surfaces of the kitchen units gleaming, the table she was sitting at shining.

And that dazzling brilliance was in her too.

She looked at the oven clock. She was going to be late

for work, late for the job that had given her her pride and self-worth...

Matteo had already given her those things. She'd proved she could make it on her own. One day she might even be happy. But it was this wonderful man who had loved her and broken her heart who completed her and she knew with utter clarity that if she didn't swallow her new-found pride any future happiness would be stained. The bright colours evoked by his words now would fade to sepia. He was the one who brought colour to her life.

The balloon in her chest, which had been steadily growing bigger and bigger while Matteo had finally opened his heart, suddenly exploded and flooded her with the warmth she had never hoped to feel again.

He *did* love her. And he did trust her.

And then her mouth opened and she was screaming out his name, laughing and crying all at the same time, her unsteady legs racing to catch him.

But he caught her, in the small hallway by the front door, capturing her in his strong arms and holding her so tightly her feet left the floor.

'Don't you dare go,' she said, before finding his mouth and smothering it and his entire face with kisses. 'Don't you dare, don't you dare.'

It was a long time until he put her back down. He took her face in his hands and kissed her, before staring into her eyes, bewilderment and hope ringing from his. 'You want me to stay?'

She smiled her first real smile in so, so long. 'Only if you promise to stay for ever.'

The bleakness that had been etched on his face lifted, wonder taking its place. 'If you'll have me, I will stay with you for ever.'

She covered the hand palming her cheek. 'I will always be yours. I love you. I will always love you.'

He kissed her again, a kiss that conveyed more meaning than any words could. Into her mouth, he said, 'And I will always love you.'

With one final deep kiss, he lifted her into his arms and carried her up to the bedroom, where he proceeded to show her exactly how deep his love for her ran.

EPILOGUE

NATASHA STOOD UNDER the glorious late-summer sun at the entrance of the Pellegrini chapel at Castello Miniato and waited for the music that would cue her entrance to walk down the aisle. Holding tightly to her arm, as proud as punch to be the one giving her away, stood her brother-in-law Daniele, now the legal owner of the *castello* and who in approximately one hour would become her cousin by marriage.

Behind her, flapping the train of Natasha's wedding dress, was Francesca, taking her duties as chief bridesmaid with a little too much enthusiasm.

The music started and were it not for Francesca deliberately treading on the train to hold her back, Natasha would have galloped down the aisle. As far as she was concerned, she'd waited long enough to marry the man she loved, a man whose greatness had only increased in her eyes since he'd admitted his love for her. Matteo had sold his chain of vanity clinics to a hedge fund manager for an obscene amount of money.

When they returned from their honeymoon he would be opening a new type of clinic in Miami, a specialist hospital dedicated to performing surgery on the most severely disfigured people, adults and children alike. He would be funding the building and running costs and staff wages himself. It would be the first of what he planned to be many such specialist hospitals. Natasha would be in charge of the interior design, her brief to make it as homely and comforting as a hospital could be.

Forcing herself to walk sedately, she put one foot in front of the other and beamed her way towards Matteo. By his side stood Felipe, his best man, who, naturally, didn't look once at her as his eyes were too busy fixing on his wife. The Lorenzis had beaten them down the aisle by four months.

She smiled at her parents, sitting in the second row, and wondered if they'd asked Matteo for more money yet. She couldn't find it in her heart to hate them. They might be contenders for worst parents in the world, but they were *her* worst parents in the world and she looked on them as an example of how not to parent her own child. As she and Matteo lived in Miami and her parents were perpetually skint despite the regular large deposits Matteo transferred into their account, she rarely saw them. It was no loss, just as Matteo no longer felt the loss of his own parents. They'd created such a tight family unit of their own they had no need to wish for things that could never be.

The squeals of a bored, grumpy baby mingled with the music. Vanessa, sitting in the front row rocking baby Lauren, smiled when Natasha met her eye and blew her a kiss before attempting to soothe the fractious child.

Natasha blew a kiss back and then aimed one at her two-month-old daughter. As if by a miracle, the kiss landed and Lauren quietened. Or maybe it was Vanessa's magic touch.

Slowly the family had pulled back together, drawing comfort and understanding from each other. Natasha and Matteo had been pulled back into the bosom of the Pellegrini family too, and Francesca and Felipe had been delighted to accept the honour of being Lauren's godparents and guardians.

And then she was at Matteo's side and they were exchanging their vows and sliding on the rings that would cement their love and declare to the world that they did belong to each other and that no one and nothing could ever tear them apart again.

* * * * *

If you enjoyed
CLAIMING HIS ONE-NIGHT BABY,
make sure you read the first part of
Michelle Smart's
BOUND TO A BILLIONAIRE *trilogy,*
PROTECTING HIS DEFIANT INNOCENT
Available now!

And look for
BUYING HIS BRIDE OF CONVENIENCE,
coming October 2017.

In the meantime, why not explore another
Michelle Smart trilogy
THE KALLIAKIS CROWN?

TALOS CLAIMS HIS VIRGIN
THESEUS DISCOVERS HIS HEIR
HELIOS CROWNS HIS MISTRESS

Available now!

'You can't just…just *kidnap* me for weeks on end because you have a deal to complete! That's a crime!'

'Incendiary words, Miss Brennan.'

Lucas leaned over and placed both hands on either side of her chair, caging her in so that she automatically cringed back. The power of his personality was so suffocating that she had to make an effort to remember how to breathe.

'I won't be kidnapping you. Far from it. You can walk out of here, but you know the consequences if you do. I am an extremely powerful man, for my sins. Please do us both a favour by not crossing me.'

'Arrogant!' Katy's green eyes narrowed in a display of bravado she was inwardly far from feeling. 'That's what you are, Mr Cipriani! You're an arrogant, domineering bully!' She collided with eyes that burned with the heat of molten lava.

Lucas's eyes drifted to her full lips and for a second he was overwhelmed by a powerful, crazy urge to crush them under his mouth. He drew back, straightened and resumed his seat behind his desk.

'I can't just be *kept under watch* for *two weeks*. How is it going to work?'

'It's simple.' He leaned forward, the very essence of practicality. 'You will be accommodated, without benefit of your phone or personal computer, for a fortnight. You can consider it a pleasant holiday without the nuisance of having your time interrupted by gadgets.'

'A *pleasant holiday*?' Her breathing was ragged and her imagination, released to run wild, was coming up with all sorts of giddying scenarios…

Cathy Williams can remember reading Mills & Boon books as a teenager, and now that she is writing them she remains an avid fan. For her, there is nothing like creating romantic stories and engaging plots, and each and every book is a new adventure. Cathy lives in London. Her three daughters—Charlotte, Olivia and Emma—have always been, and continue to be, the greatest inspirations in her life.

Books by Cathy Williams

Mills & Boon Modern Romance

The Secret Sanchez Heir
Bought to Wear the Billionaire's Ring
Snowbound with His Innocent Temptation
A Virgin for Vasquez
Seduced into Her Boss's Service
The Wedding Night Debt
A Pawn in the Playboy's Game
At Her Boss's Pleasure
The Real Romero
The Uncompromising Italian
The Argentinian's Demand
Secrets of a Ruthless Tycoon

The Italian Titans

Wearing the De Angelis Ring
The Surprise De Angelis Baby

One Night With Consequences

Bound by the Billionaire's Baby

Seven Sexy Sins

To Sin with the Tycoon

Visit the Author Profile page
at millsandboon.co.uk for more titles.

CIPRIANI'S INNOCENT CAPTIVE

BY
CATHY WILLIAMS

First Published in Great Britain 2017
By Mills & Boon, an imprint of HarperCollins*Publishers*
1 London Bridge Street, London, SE1 9GF

© 2017 Cathy Williams

ISBN: 978-0-263-92536-4

Our policy is to use papers that are natural, renewable and recyclable
products and made from wood grown in sustainable forests. The logging
and manufacturing processes conform to the legal environmental
regulations of the country of origin.

Printed and bound in Spain
by CPI, Barcelona

CIPRIANI'S
INNOCENT
CAPTIVE

CHAPTER ONE

'MR CIPRIANI IS ready for you now.'

Katy Brennan looked up at the middle-aged, angular woman who had earlier met her in the foyer of Cipriani Head Office and ushered her to the directors' floor, where she had now been waiting for over twenty minutes.

She didn't want to feel nervous but she did. She had been summoned from her office in Shoreditch, where she worked as an IT specialist in a small team of four, and informed that Lucas Cipriani, the ultimate god to whom everyone answered, requested her presence.

She had no idea why he might want to talk to her, but she suspected that it concerned the complex job she was currently working on and, whilst she told herself that he probably only wanted to go through some of the finer details with her, she was still...*nervous*.

Katy stood up, wishing that she had had some kind of advance warning of this meeting, because if she had she would have dressed in something more in keeping with the über-plush surroundings in which she now found herself.

As it was, she was in her usual casual uniform of jeans and a tee-shirt, with her backpack and a lightweight bomber jacket, perfect for the cool spring weather, but utterly inappropriate for this high-tech, eight-storey glasshouse.

She took a deep breath and looked neither left nor right as she followed his PA along the carpeted corridor, past the hushed offices of executives and the many boardrooms where deals worth millions were closed, until the corridor ballooned out into a seating area. At the back of this was a closed eight-foot wooden door which was enough to send a chill through any person who had been arbitrarily summoned by the head of her company—a man whose ability to make deals and turn straw into gold was legendary.

Katy took a deep breath and stood back as his PA pushed open the door.

Staring absently through the floor-to-ceiling pane of reinforced glass that separated him from the streets below, Lucas Cipriani thought that this meeting was the last thing he needed to kick off the day.

But it could not be avoided. Security had been breached on the deal he had been working on for the past eight months, and this woman was going to have to take the consequences—pure and simple.

This was the deal of a lifetime and there was no way he was going to allow it to be jeopardised.

As his PA knocked and entered his office, Lucas slowly turned round, hand in trouser pocket, and looked at the woman whose job was a thing of the past, if only she knew it.

Eyes narrowed, it hit him that he really should catch up on the people who actually worked for him, because he hadn't expected this. He'd expected a nerd with heavy spectacles and an earnest manner, whilst the girl in front of him looked less like a computer whizz-kid and more like a hippy. Her clothes were generic: faded jeans and a tee-shirt with the name of a band he had never heard of. Her shoes were masculine black boots, suitable for heavy-duty construction work. She had a backpack slung over her shoulder, and stuffed into the top of it was some kind of jacket, which she had clearly just removed. Her entire dress code contradicted every single thing he associated with a woman, but she had the sort of multi-coloured coppery hair that would have had artists queuing up to commit it to canvas, and an elfin face with enormous bright-green eyes that held his gaze for reasons he couldn't begin to fathom.

'Miss Brennan.' He strolled towards his desk as Vicky, his secretary, clicked the heavy door to his office shut behind her. 'Sit, please.'

At the sound of that deep, dark, velvety voice, Katy started and realised that she had been holding her breath. When she had entered the office she'd thought that she more or less knew what to expect. She vaguely knew what her boss looked like because she had seen pictures of him in the company magazines that occasionally landed on her desk in Shoreditch, far away from the cutting-edge glass building that housed the great and the good in the company: from Lucas Cipriani, who sat at the very top like a god atop Mount Olympus, to his team of powerful executives who made sure that his empire ran without a hitch.

Those were people whose names appeared on letterheads and whose voices were occasionally heard down the end of phone lines, but who were never, ever seen. At least, not in Shoreditch, which was reserved for the small cogs in the machine.

But she still hadn't expected *this*. Lucas Cipriani was, simply put, beautiful. There was no other word to describe him. It wasn't just the arrangement of perfect features, or the burnished bronze of his skin, or even the dramatic masculinity of his physique: Lucas Cipriani's good looks went far beyond the physical. He exuded a certain power and charisma that made the breath catch in your throat and scrambled your ability to think in straight lines.

Which was why Katy was here now, in his office, drawing a blank where her thoughts should be and with her mouth so dry that she wouldn't have been able to say a word if she'd wanted to.

She vaguely recalled him saying something about sitting down, which she badly wanted to do, and she shuffled her way to the enormous leather chair that faced his desk and sank into it with some relief.

'You've been working on the Chinese deal,' Lucas stated without preamble.

'Yes.' She could talk about work, she could answer any question he might have, but she was unsettled by a dark, brooding, in-your-face sensuality she hadn't expected, and when she spoke her voice was jerky and nervous. 'I've been working on the legal side of the deal, dedicating all the details to a programme that will enable instant access to whatever is required, without having to sift through reams of documentation. I hope there isn't a problem. I'm running ahead of schedule, in actual fact. I'll be honest with you,

Mr Cipriani, it's one of the most exciting projects I've ever worked on. Complex, but really challenging.'

She cleared her throat and hazarded a smile, which was met with stony silence, and her already frayed nerves took a further battering. Stunning dark eyes, fringed with inky black, luxuriant lashes, pierced through the thin veneer of her self-confidence, leaving her breathless and red-faced.

Lucas positioned himself at his desk, an enormous chrome-and-glass affair that housed a computer with an over-sized screen, a metallic lamp and a small, very artfully designed bank of clocks that made sure he knew, at any given moment, what time it was in all the major cities in which his companies were located.

He lowered his eyes now and, saying nothing, swivelled his computer so that it was facing her.

'Recognise that man?'

Katy blanched. Her mouth fell open as she found herself staring at Duncan Powell, the guy she had fallen for three years previously. Floppy blond hair, blue eyes that crinkled when he grinned and boyish charm had combined to hook an innocent young girl barely out of her teens.

She had not expected this. Not in a million years. Confused, flustered and with a thousand alarm bells suddenly ringing in her head, Katy fixed bewildered green eyes on Lucas.

'I don't understand…'

'I'm not asking you to understand. I'm asking you whether you know this man.'

'Y-yes,' she stammered. 'I… Well, I knew him a few years ago…'

'And it would seem that you bypassed certain security systems and discovered that he is, these days, employed by the Chinese company I am in the process of finalising a deal with. Correct? No, don't bother answering that. I have a series of alerts on my computer and what I'm saying does not require verification.'

She felt dazed. Katy's thoughts had zoomed back in time to her disastrous relationship with Duncan.

She'd met him shortly after she had returned home to her parents' house in Yorkshire. Torn between staying where she was and facing the big, brave world of London, where the lights were bright and the job prospects were decidedly better, she had taken up a temporary post as an assistant teacher at one of the local schools to give herself some thinking time and to plan a strategy.

Duncan had worked at the bank on the high street, a stone's throw from the primary school.

In fairness, it had not been love at first sight. She had always liked a quirky guy; Duncan had been just the opposite. A snappy dresser, he had homed in on her with the single-minded focus of a heat-seeking missile with a pre-set target. Before she'd even decided whether she liked him or not, they had had coffee, then a meal, and then they were going out.

He'd been persistent and funny, and she'd started rethinking her London agenda when the whole thing had fallen apart because she'd discovered that the man who had stolen her heart wasn't the honest, sincere, single guy he had made himself out to be.

Nor had he even been a permanent resident in the little village where her parents lived. He'd been there on a one-year secondment, which was a minor detail he had cleverly kept under wraps. He had a wife and twin daughters keeping the fires warm in the house in Milton Keynes he shared with them.

She had been a diversion and, once she had discovered the truth about him, he had shrugged and held his hands up in rueful surrender and she had known, in a flash of pure gut instinct, that he had done that because she had refused to sleep with him. Duncan Powell had planned to have fun on his year out and, whilst he had been content to chase her for a few months, he hadn't been prepared to take the chase to a church and up an aisle, because he had been a fully committed family man.

'I don't understand.' Katy looked away from the reminder of her steep learning curve staring out at her from Lucas's computer screen. 'So Duncan works for their company. I honestly didn't go hunting for that information.' Although, she *had* done some basic background checks, just out of sheer curiosity, to see whether it was the same creep once she'd stumbled upon him. A couple of clicks of a button was all it had taken to confirm her suspicion.

Lucas leaned forward, his body language darkly, dangerously menacing. 'That's as may be,' he told her, 'but it does present certain problems.'

With cool, clear precision he presented those *certain problems* to her and she listened to him in ever-increasing alarm. A deal done in complete secrecy…a family company rooted in strong values of tradition… a variable stock market that hinged on nothing being leaked and the threat her connection to Duncan posed at a delicate time in the negotiations.

Katy was brilliant with computers, but the mysteries of high finance were lost on her. The race for money had never interested her. From an early age, her parents had impressed upon her the importance of recognising value in the things that money couldn't buy. Her father was a parish priest and both her parents lived a life that was rooted in the fundamental importance of putting the needs of other people first. Katy didn't care who earned what or how much money anyone had. She had been brought up with a different set of values. For better or for worse, she occasionally thought.

'I don't care about any of that,' she said unevenly, when there was a brief lull in his cold tabulation of her transgressions. It seemed a good moment to set him straight because she was beginning to have a nasty feeling that he was circling her like a predator, preparing to attack.

Was he going to sack her? She would survive. The bottom line was that that was the very worst he could do. He wasn't some kind of mediaeval war lord who could have her hung, drawn and quartered because she'd disobeyed him.

'Whether you care about a deal that isn't going to impact on you or not is immaterial. Either by design or incompetence, you're now in possession of information that could unravel nearly a year and a half of intense negotiation.'

'To start with, I'm obviously very sorry about what happened. It's been a very complex job and, if I accidentally happened upon information I shouldn't have, then I apologise. I didn't mean to. In fact, I'm not at all interested in your deal, Mr Cipriani. You gave me a job to do and I was doing it to the best of my ability.'

'Which clearly wasn't up to the promised standard, because an error of the magnitude of the one you made is inexcusable.'

'But that's not fair!'

'Remind me to give you a life lesson about what's fair and what isn't. I'm not interested in your excuses, Miss Brennan. I'm interested in working out a solution to bypass the headache you created.'

Katy's mind had stung at his criticism of her ability. She was good at what she did. Brilliant, even. To have her competence called into question attacked the very heart of her.

'If you look at the quality of what I've done, sir, you'll find that I've done an excellent job. I realise that I may have stumbled upon information that should have not been available to me, but you have my word that anything I've uncovered stays right here with me.'

'And I'm to believe you because…?'

'Because I'm telling you the truth!'

'I'm sorry to drag you into the world of reality, Miss Brennan, but taking things at face value, including other people's *sincerely meant promises*, is something I don't do.' He leaned back into his chair and looked at her.

Without trying, Lucas was capable of exuding the sort of lethal cool that made grown men quake in their shoes. A chit of a girl who was destined for the scrapheap should have been a breeze but for some reason he was finding some of his formidable focus diluted by her arresting good looks.

He went for tall, career-driven brunettes who were rarely seen without their armour of high-end designer suits and killer heels. He enjoyed the back and forth of intellectual repartee and had oftentimes found himself embroiled in heated debates about work-related issues.

His women knew the difference between a bear market and a bull market and would have sneered at anyone who didn't.

They were alpha females and that was the way he liked it.

He had seen the damage caused to rich men by airheads and bimbos. His fun-loving, amiable father had had ten good years of marriage to Lucas's mother and then, when Annabel Cipriani had died, he had promptly lost himself in a succession of stunningly sexy blondes, intelligence not a prerequisite.

He had been taken to the cleaners three times and it was a miracle that any family money, of which there had been a considerable sum at the starting block, had been left in the coffers.

But far worse than the nuisance of having his bank accounts bled by rapacious gold-diggers was the *hope* his father stupidly had always invested in the women he ended up marrying. Hope that they would be there for him, would somehow give him the emotional support he had had with his first wife. He had been looking for love and that weakness had opened him up to being used over and over again.

Lucas had absorbed all this from the side lines and had learned the necessary lessons: avoid emotional investment and you'd never end up getting hurt. Indeed, bimbos he could handle, though they repulsed him. At least they were a known quantity. What he really didn't do were women who demanded anything from him he knew he was incapable of giving, which was why he always went for women as emotionally and financially independent as him. They obeyed the same rules that he did and were as dismissive of emotional, overblown scenes as he was.

The fact was that, if you didn't let anyone in, then you were protected from disappointment, and not just the superficial disappointment of discovering that some replaceable woman was more interested in your bank account than she was in *you*.

He had learned more valuable lessons about the sort of weaknesses that could permanently scar and so he had locked his heart away and thrown away the key and, in truth, he had never had a moment's doubt that he had done the right thing.

'Are you still in contact with the man?' he murmured, watching her like a hawk.

'No! I am *not*!' Heated colour made her face burn. She found that she was gripping the arms of the chair for dear life, her whole body rigid with affront that he would even ask her such a personal question. 'Are you going to sack me, Mr Cipriani? Because, if you are, then perhaps you could just get on with it.'

Her temples were beginning to throb painfully. Of course she was going to be sacked. This wasn't going to be a ticking off before being dismissed back to Shoreditch to resume her duties as normal, nor was she simply going to be removed from the task at which inadvertently she had blundered.

She had been hauled in here like a common criminal so that she could be fired. No one-month's notice, no final warning, and there was no way that she could even consider a plea of unfair dismissal. She would be left without her main source of income and that was something she would just have to deal with.

And the guy sitting in front of her having fun being judge, jury and executioner didn't give a hoot as to whether she was telling the truth or not, or whether her life would be affected by an abrupt sacking or not.

'Regrettably, it's not quite so straightforward—'

'Why not?' Katy interrupted feverishly. 'You obviously don't believe a word I've told you and I know I certainly wouldn't be allowed anywhere near the project again. If you just wanted me off it, you would have probably told Tim, my manager, and let him pass the message on to me. The fact that I've been summoned here tells me that you're going to give me the boot, but not before you make sure I know why. Will you at the very least give me a reference, Mr Cipriani? I've worked extremely hard for your company for the past year and a half and I've had nothing but glowing reports on the work I've done. I think I deserve some credit for that.'

Lucas marvelled that she could think, for a minute, that he had so much time on his hands that he would personally call her in just to sack her. She was looking at him with an urgent expression, her green eyes defiant.

Again distracted, he found himself saying, 'I noticed on your file that you only work two days a week for my company. Why is that?'

'Sorry?' Katy's eyes narrowed suspiciously.

'It's unusual for someone of your age to be a part-time employee. That's generally the domain of women with children of school age who want to earn a little money but can't afford the demands of a full-time job.'

'I… I have another job,' she admitted, wondering where this was heading and whether she needed to be on her guard. 'I work as an IT teacher at one of the secondary schools near where I live.'

Lucas was reluctantly fascinated by the ebb and flow of colour that stained her cheeks. Her face was as transparent as glass and that in itself was an unusual enough quality to hold his attention. The tough career women he dated knew how to school their expressions because, the higher up the ladder they climbed, the faster they learned that blushing like virginal maidens did nothing when it came to career advancement.

'Can't pay well,' he murmured.

'That's not the point!'

Lucas had turned his attention to his computer and was very quickly pulling up the file he had on her, which he had only briefly scanned before he had scheduled his meeting with her. The list of favourable references was impressively long.

'So,' he mused, sitting back and giving her his undivided attention. 'You work for me for the pay and you work as a teacher for the enjoyment.'

'That's right.' She was disconcerted at how quickly he had reached the right conclusions.

'So the loss of your job at my company would presumably have a serious impact on your finances.'

'I would find another job to take its place.'

'Look around the market, Miss Brennan. Well paid part-time work is thin on the ground. I make it my duty to pay my employees over the odds. I find that tends to engender commitment and loyalty to the company. You'd be hard pressed to find the equivalent anywhere in London.'

Lucas had planned on a simple solution to this unexpected problem. Now, he was pressed to find out a bit more about her. As a part-time worker, it seemed she contributed beyond the call of duty, and both the people she answered to within the company and external clients couldn't praise her enough. She'd pleaded her innocence, and he wasn't gullible enough to wipe the slate clean, but a more detailed hearing might be in order. His initial impressions weren't of a thief who might be attracted to the lure of insider trading but, on the other hand, someone with a part-time job might find it irresistible to take advantage of an unexpected opportunity, and Duncan Powell represented that unexpected opportunity.

'Money doesn't mean that much to me, Mr Cipriani.' Katy was confused as to how a man whose values were so different from hers could make her go hot and cold and draw her attention in a way that left her feeling helpless and exposed. She was finding it hard to string simple sentences together. 'I have a place to myself but, if I had to share with other people, then it wouldn't be the end of the world.'

The thought of sharing space with a bunch of strangers was only slightly less appalling to Lucas than incarceration with the key thrown away.

Besides, how much did she mean that? he wondered with grim practicality, dark eyes drifting over her full, stubborn mouth and challenging angle of her head. What had been behind that situation with Powell, a married man? It wasn't often that Lucas found himself questioning his own judgements but in this instance he did wonder whether it was just a simple tale of a woman who had been prepared to overlook the fact that her lover was a married man because of the financial benefits he could bring to the table. Although, he'd seen enough of that to know that it was the oldest story in the world.

Maybe he would test the waters and see what came out in the wash. If this had been a case of hire and fire, then she would have been clearing out her desk eighteen hours ago, but it wasn't, because he couldn't sack her just yet, and it paid to know your quarry. He would not allow any misjudgements to wreck his deal.

'You never thought about packing in the teaching and taking up the job at my company full time?'

'No.' The silence stretched between them while Katy frantically tried to work out where this sudden interest was leading. 'Some people aren't motivated by money.' She finally broke the silence because she was beginning to perspire with discomfort. 'I wasn't raised to put any value on material things.'

'Interesting. Unique.'

'Maybe in *your* world, Mr Cipriani.'

'Money, Miss Brennan, is the engine that makes everything go, and not just in my world. In everyone's world. The best things in life are not, as rumour would have it, free.'

'Maybe not for you,' Katy said with frank disapproval. She knew that she was treading on thin ice. She sensed that Lucas Cipriani was not a man who enjoyed other people airing too many contradictory opinions. He'd hauled her in to sack her and was now subjecting her to the Spanish Inquisition because he was cold, arrogant and because *he could*.

But what was the point of tiptoeing around him when she was on her way out for a crime she hadn't committed?

'That's why you don't believe what I'm saying,'

she expanded. 'That's why you don't trust me. You probably don't trust anyone, which is sad, when you think about it. I'd hate to go through life never knowing my friends from my enemies. When your whole world is about money, then you lose sight of the things that really matter.'

Lucas's lips thinned disapprovingly at her directness. She was right when she said that he didn't trust anyone but that was exactly the way he liked it.

'Let me be perfectly clear with you, Miss Brennan.' He leaned forward and looked at her coolly. 'You haven't been brought here for a candid exchange of views. I appreciate you are probably tense and nervous, which is doubtless why you're cavalier about overstepping the mark, but I suggest it's time to get down from your moral high ground and take a long, hard look at the choices you have made that have landed you in my office.'

Katy flushed. 'I made a mistake with Duncan,' she muttered. 'We all make mistakes.'

'You slept with a married man,' Lucas corrected her bluntly, startling her with the revelation that he'd discovered what he clearly thought was the whole, shameful truth. 'So, while you're waxing lyrical about my tragic, money-orientated life, you might want to consider that, whatever the extent of my greed and arrogance, I would no more sleep with a married woman than I would jump into the ocean with anchors secured to my feet.'

'I...'

Lucas held up one hand. 'No one speaks to me the way you do.' He felt a twinge of discomfort because that one sentence seemed to prove the arrogance of which he had been accused. Since when had he become so *pompous*? He scowled. 'I've done the maths, Miss Brennan and, however much you look at me with those big, green eyes, I should tell you that taking the word of an adulterer is something of a tall order.'

Buffeted by Lucas's freezing contempt and outrageous accusations, Katy rose on shaky legs to direct the full force of her anger at him.

'How *dare you*?' But even in the midst of her anger she was swamped by the oddest sensation of vulnerability as his dark eyes swept coolly over her, electrifying every inch of her heated body.

'With remarkable ease.' Lucas didn't bat an eyelid. 'I'm staring the facts in the face and the facts are telling me a very clear story. You want me to believe that you have nothing to do with the man. Unfortunately, your lack of principles in having anything to do with him in the first place tells a tale of its own.'

The colour had drained away from her face. She hated this man. She didn't think it would be possible to hate anyone more.

'I don't have to stay here and listen to this.' But uneasily she was aware that, without her laying bare her sex life, understandably he would have jumped to the wrong conclusions. Without her confession that she had never slept with Duncan, he would have assumed the obvious. Girls her age had flings and slept with men. Maybe he would be persuaded into believing her if she told him the truth, which was that she had ended their brief relationship as soon as she had found out about his wife and kids. But even if he believed that he certainly wouldn't believe that she hadn't *slept* with the man.

Which would lead to a whole other conversation and it was one she had no intention of having. How would a man like Lucas Cipriani believe that the hussy who slept with married guys was in fact a virgin?

Even Katy didn't like thinking about that. She had never had the urge to rush into sex. Her parents hadn't stamped their values on her but the drip, drip, drip of their gentle advice, and the example she had seen on the doorstep of the vicarage of broken-hearted, often pregnant young girls abandoned by men they had fallen for, had made her realise that when it came to love it paid to be careful.

In fairness, had temptation knocked on the door, then perhaps she might have questioned her old-fashioned take on sex but, whilst she had always got along just fine with the opposite sex, no one had ever grabbed her attention until Duncan had come along with his charm, his overblown flattery and his *persistence*. She had been unsure of where her future lay, and in that brief window of uncertainty and apprehension he had burrowed in and stolen her heart. She had been ripe for the picking and his betrayal had been devastating.

Her virginity was a millstone now, a reminder of the biggest mistake she had ever made. Whilst she hoped that one day she would find the guy for her, she was resigned to the possibility that she might never do so, because somehow she was just out of sync with men and what they wanted.

They wanted sex, first and foremost. To get to the prince, you seemed to have to sleep with hundreds of frogs, and there was no way she would do that. The thought that she might have slept with *one* frog was bad enough.

So what would Lucas Cipriani make of her story? She pictured the sneer on his face and shuddered.

Disturbed at the direction of her thoughts, she tilted her chin and looked at him with equal cool. 'I expect, after all this, I'm being given the sack and that Personnel will be in touch—so there can't be any reason for me to still be here. And you can't stop me leaving. You'll just have to trust me that I won't be saying anything to anyone about your deal.'

CHAPTER TWO

SHE DIDN'T GET FAR.

'You leave this office, Miss Brennan, and regrettably I will have to commence legal proceedings against you on the assumption that you have used insider information to adversely influence the outcome of my company's business dealings.'

Katy stopped and slowly turned to look at him.

His dark eyes were flat, hard and expressionless and he was looking right back at her with just the mildest of interest. His absolute calm was what informed her that he wasn't cracking some kind of sick joke at her expense.

Katy knew a lot about the workings of computers. She could create programs that no one else could and was downright gifted when it came to sorting out the nuts and bolts of intricate problems when those programs began to get a little temperamental. It was why she had been carefully headhunted by Lucas's company and why they'd so willingly accommodated her request for a part-time job only.

In the field of advanced technology, she was reasonably well-known.

She didn't, however, know a thing about law. What

was he going on about? She didn't really understand what he was saying but she understood enough to know that it was a threat.

Lucas watched the colour flood her face. Her skin was satiny smooth and flawless. She had the burnished copper-coloured hair of a redhead, yet her creamy complexion was free of any corresponding freckles. The net result was an unusual, absurdly striking prettiness that was all the more dramatic because she seemed so unaware of it.

But then, his cynical brain told him, she was hardly a shrinking violet with no clue of her pulling power, because she *had* had an affair with a married guy with kids.

He wondered whether she thought that she could turn those wide, emerald-green eyes on him and get away scot-free.

If she did, then she had no idea with whom she was dealing. He'd had a lifetime's worth of training when it came to spotting women who felt that their looks were a passport to getting whatever they wanted. He'd spent his formative years watching them do their numbers on his father. This woman might not be an airhead like them, but she was still driven by the sort of emotionalism he steered well clear of.

'Of course—' he shrugged '—my deal would be blown sky-high out of the water, but have you any idea how much damage you would do to yourself in the process? Litigation is something that takes its time. Naturally, your services would be no longer required at my company and your pay would cease immediately. And then there would be the small question of your legal costs. Considerable.'

Her expression was easy to read and Lucas found that he was enjoying the show.

'That's—that's ridiculous,' Katy stuttered. 'You'd find out that I haven't been in touch with…with Duncan for years. In fact, since we broke up. Plus, you'd *also* find out that I haven't breathed a word about the Chinese deal to…well, to anybody.'

'I only have your word for it. Like I said, discovering whether you're telling the truth or not would take time, and all the while you would naturally be without a penny to your name, defending your reputation against the juggernaut of my company's legal department.'

'I have another job.'

'And we've already established that teaching won't pay the rent. And who knows how willing a school would be to employ someone with a potential criminal record?'

Katy flushed. Bit by bit, he was trapping her in a corner and, with a feeling of surrendering to the inexorable advance of a steamroller, she finally said, 'What do you want me to do?'

Lucas stood up and strolled towards the wall of glass that separated him from the city below, before turning to look at her thoughtfully.

'I told you that this was not a straightforward situation, Miss Brennan. I meant it. It isn't a simple case of throwing you out of my company when you can hurt me with privileged information.' He paced the enormous office, obliging her to follow his progress, and all the time she found herself thinking, *he's almost too beautiful to bear looking at.* He was very tall and very lean, and somehow the finely cut, expensive suit did little to conceal something raw and elemental in his physique.

She had to keep dragging her brain back to what he was telling her. She had to keep frowning so that she could give the appearance of not looking like a complete nitwit. She didn't like the man, but did he have this effect on *all* the women he met?

She wondered what sort of women he met anyway, and then chastised herself for losing the thread when her future was at stake.

'The deal is near completion and a fortnight at most should see a satisfactory conclusion. Now, let's just say that I believe you when you tell me that you haven't been gossiping with your boyfriend...'

'I told you that Duncan and I haven't spoken for years! And, for your information, we broke up because *I found out that he was married.* I'm not the sort of person who would ever dream of going out with a married guy—!'

Lucas stopped her in mid-speech. 'Not interested. All I'm interested in is how this situation is dealt with satisfactorily for me. As far as I am concerned, you could spend all your free time hopping in and out of beds with married men.'

Katy opened her mouth and then thought better of defending herself, because it wasn't going to get her anywhere. He seemed ready to hand down her sentence.

'It is imperative that any sensitive information you may have acquired is not shared, and the only way that that can be achieved is if you are incommunicado to the outside world. Ergo that is how it is going to be for the next fortnight, until my deal is concluded.'

'Sorry, Mr Cipriani, but I'm not following you.'

'Which bit, exactly, Miss Brennan, are you not following?'

'The *fortnight* bit. What are you talking about?'

'It's crystal clear, Miss Brennan. You're not going to be talking to anyone, and I mean *anyone,* for the next two weeks until I have all the signatures right where I want them, at which point you may or may not return to your desk in Shoreditch and we can both forget that this unfortunate business ever happened. Can I get any clearer than that? And by "incommunicado", I mean no mobile phone and no computer. To be blunt, you will be under watch until you can no longer be a danger to me.'

'But you can't be serious!'

'Do I look as though I'm doing a stand-up routine?'

No, he didn't. In fact, without her even realising it, he had been pacing the office in ever decreasing circles and he was now towering right in front of her; the last thing he resembled was a man doing a stand-up routine.

Indeed, he looked about as humorous as an executioner; she quailed inside.

Mentally, she added 'bully' to the growing list of things she loathed about him.

'Under watch? What does that even mean? You can't just…just *kidnap* me for weeks on end because you have a deal to complete! That's a crime!'

'Incendiary words, Miss Brennan.' He leaned over and placed both hands on either side of her chair, caging her in so that she automatically cringed back. The power of his personality was so suffocating that she had to make an effort to remember how to breathe. 'I won't be kidnapping you. Far from it. You can walk out of here, but you know the consequences of that if you do. The simple process of consulting a lawyer would start racking up bills you could ill afford, I'm sure. Not to mention the whiff of unemployability that would be attached to you at the end of the long-winded and costly business. I am an extremely powerful man, for my sins. Please do us both a favour by not crossing me.'

'Arrogant.' Katy's green eyes narrowed in a display of bravado she was inwardly far from feeling. 'That's what you are, Mr Cipriani! You're an arrogant, domineering bully!' She collided with eyes that burned with the heat of molten lava, and for a terrifying moment her anger was eclipsed by a dragging sensation that made her breathing sluggish and laborious.

Lucas's eyes drifted to her full lips and for a second he was overwhelmed by a powerful, crazy urge to crush them under his mouth. He drew back, straightened and resumed his seat behind his desk.

'I'm guessing that you're beginning to see sense,' he commented drily.

'It's not ethical,' Katy muttered under her breath. She eyed him with mutinous hostility.

'It's perfectly ethical, if a little unusual, but then again I've never been in the position of harbouring suspicions about the loyalties of any of my employees before. I pay them way above market price and that usually works. This is a first for me, Miss Brennan.'

'I can't just be *kept under watch* for *two weeks*. I'm not a specimen in a jam jar! Plus, I have responsibilities at the school!'

'And a simple phone call should sort that out. If

you want, I can handle the call myself. You just need to inform them that personal circumstances will prevent you from attending for the next fortnight. Same goes for any relatives, boyfriends and random pets that might need sorting out.'

'I can't believe this is happening. How is it going to work?'

'It's simple.' He leaned forward, the very essence of practicality. 'You will be accommodated without benefit of your phone or personal computer for a fortnight. You can consider it a pleasant holiday without the nuisance of having your time interrupted by gadgets.'

'A *pleasant holiday*?' Her breathing was ragged and her imagination, released to run wild, was coming up with all sorts of giddying scenarios.

Lucas had the grace to flush before shrugging. 'I assure you that your accommodation will be of the highest quality. All you need bring with you are your clothes. You will be permitted to return to your house or flat, or wherever it is you live, so that you can pack what you need.'

'Where on earth will I be going? This is mad.'

'I've put the alternative on the table.' Lucas shrugged elegantly.

'But where will I be *put*?'

'To be decided. There are a number of options. Suffice to say that you won't need to bring winter gear.' In truth, he hadn't given this a great deal of thought. His plan had been to delegate to someone else the responsibility of babysitting the headache that had arisen.

Now, however, babysitting her himself was looking good.

Why send a boy to do a man's job? She was lippy, argumentative, stubborn, in short as unpredictable as a keg of dynamite, and he couldn't trust any of his guys to know how to handle her.

She was also dangerously pretty and had no qualms when it came to having fun with a married guy. She said otherwise, but the jury was out on that one.

Dangerously pretty, rebellious and lacking in a moral compass was a recipe for disaster. Lucas looked at her with veiled, brooding speculation. He frankly couldn't think of anyone who would be able to handle this. He had planned to disappear for a week or so to consolidate the finer details of the deal, without fear of constant interruption, and this had become even more pressing since the breach in security. He could easily kill two birds with one stone, rather than delegating the job and then wasting his time wondering whether the task would go belly up.

'So, to cut to the chase, Miss Brennan...' He buzzed and was connected through to his PA. In a fog of sick confusion, and with the distinct feeling of being chucked into a tumble drier with the cycle turned to maximum spin, Katy was aware of him instructing the woman who had escorted her to his office to join them in fifteen minutes.

'Yes?' she said weakly.

'Vicky, my secretary, is going to accompany you back to...wherever you live...and she will supervise your immediate packing of clothes to take with you. Likewise, she will oversee whatever phone calls you feel you have to make to your friends. Needless to say, these will have to be cleared with her.'

'This is ridiculous. I feel as though I'm starring in a low-grade spy movie.'

'Don't be dramatic, Miss Brennan. I'm taking some simple precautions to safeguard my business interests. Carrying on; once you have your bags packed and you've made a couple of calls, you will be chauffeured back here.'

'Can I ask you something?'

'Feel free.'

'Are you always this…*cold*?'

'Are you always this outspoken?' Eyes as black as night clashed with emerald-green. Katy felt something shiver inside her and suddenly, inexplicably, she was aware of her body in a way she had never been in her life before. It felt heavy yet acutely sensitive, tingly and hot, aching as though her limbs had turned to lead.

Her mouth went dry and for a few seconds her mind actually went completely blank. 'I think that, if I have something to say, then why shouldn't I? As long as I'm not being offensive to anyone, we're all entitled to our opinions.' She paused and tilted her chin at a challenging angle. 'To answer your question.'

Lucas grunted. Not even the high-powered women who entered and exited his life made a habit of disagreeing with him, and they certainly never criticised. No one did.

'And to answer yours,' he said coolly, 'I'm cold when the occasion demands. You're not here on a social visit. You're here because a situation has arisen that requires to be dealt with and you're the root cause of the situation. Trust me, Miss Brennan, I'm the opposite of cold, given the right circumstances.'

And then he smiled, a long, slow, lazy smile and her senses shot into frantic overdrive. She licked her lips and her body stiffened as she leant forward in the chair, clutching the sides like a drowning person clutches a lifebelt.

That smile.

It seemed to insinuate into parts of her that she hadn't known existed, and it took a lot of effort actually to remember that the man was frankly insulting her and that sexy smile was not directed at her. Whoever he was thinking of—his current girlfriend, no doubt—had instigated that smile.

Were he to direct a smile at her, it would probably turn her to stone.

'So you stuff me away somewhere...' She finally found her voice and thankfully sounded as composed as he did. 'On a two week *holiday*, probably with those bodyguards of yours who brought me from the office, where I won't be allowed to do anything at all because I'll be minus my mobile phone and minus my computer. And, when you're done with your deal, you might just pop back and collect me, provided I've survived the experience.'

Lucas clicked his tongue impatiently. 'There's no need to be so dramatic.' He raked his fingers through his hair and debated whether he should have taken a slightly different approach.

Nope. He had taken the only possible approach. It just so happened that he was dealing with someone whose feet were not planted on the ground the way his were.

'The bodyguards won't be there.'

'No, I suppose it would be a little *chancy* to stuff

me away with men I don't know. Not that it'll make a
scrap of difference whether your henchmen are male
or female. I'll still be locked away like a prisoner in
a cell with the key thrown away.'

Lucas inhaled deeply and slowly, and hung on to
a temper that was never, ever lost. 'No henchmen,'
he intoned through gritted teeth. 'You're going to be
with me. I wouldn't trust anyone else to keep an eye
on you.'

Not without being mauled to death in the process.

'With *you*?' Shot through with an electrifying
awareness of him, her heart sped up, sending the
blood pulsing hotly through her veins and making it
difficult to catch her breath. *Trapped somewhere with
him?* And yet the thought, which should have filled
her with unremitting horror, kick-started a dark, in-
surgent curiosity that frankly terrified her.

'I have no intention of having any interaction with
you at all. You will simply be my responsibility for a
fortnight and I will make sure that no contact is made
with any outside parties until the deal is signed, sealed
and delivered. And please don't tell me the prospect
of being without a mobile phone or computer for a
handful of days amounts to nothing short of torture,
an experience which you may or may not survive!
It *is* possible to live without gadgets for a fortnight.'

'Could *you*?' But her rebellious mind was somewhere else, somewhere she felt it shouldn't be.

'This isn't about me. Bring whatever books you
want, or embroidery, or whatever you might enjoy
doing, and think about it positively as an unexpected
time out for which you will continue to be paid. If
you're finding it difficult to kick back and enjoy the

experience, then you can always consider the alternative: litigation, legal bills and no job.'

Katy clenched her fists and wanted to say something back in retaliation, even though she was dimly aware of the fact that this was the last person on the planet she wanted to have a scrap with, and not just because he was a man who would have no trouble in making good on his threats. However, the door was opening and through the haze of her anger she heard herself being discussed in a low voice, as if she wasn't in the room at all.

'Right.'

She blinked and Lucas was staring down at her, hands shoved in his trouser pockets. Awkwardly she stood up and instinctively smiled politely at his secretary, who smiled back.

He'd rattled off a chain of events, but she'd only been half listening, and now she didn't honestly know what would happen next.

'I'll have to phone my mum and dad,' she said a little numbly and Lucas inclined his head to one side with a frown.

'Of course.'

'I talk with them every evening.'

His frown deepened, because that seemed a little excessive for someone in her twenties. It didn't tally with the image of a raunchy young woman indulging in a steamy affair with a married man, not that the details of that were his business, unless the steamy affair was ongoing.

'And I don't have any pets.' She gathered her backpack from the ground and headed towards the door in the same daze that had begun settling over her the second his secretary had walked into the room.

'Miss Brennan…'

'Huh?' She blinked and looked up at him.

She was only five-three and wearing flats, so she had to crane her neck up. Her hair tumbled down her back in a riot of colour. Lucas was a big man and he felt as though he could fit her into his pocket. She was delicate, her features fine, her body slender under the oversized white shirt. Was that why he suddenly felt himself soften after the gruelling experience he had put her through? He had never in his life done anything that disturbed his conscience, had always acted fairly and decently towards other people. Yes, undeniably he could be ruthless, but never unjustly so. He felt a little guilty now.

'Don't get worked up about this.' His voice was clipped because this was as close as he was going to get to putting her mind at ease. By nature, he was distrustful, and certainly the situation in which he had encountered her showed all the hallmarks of being dangerous, as she only had to advertise what she knew to her ex. Yet something about her fuelled an unexpected response in him.

Her eyes, he noted as he stared down into them, were a beguiling mix of green and turquoise. 'This isn't a trial by torture. It's just the only way I can deal with a potential problem. You won't spend the fortnight suffering, nor is there any need to fear that I'm going to be following you around every waking moment like a bad conscience. Indeed, you will hardly notice my presence. I will be working all day and you'll be free to do as you like. Without the tools for communicating with the outside world, you can't get up to any mischief.'

'But I don't even know where I'm going!' Katy cried, latching on to that window of empathy before it vanished out of sight.

Lucas raised his eyebrows, and there was that smile again, although the empathy was still there and it was tinged with a certain amount of cool amusement. 'Consider it a surprise,' he murmured. 'A bit like winning the lottery which, incidentally, pretty much sums it up when you think about the alternative.' He nodded to his secretary and glanced at his watch. 'Two hours, Vicky. Think that will do it?'

'I think so.'

'In that case, I will see you both shortly. And, Miss Brennan...don't even think about doing a runner.'

Over the next hour and a half Katy experienced what it felt like to be kidnapped. Oh, he could call it what he liked, but she was going to be held prisoner. She was relieved of her mobile phone by Lucas's secretary, who was brisk but warm, and seemed to see nothing amiss in following her boss's high-handed instructions. It would be delivered to Lucas and held in safekeeping for her.

She packed a bunch of clothes, not knowing where she was going. Outside, it was still, but spring was making way for summer, so the clothes she crammed into her duffel bag were light, with one cardigan in case she ended up somewhere cold.

Although how would she know what the weather was up to when she would probably be locked in a room somewhere with views of the outside world through bars?

And yet, for all her frustration and downright *anger,* she could sort of see why he had reacted the way he had. Obviously the only thing that mattered to Lucas Cipriani was making money and closing deals. If this was to be the biggest deal of his career—and dipping his corporate toes into the Far East would be—then he would be more than happy to do what it took to safeguard his interest.

She was a dispensable little fish in the very big pond in which he was the marauding king of the water.

And the fact that she knew someone at the company he was about to take over, someone who was so far ignorant of what was going on, meant she had the power to pass on highly sensitive and potentially explosive information.

Lucas Cipriani, being the sort of man he was, would never believe that she had no ongoing situation with Duncan Powell because he was suspicious, distrustful, power hungry, arrogant, and would happily feed her to the sharks if it suited him, because he was also ice-cold and utterly emotionless.

'Where am I being taken?' she asked Vicky as they stepped back into the chauffeur-driven car that had delivered her to her flat. 'Or am I going to find myself blindfolded before we get there?'

'To a field on the outskirts of London.' She smiled. 'Mr Cipriani has his own private mode of transport there. And, no, you won't be blindfolded for any of the journey.'

Katy subsided into silence and stared at the scenery

passing by as the silent car left London and expertly took a route with which she was unfamiliar. She seldom left the capital unless it was to take the train up to Yorkshire to see her parents and her friends who still lived in the area. She didn't own a car, so escaping London was rarely an option, although, on a couple of occasions, she *had* gone with Tim and some of the others to Brighton for a holiday, five of them crammed like sardines into his second-hand car.

She hadn't thought about the dynamics of being trapped in a room with just Lucas acting as gaoler outside, but now she did, and she felt that frightening, forbidding tingle again.

Would other people be around? Or would there just be the two of them?

She hated him. She loathed his arrogance and the way he had of assuming that the world should fall in line with whatever he wanted. He was the boss who never made an effort to interact with those employees he felt were beneath him. He paid well not because he was a considerate and fair-minded guy who believed in rewarding hard work, but because he knew that money bought loyalty, and a loyal employee was more likely to do exactly what he demanded without asking questions. Pay an employee enough, and they lost the right to vote.

She hoped that he'd been telling the truth when he'd said that there would be no interaction between them because she couldn't think that they would have anything to talk about.

Then Katy thought about seeing him away from the confines of office walls. Something inside trembled and she had that whooshing feeling again, as if she had been sitting quietly on a chair, only to find that the chair was attached to a rollercoaster and the switch had suddenly been turned on. Her tummy flipped over; she didn't get it, because she really and truly didn't like the guy.

She surfaced from her thoughts to find that they had left the main roads behind and were pulling into a huge parking lot where a long, covered building opened onto an air field.

'I give you Lucas's transport...' Vicky murmured. 'If you look to the right, you'll see his private jet. It's the black one. But today you'll be taking the helicopter.'

Jet? Helicopter?

Katy did a double-take. Her eyes swivelled from private jet to helicopter and, sure enough, there he was, leaning indolently against a black and silver helicopter, dark shades shielding his eyes from the early-afternoon glare.

Her mouth ran dry. He was watching her from behind those shades. Her breathing picked up and her heart began to beat fast as she wondered what the heck she had got herself into, and all because she had stumbled across information she didn't even care about.

She didn't have time to dwell on the quicksand gathering at her feet, however, because with the sort of efficiency that spoke of experience the driver was pulling the car to a stop and she was being offloaded, the driver hurrying towards the helicopter with her bag just as the rotary blades of the aircraft began to *whop, whop, whop* in preparation for taking off, sending a whirlwind of flying dust beneath it.

Lucas had vanished into the helicopter.

Katy wished that she could vanish to the other side of the world.

She was harried, panic-stricken and grubby, because she hadn't had a chance to shower, and her jeans and shirt were sticking to her like glue. When she'd spoken to her mother on the phone, under the eagle eye of Vicky, she had waffled on with some lame excuse about being whipped off to a country house to do an important job, where the reception might be a bit dodgy, so they weren't to worry if contact was sporadic. She had made it sound like an exciting adventure because her parents were prone to worrying about her.

She hadn't thought that she really *would* end up being whipped off to anywhere.

She had envisaged a laborious drive to a poky holding pen in the middle of nowhere, with Internet access cruelly denied her. She hadn't believed him when he had told her to the contrary, and she certainly had not been able to get her head around any concept of an unplanned holiday unless you could call *incarceration* a holiday.

She was floored by what seemed to be a far bigger than average helicopter, but she was still scowling as she battled against the downdraft from the blades to climb aboard.

Lucas had to shout to be heard. As the small craft spun up, up and away, he called out, 'Small bag, Miss Brennan. Where have you stashed the books, the sketch pads and the tin of paints?'

Katy gritted her pearly teeth together but didn't say anything, and he laughed, eyebrows raised.

'Or did you decide to go down the route of being

a good little martyr while being held in captivity against your will? No books...no sketch pads...no tin of paints...and just the slightest temptation to stage a hunger strike to prove a point?'

Clenched fists joined gritted teeth and she glared at him, but he had already looked away and was flicking through the papers on his lap. He only glanced up when, leaning forward and voice raised to be heard above the din, she said, 'Where are you taking me?'

Aggravatingly seeming to read her mind, privy to every dark leap of imagination that had whirled through her head in a series of colourful images, Lucas replied, 'I'm sure that you've already conjured up dire destinations. So, instead of telling you, I'll leave you to carry on with your fictitious scenarios because I suspect that where you subsequently end up can only be better than what you've wasted your time imagining. But to set your mind at rest...'

He patted the pocket of the linen jacket which was dumped on the seat next to him. 'Your mobile phone is safe and sound right there. As soon as we land, you can tell me your password so that I can check every so often: make sure there are no urgent messages from the parents you're in the habit of calling on a daily basis...'

'Or from a married ex-boyfriend?' She couldn't resist prodding the sleeping tiger and he gave her a long, cool look from under the dark fringe of his lashes.

'Or from a married ex-boyfriend,' he drawled. 'Always pays to be careful, in my opinion. Now why don't you let me work and why don't you...enjoy the ride?'

CHAPTER THREE

THE RIDE PROBABLY TOOK HOURS, and felt even longer, with Katy doing her best to pretend that Lucas wasn't sitting within touching distance. When the helicopter began descending, swinging in a loop as it got lower, all she could see was the broad expanse of blue ocean.

Panicked and bewildered, she gazed at Lucas, who hadn't looked up from his papers and, when eventually he did, he certainly didn't glance in her direction.

After a brief hovering, the helicopter delicately landed and then she could see what she had earlier missed.

This wasn't a shabby holding pen.

Lucas was unclicking himself from his seat belt and then he patiently waited for her to do the same. This was all in a day's work for him. He turned to talk to the pilot, a low, clipped, polite exchange of words, then he stood back to allow her through the door and onto the super-yacht on which the helicopter had landed.

It was much, much warmer here and the dying rays of the sun revealed that the yacht was anchored at some distance from land. No intrusive boats huddled anywhere near it. She was standing on a yacht

that was almost big enough to be classified as a small
liner—sleek, sharp and so impressive that every single left wing thought about money not mattering was
temporarily wiped away under a tidal wave of shame-
less awe.

The dark bank of land rose in the distance, reveal-
ing just some pinpricks of light peeping out between
the trees and dense foliage that climbed up the side
of the island's incline.

She found herself following Lucas as behind them
the helicopter swung away and the deafening roar
of the rotary blades faded into an ever-diminishing
wasp-like whine. And then she couldn't hear it at all
because they had left the helipad on the upper deck
of the yacht and were moving inside.

'How does it feel to be a prisoner held against your
will in a shabby cell?' Lucas drawled, not looking
at her at all but heading straight through a vast expanse of polished wood and expensive cream leather
furniture. A short, plump lady was hurrying to meet
them, her face wreathed in smiles, and they spoke in
rapid Italian.

Katy was dimly aware of being introduced to the
woman, who was Signora Maria, the resident chef
when on board.

Frankly, all she could take in was the breath-taking,
obscene splendour of her surroundings. She was on
board a billionaire's toy and, in a way, it made her feel
more nervous and jumpy than if she had been dumped
in that holding pen she had created in her fevered, over-
imaginative head.

She'd known the guy was rich but when you were

as rich as this, rich enough to own a yacht of this calibre, then you could do whatever you wanted.

When he'd threatened her with legal proceedings,
it hadn't been an empty threat.

Katy decided that she wasn't going to let herself
be cowed by this display. She wasn't guilty of anything and she wasn't going to be treated like a criminal because Lucas Cipriani was suspicious by nature.

She had always been encouraged by her parents
to speak her mind and she wasn't going to be turned
into a rag doll because she was overwhelmed by her
surroundings.

'Maria will show you to your suite.' He turned
to her, his dark eyes roving up and down her body
without expression. 'In it you will find everything
you need, including an *en suite* bathroom. You'll be
pleased to hear that there is no lock on the outside
of your room, so you're free to come and go at will.'

'There's no need to be sarcastic,' Katy told him,
mouth set in a sullen line. Her eyes flicked to him
and skittered away just as fast before they could dwell
for too long on the dark, dramatic beauty of his lean
face because, once there, it was stupidly hard to tear
her gaze away.

'Correction—there's *every* need to be sarcastic
after you've bandied around terms such as *kidnapped*.
I told you that you should look on the bright side and
see this as a fully paid two-week vacation.' He dismissed Maria with a brief nod, because this looked as
though it was shaping up to be another one of *those*
conversations, then he shoved his hands in his pockets and stared down at her. She looked irritatingly
unrepentant. 'In the absence of your books, you'll

find that there is a private home cinema space with a comprehensive selection of movies. There are also two swimming pools—one indoor, one on the upper deck. And of course a library, should you decide that reading is a worthwhile option in the absence of your computer.'

'You're not very nice, are you?'

'Nice people finish last so, yes, that's an accolade I've been more than happy to pass up, which is something you'd do well to remember.'

Katy's eyes narrowed at the bitterness in his voice. Was he speaking from experience? What experience? She didn't want to be curious about him, but she suddenly was. Just for a moment, she realised that underneath the ruthless, cool veneer there would be all sorts of reasons for him being the man he was.

'Nice people don't always finish last,' she murmured sincerely.

'Oh, but they do.' Lucas's voice was cool and he was staring at her, his head at an angle, as if examining something weird he wasn't quite sure about. 'They get wrapped up in pointless sentimentality and emotion and open themselves up to getting exploited, so please don't think I'll be falling victim to that trait while we're out here.'

'Get exploited?' Katy found that she was holding her breath as she waited for his answer.

'Is that the sound of a woman trying to find out what makes me tick?' Lucas raised his eyebrows with wry amusement and began walking. 'Many have tried and failed in that venture, so I shouldn't bother if I were you.'

'It's very arrogant of you to assume that I want

to find out about you,' Katy huffed. 'But, as you've reminded me, we're going to be stuck here together for the next two weeks. I was just trying to have a conversation.'

'Like I said, I don't intend to be around much. When we do converse, we can keep it light.'

'I'm sorry.' She sighed, reaching to loop her long hair over one shoulder. 'Believe it or not, I can almost understand why you dragged me out here.'

'Well, at least *drag* is an improvement on *kidnap,*' Lucas conceded.

'I'm hot, tired and sticky, and sitting quietly at my desk working on my computer feels like a lifetime ago. I'm not in the best of moods.'

'I can't picture you sitting quietly anywhere. Maybe I've been remiss in not getting out and seeing what my employees are doing. What do you think? Should I have left my ivory tower and had a look at which of my employees were sitting and meekly doing their jobs and which ones were pushing the envelope?'

Katy reddened. His voice was suddenly lazy and teasing and her pulses quickened in response. How could he be so ruthless and arrogant one minute and then, in a heartbeat, make the blood rush to her head because of the way he was able to laugh at himself unexpectedly?

She didn't know whether it was because she had been yanked out of her comfort zone, but he was turning her off and on like a tap, and it unsettled her.

After Duncan, she had got her act together; she had looked for the silver lining and realised that he had pointed her in the right direction of what to look for in a man: someone down-to-earth, good-natured, genuine. Someone *normal*. When she found that man, everything else would fall into place, and she was horrified that a guy like Lucas Cipriani could have the sort of effect on her that he did. It didn't make sense and she didn't like it.

'I think my opinion doesn't count one way or another,' she said lightly. 'I can't speak for other people, but no one in my office actually expects you to swoop down and pay a visit.'

'You certainly know how to hit below the belt,' Lucas imparted drily. 'This your normal style when you're with a man?'

'You're not a man.'

Lucas laughed, a rich, throaty laugh that set her senses alight and had her pulses racing. 'Oh, no,' he murmured seriously. 'And here I was thinking that I was…'

'You know what I mean.' Rattled, Katy's gaze slid sideways and skittered away in confusion.

'Do I? Explain.' This wasn't the light conversation he had had in mind, but that wasn't to say that he wasn't enjoying himself, because he was. 'If I'm not a man, then what am I?'

'You're…you're my *captor*.'

Lucas grinned. 'That's a non-answer if ever there was one, but I'll let it go. Besides, I thought we'd got past the kidnap analogy.'

Katy didn't answer. He was being nice to her, teasing her. She knew that he still probably didn't trust her as far as he could throw her, but he was worldly wise and sophisticated, and knew the benefits of smoothing tensions and getting her onside. Constant sniping would bore him. He had been forced into a situation he hadn't banked on, just as she had, but he wasn't throwing temper tantrums. He wasn't interested in having meaningful conversations, because he wasn't interested in her and had no desire to find out anything about her, except what might impact on his business deal; but he would be civil now that he had told her in no uncertain terms what the lay of the land was. He had laughed about being called her captor, but he was, and he called the shots.

Instead of getting hot and bothered around him, she would have to step up to the plate and respond in kind.

They had reached the kitchen and she turned her attention away from him and looked around her. 'This is wonderful.' She ran her fingers over the counter. 'Where is Maria, your...chef?' She remained where she was, watching as he strolled to an over-sized fridge, one of two, and extracted a bottle of wine.

He poured them both a glass and nodded to one of the grey upholstered chairs tucked neatly under the metal kitchen table. Katy sat and sipped the wine very slowly, because she wasn't accustomed to drinking.

'Has her own quarters on the lower deck. I dismissed her rather than let her hang around listening to...a conversation she would have found puzzling. She might not have understood the meaning but she would have got the gist without too much trouble.'

Lucas sat opposite her. 'It is rare for me to be on this yacht with just one other person. It's generally used for client entertaining and occasionally for social gatherings. Under normal circumstances, there would be more than just one member of staff present, but there seemed little need to have an abundance of crew for two people. So, while we're here, Maria will clean and prepare meals.'

'Does she know why I'm here?'

'Why would she?' Lucas sounded genuinely surprised. 'It's none of her business. She's paid handsomely to do a job, no questions asked.'

'But wouldn't she be curious?' Katy couldn't help asking.

Lucas shrugged. 'Do I care?'

'*You* might not care,' she said tartly. 'But maybe *I* do. I don't want her thinking that I'm... I'm...'

'What?'

'I wouldn't want her thinking that I'm one of your women you've brought here to have a bit of fun with.'

Lucas burst out laughing. When he'd sobered up, he stared at her coolly.

'Why does it matter to you what my chef thinks of you? You'll never lay eyes on her again once this two-week stint is over. Besides...' he sipped his wine and looked at her over the rim of his glass '...I often fly Maria over to my place in London and occasionally to New York. She has seen enough of my women over the years to know that you don't fit the mould.'

Katy stared at him, mortified and embarrassed, because somehow she had ended up giving him the impression that...*what*? That she thought he might fancy her? That she thought her precious virtue might be *compromised* by being alone with him on this yacht, when she was only here because of circumstances? The surroundings were luxurious but this wasn't a five-star hotel with the man of her dreams. This was a prison in all but name and he was her gaoler...and since when did gaolers fancy their captives?

'Don't fit the mould?' she heard herself parrot in a jerky voice, and Lucas appeared to give that some consideration before nodding.

'Maria has been with me for a very long time,' he said without a shade of discomfort. 'She's met many of my women over the years. I won't deny that you have a certain appeal, but you're not my type, and she's savvy enough to know that. Whatever she thinks, it won't be that you're here for any reasons other than work. Indeed, I have occasionally used this as a work space with colleagues when I've needed extreme privacy in my transactions, so I wouldn't be a bit surprised if she puts that spin on your presence here.' He tried and failed to think of the woman sitting opposite him in the capacity of *work colleague*.

You have a certain appeal. Katy's brain had clunked to a stop at that throwaway remark and was refusing to budge. Why did it make her feel so flustered; hadn't she, two seconds ago, resolved not to let him get to her? She wanted to be as composed and collected as he was but she was all over the place.

Why was that? Was it the unsettling circumstances that had thrown them together? Lucas was sexy and powerful, but he was still just a man, and male attention, in the wake of Duncan, left her cold. So why did half a sentence from a man who wasn't interested in her make her skin prickle and tingle?

She forced her brain to take a few steps forward and said faintly, 'I didn't realise men had a type.' Which wasn't what she had really wanted to say. What she had *really* wanted to say was '*what's your type?*'

Rich men were always in the tabloids with women dripping from their arms and clinging to them like limpets. Rich men led lives that were always under the microscope, because the public loved reading about the lifestyles of the rich and famous, but she couldn't recall ever having seen Lucas Cipriani in any scandal sheets.

'All men have a *type*,' Lucas informed her. He had a type and he was clever enough to know *why* he had that particular type. As far as he was concerned, knowledge in that particular area was power. He would never fall victim to the type of manipulative women that his father had. He would always be in control of his emotional destiny. He had never had this sort of conversation with a woman in his life before, but then again his association with women ran along two tracks and only two. Either there was a sexual connection or else they were work associates.

Katy was neither. Yes, she worked for him, but she was not his equal in any way, shape or form.

And there was certainly no sexual connection there.

On cue, he gazed away from her face to the small jut of her breasts and the slender fragility of her arms. She really was tiny. A strong wind would knock her off her feet. She was the sort of woman that men instinctively felt the need to protect.

It seemed as good a time as any to remember just the sort of women he went for and, he told himself, keeping in the practical vein, to tell *her,* because, work or no work, aside from his chef there were only the two of them on board his yacht and he didn't want her to start getting any ideas.

She was a nobody suddenly plunged into a world of extreme luxury. He'd had sufficient experience over the years with women whose brains became scrambled in the presence of wealth.

'Here's *my* type,' he murmured, refilling both their glasses and leaning towards her, noting the way she reflexively edged back, amused by it. 'I don't do clingy. I don't do gold-diggers, airheads or any women who think that they can simper and preen their way to my bank balance—but, more than that, I don't care for women who demand more than I am capable of giving them. I lead an extremely pressurised working life. When it comes to my private life, I like women to be soothing and compliant. I enjoy the company of high fliers, career women whose independence matches my own. They know the rules of my game and there are never any unpleasant misunderstandings.'

He thought of the last woman in his life, a raven-haired beauty who was a leading light in the field of international law. In the end their mutually busy schedules had put paid to anything more than a six-month dalliance although, in fairness, he hadn't wanted more. Even the most highly intelligent and ferociously independent woman had a sell-by date in his life.

Katy was trying to imagine these high-flying, saintly paragons who didn't demand and who were also soothing and compliant. 'What would constitute them demanding more than you're capable of giving them?' she asked impulsively and Lucas frowned.

'Come again?'

'You said that you didn't like women who demanded more than you were capable of giving them. Do you mean *love and commitment*?'

'Nicely put,' Lucas drawled. 'Those two things are

off the agenda. An intellectually challenging relation-ship—with, of course, ample doses of fun—is what I look for and, fortunately, the women I go out with are happy with the arrangement.'

'How do you know?'

'How do I know what?'

'That they're happy. Maybe they really want more but they're too scared to say that because you tell them that you don't want a committed relationship.'

'Maybe. Who knows? We're getting into another one of those deep and meaningful conversations again.' He stood up and stretched, flexing muscles that rippled under his hand-tailored clothes. 'I've told you this,' he said, leaning down, hands planted squarely on the table, 'Because we're here and I wouldn't want any *wow* moments to go to your head.'

'I beg your pardon?'

'You're here because I need to keep an eye on you and make sure you don't do anything that could jeop-ardise a deal I've been working on for the past year and a half,' he said bluntly, although his voice wasn't unkind. He was unwillingly fascinated by the way her face could transmit what she was thinking, like a shining beacon advertising the lay of the land. 'I know you're out of your comfort zone but I wouldn't want you to get any ideas.'

Comprehension came in an angry rush...although, a little voice whispered treacherously in her head, *hadn't* she been looking at him? Had he spotted that and decided to nip any awkwardness in the bud by putting down 'no trespass' signs? She wasn't his type and he was gently but firmly telling her not to start thinking that she might be. 'You're right.' Katy sat back and folded her arms. 'I *am* out of my comfort zone and I *am* impressed. Who wouldn't be? But it takes more than a big boat with lots of fancy gadgets to suddenly turn its owner into someone I could *ever* be attracted to.'

'Is that a fact?'

'Yes, it is. I know my place and I'm perfectly happy there. You asked me why do I continue to work in a school? Because I enjoy giving back. I only work for your company, Mr Cipriani, because the pay enables me to afford my rent. If I could somehow be paid more as a teacher, then I would ditch your job in a heartbeat.' Katy thought that, at the rate she was going, she wouldn't have to ditch his job because *it* would be ditching *her*. 'You don't have to warn me off you and you don't have to be afraid that I'm going to start suddenly wanting to have a big boat like this of my own...'

'For goodness' sake, it's a *yacht*, not a *boat*.' And the guy who had overseen its unique construction and charged mightily for the privilege would be incandescent at her condescending referral to it as a boat. Although, Lucas thought, his lips twitching as he fought off a grin, it would certainly be worth seeing. The man, if memory served him right, had embodied all the worst traits of someone happy to suck up to the rich while stamping down hard on the poor.

Katy shrugged. 'You know what I mean. At any rate, Mr Cipriani, you don't want to be stuck here with me and I don't want to be stuck here with you either.'

'Lucas.'

'Sorry?'

'I think it's appropriate that we move onto first names. The name is Lucas.'

Flustered, Katy stared at him. 'I wouldn't feel right calling you by your first name,' she muttered, bright red. 'You're my boss.'

'I'll break the ice. Are you hungry, Katy? Maria will have prepared food and she will be unreasonably insulted if we don't eat what she has cooked. I'll call her up to serve us, after which she'll show you to your quarters.'

'Call her up?'

'The food won't magically appear on our plates.'

'I don't feel comfortable being waited on as though I'm royalty,' Katy told him honestly. 'If you direct me, I'm sure I can do whatever needs doing.'

'You're not the hired help, Katy.'

Katy shivered at the use of her name. It felt…*intimate*. She resolved to avoid calling him by his name unless absolutely necessary: perhaps if she fell overboard and was in the process of drowning. Even then she knew she would be tempted to stick to Mr Cipriani.

'That's not the point.' She stood up and looked at him, waiting to be directed, then she realised that he genuinely had no idea in which direction he should point her. She clicked her tongue and began rustling through the drawers, being nosy in the fridge before finding casserole dishes in the oven.

She could feel his dark, watchful eyes following her every movement, but she was relieved that he hadn't decided to fetch Maria, because this was taking away some of her jitters. Instead of sitting in front of him, perspiring with nerves and with nowhere to

rest her eyes except on *him,* which was the least rest-
ful place they could ever land, busying herself like
this at least occupied her, and it gave her time to get
her thoughts together and forgive herself for behav-
ing out of character.

It was understandable. Twenty-four hours ago,
she'd been doing her job and going through all the
usual daily routines. Suddenly she'd been thrown
blindfolded into the deep end of a swimming pool
and it was only natural for her to flounder before she
found her footing.

She could learn something from this because,
after Duncan, being kind to herself had come hard.
She had blamed herself for her misjudgements. How
could she have gone so wrong when she had spent a
lifetime being so careful and knowing just what she
wanted? She had spent months beating herself up for
her mistake in not spotting the kind of man he had
been. She had been raised by two loving parents who
had instilled the right values in her, so how had she
been sucked into a relationship with a man who had
no values at all?

So here she was, acting out of character and going
all hot and cold in the company of a man she had just
met five seconds ago. It didn't mean anything and
she wasn't going to beat herself up over it. There was
nothing wrong with her. It was all a very natural reaction to unforeseen circumstances.

Watching her, Lucas thought that this was just the
sort of domestic scene he had spent a lifetime avoiding. He also thought that, despite what he had said
about his high-flying career women wanting no more
than he was willing to give them, many of them had

tentatively broached the subject of a relationship that would be more than simply a series of fun one-night stands. He had always shot those makings of uncomfortable conversations down in flames. But looking at the way Katy was pottering in this kitchen, making herself at home, he fancied that many an ex would have been thrilled to do the same.

'I like cooking,' she told him, bringing the food to the table and guilt-tripping him into giving her a hand because, as he had pointed out with spot-on accuracy, she *wasn't* the hired help. 'It's not just because it feels wrong to summon Maria here to do what I could easily do, but I honestly enjoy playing around with food. This smells wonderful. Is she a qualified chef?'

'She's an experienced one,' Lucas murmured.

'Tell me where we're anchored,' Katy encouraged. 'I noticed an island. How big is it? Do you have a house there?'

'The island is big enough for essentials and, although there is some tourism, it's very exclusive, which is the beauty of the place. And, yes, I have a villa there. In fact, I had planned on spending a little time there on my own, working flat-out on finalising my deal without interruptions, but plans changed.'

He didn't dwell on that. He talked, instead, about the island and then, as soon as he was finished eating, he stood up and took his plate to the sink. Katy followed his lead, noticing that his little foray into domesticity didn't last long, because he remained by the sink, leaning against it with his arms folded. She couldn't help but be amused. Just like the perplexed frown when he had first entered the kitchen, his obvious lack of interest in anything domestic was something that came across as ridiculously macho yet curiously endearing. If a man like Lucas Cipriani could ever be *endearing,* she thought drily.

'You can leave that,' was his contribution. 'Maria will take care of it in the morning.'

Katy paused and looked up at him with a half-smile. Looking down at her, he had an insane urge to...to *what?*

She had a mouth that was lush, soft and ripe for kissing. Full, pink lips that settled into a natural, sexy pout. He wondered whether they were the same colour as her nipples, and he inhaled sharply because bringing her here was one thing, but getting ideas into his head about what she might feel like was another.

'I'll show you to your cabin,' he said abruptly, heading off without waiting while she hurriedly stacked the plates into the sink before tripping along behind him.

Let this be a lesson in not overstepping the mark, she thought firmly. They'd had some light conversation, as per his ground rules, but it would help to remember that they weren't pals and his tolerance levels when it came to polite chit chat would only go so far. Right now, he'd used up his day's quota, judging from the sprint in his step as he headed away from the kitchen.

'Have you brought swimsuits?' he threw over his shoulder.

'No.' She didn't even know what had happened to her bag.

Maria, as it turned out, had taken it and delivered it to the cabin she had been assigned. Lucas pushed open the door and Katy stood for a few seconds, looking at the luxurious bedroom suite, complete with a proper king-sized bed and a view of the blue ocean, visible through trendy oversized port holes. Lucas showed her a door that opened out onto a balcony and she followed him and stood outside in a setting that was impossibly romantic. Balmy air blew gently through her hair and, looking down, she saw dark waves slapping lazily against the side of the yacht. She was so conscious of him leaning against the railing next to her that she could scarcely breathe.

'In that case, there's an ample supply of laundered swimsuits and other items of clothing in the walk-in wardrobe in the cabin alongside yours. Feel free to help yourself.'

'Why would that be?'

'People forget things. Maria digs her heels in at throwing them out. I've stopped trying to convince her.' He raked his fingers through his hair and watched as she half-opened her mouth, and that intensely physical charge rushed through him again.

'Okay.'

'You have the freedom of my yacht. I'll work while I'm here and the time will fly past, just as long as we don't get in one another's way...'

CHAPTER FOUR

LUCAS LOOKED AT the document he had been editing for half an hour, only to realise that he had hardly moved past the first two lines.

At this point in time, and after three days of enforced isolation on his yacht, he should have been powering through the intense backlog of work he had brought with him. Instead, he had been wasting time thinking about the woman sharing his space on his yacht.

Frustrated, he stood up, strolled towards the window and stared out, frowning, at a panoramic view of open sea. Every shade of blue and turquoise combined, in the distance, into a dark-blue line where the sea met the skyline. At a little after three, it was still very hot and very still, with almost no breeze at all rippling the glassy surface of the water.

He'd looked at this very skyline a hundred times in the past, stared through this very window of his office on the lower deck, and had never been tempted to leave it for the paradise beckoning outside. He'd never been good at relaxing, and indeed had often found himself succumbing to it more through necessity than anything else. Sitting around in the sun doing nothing was a waste of valuable time, as far as he was concerned; and on the few occasions he had been on weekend breaks with a woman he had found himself enduring the time spent playing tourist with a certain amount of barely concealed impatience.

He was a workaholic and the joys of doing nothing held zero appeal for him.

Yet, he was finding it difficult to concentrate. If he had noticed Katy's delicate, ridiculous prettiness on day one, and thought he could studiously file it away as something he wasn't going to allow to distract him, then he'd made a big mistake because the effect she was having on him was increasing with every second spent in her company.

He'd done his best to limit the time they were together. He'd reminded himself that, were it not for an unfortunate series of events, the woman wouldn't even be on his yacht now, but for all his well-constructed, logical reasons for avoiding her his body remained stubbornly recalcitrant.

Perversely, the more uptight he felt in her company, the more relaxed she seemed to be in his.

Since when had the natural order of things been rearranged? For the first time in his life, he wasn't calling the shots, and *that* was what was responsible for his lack of focus.

Being stuck on the yacht with Katy had made him realise that the sassy, independent career women he dated had not been as challenging as he had always liked to think they were. They'd all been as subservient and eager to please as any vacuous airhead keen to burn a hole in his bank account. In contrast, Katy didn't seem to have a single filter when it came to telling him what she thought about…anything and everything.

So far, he had been regaled with her opinions on money, including his own. She had scoffed at the foolishness of racing towards power and status, without bothering to hide the fact that he was top of her list as a shining example of someone leading the race. She had quizzed him on what he did in his spare time, and demanded to know whether he ever did anything that was actually *ordinary*. She seemed to think that his lack of knowledge of the layout of his own private yacht's kitchen was a shocking crime against humanity, and had then opined that there was such a thing as more money than sense.

In short, she had managed to be as offensive as any human being was capable of being and, to his astonishment, he had done nothing to redress the balance by exerting the sort of authority that would have stalled her mid-sentence.

He had the power in his hands to ruin her career but the thought had not crossed his mind.

She might have been in his company for all the wrong reasons, but he was no longer suspicious of her motives, especially when she had no ability to contact anyone at all, and her openness was strangely engaging.

It was also an uncomfortable reminder as to how far he normally went when it came to getting exactly what he wanted, and that he had surrounded himself with people who had forgotten how to contradict him.

Without giving himself a chance to back out, he headed to his quarters and did the unthinkable: he swapped his khakis for a pair of swimming trunks that hadn't seen the light of day in months, if not years, and a tee-shirt.

Barefoot, grabbing a towel on the way, he headed up to the pool area where he knew Katy was going to be.

She had been oddly reticent about using the swimming pool and, chin tilted at the mutinous angle he was fast becoming accustomed to, she had finally confessed that she didn't like using stuff that didn't belong to her.

'Would you rather the swimsuits all sit unused in cupboards until it's time for the lot to be thrown away?'

'Would you throw away perfectly good clothes?'

'I would if it was cluttering up my space. You wouldn't have to borrow them if you'd thought ahead and brought a few of your own.'

'I had no idea I would be anywhere near a pool,' she had been quick to point out, and he had dealt her a slashing grin, enjoying the way the colour had rushed into her cheeks.

'And now you are. Roll with the punches, would be my advice.'

His cabin was air-conditioned, and as he headed up towards the pool on the upper deck he was assailed by heat. It occurred to him that she might not be there, that she might have gone against her original plan of reading in the afternoon and working on ideas for an app to help the kids in her class with their homework, something he had discovered after some probing. If she wasn't there, he'd be bloody disappointed, and that nearly stopped him in his tracks because disappointment wasn't something he associated with the opposite sex.

He enjoyed the company of women. He wasn't promiscuous but the truth was that no woman had ever had the power to hold his attention for any sustained length of time, so he had always been the first to do the dispatching. By which point, he was always guiltily relieved to put the relationship behind him. In that scenario, disappointment wasn't something that had ever featured.

Katy, with her quirky ways and forthright manner, was yanking him along by some sort of invisible chain and he was uneasily aware that it was something he should really put a stop to.

Indeed, he paused, considering that option. It would take him less than a minute to make it back down to his office where he could resume work.

Except...would he be able to? Or would he sit at his desk allowing his mind idly to drift off to the taboo subject of his sexy captive?

Lucas had no idea what he hoped to gain by hitting the upper deck and joining her by the pool. So what if she was attractive? The world was full of attractive women and he knew, without a shred of vanity, that he could have pretty much any of them he wanted.

Playing with his reluctant prisoner wasn't on the cards. He'd warned her off getting any ideas into her head so there was no way he was going to try to get her into his bed now.

Just thinking about that, even as he was fast shoving it out of his head, conjured up a series of images that sent his pulses racing and fired up his libido as though reacting to a gun at the starting post.

He reached out one hand and supported himself heavily against the wall, allowing his breathing to settle. His common sense was fighting a losing battle with temptation, telling him to hot foot it back to the office and slam the metaphorical door on the siren lure of a woman who most definitely wasn't his sort.

He continued on, passing Maria in the kitchen preparing supper, and giving a brief nod before heading up. Then the sun was beating down on him as he took a few seconds to appreciate the sight of the woman reclining on a deck chair, eyes closed, arms hanging loosely over the sides of the chair, one leg bent at the knee, the other outstretched.

She had tied her long, vibrant hair into some kind of rough bun and a book lay open on the ground next to her.

Lucas walked softly towards her. He hadn't seen her like this, only just about decently clothed, and his breathing became sluggish as he took in the slender daintiness of her body: flat stomach, long, smooth legs, small breasts.

He cleared his throat and wondered whether he would be able to get his vocal cords to operate. 'Good job I decided to come up here…' He was inordinately thankful for the dark sunglasses that shielded his expression. 'You're going pink. Where's your sunblock? With your skin colouring, too much sun and you'll end up resembling a lobster—and your two-week prison sentence might well end up being longer than you'd bargained for. Sun burn can be a serious condition.'

'What are you *doing* here?' Katy jack-knifed into a sitting position and drew her knees up to her chest, hugging herself and glowering from a position of disadvantage as he towered over her, all six-foot-something of bronzed, rippling muscle.

Her eyes darted down to his legs and darted away again just as fast. Something about the dark, silky hair shadowing his calves and thighs brought her out in a sweat.

She licked her lips and steadied her racing pulse. She'd kept up a barrage of easy chatter for the past few days, had striven to project the careless, outspoken insouciance that she hoped would indicate to him that she wasn't affected by him, *not at all,* and she wasn't going to ruin the impression now.

He'd warned her not to go getting any ideas and that had been the trigger for her to stop gaping and allowing him to get under her skin. She was sure that the only reason he had issued that warning was because he had noticed her reaction to him and, from that moment onwards, she had striven to subdue any wayward reactions under a never-ending stream of small talk.

To start with, she'd aimed to keep the small talk *very* small, anything to break the silence as they had shared meals. In the evenings, before he left to return to the bowels of the yacht, they'd found themselves continuing to talk over coffee and wine.

Her aim had been harder to stick to than she'd thought because something about him fired her up. Whilst she managed to contain her body's natural impulse to be disobedient—by making sure she was physically as far away from him as possible without being too obvious—she'd been seduced into provoking him, enjoying the way he looked at her when she said something incendiary, head to one side, his dark eyes veiled and assessing.

It was a subtle form of intellectual arousal that

kept her on a permanent high and it was as addictive as a drug.

In Lucas's presence, Duncan no longer existed.

In fact, thanks to Lucas's all-consuming and wholly irrational ability to rivet her attention, Katy had reluctantly become aware of just how affected she had been by Duncan's betrayal. Even when she had thought she'd moved on, he had still been there in the background, a troubling spectre that had moulded her relationships with the opposite sex.

'I own the yacht,' Lucas reminded her lazily. He began stripping off the tee-shirt and tossed it onto a deckchair, which he pulled over with his foot so that it was right next to her. 'Do you think I should have asked your permission before I decided to come up here and use the pool?'

'No, of course not,' Katy replied, flustered. 'I just thought that you had your afternoon routine and you worked until seven in the evening...'

'Routines are made to be broken.' He settled down onto the deck chair and turned so that he was looking at her, still from behind the dark shades that gave him a distinct advantage. 'Haven't you been lecturing me daily on my evil workaholic ways?'

'I never said that they were *evil*.'

'But you were so persuasive in convincing me that I was destined for an early grave that I decided to follow your advice and take some time out.' He grinned and tilted his shades up to look at her. 'You're not reacting with the sort of smug satisfaction I might have expected.'

'I didn't think that you would actually listen to

what I said,' Katy muttered, her whole body as rigid as a plank of wood.

She wanted to look away but her greedy eyes kept skittering back to him. He was just so unbelievably perfect. More perfect than anything she had conjured up in her fevered imaginings. His chest was broad and muscular, with just the right dusting of dark hair that made her draw her breath in sharply, and the line of dark hair running down from his belly button electrified her senses like a live wire. How was it possible for a man to be so sexy? So sinfully, darkly and *dangerously* sexy?

Every inch of him eclipsed her painful memories of Duncan and she was shocked that those memories had lingered for as long as they had.

Watching him, her imagination took flight. She thought of those long, clever fingers stroking her, touching her breasts, lingering to circle her nipples. She felt faint. Her nipples were tight and pinched, and between her legs liquid heat was pooling and dampening her bikini bottoms.

She realised that she had been fantasising about this man since they had stepped foot on the yacht, but those fantasies had been vague and hazy compared to the force of the graphic images filling her head as she looked away with a tight, determined expression.

It was his body, she thought. Seeing him like that, in nothing but a pair of black trunks, was like fodder for her already fevered imagination.

Under normal circumstances, she might have looked at him and appreciated him for the drop-dead, gorgeous guy that he was, but actually she wouldn't have turned that very natural appreciation into a full-on mental sexual striptease that had him parading naked in her head.

But these weren't normal circumstances and *that* was why her pragmatic, easy-going and level-headed approach to the opposite sex had suddenly deserted her.

'Tell me about the deal.' She launched weakly into the first topic of conversation that came into her head, and Lucas flung himself back into the deck chair and stared up at a faultlessly blue, cloudless sky.

He was usually more than happy to discuss work-related issues, except right now and right here that was the last thing he wanted to do. 'Persuade me that you give a damn about it.' He slanted a sideways look at her and then kept looking as delicate colour tinged her cheeks.

'Of course I do.' Katy cleared her throat. 'I'm here *because* of it, aren't I?'

'Are you enjoying yourself?' He folded his arms behind his head and stared at her. 'You're only here because of the deal but, now that you *are* here, are you having a good time?'

Katy opened her mouth to ask him what kind of question that was, because how on earth could she be having a good time when life as she knew it had been turned upside down? Except she blinked and thought that she *was* having a good time. 'I've never been anywhere like this before,' she told him. 'When I was a kid, holidays were a week in a freezing-cold British seaside town. Don't get me wrong, I adored my holidays, but this is…out of this world.'

She looked around her and breathed in the warm breeze, rich with the salty smell of the sea. 'It's a different kind of life having a father who's the local parish priest,' she confided honestly. 'On the one hand, it was brilliant, because I never lacked love and support from both my parents, especially as I was an only child. They wanted more but couldn't have them. My mum once told me that she had to restrain herself from lavishing gifts on me, but of course there was always a limit to what they could afford. And besides, as I've told you, they always made sure to tell me that money wasn't the be-all and end-all.' She looked at Lucas and smiled, somewhat surprised that she was telling him all this, not that any of it was a secret.

Never one to encourage confidences from women, Lucas was oddly touched by her confession because she was usually so outspoken in a tomboyish, challenging way.

'Hence your entrenched disregard for money,' he suggested drily. 'Tell me about the down sides of life in a vicarage. I'll be honest with you, you're the first daughter of a man of the cloth I've ever met.'

The image of the happy family stuck in his mind and, in a rare bout of introspection, he thought back to his own troubled youth after his mother had died. His father had had the love, but he had just not quite known how to deliver it and, caught up in his own grief and his never-ending quest to find a substitute for the loss of his wife, he had left a young Lucas to find his own way. The independence Lucas was now so proud of, the mastery over his own emotions and his talent for self-control, suddenly seemed a little tarnished at the edges, too hard-won to be of any real value.

He dismissed the worrying train of thought and

encouraged her to keep talking. She had a very melodic voice and he enjoyed the sound of it as much as he enjoyed the animation that lit up her ravishingly pretty, heart-shaped face.

'Down sides... Well, now, let me have a think...!' She smiled and lay down on the deck chair so that they were now both side by side, faces upturned to the brilliant blue sky above. She glanced across at him, expecting to see amusement and polite interest, just a couple of people chatting about nothing in particular. Certainly nothing that would hold the interest of a man like Lucas Cipriani. But his dark, fathomless eyes were strangely serious as he caught her gaze and held it for a few seconds, and she shivered, mouth going dry, ensnared by the gravity of his expression.

'So?' Lucas murmured, closing his eyes and enjoying the warmth and the rarity of not doing anything.

'So...you end up always knowing that you have to set a good example because your parents are pillars of the community. I could never afford to be a rebel.'

Even when she had gone to university her background had followed her. She'd been able to have a good time, and stay out late and drink with the best of them, but she had never slept around or even come close to it. Maybe if she hadn't had so many morals drilled into her from an early age she would have just got sex out of the way and then would have been relaxed when it came to finding relationships. Maybe she would have accepted that not all relationships were serious, that some were destined to fall by the wayside, but that didn't mean they weren't worthwhile.

It was a new way of thinking for Katy and she gave

it some thought because she had always assumed, post-Duncan, that she would hang on to her virginity, would have learned her lesson, would be better equipped to make the right judgement calls.

Thinking that she could deviate from that path gave her a little frisson of excitement.

'Not that I was ever tempted,' she hurriedly expanded. 'I had too much experience of seeing where drugs and drink and casual sex could lead a person. My dad is very active in the community and does a lot outside the village for down-and-outs. A lot of them ended up where they did because of poor choices along the way.'

'I feel like I'm talking to someone from another planet.'

'Why?'

'Because your life is so vastly different from anything I've come across.'

Katy laughed. Lying side by side made it easier to talk to him. If they'd been sitting opposite one another at the table in the kitchen, with the yacht rocking softly as they ate, she wasn't sure she would have been able to open up like this. She could spar with him and provoke him until she could see him gritting his teeth in frustration—in fact, she got a kick out of that—but this was different.

She couldn't even remember having a conversation like this with Duncan, who had split his time talking about himself and flirting relentlessly with her.

'What do you come across?' she asked lightly, dropping her hands to either side of the deck chair and tracing little circles on the wooden decking.

'Tough career women who don't make a habit of

getting too close to down-and-outs,' Lucas told her wryly. 'Unless, in the case of at least a couple of them who were top barristers, a crime had been committed and they happened to be confronted with one of those down-and-outs in a court of law.'

'I remember you telling me,' Katy murmured, 'About those tough career women who never wanted more than you were prepared to give them and were always soothing and agreeable.'

Lucas laughed. That had been when he'd been warning her off him, just in case she got ideas into her head. On cue, he inclined his head slightly and looked at her. She was staring up at the sky, eyes closed. Her long, dark lashes cast shadows on her cheeks and her mouth, in repose, was a full, pink pout. The sun had turned her a pale biscuit-gold colour and brought out shades of strawberry blonde amidst the deep russets and copper of her hair. Eyes drifting down, he followed the line of her shoulders and the swell of her breasts under the bikini, which he had not really been able to appreciate when she had been hugging her knees to herself, making sure that as little of her body was on show as humanly possible.

The bikini was black and modest by any modern standard but nothing could conceal the tempting swell of her pert, small breasts, the barely there cleavage, the jut of her hip bones and the silky smoothness of her thighs.

Lucas didn't bother to give in to consternation at the hot, pulsing swell of his arousal which, had she only opened her big green eyes and cast a sideways glance at him, she'd have noticed was distorting his swimming trunks.

He'd acknowledged her appeal from day one, from the very second she had walked into his office. No red-blooded male could have failed to. He'd also noted her belligerence and lack of filter when it came to speaking her mind, which was why he had decided to take on babysitting duties personally until his deal was safely in the bag. When you took into account that she had shimmered into his line of vision as a woman not averse to sleeping with married men, one who could not be trusted, it had seemed the obvious course of action.

But he knew, deep down, that even though he had dismissed any notion of going anywhere near Katy the prospect of being holed up with her for a fortnight had not exactly filled him with distaste.

He wondered whether he had even played with the forbidden thought of doing what his body wanted against the wishes of his brain. Or maybe he had been invigorated just by the novelty of having that mental tussle at all. In his well-ordered life, getting what he wanted had never posed a challenge, and internal debates about what he should or shouldn't do rarely featured, especially when it came to women.

He thought that if she had lived down to expectations and proved herself to be the sort of girl who had no morals, and really *might* have tried her luck with him, he would have had no trouble in eating, breathing and sleeping work. However, she hadn't, and the more his curiosity about her had been piqued the more he had been drawn to her like a wanderer hearing the call of a siren.

Which was so not him *at all* that he almost didn't know how to deal with it.

Except, his body was dealing with it in the time-honoured way, he thought, and then hard on the heels of that thought he wondered what she would do if she looked and saw the kind of response she'd awakened in him.

Katy wasn't sure whether it was the sudden silence, or just something thick and electric in the air, but she opened her eyes and turned her head, her mouth already opening to say something bland and chirpy to dispel the sudden tension.

His eyes caught hers and she stopped breathing. She had a drowning sensation as she was swallowed up in the deep, dark, quiet depths of his eyes. Those eyes were telegraphing a message to her, or they seemed to be. Was she imagining it? She had no experience of a man like him. That cool, brooding, speculative expression seemed to be inviting a response, but was it? Flustered and confused, her eyes dipped...

And then there was no doubt exactly what message was being telegraphed.

For a few seconds, Katy froze while her mind went into free fall. He was *turned on*. Did he think that he could try it on and she would fall in line because she was easy? Who knew, he probably still believed that she was the sort who had affairs with married men, even though he surely should know better, because she had shared stuff with him, told him about her childhood and her parents and the morals they had instilled in her. Maybe he hadn't believed her. Maybe he had taken it all with a pinch of salt because he was suspicious and mistrustful.

She *wasn't* easy. And yet, unleashed desire flooded through her in an unwanted torrent, crashing through common sense and good intentions. *She wanted this man, this unsuitable man, and she wanted him with a craving that was as powerful as a depth charge.*

The shocking intensity of a physical response she had never, *ever* felt towards any man, including Duncan, scared the living daylights out of her. Mumbling something under her breath, she leapt to her feet, the glittering blue of the infinity pool beckoning like an oasis of safety away from the onslaught of confusion overwhelming her.

Heart hammering in her chest, she scrambled forward, missed the step that gave down to the smooth wood around the pool and found herself flying forward.

She landed with a painful thump, her knees stinging where she had grazed them after her airborne flight.

Clutching her leg, she watched in fascinated slow motion as Lucas strode towards her, every lean muscle of his body intent.

'What were you thinking?' he asked urgently, scooping her up and ignoring her protests that he put her down because she was *absolutely fine.* 'You took off like a bat out of hell. Something I said?'

He was striding away from the pool area, carrying her as easily as he would carry a couple of cushions. Katy clutched his broad shoulders, horribly aware that in this semi-folded position there were bits of her on view that made her want to die an early death from embarrassment.

One glance down and he would practically be able to see the shadow of one of her nipples.

'Where are you taking me?' she croaked. 'This is ridiculous. I tripped and fell!'

'You could have broken something.'

'I haven't broken *anything*!' Katy practically sobbed.

'How do you know?'

'Because if I had I wouldn't be able to walk!'

'You're not walking. I'm carrying you. How much do you weigh, by the way? You're as light as a feather. If I didn't see how much food you're capable of putting away, I'd be worried.'

'I've always been thin,' Katy said faintly, barely noticing where they were going because she was concentrating very hard on making sure no more of her bikini-clad body went on show. She felt she might be on the verge of passing out. 'Please just take me to my cabin. That would be fine. I can clean my knee up and I'll be as right as rain.'

'Nonsense. How could I live with myself if I didn't do the gentlemanly thing and make sure you're all right? I wasn't brought up to ignore damsels in distress.'

'I'm not one of those!'

'Here we are,' Lucas intoned with satisfaction. He kicked open the door and, when Katy tore her focus away from her excruciating attempts to keep her body safely tucked away in the swimsuit, she realised where he had taken her.

Away from the safety of the pool and straight into the hellfire of his private quarters.

CHAPTER FIVE

LUCAS'S CABIN WAS different from hers insofar as it was twice the size and unnervingly masculine: dark-grey silky throw on the bed, dark-grey pillows, built-in furniture in rich walnut that matched the wooden flooring. He laid her on the bed and she immediately wriggled into a sitting position, wishing that she had something to tug down to cover herself, but instead having to make do with arranging herself into the most modest position possible, back upright, legs rammed close together and hands primly folded on her lap.

Sick with tension, she watched him disappear into an adjoining bathroom, that made hers look like a shower cubicle, to return a minute later with a first-aid kit.

'This really isn't necessary…er… Lucas.'

'You managed the first name. Congratulations. I wondered whether you would.'

'I have a few grazes, that's all.'

He was kneeling in front of her and he began to feel her ankle with surprisingly gently fingers. 'Tell me if anything hurts.'

'Nothing,' Katy stated firmly. She gave a trial tug

of her leg so that Lucas could get the hint that this was all pretty ridiculous and overblown but he wasn't having it.

Relax, she told herself sternly; *relax and it'll be over and done with in a second and you can bolt back to your cabin.* But how could she even begin to relax when those fingers were doing all sorts of things to her body?

The feathery delicacy of his touch was stirring her up, making her breathing quicken and sending tingling, delicious sensations racing through her body like little lightning sparks. She looked at his down-bent head, the raven-black hair, and had to stop herself from reaching out and touching it just to see what it felt like between her fingers.

Then she thought of the bulge of his arousal and felt faint all over again.

'I'm surprised you have a first-aid kit to hand,' she said breathlessly, tearing her fascinated gaze away from him and focusing hard on trying to normalise the situation with pointless conversation.

'Why?' Lucas glanced up briefly before continuing with his exceedingly slow exploration of her foot.

'Because you don't seem to be the type to do this sort of thing,' Katy said honestly.

'It's essential to have a first-aid kit on board a sailing vessel. In fact, this is just one of many. There's a comprehensive supply of medical equipment in a store room on the middle deck. You would be surprised at the sort of unexpected accidents that can happen when you're out at sea, and there's no ambulance available to make a five-minute dash to collect and take you to the nearest hospital.' He was working his way gently up her calf, which was smooth, slender and sprinkled with golden hair. Her skin was like satin and still warm from the sun.

'And you know how to deal with all those unexpected accidents?' Lucas's long, clever fingers were getting higher and, with each encroaching inch, her body lit up like a Christmas tree just a tiny bit more. Any higher and she would go up in flames.

'You'd be surprised,' Lucas drawled. 'Your knees are in a pretty terrible state, but after I've cleaned them up you should be fine. You'll be pleased to know that nothing's been broken.'

'I told you that,' Katy reminded him. 'Why would I be surprised?'

He was now gently swabbing her raw, torn skin and she winced as he patted the area with some oversized alcohol wipes, making sure to get rid of every last bit of dirt.

'Because,' Lucas said wryly, not looking at her, 'I get the feeling you've pigeonholed me as the sort of money-hungry, ambitious businessman who hasn't got time for anything other than getting richer and richer and richer, probably at the expense of everyone around him. Am I right?'

'I never said that,' Katy told him faintly.

'It's hard not to join the dots when your opening words to me were to accuse me of being capable of kidnapping you.'

'You *were* kidnapping me, in a manner of speaking!'

'Tell me how it feels to be a kidnap victim.' His voice was light and teasing as he continued to tend to her knee, now applying some kind of transparent ointment, before laboriously bandaging it and then turning his attention to foot number two. 'I always wanted to be a doctor,' he surprised her and himself by saying.

'What happened?' For the first time since she had been deposited on his bed, Katy felt herself begin to relax, the nervous tension temporarily driven away by a piercing curiosity. Lucas could be many things, as she had discovered over the past few days. He could be witty, amusing, arrogant and always, always wildly, extravagantly intelligent. But confiding? No.

'My father's various wives happened,' Lucas said drily. 'One after each other. They looked alike and they certainly were all cut from the same cloth. They had their eyes on the main prize and, when their tenure ran out, my father's fortune was vastly diminished. By the time I hit sixteen, I realised that, left to his own devices, he would end up with nothing to live on. It would have killed my father to have seen the empire his grandfather had built dwindle away in a series of lawsuits and maintenance payments to greedy ex-wives.

'I knew my father had planned on my inheriting the business and taking over, and I had always thought that I'd talk to him about that change of plan when the time was right; but, as it turned out, the time never became right because without me the company would have ended up subdivided amongst a string of gold-diggers and that would have been that.'

'So you gave up your hopes and dreams?'

'Don't get too heavy on the pity card.' Lucas laughed, sitting back on his heels to inspect his work, head tilted to one side. He looked at her and her mouth went dry as their eyes tangled. 'I enjoy my life.'

'But it's a far cry from being a doctor.' She had never imagined him having anything to do with the caring profession and something else was added to the swirling mix of complex responses she was stockpiling towards him. She thought that the medical profession had lost something pretty big when he had decided to pursue a career in finance because, knowing the determination and drive he brought to his chosen field of work, he surely would have brought tenfold to the field of medicine.

'So it is,' Lucas concurred. 'Hence the fact that I actually enjoy being hands-on when it comes to dealing with situations like this.'

'And have you had to deal with many of them?' She thought of him touching another woman, one of the skinny, leggy ones to whom those thong swimsuits forgotten on the yacht belonged, carefully stored just in case someone like her might come along and need to borrow one of them.

'No.' He stood up. 'Like I said, my time on this yacht is limited, and no one to date has obliged me by requiring mouth-to-mouth resuscitation whilst out to sea.' He disappeared back into the bathroom with the kit and, instead of taking the opportunity to stand up and prepare herself for a speedy exit, Katy remained on the bed, gently flexing both her legs and getting accustomed to the stiffness where the bandages had been applied expertly over her wounds.

'So I'm your first patient?'

Lucas remained by the door to the bathroom, lounging against the doorframe.

Katy was riveted at the sight. He was still wearing his bathing trunks although, without her even noticing when he had done it, he had slung on his tee-shirt. He was barefoot and he exuded a raw, animal sexiness that took her breath away.

'Cuts and grazes don't honestly count.' Lucas grinned and strolled towards her, holding her spellbound with his easy, graceful strides across the room. He moved to stand by the window which, as did hers, looked out on the blue of an ocean that was as placid as the deepest of lakes. His quarters were air-conditioned, as were hers, but you could almost feel the heat outside because the sun was so bright and the sky was so blue and cloudless.

'I'm sorry if I ruined your down time.'

'You never told me why you leapt off your deck-chair and raced for the pool as though the hounds of hell were after you,' Lucas murmured.

She was in his bedroom and touching her had ignited a fire inside him, the same fire that had been burning steadily ever since they had been on his yacht. He knew why she had leapt off that deck chair. He had enough experience of the opposite sex to register when a woman wanted him, and it tickled him to think that she wasn't doing what every other woman would have done and flirting with him. Was that because she worked for him? Was that holding her back? Maybe she thought that he would sack her if she was too obvious. Or maybe she had paid attention to the speech he had given her at the start when he had told her not to get any crazy ideas about a relationship developing between them.

He almost wished that he hadn't bothered with that

speech because it turned him on to imagine her making a pass at him.

Lucas enjoyed a couple of seconds wondering what it would feel like to have her begin to touch him, blushing and awkward, but then his innate pragmatism kicked in and he knew that she was probably playing hard to get, which was the oldest game in the world when it came to women. She had revealed all sorts of sides to her that he hadn't expected, but the reality was that she *had* had an affair with a married man. She'd denied that she'd known about the wife and kiddies, and maybe she hadn't. Certainly there was an honesty about her that he found quite charming but, even so, he wasn't going to be putting any money on her so-called innocence any time soon.

'It was very hot out there,' Katy muttered awkwardly, heating up as she recalled the pivotal moment when raging, uncontrolled desire had taken her over like a fast-moving virus and she had just *had to escape.* 'I just fancied a dip in the pool and unfortunately I didn't really look where I was going. I should head back to my room now. I think I'll give my legs a rest just while I have these bandages on—and, by the way, thank you very much for sorting it out. There was no need, but thanks anyway.'

'How long do you think we should carry on pretending that there's nothing happening between us?' Which, frankly, was a question Lucas had never had to address to any other women because other women had never needed persuading into his bed. Actually, it was a question he had not envisaged having to ask *her,* considering the circumstances that had brought them together. But he wanted her and there was no point having a mental tussle over the whys and where-fores or asking himself whether it made sense or not.

On this occasion, self-denial probably made sense, but Lucas knew himself and he knew that, given the option of going down the route of what made sense or the less sensible route of scratching an itch, then the less sensible route was going to win the day hands down every time.

He also knew that he wasn't a man who was into breaking down barriers and jumping obstacles in order to get any woman between the sheets—and why would he do that anyway? This wasn't a game of courtship that was going anywhere. It was a case of two adults who fancied one another marooned on a yacht for a couple of weeks..

In receipt of this blunt question, presented to her without the benefit of any pretty packaging, Katy's eyes opened wide and her mouth fell open.

'I beg your pardon?'

'I've seen the way you look at me,' Lucas mur-mured, moving to sit on the bed right next to her, and depressing the mattress with his weight so that Katy had to shift to adjust her body and stop herself from sliding against him.

She should have bolted. His lazy, dark eyes on her were like lasers burning a hole right through the good, old-fashioned, grounded common sense that had dic-tated her behaviour all through her life—with the ex-ception of those few disastrous months when she had fallen for Duncan.

The slow burning heat that had been coursing through her, the exciting tingle between her legs and the tender pinching of her sensitive nipples—all responses activated by being in his presence and feeling his cool fingers on her—were fast disappearing under a tidal wave of building anger.

'The way I *look at you*?'

'Don't be embarrassed. Believe me, it isn't usually my style to force anyone's hand, but we're here and there's a sexual chemistry between us. Are you going to dispute that? It's in the air like an invisible electric charge.' He laughed with some incredulity. 'You're not going to believe this, but it's something I can't remember feeling in a very long time, if ever.'

'And you think I should be *flattered*?'

Lucas frowned because this wasn't the reaction he had been expecting. 'Frankly, yes,' he told her with complete honesty.

Katy gaped, even though she knew very well why a woman would be flattered to be the object of attention from Lucas Cipriani. He was drop-dead gorgeous and a billionaire to boot. If he made a pass at a woman, then what woman was going to stalk off in the opposite direction and slam the door in his face? He probably had a queue of them waiting to be picked.

Her lips tightened because what he saw as a flattering, complimentary approach was, to her, downright insulting.

At least the creep Duncan had had the wit to approach her a little less like a bull stampeding through a china shop.

But then, Katy concluded sourly, time wasn't on Lucas's side. They were here for a limited duration, so why waste any precious time trying to seduce her into bed the old-fashioned way?

'That's the most egotistical, arrogant thing I have ever heard *in my entire life*!'

'Because I've been honest?' But Lucas flushed darkly. 'I thought you were all in favour of the honest approach?'

'Who do you think I am?'

'I have no idea where you're going with this.'

'You think that you just have to snap your fingers and someone like me will dump all her principles and come running, don't you?'

'Someone like you?' But she had scored a direct hit, and he was guiltily aware that he *had* indeed compartmentalised her, however much he had seen evidence to the contrary.

'The sort of person,' Katy informed him with scathing distaste, 'Who needs a good, long lecture on making sure her little head doesn't get turned by being on a big, expensive boat—oh, sorry, *super-yacht*— with the great Lucas Cipriani! The sort of person,' she added for good measure, 'Who comes with a dubious reputation as someone who thinks it's okay to hop into bed with a married guy!' It made her even madder to think that she had fallen into the trap of forgetting who he really was, won over by his charm and the random confidences he had thrown her way which she had sucked up with lamentable enthusiasm.

And what made her even madder *still* was the fact that he had managed to read her so correctly! She thought she'd been the model of politeness, but he'd seen right through that and homed in laser-like on the fevered core of her that was attracted to him.

'You're over-analysing.' Lucas raked his fingers

through his hair and sprang to his feet to pace the cabin before standing by the window to look at her.

'I am *not* over-analysing,' Katy told him fiercely. 'I know what you think of me.'

'You don't.' Unaccustomed to apologising for anything he said or did, Lucas now felt...like a cad. He couldn't credit how she had taken his interest in her and transformed it into an insult, yet he had to admit to himself that his approach had hardly been handled with finesse. He'd been clumsy, and in no one's wildest imagination could it have passed for *honesty*.

'I know exactly what you think of me! And you've got a damned cheek to imagine that I would be so easy that I'd just fall into bed with you because you happened to extend the invite.'

'I... I apologise,' Lucas said heavily, and that apology was so unexpected that Katy could only stare at him with her mouth open. He looked at her with a roughened sincerity and she fought against relenting.

Glaring, she stood up. Her good intentions of sweeping out of his cabin with her head held high, now that she had roundly given him a piece of her mind, were undermined by the fact that she was wearing next to nothing and had to hobble a bit because the grazes on her knees were killing her.

'Katy,' he murmured huskily, stopping her in her tracks. He reached out to stay her and the pressure on her arm where his fingers circled her skin was as powerful as a branding iron. She had to try not to flinch. Awareness shot through her, rooting her to the spot. 'I don't, actually, think that you're easy and I certainly don't take it for granted that you're going to fall into bed with me because that's the kind of person you are. And,' he continued with grudging sincerity, 'If there's a part of me that is still wary, it's because it's my nature to be suspicious. The bottom line is that I want you, and I might be wrong but I think it's mutual. So tell me…is it?'

He took half a step closer to her, looked down and suppressed a groan at the delicious sight of her delicate breasts encased in stretchy fabric. 'If I've misread the signals,' he told her, 'Then tell me now and I'll back off. You have my word. Nor will I let it affect whatever lies down the line in terms of your position in my company. Say no, and this is never mentioned again. It will never have happened.'

Katy hesitated. She so badly wanted to tell him that, no, she most certainly was *not* interested in him *that* way, but then she thought of him backing away and leaving her alone and she realised with a jolt how much she enjoyed spending time in his company when they were tossing ideas around and sparring with one another. She also now realised that underneath that sparring had been the very thread of sexual attraction which he had picked up with his highly developed antennae.

'That's not the point,' she dodged feebly.

'What do you mean?'

'I mean…' Katy muttered *sotto voce*, red-faced and uncomfortable, 'It doesn't matter whether we're attracted to one another or not. It would be mad for us to do anything about it. Not that I would,' she continued at speed, face as red as a beetroot. 'After Duncan, I swore to myself that I would never make the mistake of throwing myself into anything with someone unless I really felt that they were perfect for me.'

'I've never heard such nonsense in my entire life,' Lucas said bluntly, and, feathers ruffled, Katy tensed and bristled.

'What's wrong with wanting the best?' she demanded, folding her arms, neither leaving the room nor returning to the bed, instead just standing in the middle as awkward as anything. He, on the other hand, looked totally at ease even though he was as scantily clad as she was. But then, he obviously wasn't the sort who gave a jot if his body was on display.

'Nothing's wrong with wanting the best,' Lucas concurred. 'But tell me, how do you intend to find it? Are you going to present each and every candidate with a questionnaire which they will be obliged to fill out before proceeding? I'm going to take a leap of faith here and assume that you didn't know about Powell's marital status. You went out with the man and presumably you believed that he was the right one for you.'

'I made a mistake,' Katy said defensively.

'And mistakes happen. Even if you're not being deliberately misled by a guy, you could both go out in good faith, thinking that it will go somewhere, only to discover that you hit obstacles along the way that make it impossible for you both to consider a life together.'

'And you're an expert because…?' Katy asked sarcastically.

'People are fond of self-deception,' Lucas delivered with all-knowing cool. 'I should know because I witnessed it first-hand with my father. You want something badly enough and you try and make it work and, if it all makes sense on paper, then you try all the harder to make it work. In a worst case scenario, you might actually walk up the aisle and then into a maternity ward, still kidding yourself that you've got the real deal, only to be forced to concede defeat, then cutting the ties is a thousand times more complicated.'

'You're so cynical…about *everything*.' She harked back to the lack of trust that had made him think that the only solution to saving his deal was to isolate her just in case.

'There's no such thing as the perfect man, Katy. With Powell, you got someone who deliberately set out to deceive you.' He shrugged. 'You might think I'm cynical but I'm also honest. I have never in my life set out to deceive anyone. I've never promised a bed of roses or a walk up the aisle.' He looked at her thoughtfully. 'You had a crap time with some guy who strung you along…'

'Which is why you should have believed me when I told you that I'd rather have walked on a bed of hot coals than have anything to do with him in my life again.'

'That's beside the point. At the time, I looked at the facts and evaluated them accordingly. What I'm trying to tell you is this: the world is full of men who will do whatever it takes to get a woman into bed, and that includes making promises they have no intention of keeping. With me, what you see is what you get. We're here, we're attracted to one another and that's all there is to it.'

'Sex for the sake of sex.' That was something she had never considered and surely *would* never consider. It contravened pretty much everything she had been taught to believe in. Didn't it? It was what Duncan had been after and that had repulsed her. Sex and love were entwined and to disentangle them was to reduce the value of both.

Lucas laughed at the disapproving, tight-lipped expression on her face. 'It could be worse,' he drawled. 'It could be sex for the sake of a happy-ever-after that is never going to be delivered.'

The air sizzled between them. Katy was mesmerised by the dark glitter in his eyes and could feel herself being seduced by opinions that were so far removed from her own. Yet he made them sound so plausible. Instead of giving her the freedom to enjoy a healthy and varied sex life, to take her time finding the right man for her, her experience with Duncan had propelled her ever further into a mind-set that rigidly refused to countenance anything but the guy who ticked all the boxes.

Wasn't Lucas right in many ways? How could you ever be sure of finding Mr Right unless you were prepared to bravely face down the probability that you might have to risk some Mr Wrongs first?

And who was to say that all Mr Wrongs were going to be creeps like Duncan? Some Mr Wrongs might actually be *fun*. Not marriage material, but *fun*.

Like Lucas Cipriani. He had Mr Wrong stamped all over him and yet...wouldn't he be fun?

For the first time in her life, Katy wondered when and how she had become so protective of her emotions and so incapable of enjoying herself in the way all other girls of her age would. Her parents had never laid down any hard and fast rules but she suspected now, looking back down the years, that she had picked things up in overheard conversations about some of the young women in distress they had helped. She had seen how unwanted pregnancies and careless emotional choices could destroy lives and she had consigned those lessons to the back of her mind, little knowing how much they would influence her later decisions.

Lucas could see the range of conflicting emotions shadowing her expression.

The man had really done a number on her, he thought, and along with that thought came another, which was that the first thing he would do, provided the deal went through, was to sling Powell out on his backside.

Whatever experiences she had had before the guy, he had clearly been the one she had set her sights on for a permanent relationship, and throwing herself into something only to find it was built on lies and deceit would have hit her hard.

For all her feisty, strong-willed, argumentative personality, she was a romantic at heart and that probably stemmed from her background. Sure she would have enjoyed herself as a girl, would have had the usual sexual experiences, but she would have kept her heart intact for the man she hoped to spend the rest of her life with, and it was unfortunate that that man happened to have been a married guy with a penchant for playing away.

'You may think that I don't have the sort of high moral code that you look for,' Lucas told her seriously. 'But I have my own code. It's based on honesty. I'm not in search of involvement and I don't pretend to be. You were hurt by Powell but you could never be hurt by me because emotions wouldn't enter the equation.'

Katy looked at him dubiously. She was surprised that she was even bothering to listen but a Pandora's box had been opened and all sorts of doubts and misgivings about that high moral code he had mentioned were flying around like angry, buzzing wasps.

'I'm not the type you would ever go for.' Lucas had never thought he'd see the day he actually uttered those words to a woman. 'And quite honestly, I second that, because I would be no good for you. This isn't a relationship where two people are exploring one another in the hope of taking things to the next level. This is about sex.'

'You're confusing me.'

'I'm taking you out of your comfort zone,' Lucas murmured, yearning to touch her, only just managing to keep his hands under lock and key. 'I'm giving you food for thought. That can't be a bad thing.'

Katy looked at him and collided with eyes the colour of the deepest, darkest night. Her heart did a series of somersaults inside her chest. He was temptation in a form she was finding irresistible. Every word he had said and every argument he had proffered combined to produce a battering ram that rendered her defenceless.

'You're just bored,' she ventured feebly, a last-ditch attempt to stave off the crashing ache to grab hold of what he was offering and hold on tight. 'Stuck here without a playmate.'

'How shallow do you think I am?' Lucas grinned, his expression lightening, his eyes rich with open amusement. 'Do you think I need to satisfy my raging libido every other hour or risk exploding? I'm tired of talking. I don't think I've ever spent this much time trying to persuade a woman into bed with me.'

'Should I be flattered?'

'Most definitely,' Lucas returned, without the slightest hesitation.

Then he reached out, trailed a long finger against her cheek and tucked some strands of coppery hair behind one ear. When he should have stopped and given her time to gather herself, because she was all over the place, he devastated her instead by feathering his touch along her collarbone then dipping it down to her cleavage.

Gaze welded to his darkly handsome face, Katy remained rooted to the spot. Her nipples were pinched buds straining against the bikini top. If she looked down she knew that she would see their roused imprint against the fabric. Her eyelids fluttered and then she breathed in sharply as he stepped closer to her and placed both of his big hands on her rib cage.

He had been backing her towards the bed without her even noticing and suddenly she tumbled back against the mattress and lay there, staring up at him.

She was about to break all her rules for a one-night stand and she wasn't going to waste any more time trying to tell herself not to.

CHAPTER SIX

EXCEPT KATY WASN'T entirely sure how she was going to initiate breaking all those rules. She'd never done so before and she was dealing with a man who had probably cut his teeth breaking rules. He'd made no bones about being experienced. Was he expecting a similar level of experience? Of course he was!

She quailed. Mouth dry, she stared at him in silence as he whipped off his shirt in one fluid movement and then stood there, a bronzed god, staring down at her. She greedily ate him up with her eyes, from his broad shoulders to his six-pack and the dark line of hair that disappeared under the low-slung swimming trunks.

Lucas hooked his fingers under the waistband of the trunks and Katy shot up onto her elbows, fired with a heady mixture of thrilling excitement and crippling apprehension.

What would he do if she were to tell him that she was a virgin? *Run a mile*, was the first thought that sprang to mind. Katy didn't want him to run a mile. She wanted him near her and against her and inside her. It made her feel giddy just thinking about it.

In the spirit of trying to be someone who might actually know what to do in a situation like this, she reached behind her to fumble unsuccessfully with the almost non-existent spaghetti strings that kept the bikini top in position.

Lucas couldn't have been more turned on. He liked that shyness. It wasn't something with which he was familiar. He leant over her, caging her in.

'You smell of the sun,' he murmured. 'And I don't think I've ever wanted any woman as much as I want you right now.'

'I want you too,' Katy replied huskily. She tentatively traced the column of his neck then, emboldened, his firm jawline and then the bunched muscles of his shoulder blades. Her heart was thumping hard and every jerky breath she took threatened to turn into a groan.

He eased her lips apart and flicked his tongue inside her mouth, exploring and tasting her, and setting off a dizzying series of reactions that galvanised every part of her body into furious response. Her small hands tightened on his shoulders and she rubbed her thighs together, frantic to ease the tingling between them.

Lucas nudged her with his bulging erection, gently prising her legs apart and settling himself between them, then moving slowly as he continued to kiss her.

He tugged at her lower lip with his teeth, teasing her until she was holding her breath, closing her eyes and trembling like a leaf.

Katy didn't think that anything in the world could have tasted as good as his mouth on her and she pulled him against her with urgent hands.

She wished she'd rid herself of her bikini because now it was an encumbrance, separating their bodies.

She wriggled under him, reaching behind herself and, knowing what she wanted to do, Lucas obliged, urging her up so that he could tug free the ties. Then he rose up to straddle her and looked down, his dark eyes slumberous with desire.

Katy had never thought about sex without thinking about love and she had never thought about love without painting a tableau of the whole big deal, from marriage to babies in a thirty-second fast-forward film reel in her head.

Big mistake. In all those imaginings, her body had just been something all tied up with the bigger picture and not something needing fulfilment in its own right. The fact she had never been tempted had only consolidated in her head that sex was not at all what everyone shouted about.

Even the momentous decision that desire had propelled her into making, to ditch her hard and fast principles and sleep with him, had been made with no real prior knowledge of just how wonderfully liberating it would feel for her.

Yes, she had imagined it.

In practice, it was all oh, so wildly different. She felt joyously free and absolutely certain that what she was doing was the right thing for her to do.

Burning up, she watched Lucas as he looked at her. He was so big, so dangerously, *sinfully* handsome, and he was gazing at her as though she was something priceless. The open hunger in his eyes drove away all her inhibitions and she closed her eyes on a whimper as he leaned back down to trail his tongue against her collarbone.

Then he pinned her hands to her sides, turning her

into a willing captive so that he could fasten his mouth on one nipple. He suckled, pulling it into his mouth while grazing the stiffened bud with his tongue.

This was sex as Katy had never imagined it. Wild, raw and basic, carrying her away on a tide of passion that was as forceful as a tsunami. This wasn't the physical connection from a kind, considerate and thoughtful guy who had wooed her with flowers and talked about a happy-ever-after future. This was the physical connection from a guy who had promised nothing but sex and would walk away from her the minute their stay on his yacht had come to an end.

His mouth and tongue against her nipple were sending piercing arrows of sensation through her body. She was on fire when he drew back to rid himself of his swimming trunks. The bulge she had felt pressing against her was impressively big, big enough for her to feel a moment of sheer panic, because how on earth could something so big fit inside her and actually feel good?

But that fear wasn't allowed to take root because desire was smothering it. He settled back on the bed and then tugged down the bikini bottoms.

Katy closed her eyes and heard him laugh softly.

'Don't you like what you see?' Lucas teased and she cautiously looked at him. 'Because I very much like what *I* see.'

'Do you?' Katy whispered, very much out of her depth and feverishly making all sorts of comparisons in her head between her boyish figure and the women he probably took to his bed. She wasn't going to dwell on it, but she wasn't an idiot. Lucas Cipriani could have any woman he wanted and, whilst she was confident enough about her looks, that confidence took a very understandable beating when she considered that the man in bed with her was every woman's dream guy. 'Sexy' didn't get more outrageous.

Lucas felt a spurt of pure rage against Powell, a man whose existence he had known nothing about a week ago. Not only had he destroyed Katy's faith in the opposite sex, but he had also pummelled her self-esteem. Any human being with functioning eyesight could have told her that she was a show-stopper.

He bent over to taste her pouting mouth whilst at the same time gently inserting his hand between her thighs.

She wasn't clean-shaven down there and he liked that; he enjoyed the feel of her soft, downy fluff against his fingers. He liked playing with it before inserting one long finger into her.

It was electrifying. He slid his finger lazily in long strokes, finding the core of her and the tight little bud that throbbed as he zeroed in on it. In the grip of sensations she had never known before, Katy whimpered and clutched him, all frantic need and craving. She was desperate to ride the crest of a building wave and her whimpers turned into soft, hitched moans as she began to arch her spine, pushing her slight breasts up, inviting him to tease a nipple with his tongue.

He released her briefly to fetch a condom from his wallet then he was over her, nudging her legs apart with his thigh and settling between them. Nerves firmly back in place, Katy smoothed exploratory hands along his back, tracing the hardness of muscle and sinew.

Her coppery hair was in tangles over her shoulders,

spread like flames across the pillows. Lucas stroked some of the tangles back and kissed her.

'I want you,' Katy muttered into his mouth, and she felt him smile. Desire was a raging force inside her, ripping all control out of her grasp and stripping her of her ability to think straight, or even to think at all.

She felt his impatience and his need matching hers as he pushed into her, a deep, long thrust that made her cry out. He stilled and frowned.

'Don't stop,' she begged him, rising up so that he could sink deeper into her. She was so wet for him and so ready for this.

'You're so tight,' Lucas murmured huskily in a driven undertone. 'I can't describe the sensation, *mia bella*.'

'Don't talk!' Katy gasped, urging him on until he was thrusting hard, and the tight pain gave way to a soaring sense of pleasure as he carried her higher and higher until, at last, she came…and it was the most out-of-body experience she could ever have imagined. Wracked with shudders, she let herself fly until she weakly descended back down to planet Earth. Then, all she wanted to do was wrap her arms around him and hold him tightly against her.

Lucas was amused when she hugged him. He wasn't one for hugs, but there was something extraordinarily disingenuous about her and he found that appealing.

He gently moved off her and then looked down and frowned, his brain only slowly making connections that began to form into a complete picture, one that he could scarcely credit.

There wasn't much blood, just a few drops, enough

for him to work out that none of that shyness and hesitancy had been put on. She'd blushed like a virgin because that was exactly what she was. He looked at her as the colour drained from her face.

'This is your first time, isn't it?'

For Katy, that was the equivalent of a bucket of cold water being poured over her. She hadn't thought that he would find out. She had vaguely assumed that if she didn't say anything then Lucas would never know that she had lost her virginity to him. She hadn't wanted him to know because she had sensed, with every pore of her being, that he wouldn't be thrilled.

For a man who didn't do commitment, and who gave warnings about the perils of involvement, a virgin would represent the last word in unacceptable.

She quailed and clenched her fists because making love to Lucas had been the most wonderful thing in her life, just the most beautiful, *right* thing she had ever done, and now it was going to be spoiled because, quite rightly, he was going to hit the roof.

She wriggled and tried to yank some of the covers up because there was no way she was going to have an argument with him in the nude.

'So what?' She eyed him mutinously under the thick fringe of her lashes and glowered. 'It's really no big deal.'

'No big deal?' Lucas parroted incredulously. 'Why didn't you tell me?'

'Because I know how you would have reacted,' Katy muttered, hugging her knees to her chest and refusing to meet his eyes for fear of the message she would read there.

'You know, do you?'

Katy sneaked a glance at him, and just as fast her eyes skittered away. He was sprawled indolently on the bed, an in-your-face reminder of the intimacy they had just shared. She was covering up for all she was worth but he was carelessly oblivious to his nakedness.

'I wanted to do it.' She stuck her chin up and challenged him to argue with that. 'And I knew that if I told you that I'd never slept with anyone before you'd have run a mile. Wouldn't you?'

Lucas grimaced. 'I probably would have been a little cautious,' he conceded.

'Run a mile.'

'But I would have been flattered,' he admitted with even more honesty. 'I would also have been more gentle and taken my time.' He raked his fingers through his hair and vaulted out of the bed to pace the floor, before snatching a towel which was slung over the back of a chair and loosely settling it around his waist. Then he circled to sit on the bed next to her. 'It *is* a big deal,' he said gently. He took her hands in his and stroked her wrists until her clenched fists relaxed. 'And if I was a little rough for you, then I apologise.'

'Please don't apologise.' She smiled cautiously and stroked his face, and it was such an intimate gesture that she almost yanked her hand back, but he didn't seem to mind; indeed he caught her hand and turned it over so that he could place a very tender kiss on the underside of her wrist.

'You're beautiful, *cara*. I don't understand how it is that you've remained a virgin. Surely there must have been other men before Powell?'

Katy winced at the reminder of the man who had

been responsible for landing them here together on this yacht. It was fair to say that, however hateful her memories of him were, they seemed a lot less hateful now. Maybe one day she might even mentally thank him because she couldn't see how she could ever regret having slept with Lucas.

'That was another of those down sides to having parents who were pillars of the community.' Katy let loose a laugh. 'There were always expectations. And especially in a tiny place, when you're growing up, everyone knows everyone else. Reputations are lost in the snap of a finger. I didn't really think about that, though,' she said thoughtfully. 'I just knew that I wanted the whole love and marriage thing, so my standards were maybe a bit on the high side.'

She sighed and smiled ruefully at Lucas, who was looking at her with such sizzling interest that every pulse in her body raced into overdrive.

'When Duncan came along, I'd just returned from university and I wasn't quite sure what direction my life was going to take. I remember my mother and I talking about the social scene at university, and my mum asking me about the boys, and something must have registered that I needed to take the next step, which was finding someone special.' She gazed at Lucas. 'I slept with you because I really wanted to. You said a lot of stuff…basically about seizing the day…'

'I had no idea I was addressing a girl who had no experience.'

'But, you see, that's not the point.' Katy was keen to impress this on him. 'The point is that you made me think about things differently. I know this isn't going anywhere but at least you were honest about that and you gave me a choice.' Duncan had denied her the truth about himself and, even if this was just a one night stand, which was something she had always promised herself she would never do, was it really worse to lose her virginity to Lucas than to a liar like Duncan?

She gazed up at him earnestly and Lucas lowered his head and very tenderly kissed her on the lips. He could have taken her again, right then, but she would be sore. Next time, he intended to make it up to her, to take his time. It blew his mind to think that she had come to him as a virgin. It was a precious gift and he knew that, even though he couldn't fully understand what had led her to give it to him.

'Yes, *cara,* there will be no "for ever after" with us but believe me when I tell you that, for the time we're together, I will take you to paradise and back. But before that…can I interest you in a shower?' He stood up and looked down at her slender perfection.

'With you?'

'Why not?' Lucas raised his eyebrows. 'You'd be surprised how different an experience it can be when you're in a shower with your lover.'

Katy shivered pleasurably at that word…*lover.* She shook her head and laughed. 'I think I'm going to relax here for a bit, then I'll go back to my cabin.'

Of course there would be no 'for ever after'…and she was tempted to tell him that she understood that well enough without having to be reminded of it.

'Why?' Lucas frowned and then heard himself inviting her to stay with him, which was astonishing, because he had always relished his privacy, even when he was involved with someone. Sex was a great outlet, and his appetite for it was as healthy as the next man's, but when the sex was over his craving for his own space always took precedence over post-coital closeness. He'd never spent the night with a woman.

'Because I need to be on my own for a bit.'

Right then, Lucas felt that by the time they were ready to leave this yacht he would have introduced her to the joys of sharing showers and shown her how rewarding it could be to spend the night in his bed…

Katy had fallen into something of a sleep when she heard the bang on the door to her cabin. For the first time since she had arrived on Lucas's cruiser, she had retired to bed without anything to eat, but then it had been late by the time she had eventually left his cabin.

Having intended to sneak out while he was showering, she had remained where she was and they had spent the next few hours in one another's arms. To his credit, he had not tried to initiate sex again.

'I can show you a lot of other ways we can satisfy one another,' he had murmured, and he had proceeded to do just that.

In the end, *she* had been the one whose body had demanded more than just the touch of his mouth and the feel of his long, skilful fingers. *She* had been the one to guide him into her and to demand that he come inside her.

It had been a marathon session and she had made her way back to her cabin exhaustedly, still determined not to stay the night in his room, because if she slept in her own bed then she would somehow be able to keep control of the situation.

'Katy! Open up!'

Katy jerked up with a start at the sound of Lucas's voice bellowing at her through the locked door. She leapt out of the bed, half-drugged with sleep, and yanked open the door, every fibre in her body responding with panic to the urgency in his voice.

She looked at him in consternation. He was in a pair of jeans and a black, figure-hugging tee-shirt. Not the sort of clothes anyone would consider wearing for a good night's sleep. Her already panicked antennae went into overdrive.

'Lucas! What time is it?'

'You need to get dressed immediately. It's a little after five in the morning.'

'But why?'

'Don't ask questions, Katy. Just do it.' He forged into the room and began opening drawers, yanking out a pair of jeans, quickly followed by the first tee-shirt that came to hand. Even at that hour in the morning, it would be balmy outside. 'Maria is sick.' He looked at his watch. 'Very sick. It has all the makings of acute appendicitis. Any delay and peritonitis will kick in, so you need to dress and you need to dress fast. I can't leave you on this yacht alone.'

Katy dashed into the bathroom and began stripping off the oversized tee-shirt she slept in, replacing it with the jeans and tee-shirt she had grabbed from his outstretched hand.

'Do you think I might get up to no good if you're not around to keep an eye on me?' she asked breathlessly, only half-joking because that deeply intimate step she had taken with him had clearly not been a deeply intimate step for him. He was a man who could detach, as he had made perfectly clear.

'Not now, Katy.'

'How will we get her to the hospital?' She flushed, ashamed that her thoughts had not been one hundred percent on the woman of whom she had grown fond during the short time she had been on the yacht.

'Not by helicopter,' Lucas told her, his every movement invested with speed as he took her arm and began leading her hurriedly out of the bedroom. 'Too long to get my pilot here and nowhere to land near the hospital.'

They were walking quickly to a part of the yacht Katy hadn't known existed, somewhere in the bowels of the massive cruiser.

'Fortunately, I am equipped to deal with any emergency. And to answer your earlier question...' He briefly glanced down at her, rosy, tousled and so utterly adorable that she literally took his breath away. 'I'm not taking you with me because I think you might get up to no good in my absence. I'm taking you with me because if something happened to you and I wasn't around I would never forgive myself.'

Something flared inside her and she felt a lump in her throat, then she quickly told herself not to be an idiot, because that wasn't a declaration of caring; it was a simple statement of fact. If she was left alone on the yacht and she needed help of any sort, she would be unable to swim to shore and unable to contact him. How would he, or anyone in his position, be able to live with that?

Things were happening at the speed of light now. In a move she thought was as impressive as a master magician's sleight of hand, the side of the yacht opened up to reveal a speedboat, an expensive toy within an expensive toy. Maria, clearly in a great deal of pain but smiling bravely, was waiting for them and was soon ensconced, to be taken to the island.

Dawn was breaking as they hit the island, a rosy, blushing dawn that revealed lush trees and flowers and narrow, winding roads disappearing up sloping hills.

A car was waiting for them, a four-wheel drive with an elderly man behind the wheel. They reached the town in under half an hour and then Maria was met in Accident and Emergency and whizzed through in a wheelchair, everything moving as though orchestrated.

Katy had barely had time to draw breath. Only when the older woman had been wheeled into the operating theatre, and they were sitting in the small hospital café with a cup of coffee in front of them, did she begin to pay attention to her surroundings... and then it registered.

'Your name is all over this hospital...'

Lucas shifted uncomfortably and glanced around him. 'So it would seem.'

'But why?'

'My money went towards building most of it.' He shrugged, as though that was the most natural response in the world. 'My father's family owned a villa here and he spent his holidays on the island with my mother and me when I was very young. It's about the only thing my father didn't end up giving away to one of the ex-wives who fleeced him in their divorce proceedings. I expect he had strong sentimental attachments to it. There was a prolonged period when the villa got very little use but, as soon as I was able, I began the process of renovation. I have the money, so when the head of the hospital came to me for help it was only natural for me to offer it.'

It felt odd to be offering her this slither of personal information and for a few seconds he was uncomfortable with what felt like a loss of his prized self-control.

What was it about this woman that made him behave out of character? Not in ways that should be disconcerting, because she neither said nor did anything that raised red flags, but still…

He was intensely private, not given to sharing. However, this was the first time he had been on the island with any woman. He rarely came here but, when he did, he came on his own, relishing the feeling of being swept back to happier times. Was Katy's necessary presence here the reason why he was opening up? And why was he making a big deal of it anyway? he thought with prosaic irony. She couldn't help but have noticed his name on some of the wards, just as she couldn't have failed to notice how eager the staff were to please.

'The old hospital, which was frankly far from perfect, was largely destroyed some time ago in a storm. I made sure that it was rebuilt to the highest specification. The infrastructure here is not complex but it is essential it all works. The locals depend on exporting produce, and naturally on some tourism. The tourists, in particular, are the wealthy sort who expect things to run like clockwork. Including the hospital, should one of them decide to take ill.' He grinned. 'There's nothing more obnoxious than a rich tourist who finds himself inconvenienced.'

'And I'm guessing you don't include yourself in that category?' Katy teased. Their eyes met; butterflies fluttered in her tummy and her heart lurched. They hadn't had a chance to talk about what had happened because she had disappeared off to her own quarters, and here they were now, caught up in unexpected circumstances.

She had no idea whether this was something that would be more than a one-night stand. She hoped it was. She had connected with him and she would feel lost if the connection were abruptly to be cut. It panicked her to think like that but she had to be honest with herself and admit that Lucas was not the man she had originally thought he was. He still remained the last person on earth she could ever contemplate having an emotional relationship with, but he had shown her the power of a sexual relationship and, like a starving person suddenly led to a banquet, she didn't want the experience to end. Just yet.

But nothing had been said and she wasn't going to engineer round to the conversation.

'Do *you* think I'm obnoxious?' Lucas questioned softly and she blushed and squirmed, so very aware of those dark eyes fastened to her face.

'My opinion of you *has* changed,' Katy admitted, thinking back to the ice-cold man who had forced her hand for the sake of a deal. She thought that her opinion also *kept* changing. She didn't want to dwell on that, so instead she changed the subject. 'What about Maria? When will we find out what the outcome is?'

'There's every chance it will be a positive one.'

Lucas glanced at his watch. 'I personally know the surgeon and there's no one better. I've contacted her family, who will be in the waiting area, and as soon as the operation is over I've asked to be called. I don't anticipate any problems at all. However...'

'However?'

'It does mean that there will be a small change of plan.'

'How do you mean?'

'We will no longer be based on the yacht. For a start, without Maria around, there will be no one to attend to the cooking and all the other little things she takes care of, and it's too late to find a replacement who can stay on board. So we'll have to relocate to my villa. I can get someone to come in on a daily basis and, furthermore, I will be on hand in case there are any complications following surgery.'

He paused. 'Maria worked for my father before he...began steadily going off the rails. My mother was very fond of her, so I've made sure to look out for her and her family, and also made sure to carry on employing her in some capacity when my father's various wives decided that they would rather have somewhat smarter people holding the fort in the various properties.'

His mobile phone buzzed and he held up one hand as he spoke in rapid Italian to the consultant, the concerned lines on his face quickly smoothing over in reaction to whatever was being said on the other end.

'All's gone according to plan,' he said. 'But, had she not reached the hospital when she did, then it would have been quite a different story. Now, why don't you wait here while I have a word with some of her family? I won't be long. I'll also arrange for your clothes and possessions to be transported to the villa.' He looked at her, head tilted to one side, then he patted his pocket. 'You can call your parents, if you like,' he said gruffly. 'I've been checking your phone, and I see that they've taken you at your word and not texted, but I expect they'd like to hear from you.'

He handed over the phone and her eyes shone, because more than anything else this demonstrated that he finally trusted her, and she found that that meant a great deal to her.

'What can I say to them?' she asked, riding high on the fact that she was no longer under suspicion. A barrier between them had been crossed and that felt good in the wake of what they had shared.

'Use your discretion,' Lucas told her drily. 'But it might be as well not to mention too many names, not that I think anything can go wrong with the deal at this stage. It's a hair's breadth away from being signed.' He stood up, leaving her with her mobile phone, and it felt like the greatest honour bestowed on her possible. 'I'll see you shortly and then we'll be on our way.'

CHAPTER SEVEN

LYING ON THE wooden deckchair by the side of the infinity pool that graced the lush grounds of his villa and overlooked the distant turquoise of the ocean, Lucas looked at Katy as she scythed through the water with the gracefulness of a fish.

The finalising of the deal had taken slightly longer than Lucas had anticipated, but he wasn't complaining. Indeed, he had encouraged his Chinese counterparts to take their time in sorting out all the essential details on which the takeover pivoted. In the meantime...

Katy swam to the side of the pool and gazed at him with a smile.

Up above, the sun had burnt through the early-morning clouds to leave a perfectly clear, milky, blue sky. Around them, the villa afforded absolute isolation. It was ringed with trees and perched atop a hill commanding views of the sea. Lucas had always valued his privacy and never more so than now, when he didn't want a single second of his time with her interrupted by so much as a passing tradesman. Not that any passing tradesman would be able to make it past the imposing wrought-iron gates that guarded the property.

He had dismissed all help, ensuring that the villa was stocked with sufficient food for their stay.

Just him…and her…

Right now, she was naked. He had half-expected, after that tentative surrender four days ago when she had placed her small hand on his thigh and sent his blood pressure through the roof, that a three-steps-forward, one-step-back game might ensue. He had predicted a tussle with her virtuous conscience, with lust holding the trump card, but in fact she had given herself to him without a trace of doubt or hesitation. He had admired her for that. Whatever inner battles she had fought, she had put them behind her and given generously.

'It's beautiful in here.' She grinned. 'Stop being so lazy and come and swim.'

'I hope that's not the sound of a challenge,' Lucas drawled, standing up, as naked as she was. He couldn't see her without his libido reacting like a lit rocket and now was no exception.

'Is sex *all* you ever think about, Lucas?' But she was laughing as she stepped out of the pool, the water streaming off her slick body.

'Are you complaining?' His eyes darkened and he balled his hands into fists. The urge to take her was so powerful it made him feel faint. He wanted to settle her on a towel on the ground and have her hard and fast, like a teenager in the grip of too much testosterone. Around her he lost his cool.

'Not at the moment,' Katy said breathlessly, walking straight into his arms. They had a lot of sex but, in fact, they also talked as well, and laughed, and enjoyed a level of compatibility she would never have thought possible when she had first met him.

He was still the most arrogant man she had ever met but there was so much more to him as well. She had no idea what was going to happen when they returned to London and she didn't think about it. Maybe they would carry on seeing one another...although how that would work out when she was his employee she couldn't quite fathom. The gossip would be out of control and he would loathe that.

For the first time in her life, Katy was living in the moment, and she wasn't going to let fear of what might or might not lie round the corner destroy her happiness.

Lucas cupped her pert bottom, which was wet from swimming, and kneaded it between his hands, driving her closer to him so that his rock-hard erection pushed against her belly.

She held him, played with him, felt the way his breathing changed and his body stiffened. She couldn't stop loving the way he reacted to her. It made her feel powerful and sexy and very, very feminine.

'I'm too big for deck-chair sex,' Lucas murmured.

'Who said anything about sex?' Katy breathed. 'We could just...you know...'

'I think I'm getting the picture.' He emitted a low, husky laugh and settled her on the cushioned deck chair, arranging her as carefully as an artist arranging a model he was about to paint, lying her in just the right place with her legs parted, hanging over either side of the chair, leaving her open for his attentive ministrations.

Then, sitting at the foot of the chair on his over-sized beach towel, he tugged her gently down towards his mouth and began tasting her. He slid his tongue into her, found the bud of her clitoris and licked it delicately, feathering little explosions of sensation through her, and he continued licking and teasing, knowing at which point she would begin to buck against his mouth as those little explosions became more and more impossible to control.

When he glanced up, he could see her small breasts, pointed and crowned with the dusky pink of her nipples, which were pinched from the water cooling on them. Her lips were parted, her nostrils flared as she breathed laboriously and her eyes were closed.

A thought flashed through his head. His condoms were nowhere to hand. What would happen if he were to sweep her up right now, hoist her onto him and let her ride them both to one of the body-shattering orgasms that they seemed strangely adept at giving one another? What if he were to feel himself in her without the barrier of a condom? Would it be such a bad thing? It wasn't as if pregnancy would be a certainty.

Shock at even thinking such a thing stilled him for a second. He'd never had thoughts like that in his life before and it implied a lack of self-control he found disturbing.

He killed the wayward thought that had sprung from nowhere and drove a finger into her, rousing her deep inside, and feeling her begin to spasm as she began to soar towards a climax.

She came against his mouth, arching up with an

abandoned cry of intense satisfaction, and then and only then did he allow her to touch him, with her mouth and with her hands.

The errant desire to take her without protection had been ruthlessly banished from his head but it left a lingering taste of unease in his mouth as they both subsided and flopped back into the pool to cool off.

Katy swam to Lucas but he stiffened and turned away, striking out into the water and rapidly swimming four lengths, barely surfacing for air as she watched from the side. He'd rejected her just then. Or maybe she'd been imagining it. Had she? He certainly hadn't done the usual and held her against him, coming down from a high with his body still pressed up against hers.

Sensitive to the fact that this was not a normal situation, that it was the equivalent of a one-night stand stretched out for slightly longer than the one night, Katy got out of the pool and walked over to her towel, anchoring it firmly around her so that she was covered up. Then she watched him as he continued swimming, his strong, brown body slicing through the water with speed and efficiency.

He didn't spare her a glance and after five minutes she retired to the villa and to the *en suite* bathroom which had been designated for her but rarely used, now she and Lucas were lovers.

The villa was magnificent, interestingly laid out with lots of nooks and crannies in which to relax, and huge, open windows through which breezes could circulate freely through the house. It lacked the slick sophistication of his yacht and was rather colonial in style with a stunning mixture of wood, billowing muslin at the windows, shutters and over-head fans. Katy loved it. She settled with her book into a rocking chair on the wide veranda that fronted the villa.

She kept waiting for Lucas to show up but eventually she gave up and nodded off. It was a little after four but still baking hot and, as always, cloudless.

Allowing her mind to drift, yanking it back every time it tried to break the leash and worry away at Lucas's reaction earlier on, she was scarcely aware of time going by, and it was only when she noticed the tell-tale signs of the sun beginning to dip that she realised that several hours must have passed.

In a panic, she scrambled to her feet and turned round, to find the object of her feverish imaginings standing framed in the doorway…and he wasn't smiling. Indeed, the humorous, sexy guy she had spent the past week with was noticeably absent.

'Lucas!' She plastered a smile on her face. 'How long have you been standing there? I was reading… er… I must have nodded off…'

Lucas saw the hurt beneath the bright smile and he knew that he had put it there. He had turned his back on her and swam off, and he had carried on swimming because he had needed to clear his head. When he'd finally stopped, she was gone and he had fought against the desire to seek her out because he was not going to allow a simple sexual liaison to get out of control. When they returned to London, this would finish and his life would return to normal, which was exactly as it should be. So he'd kept his distance and that would have upset her. He clenched his jaw and focused on what really mattered now, which was a turn of events that neither of them could have predicted.

'You've been talking to your parents. What, exactly, have you told them?'

'Lucas, I have no idea what you're talking about.'

'Just try and think.' He moved to stand in front of her, the beautiful lines of his handsome face taut and forbidding. 'Did you tell either of them where you were? What you were doing here? Who you were with?'

'I…you're making me nervous, Lucas. Let me think…no; *no*. I just told Mum that I was in Italy and that it was lovely and warm and that I was fine and having a good time…'

'I have just spent the past hour on the phone with the Chinese company. It seems that they were told by Powell that I was the wrong kind of person to be doing business with—that I was the sort of guy who seduces innocent girls and shouldn't be trusted as far as I can be thrown. It would seem that news travelled and connections were made. Someone, somewhere, figured out that we're here together and social media has taken the information right into Powell's hands and given the man ammunition to blow my deal sky-high at the last minute.'

The colour drained from Katy's face. When he said that 'connections were made', it was easy to see how. They had been into the little town several times over the past few days, checking on Maria and doing all sorts of touristy things. He could have been recognised and, whilst *she* wouldn't have been, someone could have sneakily taken a picture of them together and tagged them in something they posted online. The mind boggled.

'This is *not* my fault, Lucas. You know how pervasive social media is.' But it *was* her fault. She was the one with the connection to Duncan and, if gossip had been spread, then who knew what her mum might have mentioned to anyone in the village? Someone might be friends with Duncan on Facebook or whatever. Guilt pinked her cheeks, but before she could go on the defensive he held up one imperious hand to close down her protest.

'I'm not going to waste time going back and forth with this.' He frowned down at her and sighed. 'I'm not playing blame games here, Katy, and you're right: there's no privacy left anywhere. If anyone is to blame, then it's me, because I should have been more circumspect in my movements here. The place is small, I'm a well-known face, it's close to the busiest time of year for tourists and they have smart phones. But the fact remains that I have now been left with a considerable problem.

'No, perhaps I should amend that: when I say that *I* have a considerable problem, it might be fairer to say that we *both* have a considerable problem. Your ex approached Ken Huang and told him a story, and there's an underlying threat to go to the press and take public this sordid tale of a young, innocent girl being taken advantage of by an unscrupulous billionaire womaniser.'

Katy paled. 'Duncan wouldn't…'

But he would.

'He's played up your innocence to the hilt.'

'He knew…' Katy swallowed painfully. 'He knew

that I was inexperienced. I never thought that he would use the information against me. I trusted him when I confided in him.'

In the midst of an unfolding nightmare, Lucas discovered that the deal which should have been uppermost in his mind was overshadowed by a gut-wrenching sympathy for her vulnerability, which Powell had thoroughly taken advantage of.

Lucas dragged over a chair to join hers and sat heavily, closing his eyes for a few seconds while he sifted through the possibilities for damage limitation. Then he looked at her.

'The man has an axe to grind,' Lucas stated flatly. 'Tell me why.'

'Does it matter?'

'In this instance, everything matters. If I need to use leverage, then I need to know where to apply it. I don't play dirty but I'm willing to make an exception in this case.'

'It ended really badly between me and Duncan.' She shot him a guilty, sidelong look before lowering her eyes. 'As you may have gathered. It wouldn't have been so bad if I'd found out about his wife and children *after* I'd slept with him, but I think he was doubly enraged that, not only did I find out that he was married, but he hadn't even succeeded in getting me into bed *before* I'd had a chance to find out.'

'Some men are bastards,' Lucas told her in a matter-of-fact voice. 'It has to be said that some women leave a lot to be desired as well. It's life.'

'You mean those women your father married,' Katy murmured, distracted, thinking that on some level their approaches to life had been similarly tarnished by unfortunate experiences with the opposite sex. It was easy to think that, because you came from a wildly different background from someone, the things that affected the decisions you made had to be different, but that wasn't always the case. Money and privilege had been no more guarantee of a smooth ride in his case than a stable family background had been in hers.

Lucas shrugged. 'I have no more time for the gold-diggers,' he gritted. 'At least a guy with his head screwed on has a fighting chance of recognising them for what they are and can take the necessary precautions. You, I'm guessing, had no chance against a skilled predator. Continue.'

'I'd confided in my best friend,' Katy said, with a grimace. 'I felt such a fool. Claire was far more experienced than me, and she was livid when I told her about the messages I'd accidentally seen on his phone from his wife. He'd made a mistake in leaving it on the table while he vanished off to the toilet when we'd been having a meal out. Up popped a reminder to phone the kids to say good night and to remember some party they were going to on the weekend. He'd told me he was going to be away on business. Weekends, he'd always said, were tricky for him because he was trying to kick-start a photography business and they were the only times he could do whatever he had to do—networking and the like—because he was at the bank during the week.'

'A skilled excuse,' Lucas said drily. 'The man obviously came with form.'

'That was what Claire said. She told me that I was

probably not the first, which needless to say didn't make me feel at all better.'

It was as though she was looking at a very young, very naïve stranger from the advantageous position of someone who was much older and wiser. And she had Lucas to thank for that.

'Anyway, she started doing a little digging around. The world's a small place these days.' Katy grimaced. 'She found that he was a serial womaniser and she went to see his wife.'

'Ah.'

'I had no idea at the time that that was her plan, and afterwards she confessed that she didn't quite know what had prompted her to take such drastic action. But she was upset on my behalf and, in a weird way, upset on behalf of all the other girls he had conned into sleeping with him. His marriage fell apart on the back of that, so...'

'I'm getting the picture loud and clear. The ex who hates you and holds you responsible for the break-down of his marriage now has the perfect vehicle for revenge put into his hands.'

'If I had told you the whole story in the first place, you would have realised that there was no chance I could have been any kind of mole. Then we wouldn't have ended up here and none of this would be hap-pening now.'

Lucas smiled wryly. 'Really think that would have been how it would have worked?'

'No,' Katy answered honestly. 'You wouldn't have believed me. I would have been guilty until proven innocent.' At that point in time, he'd been a one-dimensional autocrat—ruthless, suspicious, arrogant. At this point in time…

She didn't know what he was and she didn't want to think too hard about it. They had a situation and she began to see all the nooks and crannies of it. If Duncan decided to take his revenge by publicising a tale of some sordid love tryst between Lucas and herself, not only would Lucas's deal be ruined but he would have to face the horror of the world gossiping about him behind his back. His reputation would be in tatters because, however much a lie could be disproved, mud inevitably stuck. He was the sort of guy who would claim to shrug off the opinions of other people, but that would be a heck of a lot to shrug off.

And it would all have been *her* fault.

Could she allow that to happen?

And then, aside from Lucas, there was the matter of her and her parents. They would never live it down. She felt sick thinking about their disappointment and the whispers that would circulate around the village like a raging forest fire blazing out of control. When she returned to see them, people would stare at her. Her parents would shy away from discussing it but she would see the sadness in their eyes.

She would be at the heart of a tabloid scandal: 'desperate virgin in sordid tryst with billionaire happy to use her for a few days before discarding her'. 'Sad and gullible innocent lured to a villa for sex, too stupid to appreciate her own idiocy'.

'Marry me!' she blurted out and then looked at him with wide-eyed dismay.

She jumped to her feet and began pacing the veranda, before curling onto the three-seater wicker sofa and drawing her knees up.

'Forget I said that.'

'Forget that I've received a marriage proposal?' Lucas drawled, strolling over to the sofa and sitting down, body angled towards her. 'It's the first I ever have…'

'It wasn't a marriage proposal,' Katy muttered, eyeing him with a glower, her cheeks tinged with heated colour.

'Sure about that? Because I distinctly heard the words "marry me".'

'It wasn't a *real* marriage proposal,' Katy clarified, hot all over. 'It just seemed that…if Duncan does what he's threatening to do—and I guess he will, if he's already started dropping hints to your client—then it's not just that your deal will be jeopardised—'

'Ruined,' Lucas elaborated for good measure. 'Shot down in flames…dead in the water and beyond salvation…'

'All those things,' Katy mumbled, guilt washing over her with tidal force. She breathed in deeply and looked him directly in the eyes. 'It's not even a marriage proposal,' she qualified. 'It's an *engagement* proposal. If we're engaged then Duncan can't spread any rumours about sordid trysts and he can't take your reputation away from you by implying that you're the sort of womaniser who's happy to take advantage of… of…an inexperienced young girl…'

He wasn't saying anything and she wished he would. In fact, she couldn't even read what he was thinking because his expression was so shuttered.

'Your deal can go ahead,' she plunged on. 'And you

won't have to worry about people gossiping about you behind your back.'

'That sort of thing has never bothered me.'

Katy almost smiled, because that was just *such* a predictable response, then she thought about people gossiping about him and her heart clenched.

'What's in it for you?' Lucas asked softly.

'Firstly,' Katy told him with absolute honesty, 'You're here because of me, so this is pretty much my fault. Secondly, I know how much this deal means to you. Thirdly, it's not just about you. It's also about me. My parents would be devastated and I can't bear the thought of that. And *you* might not care about what other people think of you, but *I* care what other people think of me. I wouldn't be able to stay on at either of my jobs because of the shame, and I would find it really hard to face people at home who have known me all my life.'

It was slowly dawning on her that there had been something in his softly spoken words when he had asked her what would be in it for her, something she hadn't registered immediately but which she was registering fast enough now.

'It would work.' She tilted her chin at a defiant angle to rebut the hidden insinuation she had read behind his words. She might have been wrong in her interpretation but she didn't think so. 'And it would work brilliantly because there's no emotional bond between us. I mean, there's no danger that I would get it into my head that I was doing anything but role-playing. You could get your deal done, we could defuse a potential disaster and I would be able to live with myself.'

'You're presenting me with a business proposition, Katy?' He dealt her a slashing smile that threatened to knock her sideways. 'You, the ultimate romantic, are presenting me with a business proposition that involves a phoney engagement?'

'It makes sense,' she defended.

'So it does,' Lucas murmured. 'And tell me, how long is this phoney engagement supposed to last?' He couldn't help but be amused by this from the girl who typified everything that smacked of flowers, chocolates, soul mates and walks up the aisle in a frothy, meringue wedding dress. Then he sobered up as he was struck by another, less amusing thought.

Had he changed her into something she was never meant to be? He had shown Katy the marvels of sex without strings because it was something that worked for him, but had he, in the process, somehow *changed* her? For reasons he couldn't explain, he didn't like the thought of that, but he pushed those uneasy reservations to one side, choosing instead to go for the straightforward explanation she had given, which was that it was a solution that would work for her as well as it would work for him.

Katy shrugged. 'You still haven't said whether you think it's a good idea or not.'

'I couldn't have come up with something better myself.' Lucas grinned, then looked at her seriously. 'But you should know that I wouldn't ask you to do anything you feel uncomfortable about.'

Katy's heart did that weird, clenching thing again. 'I feel very comfortable about this and, as for how long it would last, I haven't given much thought to that side of things.'

'You'd be deceiving your parents,' Lucas pointed out bluntly.

'I realise that.' She sighed and fiddled with the ends of her long hair, frowning slightly. 'I never thought that the ends justified the means, and I hate the thought of deception, but, between the devil and the deep blue sea, this seems the less hurtful option.'

Lucas looked at her long and hard. 'So we're a loved-up couple,' he murmured, his dark eyes veiled. 'And in fact, so irresistibly in love with one another that we escaped for some heady time to my yacht where we could be together free from interruption from the outside world. Your colleagues at work might find it a little hard to swallow.'

'You'd be shocked at how many people believe in love at first sight.' Katy smiled. 'You know, just because *you're* such a miserable cynic when it comes to love, doesn't mean that the rest of us are as well...'

'So now I'm a miserable cynic,' Lucas drawled, reaching out to tug her towards him. 'Tell me how likely it is that you would fall head over heels for a miserable cynic?'

'Not likely at all!' Katy laughed, looking up at him, and her heart did that funny thing again, skipping a beat, which made her feel as though she'd been cruising along quite nicely only to hit a sudden patch of violent turbulence. 'I'm afraid what you have is a girl who could only fall head over heels for someone as romantic as she is!' She frowned and tried to visualise this special person but the only face to fill her head was Lucas's dark and devastatingly handsome one.

'If we're going to be engaged, then we need to get

to know one another a whole lot better,' Lucas told her, still admiring the very practical streak which had led her to propose this very practical solution. Although, why should he be that surprised? She was a whizz at IT and that, surely, indicated a practical side to her that she herself was probably not even aware of.

He stood up, his fingers still linked with hers, and led her back through the villa and in the direction of his bedroom.

'What are you going to do with me once the engagement is over?' he murmured, toeing open his bedroom door, and then propelling her backwards to his bed while she tried to contain her laughter. 'I mean...' he lowered his head and kissed her, flicking his tongue into her mouth and igniting a series of fireworks inside her '... I'm assuming that, since you are the one with the clever plan to stage a fake engagement, you'll likewise be the one with the clever plan when it comes to wriggling out of it. So how will you dispose of me?'

He slid his hand under her tee-shirt and the warmth of her skin sent his body immediately into outer orbit. She wasn't wearing a bra, and he curved his big hand over her breast and gently teased her nipple until it was ripe and throbbing between his skilful fingers. They tumbled onto the bed, he settled her under him and straddled her so that he could see her face as he continued to tease her.

As usual, Katy's brain was losing the ability to fire on all cylinders, especially when he pushed up the tee-shirt and lowered himself to suckle her nipple. He looked up and caught her eyes, then flicked his tongue over the stiffened bud before devoting his attention to her pouting lips, kissing her again until she felt as though she was coming apart at the seams.

'Well?' He nuzzled the side of her neck and she wriggled and squirmed underneath him, hands on his waist, pushing into the waistband of his trousers and feeling his buttocks.

'Oh, I think we'll just drift apart,' Katy murmured. 'You know the sort of thing. You'll be working far too hard and you'll be spending most of your time in the Far East because of the deal you've managed to secure. I'll grow lonely and…who knows?…maybe I'll find some hunky guy to help me deal with my loneliness…'

'Not if I have any say in the matter,' Lucas growled, cupping her between her legs and rubbing until the pressure of his hand did all sorts of things through the barrier of her clothes.

'No,' Katy panted, bucking against his hand as she felt the stirrings of an orgasm building. 'I have to admit,' she gasped, her fingers digging into his shoulders, 'That finding another man wouldn't work, so perhaps you'll have to tire of me not being around and find someone else instead…'

And how she hated the thought of that although, she laughed shakily to herself, in the game of make-believe, what was the big deal? 'Let's not talk about this.' She tugged apart the button on his trousers and awkwardly tried to pull down the zipper. She looked at him and met his eyes. 'We can be engaged…for two months. Long enough to find out that we're not really compatible and short enough for no lasting damage.'

'You're the one calling the shots.' Lucas nipped her

neck, reared up and yanked off his shirt, before proceeding to undress her very, very slowly and, when she was completely naked, pushing apart her thighs and gazing down for a few charged seconds at her stupendous nudity. 'And I like it… Now, stop talking. It's time for action, my wife-to-be…'

CHAPTER EIGHT

KATY HAD A week to think about what would happen when they arrived back in London. The surprise announcement of their engagement had hit the headlines with the fanfare of a royal proclamation. Sitting in the little square in the island's town, whilst they sipped coffees in the sunshine, she had scrolled through the newspapers on her phone and read out loud some of the more outrageous descriptions of the 'love at first sight' scenario which Lucas had vaguely hinted at when he had called, firstly, the anxious Ken Huang and then his personal assistant, who had been instructed to inform various elements of the press.

Lucas had been amused at her reaction to what, for him, was not entirely surprising, considering the extent of his wealth and eligibility.

Now, finally on the way back to London, with the helicopter that had delivered them to his super-yacht due to land in under half an hour, the events of the past few days no longer felt like a surreal dream that wasn't quite happening.

It was one thing to read the centre pages of the tabloids and marvel that she was actually reading about herself. It was quite another to be heading straight into the eye of the hurricane where, she had been warned by Lucas, there might still be some lingering press attention.

'At least there's been some time for the story to calm down a bit,' he had told her. 'Although there's nothing the public loves more than a good, old-fashioned tale of romance.'

'Except,' Katy had quipped, 'A good, old-fashioned tale of a break-up.'

Lucas had laughed but, now that the story was out in the open, now that her parents had been told and had doubtless told every single person in the village and beyond, Katy was beginning to visualise the fallout when the phoney engagement came to an end. In short, her theory about the end justifying the means was beginning to look a little frayed at the edges.

She had spoken to her parents every single day since the announcement and had played fast and loose with fairy stories about the way her heart had whooshed the minute she had clapped eyes on Lucas, the second she had *known* that it was the real thing. They had wanted details and she had given them details.

Katy knew that she would have to face all sorts of awkward questions when this charade was over. No doubt, she would be an object of pity. Her parents would be mortified that yet again she had been short-sighted enough to go for the wrong guy. If they ever happened to meet Lucas in the flesh, then they would probably suss that he was the wrong guy before the fairy tale even had time to come crashing down.

The world would feel sorry for her. Her friends would shake their heads and wonder if there was something wrong with her. And, inevitably, there would be malicious swipes at her stupidity in thinking that she could ever have thought that a relationship with someone like Lucas Cipriani could ever last the distance.

Who did she think she was?

And yet she was happy to close the door on reality because the thrill of living for the moment was so intense. It ate everything up. All her incipient doubts, and all her darkest imaginings about what lay beyond that two-month time line they had agreed upon, were swept aside and devoured by the intensity of appreciating every single second she had with him.

The timer had been set and every feeling, every sensation and every response was heightened to an excruciating pitch.

'I have something to tell you.' Lucas pulled her towards him. It still surprised him the way he couldn't get enough of her. 'Tonight we will be the main event at a black-tie ball.'

Katy stared at him in consternation. 'Tonight?'

'The Chinese company's throwing it. It seems that Ken Huang is keen to meet you, as are all the members of his family—and, in all events, with signatures now being put to paper, it's a fitting chance to celebrate our engagement publicly as well as the closing of the deal. Your parents, naturally have been invited to attend, as have your friends and other family members. Have you got any other family, as a matter of interest?'

Katy laughed. 'Shouldn't you know that?'

'I should,' Lucas said gravely, 'But these things sometimes get overlooked in a hectic whirlwind romance.' She was wearing a little blue top and some faded cut-off jeans and, if they had been anywhere remotely private, he would have enjoyed nothing better than getting her out of both items of clothing.

'I've never been to a ball in my life before,' Katy confided, brushing aside her unease because not only would she have to mix with people she had no experience of mixing with but she would also be *on show*. 'It would be nice if Mum and Dad came, but honestly, I doubt they will. It wouldn't be their thing at all, and my dad's calendar is so packed with community stuff that he will struggle to free up the time without more advance warning.' She sighed and looked at him a little worriedly.

Lucas was overwhelmed by a sudden surge of protectiveness that came from nowhere and left him winded. He drew back slightly, confused by an emotion that had no place within his vocabulary. 'It's no big deal.'

'It's no big deal *for you*,' Katy told him gently. 'It's a huge deal *for me*.'

Lucas frowned. 'I thought everyone liked that sort of thing,' he admitted. 'There'll be a host of well-known faces there.'

Katy laughed because his self-assurance was so deeply ingrained that it beggared belief. 'Part of me didn't really think about how this would play out when we returned to London,' she admitted. 'It felt very... unreal when we were in Italy.'

'Yes it did,' Lucas agreed. 'Yet surely you would have expected a certain amount of outside attention focused on us...?'

He knew that this very naivety was something he

found intensely attractive about her. Having experienced all the trappings of extreme wealth for the past fortnight, she still hadn't joined the dots to work out what came as part and parcel of that extreme wealth, and intrusive media coverage at a time like this was one of those things. Not to mention a very necessary and unfortunately inevitable black-tie event. He decided that it would be unwise to mention just how much attention would be focused on her, and not just from reporters waiting outside the venue.

'You're going to tell me I'm an idiot.'

'I've discovered I quite like idiots.' He touched her thigh with his finger and Katy shivered and came close to forgetting all her apprehensions and doubts. They might be acting out a charade when it came to an emotional involvement with one another, or at least the sort of emotional involvement that came under the heading of 'love', but when it came to physical involvement there was no reporter who wouldn't be convinced that what they had was the real deal.

'When we get to the airfield, don't be surprised if there are one or two reporters waiting and just follow my lead. Don't say anything. I've given them enough fodder to be getting on with. They can take a couple of pictures and that'll have to do. In a week, we'll be yesterday's salacious gossip. And don't worry—you'll be fine. You never run yourself down, and you're the only woman I've ever met who gets a kick out of telling me exactly what she thinks of me. Don't be intimidated by the occasion.' He laughed and said, only partly in jest, 'If you're not intimidated by me, then you can handle anything.'

Buoyed up by Lucas's vote of confidence, Katy

watched as the door of the helicopter was pushed open to blue sky, a cooler temperature than they had left behind and a fleet of reporters who flocked towards them like a pack of wolves scenting a fresh kill.

Katy automatically cringed back and felt his arm loop through hers, gently squeezing her reassuringly as he batted aside questions and guided her towards the black car waiting for them.

A reporter yelled out asking to see the engagement ring. Katy gazed in alarm at her ring-free finger and began stumbling out something vague when Lucas cut into her stammering non-answer, drawing briefly to a halt and smoothly explaining that the jeweller's was going to be their first stop as soon as they were back in the city.

'But it won't be, will it?' she asked as soon as they were settled into the back of the car with the glass partition firmly shut between the driver and them.

'Do you think you're going to be able to get away without a ring on your finger at the ball?' Lucas said wryly. 'Brace yourself for a lot more attention than you got from those reporters back there at the air field.' He settled against the door, inclining his big body towards her.

She was waking up to life in *his world*. Not the bubble they had shared in the villa, and even more so on his yacht, where they'd been secluded and tucked away from prying eyes, but the real world in which he moved. She was going to be thrown into the deep end and it couldn't be helped. Would she be able to swim or would she flounder?

He had told her that she would be fine and again he felt it—that strong streak of protectiveness when he

thought about her lost and trying to find her way in a
world that was probably alien to her. He knew from
experience that the people who occupied his world
could be harsh and critical. He disliked the thought
of seeing her hurt, even though the practical side of
him knew that the disingenuousness that he found
so intensely appealing would be a possible weakness
under the harsh glare of real life, away from the pleasant bubble in which they had been cocooned.

'We can stop for a bite to eat, get freshened up at
my place and then head out to the jeweller's, or else
we can go directly there. And, on the subject of things
to be bought, there'll be a small matter of something
for you to wear this evening.'

'Something to wear...'

'Fancy. Long.' He shrugged. 'Naturally you won't
be expected to foot the bill for whatever you get,
Katy.' He wondered whether he should go with her,
hold her hand.

Katy stilled and wondered how the insertion of
money into the conversation could make the hairs on
the back of her neck stand on end. It felt as though
something was shifting between them, although she
couldn't quite put her finger on what that *something*
was.

'Of course.' Politeness had crept into her voice
where before there had only been teasing warmth,
and she didn't like it. But how could she pretend that
things hadn't changed between them? They had embarked on a course of action that wasn't *real* and
perhaps that was shaping her reactions towards him,
making her prickly and on edge.

Yes, she was free to touch, but there were now in-built constraints to their relationship. They were supposed to project a certain image, and that image would require her to step out of her comfort zone and do things she wasn't accustomed to doing. She was going to be on show and Lucas was right—she wasn't in the habit of running herself down and she wasn't going to start now. If she was hesitant and apprehensive, then that was understandable, but she wasn't going to let sudden insecurities dictate how she behaved.

'I think I'd rather get the ring and the outfit out of the way, then at least I can spend the afternoon relaxing, although I don't suppose I'll have much time to put my feet up.' She sighed and said with heartfelt honesty, 'I never thought I'd be getting an engagement ring under these circumstances.' She looked at her finger and tried to think back to those days when she had stupidly believed that Duncan was the man for her. Then she glanced across at Lucas and shivered. He was so ridiculously handsome, so madly self-assured. He oozed sex appeal and her body wasn't her own when she was around him. When she was around him, her body wanted to be his and only his.

What if this were a real engagement, not some crazy charade to appease other people?

She was suddenly filled with a deep, shattering yearning for a real relationship and for everything that came with it. This time it wasn't just for a relationship to rescue her from making decisions about her future, which had been the reason she'd allowed herself to be swept away by fantasies about tying the knot with Duncan.

Time slowed. It felt so right with Lucas and yet he was so wrong. How was that possible? She had proposed a course of action that had made sense, and she had imagined she could handle it with cool and aplomb because what she felt for Lucas was lust and lust was a passing fever. But looking at him now, feeling his living, breathing warmth next to her... The time they had spent together flickered like a slow-motion movie in her head: the laughter they had shared; the conversations they had had; their lazy love-making and the soaring happiness that had engulfed her when she had lain, warm and sated, in his arms.

Katy was overcome with *wanting more*. She transferred her gaze blindly down to her finger and pictured that ring on it, and then her imagination took flight and she thought of so much more. She imagined him on bended knee...smiling up at her...wanting her to be his wife *for real* and not a pretend fiancée for two months...

She loved him. She loved him and he certainly didn't love her. Sick panic filled her at the horror that she might have opened the door for hurt, and on a far bigger scale than Duncan had delivered. Indeed, next to Lucas, Duncan was a pale, ineffectual ghost and obviously one who had not taught her any lessons at all.

Lucas noted the emotions flickering across her face and instantly barriers that had been carefully crafted over many years fell back into place. He didn't do emotion. Emotions made you lose focus, sapped your strength, made you vulnerable in ways that were destructive. Gold-diggers had come close to destroying his business, but it had been his father's own emotions that had finally let him down. Lucas could feel himself mentally stepping back and he had the oddest feeling that just for a while there he had been standing too close to an inferno, the existence of which he had been unaware.

He leaned forward, slid the glass partition to one side and instructed the driver to deliver them to a jeweller Katy had never heard of but which, she guessed, would be the sort of place to deal with very, very exclusive clients.

'Where are we?' she asked forty-five minutes later, during which time Lucas had worked on his computer, catching up on transactions he had largely ignored while they had been in Italy, he'd told her without glancing at her.

'Jeweller's,' he said. 'Stop number one.'

'It doesn't look like a jeweller's…'

'We wealthy folk like to think that we don't frequent the sort of obvious places every other normal person does,' Lucas said, back in his comfort zone, back in control.

'Interesting story here,' he expanded as the car drew to a smooth halt and the driver stepped out to open the door for her. 'The woman who owns the place, Vanessa Bart, inherited it from her father and employed a young girl to work here—Abigail Christie. Long story but, to summarise, it turned out that she had a child from my friend Leandro, unbeknown to him, and like star-crossed lovers they ended up meeting again quite by chance, falling in love and getting married a while back.'

'The fairy tale,' Katy said wistfully as they were allowed into a shop that was as wonderful as Aladdin's cave. 'It's nice that it happens now and again.' She smiled and whispered, 'There's hope for me yet.'

'Wrong sentiment for a woman on the verge of wearing an engagement ring from the man of her dreams.' Lucas's voice was less amused than he would have liked. He laughed shortly and then they were being ushered into the wonderful den of exquisite gems and jewels, tray after tray of diamond rings being brought out for her to inspect, none of them bearing anything so trashy as a price tag.

Lucas watched her down-bent head as she looked at the offerings. He was a man on the verge of an engagement and, whether it was phoney or not, he suddenly had that dangerous, destabilising feeling again…the sensation of getting close to a raging inferno, an inferno he couldn't see and therefore could not protect himself against. He shifted uneasily and was relieved when she finally chose the smallest, yet as it turned out one of the dearest, of the rings.

'Rest assured,' Katy said quietly as they were once again passengers in the back seat of the car, 'That I won't be taking the ring with me when this is all over.'

'Let's just live a day at a time.' Lucas was still unsettled and frankly eager now to get to his office where he wouldn't be inconvenienced by feelings he couldn't explain. 'Before we start deciding who gets what when we're dividing the spoils.'

'Where do we go for the dress?'

'Selfridges. I've already got my PA to arrange a personal shopper for you.'

'A personal shopper…'

'I have to get to my office, so will be unable to accompany you.'

As their eyes tangled, Katy felt the thrill of being

here next to him, even if that thrill was underlain with the presence of danger and the prospect of unhappiness ahead. 'I wouldn't expect you to come with me. I don't need you to hold my hand. If you let me have the name of the person I'm supposed to meet, then I can take it from there. And, after I've done all the other stuff I'm supposed to do, then I think I'm going to head back to my place and get changed there.'

Begin stepping away, she thought sadly. *Begin a process of detachment. Protect yourself.*

Lucas was already putting the romance of Italy behind him. There would be a ring on her finger, but he wasn't going to be hankering for all that un-diluted time in each other's company they had had at his villa. He was slipping back to his reality and that involved distancing himself from her; Katy could sense that.

'Why?' Lucas realised that he didn't want her not to be around when he returned to his apartment. He wanted her to be there for him and he was irritated with himself for the ridiculous gap in his self-control.

'Because I want to check on my place, make sure everything's in order. So I'll meet you at the venue. You can text me the details.' She sounded a lot brisker than she felt inside. Inside, she wanted so much more, wanted to take without consequence, just as she wanted to give without thought. She wanted him to love her back and she wanted to shove that feeling into a box and lock it away to protect her fragile heart.

'You'll be nervous.' Lucas raked his fingers through his hair, for once on the back foot with his legendary self-control. 'There'll be reporters there.

You won't know what to do. You'll need me to be there with you, by your side.'

Where had that come from?

'But...' His voice as smooth as silk, he regained his footing. 'I see that you might want to check your place and check your mail.' He was back on familiar ground and he relaxed. 'We've got our lives to be getting on with.' He smiled wryly. 'Why kid ourselves otherwise? Don't worry. In a few weeks' time, this will be little more than something you will one day laugh about with your kids.'

'Quite,' Katy responded faintly, sick with heartache, for which she knew that she had only herself to blame. 'I'll see you later.' She forced herself to smile and marvelled that he could be so beautiful, so cool, so composed when she was breaking up inside. But then, he hadn't crossed the lines that she had.

Katy had no idea where to start when it came to looking for something to wear to a black-tie event because she had never been to one in her life before, and certainly, in her wildest imagination, had never dreamt that she would be cast in the starring role at one. She had phoned her mother but, as predicted, it had been impossible at short notice, what with her father's community duties. She had promised that she would send lots of pictures. Now, suddenly, she felt quite alone as she waited for her personal shopper to arrive.

It took over two hours for a dress to be chosen and, no matter how much she told herself that this was all an act, she couldn't help wondering what it would feel like to be trying these clothes on for real, to parade for a man who returned her love, at an event that would celebrate a union that wasn't a charade.

The dress she chose was slim-fitting to the waist, with a back scooped so low that wearing a bra was out of the question, but with an alluringly modest top half that fell in graceful layers to the floor. When she moved, it swirled around her like a cloud, and, staring at the vision looking back in the mirror, she felt the way Cinderella might have felt when the wand had been waved and the rags had been replaced with the ball gown that would later knock Prince Charming off his feet.

Prince Charming, however, had left her thoroughly to her own devices. He was back in the real world and already distancing himself from her without even realising it.

The Fairy Godmother would have to come up with more from her little bag of tricks than ever to turn Lucas into anything more than a guy who had fancied her and had talked her into having sex with him. He would happily sleep with her until the designated time was over, and then he would shove her back into the nearest pumpkin and head straight back to the women he was accustomed to dating, the women who slotted into his lifestyle without causing too many ripples.

She had expected the car from earlier to collect her but when the driver called for her at home, punctual to the last second, and when she went outside, it was to find that a stretch limo was waiting for her.

She felt like a princess. It didn't matter what was real or what was fake, she was floating on a cloud. But that sensation lasted just until they arrived at the hotel and she spotted the hordes of reporters, the beautiful people stopping to smile and pose for photos and the crowds milling around and gaping, as though they were being treated to a live cabaret. The limo pulled to a slow stop and nerves kicked in like a rush of adrenaline injected straight into her blood system. She feared that she wouldn't be able to push her way through the throng of people.

Then, like magic, the crowd parted and she was looking at Lucas as she had never seen him before. Her eyes weren't the only ones on him. As one, everyone turned. He had emerged from the hotel and was impeccably dressed in his white dress shirt and black trousers, everything fitting like a dream. He was so breathtakingly beautiful that Katy could scarcely bring herself to move.

The scene was borderline chaos, with guests arriving, cameras snapping, reporters jostling for prime position, but all of that faded into the background for Lucas as his eyes zeroed in on the open door of the limo and the vision that was Katy stepping out, blinking but holding her own as cameras flashed all around her.

Lucas felt a surge of hot blood rush through him. Of course she was beautiful. He knew that. He had known it from the very first minute he had set eyes on her in his office, but this Katy was a feast for sore eyes, and she held him captive. Their eyes met and he was barely aware of walking towards her, hand outstretched, gently squeezing her small hand as she placed it in his.

'You look amazing, *cara*,' he murmured with gruff honesty.

Nerves threatening to spill over, and frantically aware of the popping of camera bulbs and the rapt attention of people who were so far removed from her world that they could have been from another planet, Katy serenely gazed up at him and smiled in her most confident manner.

'Thank you, and so do you. Shall we go in?'

CHAPTER NINE

KATY HAD TO call upon every ounce of showmanship and self-confidence acquired down the years to deal with the evening.

Blinded by the flash of cameras, which was only slightly more uncomfortable than the inquisitive eyes of the hundred or so people who had been selectively invited to celebrate the engagement of the year, she held on to Lucas's hand and her fixed, glassy smile didn't waver as she was led like a queen into the hotel.

Lucas had told her that she looked amazing, and that buoyed her up, but her heart was still hammering like a drum beating against her ribcage as she took in the flamboyant décor of the five-star hotel.

It was exquisite. She had no idea how something of this calibre could be rustled up at a moment's notice, but then money could move mountains, and Lucas had oodles of it.

In a daze, she took in the acres of pale marble, the impeccable line of waiting staff in attendance, the dazzling glitter of chandeliers and an informal bar area dominated by an impressive ice sculpture, around which was an even more impressive array of canapés for those who couldn't wait for the waitresses to swing by. There was a buzz of interest and curiosity all around them.

'You'll be fine,' Lucas bent to murmur into her ear. 'After an hour, you'll probably be bored stiff and we'll make our departure.'

'How can we?' Katy queried, genuinely bewildered. 'Aren't *we* the leading actors in the production?'

'I can do whatever I like.' Lucas didn't crack a smile but she could hear the rich amusement in his lowered voice. 'And, if you feel nervous, rest assured that you outshine every other woman here.'

'You're just saying that…they'll all be wondering how on earth you and I have ended up engaged.'

'Then we'd better provide them with an explanation, hadn't we?' He lowered his head and kissed her. His hand was placed protectively on the small of her back and his mouth on hers was warm, fleeting and, oh, so good. Everything and everyone disappeared and Katy surfaced, blinking, ensnared by his dark gaze, her body keening towards his.

She wanted to cling and carry on clinging. Instead, she stroked his cheek briefly with her fingers and then stepped back, recalling the way he had reminded her earlier that what was happening here was just a show.

'Perhaps you could introduce me to the man you're doing the deal with.' She smiled, looking around her and doing her best to blank out the sea of beautiful faces. 'And thanks,' she added in a low voice, while her body continued to sizzle in the aftermath of that kiss. 'That was an inspired way to provide an explanation. I think you're going to be far better at this than I could ever hope to be.'

'I'll take that as a compliment,' Lucas drawled, wanting nothing more than to escort her right back into his limo and take her to his bed. 'Although I'm not entirely sure whether it was meant to be. Now, shall we get this party started?'

Having been introduced to Ken Huang, who was there with his family and two men who looked very much like bodyguards, Katy gradually edged away from the protective zone around Lucas.

Curiosity warred with nerves and won. She was surrounded by the beautiful people you saw in the gossip magazines and, after a while, she found that she was actually enjoying the experience of talking to some of those famous faces, discovering that they were either more normal than she had thought or far less so.

Every so often she would find herself drifting back towards Lucas but, even when she wasn't by his side, she was very much aware of his dark gaze on her, following her movements, and that made her tingle all over. There was something wonderfully possessive about that gaze and she had to constantly stop herself from luxuriating in the fallacy that it was heartfelt rather than a deliberate show of what was expected from a man supposedly in love with the woman wearing his ring.

Katy longed to glue herself to his side but she knew that circulating would not only remind Lucas that she was independent and happy to get on with the business of putting on a good show for the assembled crowd, just as he was, but would also shore up the barriers she knew she should mentally be erecting between them.

Everything had been so straightforward when she had been living with the illusion that what she felt for him was desire and nothing more.

With that illusion stripped away, she felt achingly vulnerable, and more than once she wondered how she was going to hold on to this so-called relationship for the period of time they had allotted to it.

In theory, she would have her window, during which she could allow herself to really enjoy him, even if she knew that her enjoyment was going to be short-lived.

In practice, she was already quailing at the prospect of walking away from him. He would probably pat her on the back and tell her that they could remain good friends. The truth was that she wasn't built to live in the moment, to heck with what happened next. Investing in a future was a by-product of her upbringing and, even though she could admit to the down side of that approach, she still feverishly wondered whether she would be able to adopt the right attitude, an attitude that would allow her to live from one moment to the next.

Thoughts buzzing in her head like a horde of hornets released from their nest, she swirled the champagne in her glass and stared down at the golden liquid while she pictured that last conversation between them. She dearly wished that she had the experience and the temperament to enjoy what she had now, instead of succumbing to dark thoughts about a future that was never going to be.

From across the crowded room, Lucas found his fiancée with the unerring accuracy of a heat-seeking missile. No matter where she was, he seemed to possess the uncanny ability to locate her. She wasn't taller than everyone else, and her outfit didn't stand out as being materially different from every other fancy long, designer dress, but somehow she emanated a light that beckoned to him from wherever she was. It was as if he was tuned into her on a wave length that was inaudible to everyone except him.

Right now, and for the first time that evening, she was on her own, thoughtfully staring down into a flute of champagne as though looking for answers to something in the liquid.

Abruptly bringing his conversation with two top financiers to an end, Lucas weaved his way towards her, approaching her from behind.

'You're thinking,' he murmured, leaning down so that he could whisper into her ear.

Katy started and spun round, and her heart began to beat faster. *Thud, thud, thud.*

She had shyly told the three colleagues who'd been invited to the ball about Lucas, glossing over how they had met and focusing instead on how they had been irresistibly drawn towards one another.

'You know how it is,' she had laughed coquettishly, knowing that she was telling nothing but the absolute truth, 'Sometimes you get hit by something and, before you know it, you're going along for the ride and nothing else matters.'

Lucas's stunning eyes on her now really did make her feel as though she had been hit head-on by a speeding train and she had to look down just in case he caught the ghost of an expression that might alert him to the way she really felt about him.

'Tired?' Lucas asked, drawing her towards the dance floor.

A jazz band had been playing for the past forty-five minutes, the music forming a perfect backdrop to the sound of voices and laughter. The musicians were on a podium, in classic coat and tails, and they very much looked as though they had stepped straight out of a twenties movie set.

'A little,' Katy admitted. His fingers were linked through hers and his thumb was absently stroking the side of hers. It made her whole body feel hot and she was conscious of her bare nipples rubbing against the silky fabric of her dress. The tips were stiff and sensitive and, the more his thumb idly stroked hers, the more her body went into melt down.

This was what he did to her and she knew that if she had any sense at all she would enjoy it while she had it. Instead of tormenting herself with thoughts of what life would be like when he disappeared from it, she should be relishing the prospect of climbing into bed with him later and making love until she was too exhausted to move a muscle.

'It's really tiring talking to loads of people you don't know,' she added breathlessly as he drew her to the side of the dance floor and turned her to face him.

The lighting had been dimmed and his gorgeous face was all shadows and angles.

'But you've been doing a pretty good job of it,' Lucas assured her with a wry smile. 'And here I was imagining that you would be a little out of your depth.'

Katy laughed, eyes dancing as she looked up at him. 'That must have been a blessed relief for you.'

'What makes you say that?' After spending the

past hour or so doing the rounds, Lucas felt relaxed for the first time that evening. No one had dared ask him any direct questions about the engagement that had sprung from nowhere, and he had not enlightened anyone, aside from offering a measured explanation to Ken Huang and his wife, both of whom, he had been amused to note, were full of praise for the romance of the situation. He had thought them far too contained for flowery congratulations but he'd been wrong on that point.

Under normal circumstances, he would have used the time to talk business. There were a number of influential financiers there, as well as several political figures with whom interesting conversations could have been initiated. However, his attention had been far too taken up with Katy and following her progress through the room.

People were keen to talk to her; he had no idea what she'd told them, but whatever it was, she had obviously struck the right note.

With women and men alike. Indeed, he hadn't failed to notice that some of the men had seemed a lot busier sizing her up than listening to whatever she had had to say. From a distance, Lucas had had to swallow down the urge to muscle in on the scene and claim his property—because she wasn't his and that was exactly how it ought to be. Possessiveness was a trait he had no time for and he refused to allow it to enter into the arrangement they had between them.

But several times he had felt his jaw tighten at the way her personal space had been invaded by men who probably had wives or girlfriends somewhere in the room, creeps with fancy jobs and flash cars who figured that they could do what they wanted with whomever they chose. Arrangement or no arrangement, Lucas had been quite prepared to land a punch if need be, but he knew that not a single man in the room would dare cross him by overstepping the mark.

Still.

Had she even noticed the over-familiarity of some of those guys? Should he have warned her that she might encounter the sort of men who made her odious ex pale in comparison?

'I can't imagine you would have wanted to spend the evening holding my hand,' she teased with a catch in her voice. 'That kiss of yours did the trick, and I have to say no one expressed any doubt about the fact that the most unlikely two people in the world decided to get engaged.'

'Even the men who had their eyes on stalks when they were talking to you?'

Katy looked at him, startled. 'What on earth are you talking about?'

'Forget it,' Lucas muttered gruffly, flushing.

'Are you *jealous*?'

'I'm not the jealous type.' He downed his whisky in one long swallow and dumped the empty glass, along with her champagne flute, on a tray carried by one of the glamorous waitresses who seemed to know just where to be at the right time to relieve important guests of their empty glasses.

'No.' Katy was forced to agree because he really wasn't, and anyway, jealousy was the domain of the person who actually *felt* something. She smiled but it was strained. 'No need to point out the obvious!'

Lucas frowned even though she was actually saying all the right things. 'That kiss, by the way,' he murmured, shifting his hand to cup the nape of her neck, keen to get off a subject that was going nowhere, 'Wasn't just about making the right impression.'

'It wasn't?'

'Have you stopped to consider that I might actually have wanted to kiss you?'

Katy blushed and said with genuine honesty, 'I thought it was more of a tactical gesture.'

'Then you obviously underestimated the impact of your dress,' Lucas delivered huskily. 'When I saw you get out of the back of my limo, my basic instinct was to get in with you, slam the door and get my driver to take us back to my apartment.'

'I don't think your guests would have been too impressed.' But every word sent a powerful charge of awareness racing through her already heated body. He was just talking about sex, she told herself weakly. Okay, so he was looking at her as though she was a feast for the eyes, but that had nothing to do with anything other than desire.

Lucas was excellent when it came to sex. He was just lousy when it came to emotion. Not only was he uninterested in exploring anything at all beyond the physical, but he was proud of his control in that arena. If he had foresworn involvement on an emotional level because of one bad experience with a woman, then Katy knew that somehow she would have tried to find a way of making herself indispensable to him. A bad experience left scars, just as Duncan had left her with scars, but scars healed over, because time moved on and one poor experience would always end up buried under layers of day-to-day life.

But Lucas wasn't like that. He wasn't a guy who had had one bad experience but was essentially still interested in having a meaningful relationship with a woman. He wasn't a guy who, even deep down, had faith in the power of love.

Lucas's cynicism stemmed from a darker place and it had been formed at so young an age that it was now an embedded part of his personality.

'Do I look like the kind of man who lives his life to impress other people?' he asked, libido kicking fast into gear as his eyes drifted down to her breasts. Knowing what those breasts looked like and tasted like added to the pulsing ache in his groin. 'Quite honestly, I can't think of anything I'd rather do than leave this room right now and head back to my apartment. Failing that, rent a bloody room in the hotel and use it for an hour.'

'That would be rude.' But her eyes were slumberous as she looked at him from under her lashes. 'We should dance instead.'

'You think that dancing is a good substitute for having mind-blowing sex?'

'Stop that!' She pulled him onto the dance floor. The music's tempo had slowed and the couples who were dancing in the half-light were entwined with one another.

It was almost midnight. Where on earth had the time gone? Lucas pulled Katy onto the dance floor and then held her so close to him that she could feel the steady beat of his heart and the pressure of his body, warm and so, so tempting.

She rested her head on his chest and he curled his fingers into her hair and leant into her.

This was heaven. For the duration of this dance, with his arms around her, she could forget that she wasn't living the dream.

Lucas looked down and saw the glitter of the diamond on her finger. The ring had fitted her perfectly, no need to be altered. He had slipped it onto her finger and it had belonged there.

Except, it didn't. Did it?

They had started something in full knowledge of how and when it would end. Katy had proposed a course of action that had been beneficial to them both and at the time, which was only a matter of days ago, Lucas had admired the utter practicality of the proposal.

She had assured him that involvement was not an issue for either of them because they were little more than two people from different planets who had collided because of the peculiar circumstances that had hurled them into the same orbit.

They had an arrangement and it was an arrangement that both of them had under control.

Except, was it?

Lucas didn't want to give house room to doubt, but that ring quietly glittering on her finger was posing questions that left him feeling uneasy and a little panicked, if truth be known.

The song came to an end and he drew away from her.

'We should go and say goodbye to Huang and his family. I've spotted them out of the corner of my eye and they've gathered by the exit. Mission accomplished, I think.'

Katy blinked, abruptly yanked out of the pleasant little cloud in which she had been nestled.

For all that common sense was telling her to be wary of this beautiful man who had stolen her heart like a thief in the night, her heart was rebelling at every practical step forward she tried to take.

She should pull back, yet here she was, wanting nothing more than to linger in his arms and for the music to never end.

She should remember Duncan and the hurt he had caused because, however upset she had been—and she now realised it had been on the mild end of the scale—whatever she had thought at the time, it would be nothing compared to what she would suffer when Lucas walked away from her. But nothing could have been less important in that moment than her cheating ex. In fact, she could barely remember what he looked like, and it had been that way for ages.

She had weeks of this farce to go through! She should steel herself against her own cowardly emotions and do what her head was telling her made sense—which was appreciate him while she could; which was gorge herself on everything he had to offer and look for no more than that.

But her own silly romanticism undermined her at every turn.

She gazed up at him helplessly. 'Mission accomplished?'

'We did what we set out to do,' Lucas said flatly. 'You only spent a short while with Ken Huang and his family, but let me tell you that he was charmed by our tale of love at first sight.'

'Oh, good.' He had already turned away and she

followed him, hearing herself say all the right things to the businessman while sifting through her conflicting emotions to try and find a path she could follow. In a show of unity, Lucas had his arm around her waist lovingly, and she could see how thrilled Ken Huang and his wife were by the romance.

Mission accomplished, indeed.

'Time to go, I think.' Lucas turned to her the second Huang had departed.

'Where?'

'Where do you think? We're engaged, Katy. Getting my driver to deliver you back to your flat is a sure-fire way of getting loose tongues wagging.'

'We're going back to your place?'

'Unless you have a better idea?' He shot her a wolfish smile but this time her blood didn't sizzle as it would have normally. This time she didn't give that soft, yielding sigh as her body took over and her ability to think disappeared like water down a plughole.

Mission accomplished. It was back to business for Lucas, and for that read 'sex'. They would go to his apartment, like the madly in love couple they weren't, and he would take her to his bed and do what he did so very, very well. He would send her pliant body into the stratosphere but would leave her heart untouched.

'We need to talk.' Nerves poured through her. She couldn't do this. She'd admitted how she felt about Lucas to herself and now she couldn't see a way of continuing what they had, pretending that nothing had changed.

'What about?'

'Us,' Katy told him quietly, and Lucas stilled.

'Follow me.'

'Where are we going? I mean, I'd rather not have this conversation in your apartment.'

'I'm on nodding acquaintance with the manager of this hotel. I will ensure we have privacy for whatever it is you feel you need to talk about.'

The shutters had dropped. Katy could feel it in his body language. Gone was the easy warmth and the sexy teasing. She followed him away from the ball room, leaving behind the remaining guests. He had said his goodbyes to the people who mattered and, where she would have at least tried to circulate and make some polite noises before leaving, Lucas had no such concerns.

She hung back as he had a word with the manager, who appeared from nowhere, as though his entire evening had been spent waiting to see if there was anything he could do for Lucas. There was and he did it, leading them to a quiet seating area and assuring them that they would have perfect privacy.

'Will I need something stiff for this *talk*?' Lucas asked once the door was closed quietly behind them. On the antique desk by the open fireplace, there was an assortment of drinks, along with glasses and an ice bucket. Without waiting for an answer, he helped himself to a whisky and then remained where he was, perched against the desk, his dark eyes resting on her without any expression at all.

Katy gazed helplessly at him for a few seconds then took a deep, steadying breath.

'I can't do this.' She hadn't thought out what she was going to say but, now the words had left her mouth, she felt very calm.

'You can't do what?'

'This. *Us*.' She spread her arms wide in a gesture of frustration. His lack of expression was like an invisible force field between them and it added strength to the decision she had taken impulsively to tell him how she felt.

'This is as far as I can go,' she told him quietly. 'I've done the public appearance thing and I've had the photos taken and I… I can't continue this charade for any longer. I can't pretend that…that…'

Lucas wasn't going to help her out. He knew what she was saying, he knew why she was saying it and he also knew that it was something he had recognised over time but had chosen to ignore because it suited him.

'You love me.'

Those three words dropped like stones into still water, sending out ripples that grew bigger and bigger until they filled the space between them.

Stressed out, stricken and totally unable to tell an outright lie, Katy stared at him, her face white, her arms folded.

'I wish I could tell you that that wasn't true, but I can't. I'm sorry.'

'You knew how I felt about commitment…'

'Yes, I knew! But sometimes the heart doesn't manage to listen to the head!'

'I told you I wasn't in the market for love and commitment.' He recalled what he had felt when he had seen other men looking at her and then later, when his gaze had dropped to that perfect diamond on her finger, and something close to fear gripped him. 'I will *never* love you the way you want to be loved and the way you deserve to be loved, *cara*. I can desire you but I am incapable of anything more.'

'Surely you can't say that?' she heard herself plead in a low, driven voice, hating herself, because she should have had a bit more pride.

Lucas's mouth twisted. In the midst of heightened emotions, he could still grudgingly appreciate her bravery in having a conversation that was only ever going to go in a pre-ordained direction. But then she *was* brave, wasn't she? In the way she always spoke her mind, the way she would dig her heels in and defend what she believed in even if he was giving her a hard time. In the way she acted, as she had at an event which would have stretched her to the limits and taken her far out of her comfort zone.

'I can't feel the way you do,' Lucas said, turning away from her wide, green, honest eyes and feeling a cad. But it wasn't his fault that he just couldn't give her what she wanted, and it was better for him to be upfront about that right now!

And maybe this was a positive outcome. What would the alternative have been—that a charade born of necessity dragged on and on until he was forced to prise her away from him? She had taken the bull by the horns and was doing the walking away herself. She was rescuing him from an awkward situation and he wondered why he wasn't feeling better about that.

He hated 'clingy' and he didn't do 'needy' and a woman who was bold enough to declare her love was both. He should be feeling relieved!

'I've seen how destructive love can be,' he told her harshly. 'And I've sworn to myself that I would never allow it to enter my life, never allow it to destroy me.' He held up one hand, as though she had interrupted him in mid-flow when in fact she hadn't said a word.

'You're going to tell me that you can change me. I can't change. This is who I am—a man with far too many limitations for someone as romantic and idealistic as you.'

'I realise that,' Katy told him simply. 'I'm not asking you to change.'

Suddenly restless, Lucas pushed himself away from the desk to pace the room. He felt caged and trapped—two very good indications that this was a situation that should be ended without delay because, for a man who valued the freedom of having complete control over his life, *caged and trapped* didn't work.

'You'll meet someone…who can give you what you want and need,' he rasped, his normally graceful movements jerky as he continued to pace the room, only stopping now and again to look at her where she had remained standing as still as a statue. 'And of course, you'll be compensated,' he told her gruffly.

'I'm not following you.'

'Compensated. For what you've done. I'll make sure that you have enough money so that you can build your life wherever you see fit. Rest assured that you will never want for anything. You will be able to buy any house you want in any part of London, and naturally I will ensure that you have enough of a comfort blanket financially so that you need not rush to find another job. In fact, you will be able to teach full-time, and you won't have to worry about finding something alongside the teaching because you won't have to pay rent.'

'You're offering me money,' Katy said numbly, frozen to the spot and stripped bare of all her defences. Had he any idea how humiliating this was for her—

to be told that she would be *paid off* for services rendered? She wanted the ground to open up and swallow her. She was still wearing the princess dress but she could have been clothed in rags because she certainly didn't feel like Cinderella at the ball.

'I want to make sure that you're all right at the end of this,' Lucas murmured huskily, dimly unsettled by her lack of expression and the fact that she didn't seem to hear what he was saying. The colour had drained from her face. Her hair, in contrast, was shockingly vibrant, hanging over her shoulders in a torrent of silken copper.

'And of course, you can keep the ring,' he continued in the lengthening silence. 'In fact, I insist you do.'

'As a reminder?' Katy asked quietly. 'Of the good old days?'

The muscles in her legs finally remembered how to function and she walked towards him stiffly.

For one crazy, wild moment, Lucas envisaged her arms around him, but the moment didn't last long, because she paused to meet his eyes squarely and directly.

'Oh, Lucas. I don't want your money.' She felt the engagement ring with her finger, enjoying the forbidden thought of what it would feel like for the ring to be hers for real, and then she gently pulled it off her finger and held it out towards him. 'And I don't want your ring either.'

Then she turned and left the room, noiselessly shutting the door behind her.

CHAPTER TEN

BEHIND THE WHEEL of his black sports car, Lucas was forced to cut his speed and to slow down to accommodate the network of winding roads that circled the village where Katy's parents lived like a complex spider's web.

Since leaving the motorway, where he had rediscovered the freedom of not being driven by someone else, he had found himself surrounded on all sides by the alien landscape of rural Britain.

He should be somewhere else. In fact, he should be on the other side of the world. Instead, however, he had sent his next in command to do the honours and finalise work on the deal that had been a game changer.

Lucas didn't know when or how the thing he had spent the better part of a year and a half consolidating had faded into insignificance. He just knew that two days ago Katy had walked out of his life and, from that moment on, the deal that had once upon a long time ago commandeered all his attention no longer mattered.

The only thing that had mattered was the driving need to get her back and, for two days, he had fought that need with every tool at his disposal. For two days, Lucas had told himself that Katy was the very epitome of what he had spent a lifetime avoiding. She lived and breathed a belief in a romantic ideal that he had always scorned. Despite her poor experience, she nurtured a faith in love that should have been buried under the weight of disappointment. She was the sort of woman who terrified men like him.

And, more than all of that put together, she had come right out and spoken words that she surely must have known would be taboo for him.

After everything he had told her.

She had fallen in love with him. She had blatantly ignored all the 'do not trespass' signs he had erected around himself and fallen in love with him. He should have been thankful that she had not wept and begged him to return her love. He should have been grateful that, as soon as she had made that announcement, she had removed the engagement ring and handed it back to him.

He should have thanked his lucky stars that she had then proceeded to exit his life without any fuss or fanfare.

There would be a little untidiness when it came to the engagement that had lasted five seconds before imploding, and the press would have a field day for a week or so, but that hadn't bothered him. Ken Huang would doubtless be disappointed, but he would already be moving on to enjoy his family life without the stress of a company he had been keen to sell to the right bidder, and would not lose sleep over it because it was a done deal.

Life as Lucas knew it could be returned to its state of normality.

Everything was positive, but Katy had left him and, stubborn, blind idiot that he was, it was only when that door had shut behind her that he had realised how much of his heart she was taking with her.

He had spent two days trying to convince himself that he shouldn't follow her, before caving in, because he just hadn't been able to envisage life without her in it, at which point he had abandoned all hope of being able to control his destiny. Along with his heart, that was something else she had taken with her.

And now here he was, desperately hoping that he hadn't left everything too late.

His satnav was telling him to veer off onto a country lane that promised a dead end, but he obeyed the instructions and, five minutes later, with the sun fading fast, the vicarage she had told him about came into view, as picturesque as something lifted from the lid of a box of chocolates.

Wisteria clambered over faded yellow stone. The vicarage was a solid, substantial building behind which stretched endless acres of fields, on which grazing sheep were blobs of white, barely moving against the backdrop of a pink-and-orange twilit sky. The drive leading to the vicarage was long, straight and bordered by neat lawns and flower beds that had obviously taken thought in the planting stage.

For the first time in his life, Lucas was in a position of not knowing what would happen next. He'd never had to beg for anyone before and he felt that he might have to beg now. He wondered whether she had decided that replacing him immediately would be a cure for the pain of confessing her love to a guy who had sent her on her way with the very considerate offer of financial compensation for any inconvenience. When Lucas thought about the way he had responded to her, he shuddered in horror.

He honestly wouldn't blame her if she refused to set eyes on him.

He drove slowly up the drive and curled his car to the side of the vicarage, then killed the engine, quietly opened the door and got out.

'Darling, will you get that?'

Propped in front of the newspaper where she had been scouring ads for local jobs for the past hour and a half, Katy looked up. Sarah Brennan was at the range stirring something. Conversation was thin on the ground because her parents were both so busy tiptoeing around her, making sure they didn't say the wrong thing.

Her father was sitting opposite her with a glass of wine in his hand, and every so often Katy would purposefully ignore the look of concern he gave her, because he was worried about her.

She had shown up, burst into tears and confessed everything. She had wanted lots of tea and sympathy, and she had got it from her parents, who had put on a brave face and said all the right things about time being a great healer, rainbows round corners and silver linings on clouds, but they had been distraught on her behalf. She had seen it in the worried looks they gave one another when they didn't think she was looking, and it was there in the silences, where before there would have been lots and lots of chat and laughter.

'I should have known better,' Katy had conceded the evening before when she had finally stopped crying. 'He was very honest. He wasn't into marriage, and the engagement was just something that served a purpose.'

'To spare us thinking you were…were…' Her mother had stumbled as she had tried to find a polite way of saying *easy*. 'Do you honestly think we would have thought that, when we know you so very well, my darling?'

Katy could have told them that sparing them had only been part of the story. The other part had been her concern for Lucas's reputation. Even then, she must have been madly in love with him, because she had cared more about his reputation than he had.

She also didn't mention the money he had offered her. She felt cheapened just thinking about that and her parents would have been horrified. Even with Lucas firmly behind her, she still loved him so much that she couldn't bear to have her parents drill that final nail in his coffin.

The doorbell rang again and Katy blinked, focused and realised that her mother was looking at her oddly, waiting for her actually to do something about getting the door.

Her father was already rising to his feet and Katy waved him down with an apologetic smile. She wondered who would be calling at this time but then, for a small place it was remarkably full of people who urgently needed to talk to her parents about something or other. Just as soon as the cat was out of the bag, the hot topic of conversation would actually be *her*, and she grimaced when she thought about that.

She was distracted as she opened the door. The biggest bunch of red roses was staring her in the face. Someone would have to have wreaked havoc in a rose garden to have gathered so many. Katy stared down, mind blank, her thoughts only beginning to sift through possibilities and come up with the right answer when she noted the expensive leather shoes.

Face drained of colour, she raised her eyes slowly, and there he was, the man whose image had not been out of her head for the past two agonising days since they had gone their separate ways.

'Can I come in?' Unfamiliar nerves turned the question into an aggressive statement of fact. Lucas wasn't sure whether flowers were the right gesture. Should he have gone for something more substantial? But then, Katy hated ostentatious displays of wealth. Uncertainty gripped him, and he was so unfamiliar with the sensation that he barely recognised it for what it was.

'What are you doing here?' Katy was too shocked to expand on that but she folded her arms, stiffened her spine and recollected what it had felt like when he had offered to pay her off. That was enough to ignite her anger, and she planted herself squarely in front of him, because there was no way she was going to let him into the house.

'I've come to see you.'

'What for?' she asked coldly.

'Please let me in, Katy. I don't want to have this conversation with you on your doorstep.'

'My parents are inside.'

'Yes, I thought they might be here.'

'Why have you come here, Lucas? We have nothing to say to one another. I don't want your flowers. I don't want you coming into this house and I don't want you meeting my parents. I've told them everything, and now I just want to get on with my life and pretend that I never met you.'

'You don't mean that.'

'Yes. I do.'

Her voice was cold and composed but she was a mess inside. She badly wanted her body to do what her brain was urgently telling it to do, but like a runaway train it was veering out of control, responding to him with frightening ferocity. More than anything in the world, she wanted to creep into his arms, rest her head against his chest and pretend that her life wasn't cracking up underneath her; she hated herself for that weakness and hated him for showing up and exposing her to it.

She glanced anxiously over her shoulder. In a minute, she knew her father would probably appear behind her, curious as to who had rung the doorbell. Lucas followed her gaze and knew exactly what she was thinking. He was here and he was going to say what he had come to say and, if forcing his way in and flagrantly taking advantage of the fact that she wouldn't be able to do a thing about it because it would create a scene in front of her parents was what it took, then so be it.

What was the point of an opportunity presenting itself if you didn't take advantage of it?

So he did just that. Hand flat against the door, he stepped forward and pushed it open and, caught unawares, Katy fell back with a look that was part surprise, part horror and part incandescent rage.

'I need to talk to you, Katy. I need you to listen to me.'

'And you think that gives you the right to barge into my house?'

'If it's the only way of getting you to listen to me...'

'I told you, I'm not interested in anything you have to say, and if you think that you can sweet talk your way back into my bed then you can forget it!' Her voice was a low, angry hiss and her colour was high.

His body was so familiar to her that she was responding to him like an engine that had been turned on and was idling, ready to accelerate.

From behind, Katy heard her mother calling out to her and she furiously stepped aside as Lucas entered the house, *her sanctuary*, with his blasted red roses, on a mission to wreck her life all over again. No way was she going to allow her parents to think that a bunch of flowers meant anything, and she took them from him and unceremoniously dumped them in an umbrella stand that was empty of umbrellas.

'I should have bought you the sports car,' Lucas murmured and Katy glared at him. 'That wouldn't have fitted into an umbrella stand.'

'You wouldn't have dared.'

'When it comes to getting what I want, there's nothing I won't do.'

Katy didn't have the opportunity to rebut that contentious statement because her mother appeared, and then shortly after her father, and there they stood in the doorway of the kitchen, mouths round with surprise, eyes like saucers and brains conjuring up heaven only knew what. Katy shuddered to think.

And, if she had anticipated Lucas being on the back foot, the wretched man managed, in the space of forty-five minutes, to achieve the impossible.

After *everything* she had told her parents—after she had filled them in on her hopeless situation, told them that she was in love with a man who could never return her love, a man whose only loyal companion would ever be his work—she seethed and fumed from the sidelines as her parents were won over by a display of charm worthy of an acting award.

Why had Lucas come? Shouldn't he have been in China working on the deal that had ended up changing *her* life more than it had changed his?

He didn't love her and, by a process of common sense and elimination, she worked out the only thing that could possibly have brought him to her parents' house would be an offer to continue their fling. Lucas was motivated by sex, so sex had to be the reason he was here.

The more Katy thought about that, the angrier she became, and by the time her parents began making noises about going out for supper so that she and Lucas could talk she was fit to explode.

'How *dare* you?' That was the first thing she said as soon as they were on their own in the comfortable sitting room, with its worn flowered sofas, framed family photos on the mantelpiece and low coffee table groaning under the weight of the magazines her mother was addicted to. 'How *dare you* waltz into my life here and try and *take over*? Do you think for a moment that if you manage to get to my parents that you'll get to me as well?'

She was standing on the opposite side of the room to him, her arms folded, the blood running hot in her veins as she tried her hardest not to be moved by the dark, sinful beauty that could get to her every time.

It infuriated her that he could just *stand there,* watching her with eyes that cloaked his thoughts, leaning indolently against the wall and not saying anything, which had the effect of propelling her into hysterical, attacking speech. She was being precisely the sort of person she didn't want to be. If she wasn't careful, she would start throwing things in a minute, and she definitely wasn't going to sink to that level.

Lucas watched her and genuinely wasn't sure how to proceed. Where did you start when it came to talking about feelings? He didn't know because he'd never been there before. But she was furious, and he didn't blame her, and standing in silence wasn't going to progress anything.

'I really like your parents,' Lucas said, a propos of nothing, and she glared at him as though he had taken leave of his senses.

'You've wasted your time,' she told him flatly. 'I'm not interested in having another fling with you, Lucas. I don't care whether my parents fell in love with you. I want you to leave and I don't want to see you ever again. I just want to be left in peace to get on with my life.'

'How can you get on with your life when you're in love with me?'

Mortification and anger coursed through her, because just like that he had cut her down at the knees. He had taken her confession and used it against her.

'How can *I* get on with my life when I'm in love with *you*?' Lucas realised that he was perspiring. Sealing multi-million-pound deals were a walk in the park compared to this.

Thrown into instant confusion, Katy gaped, unwilling to believe him. If he'd loved her, he wouldn't have let her go, she thought painfully. He would have tried to stop her. He wouldn't have offered her money to compensate for all the other things he couldn't provide.

Lucas noted the rampant disbelief on her face, and again he couldn't blame her.

'You don't believe me and I understand that.' His voice was unsteady and he raked his fingers through his hair in an unusually clumsy gesture. 'I'd made it clear that I could never be interested in having the sort of relationship I knew you wanted. You were so...so *different* that I couldn't get my head around ever falling for you. I'll be honest—I could never get my head around falling for *anyone*. I'd always equated love with vulnerability, and vulnerability with being hurt.'

'Why are you telling me this?' Katy cried jerkily. 'Don't you think I don't know all that?' But the uncertainty on his face was throwing her off-balance, and hope was unfurling and blossoming fast, yanking the ground from under her feet and setting up a drumbeat inside her that was stronger than all the caution she was desperate to impose on herself.

'What you *don't* know is that you came along and everything changed for me. You made me feel...different. When I was around you, life was in Technicolor. I put it down to the incredible sex. I put it down to the fact that I was in a state of suspended animation, far from the daily demands of my office. I never put it down to the truth, which was that I was falling for you. I was blind, but then I'd never expected to fall in love. Not with you, not with any woman.'

'You mean it? Please don't say anything you don't mean. I couldn't bear it.' Was this some ploy to try and talk her into bed? He was right, the sex *had* been incredible. Was he working up to an encore by flattering her? But, when she looked at him, the discomfort on his face was palpable and it made her breathing shallow and laborious.

'You confused me. There were times when I felt disorientated, as though the world had suddenly been turned upside down, and when that happened I just told myself that it was because you were a novelty, nothing like what I was used to. But I behaved differently when I was around you. You made me say things I've never said to anyone else and I felt comfortable doing it.'

'But you didn't try and stop me,' Katy whispered. 'I told you how I felt and you...you let me walk away. No, worse than that, you offered me money.'

'Please don't remind me,' Lucas said quietly. Somehow, he had closed the gap between them, but he was still hesitant to reach out and touch her even though he badly wanted to do just that.

'You have to understand that money is the currency I'm familiar with, not love. My father was derailed after my mother's death. I grew up watching him get carried along on emotional riptides that stripped him of his ability to function, and that taught me about the importance of self-control and the need to focus on things that were constant. Relationships, in my head, were associated with frightening inconsistency and I wanted no part of that. The only relationship I would ever consider would be one that didn't impact on the quality of my life. A relationship with a woman who wanted the same sort of thing that I did.' He smiled wryly. 'Not an emotional, outspoken and utterly adorable firebrand like you.'

Katy liked all of those descriptions. She liked the expression on his face even more, and just like that her caution faded away and her heart leapt and danced and made her want to grin stupidly at him.

'Keep talking,' she whispered, and he raised his eyebrows and smiled at her.

'So here I am,' Lucas said simply. 'I'd worked like the devil for a deal that, in the end, won't mean anything if you aren't by my side. I think that was when I was forced to accept that the only thing that mattered to me was *you*. I should have guessed when I realised how protective you made me feel and how possessive. You make me the best person I could be, and that means someone who can be hurt, who has feelings, who's willing to wear his heart on his sleeve.' He pulled her towards him and Katy sighed as she was enveloped in a hug that was so fierce that she could feel the beating of his heart. He curled his fingers into her hair and tilted her face to deliver a gentle kiss on her lips.

'I never expected to fall in love with you either,' she admitted softly. 'I was so certain that I knew the sort of guy I should end up with, and it wasn't a guy like you. But it's like you fill in the missing pieces of me and make me complete. It's weird, but when I met Duncan I was looking for love, looking for that *something else*, but I wasn't looking for anything at all when I met you—yet love found me.'

'I know what you mean. I was comfortable *wanting* you because I understood the dynamics of desire. Strangely, loving you has made me understand how my father ended up becoming entangled in a series of inappropriate relationships. He was deeply in love with my mother and he wanted to replicate that. Before I met you, I just didn't get it, but then I never understood how powerful love could be and how it can turn a black-and-white life into something filled with colour and light.'

'And when I returned home,' Katy admitted, 'And I saw the interaction between my parents, I knew that I could never settle for anything less than what they have. I was so upset when you showed up because I thought you'd come to try and persuade me into carrying on with what we had. Maybe because of the deal, or maybe because you still fancied me, even though you didn't love me.'

'Now you know the real reason I turned up with those flowers that you dumped out of sight—you want the fairy-tale romance and I want to be the lucky person who gives it to you. Will you do me the honour of marrying me, my darling? For real and for ever?'

'Just try and stop me…'

EPILOGUE

KATY PAUSED AND looked at Lucas, who was standing staring out to the sea, half-naked because he enjoyed swimming at night, something he had yet to convince her to try.

There was a full moon and the light threw his magnificent body into shadow. To think that a little over a year ago she had come aboard this very yacht, kicking and screaming and accusing him of kidnapping her.

She smiled because that felt like a lifetime ago and so much had happened since then. The engagement that wasn't an engagement had turned into the real thing and they had been married, not once, but *twice*. There was a lavish affair, held a week after the actual wedding, where reporters had jostled for prime position and celebrities had emerged from limos dressed to kill for the event of the century. But first had come something altogether smaller, in her home village, where they had married at a ceremony officiated by her father at the picturesque local church. The reception there had been warm, small and cosy.

Lavish or cosy, Katy just knew that she was the happiest person in the world.

They had had their honeymoon in Italy, where they

had stayed with Lucas's father for a few days. Katy knew that she would be seeing a great deal more of Marco Cipriani, because he had got along with her parents like a house on fire, and plans were already afoot for him to discover the joys of the northern countryside at its finest at Christmas.

And she knew that during the festive season there would certainly be reason for a great deal of celebration.

'Lucas…'

Lucas turned, and his heart stopped just for a second as he watched the woman who had so taken over his life that contemplating an existence without her was unthinkable. He smiled, held his hand out and watched her walk towards him, glorious in a casual, long dress which he knew he would be removing later.

Katy walked straight into his open arms and then looked up at him with a smile. 'I have something to say… We both have eight months to start thinking of some names…'

'Names?'

'For our baby, my darling. I'm pregnant.' She tiptoed to plant a kiss on his very sexy mouth.

'My darling, perfect wife.' Lucas closed his eyes and allowed himself to be swept away in the moment before looking down at her with love. 'I never thought that life could get any better, but I do believe it has…'

* * * * *

MILLS & BOON®

MODERN™

POWER, PASSION AND IRRESISTIBLE TEMPTATION

MILLS & BOON®

EXCLUSIVE EXTRACT

Charlotte Adair has spent her life locked away – but
once freed, she finds the one man she's ever loved,
billionaire Rafe Costa, is now blind, believes she
betrayed him, and is bent on a vengeful seduction!
Weeks after their scorching encounter he learns she's
pregnant—with twins! Rafe steals Charlotte away, but
she is a far from biddable prisoner. She is irresistible,
defiant—and Rafe must seduce her into compliance!

Read on for a sneak preview of Maisey Yates's book
THE ITALIAN'S PREGNANT PRISONER
The final part of her Once Upon a Seduction... trilogy

Charlotte hadn't touched a man since Rafe. She'd had no
interest.

She needed to find some interest. Because she was going
to have a normal life. Whatever she did, it would be her
choice. And that was the point.

She didn't know what answers she had expected to find
here. Right now, the only clear answer seemed to be that
her body, her heart, was still affected by him.

He excused himself from the group, and suddenly, he
was walking her way. And she froze. Like a deer caught in
the headlights. Or rather, like a woman staring at Rafe Costa.

She certainly wasn't the only woman staring. He moved
with fluid grace, and if she didn't know better, she would
never have known his sight was impaired at all.

He was coming closer, and as he did her heart tripped
over itself, her hands beginning to shake. She wished she
could touch him.

Oh, she wanted it more than anything. In that moment, she wanted it more than her next breath. To put her hands on Rafe Costa's face one more time. To kiss those lips again. To place her hand over his chest and see if she could still make his heart race.

It was easy to forget that her stepmother had told her how Rafe had left, taking an incentive offered by her father to end his tenure there earlier. It was easy to forget that and remember instead the way it had felt when he had kissed her. Touched her. The way she had pleaded with him to take her virginity, to make her his in every way.

Really, he had never wanted her. He had simply been toying with her.

She should remember that. Her treacherous, traitorous body should remember that well. But it didn't. Instead, it was fluttering. As if a host butterflies had been set loose inside her.

Suddenly, he was there. So close that if she wanted to she could reach out and touch the edge of his sleeve with her fingertips.

Could bump into him accidentally, just to make contact. He wouldn't know it was her. He couldn't.

Suddenly, he turned. He was looking past her, his dark eyes unseeing, unfocused. But then, he reached out and unerringly grabbed hold of her wrist, dragging her toward his muscular body.

"Charlotte."

Don't miss
THE ITALIAN'S PREGNANT PRISONER
By Maisey Yates

Available October 2017

www.millsandboon.co.uk

MILLS & BOON®

Why shop at millsandboon.co.uk?

Each year, thousands of romance readers
find their perfect read at millsandboon.co.uk.
That's because we're passionate about
bringing you the very best romantic fiction.
Here are some of the advantages of
shopping at www.millsandboon.co.uk:

* **Get new books first**—you'll be able to buy
  your favourite books one month before they
  hit the shops

* **Get exclusive discounts**—you'll also be
  able to buy our specially created monthly
  collections, with up to 50% off the RRP

* **Find your favourite authors**—latest news,
  interviews and new releases for all your
  favourite authors and series on our website,
  plus ideas for what to try next

* **Join in**—once you've bought your favourite
  books, don't forget to register with us to rate,
  review and join in the discussions

Visit **www.millsandboon.co.uk**
for all this and more today!

Join Britain's BIGGEST Romance Book Club

- **EXCLUSIVE offers every month**
- **FREE delivery direct to your door**
- **NEVER MISS a title**
- **EARN Bonus Book points**

Call Customer Services
0844 844 1358*

or visit
illsandboon.co.uk/subscriptions